continued . . .

Reader and Raelynx

"Exciting . . . Intrigue, love, and magic weave into Shinn's hallmark romantic, happy-ever-after ending." —*Publishers Weekly*

"A magnificent conclusion to Sharon Shinn's Twelve Houses series! Shinn is a master of world-building, plotting, and characterization—I loved *Reader and Raelynx* so much that I immediately started rereading the series from the beginning! Not to be missed." —Mary Jo Putney, author of *Chalice of Roses*

"Shinn continues her powerful and richly detailed Twelve Houses series with a tale of dangerous love and open rebellion." —*Library Journal*

"A vivid, spellbinding addition to the superb Twelve Houses saga . . . a beautiful adult fairy tale that readers will appreciate." —*Alternative Worlds*

"Shinn neatly and delightfully wraps up a four-volume romantic-fantasy series . . . A chocolate truffle of a novel: richly indulgent, darkly sweet, and utterly satisfying . . . There are plenty of great twists, thrilling action sequences, and long-awaited comeuppances along the way." —*Kirkus Reviews*

"The best since the first book . . . a very satisfying conclusion. The whole series is highly recommended for romance readers interested in dabbling in fantasy or fantasy readers who do not mind some mingling of the genre boundaries." —*SFRevu*

Dark Moon Defender

"Once again Shinn expertly mixes romance with traditional fantasy for a satisfying read." —*Publishers Weekly*

"Shinn continues to demonstrate her ability to write epic fantasy that leaves the reader wanting more." —*The Southern Pines (NC) Pilot*

"Combines storytelling expertise with a richly detailed fantasy world. Recommended." —*Library Journal*

The Thirteenth House

"Outstanding . . . a lyrical grace and deep appreciation of camaraderie reminiscent of Diane Duane at her best . . . [a] superior fantasy series."   —*Publishers Weekly*

"Lyrical and entertaining fantasy . . . Ideal for readers who like a little romance with their fantasy."   —*Kirkus Reviews*

"Shinn seems to have an endless ability to create plausible worlds for her stories. With a blend of adventure and romance, they almost seem based on the history of a remote time rather than a place invented in her imagination."   —*St. Louis Post-Dispatch*

"Set in a world of noble houses, shape-shifting mystics, and dexterous swordsmen, the sequel to *Mystic and Rider* further develops Shinn's new series characters and introduces new plot elements. Shinn provides a wealth of action and a balanced cast of genuinely heroic and admirable characters."
                                                        —*Library Journal*

"Shinn is a strong literary writer [and is] especially good at writing realistic characters. Readers who enjoy romance and strong characterization will enjoy this book and the Twelve Houses series."   —*SFRevu*

Mystic and Rider

"Engaging . . . an enjoyable yarn with characters who leave you wanting more."   —*Locus*

"Shinn is an engaging storyteller who moves believable characters through a fascinating landscape and interesting adventures, [and] manages to do it with deep insights that make us reach into our own souls and wonder: If we were placed in the world of these characters, what would we do and what would we believe in?"   —*St. Louis Post-Dispatch*

"*Mystic and Rider* . . . is that rarity, the opening book of a series that stands solidly as a read-alone novel. Well-developed and engaging characters, an intriguing plot, plenty of action, and unforeseen twists make *Mystic and Rider* a great book."
                                    —Robin Hobb, author of *Dragon Haven*

Quatrain

Sharon Shinn

ACE BOOKS, NEW YORK

THE BERKLEY PUBLISHING GROUP
Published by the Penguin Group
Penguin Group (USA) Inc.
375 Hudson Street, New York, New York 10014, USA
Penguin Group (Canada), 90 Eglinton Avenue East, Suite 700, Toronto, Ontario M4P 2Y3, Canada
(a division of Pearson Penguin Canada Inc.)
Penguin Books Ltd., 80 Strand, London WC2R 0RL, England
Penguin Group Ireland, 25 St. Stephen's Green, Dublin 2, Ireland (a division of Penguin Books Ltd.)
Penguin Group (Australia), 250 Camberwell Road, Camberwell, Victoria 3124, Australia
(a division of Pearson Australia Group Pty. Ltd.)
Penguin Books India Pvt. Ltd., 11 Community Centre, Panchsheel Park, New Delhi—110 017, India
Penguin Group (NZ), 67 Apollo Drive, Rosedale, North Shore 0632, New Zealand
(a division of Pearson New Zealand Ltd.)
Penguin Books (South Africa) (Pty.) Ltd., 24 Sturdee Avenue, Rosebank, Johannesburg 2196,
South Africa

Penguin Books Ltd., Registered Offices: 80 Strand, London WC2R 0RL, England

This is a work of fiction. Names, characters, places, and incidents either are the product of the author's imagination or are used fictitiously, and any resemblance to actual persons, living or dead, business establishments, events, or locales is entirely coincidental. The publisher does not have any control over and does not assume any responsibility for author or third-party websites or their content.

QUATRAIN

An Ace Book / published by arrangement with the author

PRINTING HISTORY
Ace hardcover edition / October 2009
Ace mass-market edition / October 2010

Copyright © 2009 by Sharon Shinn.
Cover art by Dominick Finelle.
Cover design by Annette Fiore DeFex.
Interior text design by Tiffany Estreicher.

ISBN: 978-0-441-01847-5

ACE
Ace Books are published by The Berkley Publishing Group,
a division of Penguin Group (USA) Inc.,
375 Hudson Street, New York, New York 10014.
ACE and the "A" design are trademarks of Penguin Group (USA) Inc.

PRINTED IN THE UNITED STATES OF AMERICA

10 9 8 7 6 5 4 3 2 1

For my readers, who have asked for
more stories in these worlds, and for Lesley,
who named Orlain for me

CONTENTS

Flight

1

Blood

85

Gold

173

Flame

253

Flight

One

Finally the rain stopped. We had gone three full weeks without seeing the sun, and, in fact, the past two months had been damp and dreary almost without interruption. The oldest hands on the farm had wearied the rest of us with endless stories about past summers in which rain had flooded the land, or drought had seared it. But within the last few days even they had seemed so sick of storms that they had given up talking about the weather.

There was great rejoicing all through the compound when the clouds parted and a sickly, apologetic sun made its first appearance. The children went running through the sodden gardens, kicking up sticky sprays of mud. The men hurried out to check the crops and see if there was anything to salvage. In the kitchen, the women talked together as they churned the butter and kneaded the bread, beginning the long preparations for dinner with more animation than they had shown in weeks. It would have to be a particularly sumptuous meal, everyone agreed, not only to celebrate the return of the sun but also to honor the guests who had arrived that morning specifically to chase away the rain.

Angels. Three of them, all from Windy Point, the angel hold a good three days' ride away. Thaddeus had left the compound nearly a week ago to beg for a weather intercession, but I had not really expected to see any angels materialize in answer to his pleas. I'm not sure why—everyone knows that one of the things angels do best is fly high above Samaria and lift their gorgeous voices to Jovah, praying for sun or storm or medicines or grain. Everyone knows that the god listens to them. Everyone knows that angels exist to mediate between mortals and the divine.

I suppose it was just that I had hoped I would never in my life see an angel again.

"The Archangel is so *handsome*!" Neri was saying to Ruth as they sat together at the table, chopping vegetables. "I never would have expected that, because he's so old, but he smiled at me and I almost fainted."

Standing at the stove stirring a pot of gravy, I smiled to myself. Raphael would hate knowing that a twenty-year-old girl thought him an old man. He was in his mid-fifties and still a spectacularly beautiful creature—tall and muscled, with flowing gold hair, tawny eyes, and those magnificent gilded wings. In the nearly eighteen years that he had been Archangel of Samaria, he had not lost an ounce of his charisma, either. He still had a smile that could melt your bones or charm you into his bed, where so many women had spent so much time.

If Neri showed him the least hint that she found him attractive, she could sleep with him tonight and perhaps be the lucky mother of an angel baby nine months from now.

I hoped she would not be so stupid.

"Oh, yes, Raphael is simply gorgeous," Ruth replied. "But I thought the other one seemed more—approachable. What was his name?"

"Saul?" Neri replied. "I thought he seemed a little intense, actually. Although I *like* that in a man sometimes."

"No, no, not Saul. The other one."

"Oh, Hiram! Yes, he had a very nice face. Did he talk to you?"

"No, but I'm sure I saw him look my way this morning when I was serving breakfast."

"I wonder how long they will stay after dinner," Neri said. "I wonder if they will spend the night. I wonder *where* they will spend the night."

"Neri!" Ruth hissed, then the two of them dissolved into giggles.

I was fairly certain that Thaddeus and Eve expected the angels to be their overnight guests. Rooms had been prepared for them, at any rate, and it would only make sense for the angels to stay. Neighbors from all the nearby farms had been invited to join the fifty or so souls who lived on Thaddeus's property, and the planned celebration would no doubt go on long into the night. I supposed it must be a four- or five-hour flight to Windy Point from here—rather a distance to cover if the angelic visitors got a late start or consumed too much wine.

Or found other inducements to stay.

"What do you think? Shall I wear my red dress?" Neri was asking. "Or is it too fine for a simple summer dinner?"

"Oh, it's too fine! What about your green dress, the one with the flowers? I think I'll wear the blue dress that matches my eyes."

"I'll lend you my sapphire earrings."

I didn't waste any time wondering what I might wear to the banquet, since I didn't plan to attend. Thaddeus was quite egalitarian in his approach to management. He expected every employee to call him by his first name, sit with him at the table, and work wholeheartedly to keep the farm profitable. While the family—Thaddeus, Eve, and their three children—sometimes dined in a more elegant state when they were entertaining company, for the most part Thaddeus didn't recognize much division between classes. And he surely knew that every man, woman, and child in the compound was dying to get a closer look at these most fabulous and exotic visitors.

But I had seen angels before. All my curiosity had been satisfied long ago.

I had even seen two of these particular angels, though it had been nearly two decades, and it seemed unlikely that Saul would recognize me after all this time. I had gained a little weight and I wore my dark hair in a much shorter style—and anyway, I had never done anything particularly memorable when Saul was around.

Raphael, of course, would know me the instant he saw my face.

Neri and Ruth continued their chattering, joined from time

to time by other girls who passed through the kitchens, their arms full of cheese or bread or freshly picked vegetables. Some of the older women joined in the speculation about what might please the angels, and a few of them touched their hands to their hair or their hips as if contemplating what *they* might do to draw the attention of the visitors.

But no one asked me which angel I found more attractive. No one asked me what I planned to wear to dinner. The other workers liked me well enough, but they didn't consider me a frivolous woman.

In fact, these days I was about as far from frivolous as it was possible to be.

During all the talk and all the work, I kept half my attention on the door, waiting for the sound of wagon wheels. My niece, Sheba, had been sent to the nearest ranch to barter for a pig that we could serve with the evening meal. Not a very glamorous commission, and the other girls her age had begged to stay home, where they might manage to throw themselves into an angel's path. But Sheba had laughed, and flipped back her thick dark hair, and told Thaddeus she didn't mind picking out pigs and sharing a cart with livestock. I supposed that one of the reasons she was so willing to go was that David was driving the wagon, and David was madly in love with her. Sheba was too much of a flirt to let David know how much she liked him—her primary purpose in life appeared to be to keep the young man in a state of hopeful agony—but she certainly wouldn't mind spending a few hours basking in his worshipful adoration as they traveled through a countryside made newly agreeable by the cessation of rain.

As soon as I heard the creak of the wagon and the clop of the horses' hooves, I made an excuse to leave the stove and move to the back door so I could watch their arrival. David pulled the cart up close to the door so that Sheba wouldn't have to dirty her shoes in the mud that covered every inch of the property that wasn't actually sown with crops. I assumed he would then take the luckless pig down to the slaughter-house where it would be readied for the meal. I saw it snorting and nosing about in the back of the wagon. It was big and mottled and fat, and I was sure it would be tasty.

David drew the wagon to a halt and clearly intended to

climb out to help Sheba down, but she was too quick for him. With a smile and a wave, she hopped to the ground, her skirts swinging and her dark hair fluttering around her face.

"That was fun!" she called carelessly to David.

"Will you sit with me at dinner?" he called back.

She only laughed and did not answer, just ducked through the door and let it fall shut behind her. Once inside, she glanced around to see who was present and what chores might be left to do. She was the most beautiful girl in the entire compound, but she was also the hardest working. Some of the other young women resented her, but the older ones loved her.

I loved her *and* I resented her. I would have given my life to keep her safe—in fact, I had practically done so. If I had not had her to care for all this time, oh, how different my last fourteen years would have been.

She loved me and resented me, too, though these days the resentment was winning out more often over the affection. She thought I was too strict, too watchful, too suspicious of her time. She wanted to travel to Luminaux or Semorrah, the most mysterious and beautiful cities of Samaria. She wanted to wear tight-fitting dresses with low necklines and highlight her eyes with liner and shadow. She wanted to be a desirable girl.

Well, I knew all about what happened to desirable girls, particularly when they were barely seventeen.

It didn't help that she resembled me so closely—as if I, and not my sister, Ann, had been her mother. Like I once did, she wore her thick, dark-brown hair past her shoulders; its lustrous waves provided the ideal frame for her flawless olive skin and brought attention to her huge hazel eyes. She affected simple styles, which just played up her perfect features and full figure. David was not the only man at the compound who couldn't keep his eyes off her; she looked luscious and unspoiled, yet rich with promise.

Pretty much exactly the way I had looked when I was seventeen.

"How was your trip to Benjamin's farm?" I asked her. "Were the roads bad?"

She pushed her hair behind her ears. "Covered in mud. We didn't have any trouble on the way out, but we got stuck twice on the way back. David said it was because the pig was so heavy."

I glanced down at the hem of her dress, which showed only the faintest smears of dirt. "It doesn't look like you had to get out and push the wheels free."

She smiled—a wicked look. "David didn't want me to get muddy. I guided the horses while he pushed."

"And how were Benjamin and his family?" I asked.

"Very excited about coming over tonight for dinner! And very happy to see the sunshine. He says he's lost everything in the southern field, because it lies so low the water would never drain."

That was the sort of detail it would never occur to Ruth or Neri to ask about, or to retain if it was offered to them. That was what made Sheba so exceptional. She was not just beautiful. She understood what was important—or at least, what mattered to other people. She had probably inquired after Benjamin's crops, her lovely face serious, her attention wholly focused on his replies. He was short and bald and old and married, but Sheba would still want him to admire her, to be pleased with himself because a pretty girl gave him a genuine smile. It was reflexive with her to figure out how to make a man like her.

"Well, I hope you got a good pig," said Lazarene, the head cook, who had lived at the compound for forty years. "I'm hungry for some pork."

Sheba laughed. "He looked like the best of the lot."

Sheba and I had a little argument shortly before dinner was served.

The kitchen staff had gone upstairs in shifts to change their clothes and style their hair and otherwise prepare themselves for the grand meal. Sheba and I no longer shared a room—two years ago, she and a girl named Hara had taken quarters together, while I inherited Lazarene as a roommate. I understood that this was a necessary step for Sheba's independence, and it was a relief to move in with someone as quiet and reasonable as Lazarene, but I couldn't help fretting. Hara was a particularly silly sixteen, a pink-cheeked blonde with an annoying giggle;

she wouldn't be the one to hold Sheba in check if my niece ever decided to be wayward. I was not above rising in the middle of the night and stalking the corridors, checking to see if any of the girls were out of their beds and engaged in illicit activities.

Although I knew well enough that if Sheba wanted to misbehave, no amount of vigilance on my part would stop her.

We headed to our rooms separately, and I went through the motions of improving my appearance just so no one would wonder why I was not dressing up for the angels. I even threaded a ribbon through my hair—still as dark as Sheba's—and put on a gold necklace to brighten my dull blue gown. I paused for a moment to study my reflection.

Tiny wrinkles around my eyes. A certain softness to my skin. I was forty now, and no mistaking. But my figure was still good—fuller than it had been when I was a girl—and my eyes were still an unusual shade of green. I remembered how it felt to turn heads when I walked into a room. Now and then, when I wanted to, I still could.

But tonight I didn't want to.

I waited in the hallway until Sheba came out of her room. She had put on a deep rose–colored dress with big pearl buttons all the way up the bodice, and she had left the last two buttons unfastened. The pendant on her silver necklace dangled just above her breasts, and the five silver bracelets she wore on her left wrist chimed together to wreathe her in music.

"You're not going to dinner looking like that," I said flatly.

She gave me a mutinous look. "Why not? I thought you liked this dress."

"I like it when it's on properly."

"You know Neri will wear that red gown that makes her bosom look huge."

"She's wearing her green dress. She said so this afternoon. Anyway, I don't care what Neri wears. I don't care if she parades around the house absolutely naked and the Archangel eats his dinner off her stomach. *You* are going to button up your dress, or you're going to change clothes."

I sometimes think how hard Ann would laugh to hear how I lecture her daughter.

I always wish that it was Ann delivering these lectures instead of me.

Sheba stamped her foot. "Everyone *else* will be wearing their most revealing clothes! Everyone *else* will be showing off for the angels. You want me to look like some prim little girl— you want me to hide in some corner, ugly and dowdy—"

"You couldn't look ugly if you spent all day trying," I said calmly. "Now, button up or go change."

Still furious, she fastened the top two buttons and then brushed past me down the hall. As if she had said the words out loud, I could tell what she was thinking. *When Aunt Salome isn't watching, I'll just undo the buttons again.* It was almost enough to make me insist that she put on something else altogether.

If I could have done it, I'd have locked her in her room for the night.

Just until the angels were gone.

◆

By most measures, the dinner was an unqualified success. Since it was common for all hands to sit down together at a meal, the dining hall was large and well stocked with tables and chairs. It was easy to accommodate the fifty workers, the three angels, and the thirty guests who had driven in from nearby properties. There was a certain amount of crowding, but that just added to the festive atmosphere—and people were already a little giddy when they first arrived, because of the day's sunshine. Lazarene and the other kitchen workers had arranged the food on two huge sideboards, and the guests were expected to serve themselves. I helped carry platters and pitchers from the kitchen to the dining room, making half a dozen trips. I just didn't leave the kitchen after my last trip back.

I had kept my head down every time I was among the diners, had turned my face away from the angels. Raphael was deep in conversation with Benjamin and his wife. I heard his gorgeous voice asking mundane questions about crop yields and acreage; I caught a glimpse of his golden wings, held tautly behind his back so that no one accidentally stepped on the trailing edges. Just a quick look, then I hurried back through the door, pretending I had one more tray to retrieve.

Then I stood with my back to the wall, breathing a little rapidly. Wishing that Raphael had chosen any other homestead to make his appearance. Hoping that he and his companions left at first light tomorrow, before I bothered to come down from my room. Praying that nothing—not weather, not plague, not appalling coincidence—would ever put me within fifty feet of the Archangel again.

"I suppose it could have been worse," I whispered, trying to calm my rapid heartbeat with an attempt at wry humor. "I suppose Raphael could have chosen Stephen to accompany him here."

❧

Much as I wanted to, I could not bring myself to leave the kitchen for the rest of the night. I just had to know what, if anything, was happening in the dining room. So I loitered near the door, nibbling on scraps of food that had been left off the platters as being too burnt or too underdone to serve. I couldn't distinguish much of the conversation, but I heard bursts of talk, frequent laughter, and now and then some distinct sentence in Raphael's mellifluous voice.

When I peeked inside, I saw Neri sitting as close to Saul as she could draw her chair, while Ruth had managed to get herself placed across from Hiram. I gave Ruth credit for finding Hiram more likable than Saul—not because I had any reason to think Hiram was a particularly admirable man, but because Saul had a dark soul and a brittle heart. He was a well-built, attractive man with coloring almost as fair as the Archangel's; like Raphael, he was dangerous and deeply flawed. I should probably find some way to tell Neri's mother that she would do well to keep her daughter away from this particular angel.

But when I scanned the crowd, I saw Neri's mother smiling with fatuous pride at the sight of her daughter cozying up to the man the Archangel trusted above all others. She would not listen to gentle hints; she might not listen to brutal facts. No, there was little I could do to stop Neri from racing headlong down a disastrous course. I would put my attention on my own charge and do what I could to keep Sheba safe.

The meal was about half over when I had a pleasant diversion. I saw Hope Danfrees, one of our near neighbors, excuse herself from the table and cross the room. Anyone watching

her probably assumed she was looking for privacy accommodations, but I was not surprised when, a few moments later,
she stepped through the kitchen door.

"Here you are, Salome," she said. "Hiding away from
everyone."

I smiled. Hope was about ten years older than I was, and
showed every day of it; she had allowed her waist to expand
and her hair to go gray and her clothing choices to evolve
from flattering to comfortable. But her eyes were filled with a
shrewdness born of much experience, and she was as worldly
as they came. I always suspected that her earlier life had been
as wild as mine, and that she regretted it less. From the very
moment we met, we had recognized kindred spirits in each
other. And despite our differences in station, we had become
good friends.

"I find I don't have much taste for fawning over angels," I
said. I waved her over to one of the small kitchen tables and
we both sat down.

"Which only shows your good sense," she replied. "I have
to say, it is times like this I'm glad I only have sons. Still, if
angels are going to come and be annoying, at least they could
do us some good by stopping the rain."

That made me laugh. "How much damage have you suffered? Thaddeus believes he can save about half his crops."

"We are probably in the same situation." She shrugged. "It
could have been worse. We are still going to take the trips we
planned, so it seems Joseph does not expect to see us beggared
anytime soon."

"Where are you going?"

"Well, of course we must attend the festival in Laban. It
was quite enjoyable last year."

I hadn't gone. Laban was a lively little town about a half
day's ride west of the compound, and for the past few years
it had hosted a midsummer fair that had won local acclaim.
"Sheba has been begging me to let her go," I said.

"Then send her with us! I'll look after her very well, and
you know my boys would be happy to have her along." Hope
grinned. "*Very* happy."

I grinned back. "She would break each of their hearts twice
before you'd even made it to Laban."

"Well, that's what youth is for," Hope said callously. "Learning how to mend your heart."

"I wouldn't want to burden you with the responsibility of looking after Sheba," I said. "But maybe we could *both* go with you? I might enjoy the festival as well."

"Oh, yes, please do! I would be delighted to have your company. But you must write away instantly to reserve a room—all the inns will be full to overflowing. I can give you the address of the place we're staying."

The more I thought about this plan, the better I liked it. "And if I take her to Laban, perhaps Sheba will think I am a loving and indulgent aunt instead of a cruel and hateful one."

Hope laughed. "No, she won't realize how good you are for at least another ten years. Young girls are stupid, but mature women are wise."

I tried not to sigh at that. "So, besides Laban, where do you plan to travel?"

She looked excited. "We're going to Velora!"

"Really! I envy you. But why?"

"Joseph wants to introduce himself to Gabriel before he becomes Archangel," she said, laughing a little and shaking her head as if to say, *Men! What odd notions they have.* "Can you believe that? But he says every Samarian landowner of any significance should make himself known to the Archangel. And he thought he should go see Gabriel *now*, before he becomes too busy with other concerns. Apparently he introduced himself to Raphael twenty years ago—as his father introduced himself to Raphael and to Michael, and his grandfather to the Archangels before him."

I just looked at her, my expression neutral. "How very enterprising."

She burst out laughing. "How very self-important! But I don't mind, as I get a trip to Velora out of it. Have you ever been there?"

Indeed, I had. For a couple of years, I had actually lived in Velora, the charming, prosperous little town situated at the foot of the Velo Mountains. It had sprung up some time ago to service the Eyrie, the angel hold in the Bethel province. It was not as sophisticated as Semorrah or as beautiful as Luminaux, but it was a lovely town where you could buy almost anything your heart desired.

If your heart desired commodities that could actually be purchased.

"Yes, but it's been years," I said. "I'm sure it has changed a great deal."

"I admit I am curious to meet Gabriel," Hope went on. "They say he is much colder and more stern than Raphael. Passionate about justice, but not particularly likable."

I gave her a straight look. "It might not be a bad thing to have an Archangel who is a little reserved," I said.

She grinned. "Oh, but the angel-seekers don't agree with you! They lament the fact that once Gabriel takes over, they will not be so welcome at the three holds to sleep with any angel who is willing."

"I find it hard to believe that Gabriel's icy attitude will keep the *rest* of the angels from taking a tumble with any girl who shows an interest," I said.

"No, and we need new angel babies, after all, so there is no use moralizing about it," Hope said. She stood up and shook out the ample skirts of her lavender gown. "You and Sheba are welcome to go with us to Velora, if you like," she added. "We are going straight there from Laban, in fact."

I came to my feet and shook my head. "I don't think Thaddeus would like us to be gone so long," I said.

"And you have no taste for fawning over angels," she repeated.

I smiled. "Exactly so. Velora holds no allure for me anymore."

She tilted her head and surveyed me. "The world might have changed since the last time you were there."

I said, "Not that much."

Two

It was at least another hour before the meal drew to a close. From my vantage point at the doorway, I could see diners folding their napkins and settling back in their chairs, expressing satisfaction with the food. A moment later, Thaddeus leaned across the table to address Raphael.

"Would it be rude for me to ask if you or your companions would be willing to sing for us?" he asked. "So many in this room have never heard an angel's voice lifted in song, but you might be tired from your long hours lifting your voices to Jovah—"

"Never too tired to sing," Raphael said instantly. The other two nodded.

"In fact, it would be an insult if you did not ask us," Saul said.

Thaddeus gestured. "This is the only room we have large enough to accommodate us all. We will work quickly to clear the tables and then turn this place into a concert hall."

That was my cue to join the others in the general bustle to clean up the dining room. We were quick and sloppy about it, stacking plates haphazardly in the kitchen and running back to get the next armload of dishes. Within fifteen minutes, the tables had been wiped down and everyone was redistributed around the room. Raphael and the other angels stood before the head table, their unfolded wings overlapping behind them in an undulating feathered wall.

They waited until the room was completely silent, then they began to sing.

Listening to Raphael perform was like wrapping yourself in liquid gold. His voice was that rich, that mellow, that seductive; it promised all sorts of delicious intimacies. Saul and Hiram added high and low harmonies, each note so perfectly pitched that the knobs of my spine tingled with pleasure. They were not singing sacred music tonight, oh no. This was a romantic song by some modern composer, designed to set girls' hearts fluttering and make young men look around for a conquest. Even I, hovering at the doorway, suspicious and hostile, felt moved and wistful and full of longing as the trio of angels sang about love.

The song came to an abrupt end in an utterly silent room. Before anyone in the audience had time to applaud, or even breathe, the angels launched into a new piece. It was entirely different. This was a marching song, or a drinking song, with a strong beat and a rousing chorus. Within ten measures, half the listeners were clapping along. A second energetic song followed the first, and then the angels offered another ballad; this time Hiram took the melody while the other two offered supporting harmonies. Their final selection was softer, sweeter, almost a lullaby—clearly a signal that the evening, or at least the entertainment portion of it, was drawing to an end.

When they concluded the last song with a final sustained major chord, the audience roared out its approbation. Everyone surged to their feet and applauded madly, some of the boys shouting and whistling. A few people pounded on the tables or stamped their feet. Raphael smiled most graciously and tilted his head forward in what was almost a bow; Hiram waved back at the crowd. Saul just smiled, an expression that was practically a sneer.

I don't know what Jovah was about giving angels such beautiful voices. Didn't the god realize how impossible it would be for mortals to resist them when they sang?

The crowd began to break up, the neighbors saying their good-byes, the residents starting to think about what the next workday might hold. Eve had approached Raphael, no doubt to explain the night's sleeping arrangements; even she, a tranquil and rather portly middle-aged matron, blushed and ducked her head when Raphael smiled in her direction. I checked to make sure Sheba was nowhere near the Archangel's vicinity, then I slipped back into the kitchen to begin scraping the plates clean. I was soon joined by Lazarene and a few of the older women. Not entirely to my surprise, all the younger girls of the estate seemed to have lingered in the dining room, no doubt angling for a private conversation with an angel.

I was relieved when Sheba joined us almost immediately in the kitchen, pushing back her sleeves before she went to work. But the small, satisfied smile on her face gave me pause.

Had she found an opportunity to talk to one of the angels? And which one? Had they made an assignation or merely indulged in an exchange of compliments?

I wondered if I should spend the night sleeping on the floor outside of Sheba's room.

It took more than an hour to put the kitchen back into some semblance of order, even with ten of us working at a steady pace. Neri and Ruth eventually drifted in to help us, whispering to each other and smiling dreamily. Most of us were yawning into our hands before the last dish was washed and the final pan was wiped dry.

"Don't forget we've got an early morning of it, too," Lazarene warned as we all took off our aprons and headed wearily out the door. "The angels will be setting off for home shortly after dawn, and the hands will work a full day in the fields, now that there's finally decent weather. So no one sleeps in."

A few voices murmured acknowledgments before the kitchen staff gradually dispersed. Neri and Ruth were still whispering together, and several of the other young girls were also trading secrets, but if Sheba had come to any conclusions about our angelic visitors, she wasn't sharing them with anybody. The more I thought about this, the more it worried me.

Accordingly, once I was in my own room, I gathered up a nightshirt and a pair of slippers and headed down the hallway to Sheba's room. "Hara," I said as I stepped inside, "I need you to stay in my room tonight, while I sleep in your bed."

Her vacuous blue eyes widened with surprise. "Why? What's wrong?"

Sheba gave me a scornful look that also held a trace of affection. "She wants to make sure I don't find my way to an angel's bed in the middle of the night."

"Sheba!" Hara exclaimed. I think she actually blushed. Not only was she a silly girl, she wasn't very ambitious if it hadn't occurred to her that she might improve her lot in life by snaring an angel lover. Still, these days I preferred simpleminded virtue to shrewd vice, so I grudgingly raised my opinion of her by the tiniest margin.

"Lazarene gets up very early in the morning," I told her. "But if you can fall back asleep, I'll come wake you up when it's time for you to be in the kitchen."

"All right," Hara said. She was already wearing a night-dress, so she just collected a few toiletries and a pair of slippers and let herself out the door.

Sheba gave me a mocking smile. "I really didn't plan to seduce an angel tonight," she said. "You're going to a lot of trouble for no reason."

I stretched out on Hara's narrow bed. "It's no trouble," I said.

She shook her head and made no answer. I was tired; I let my eyes close even before she lay down. I heard her move around the room as she got ready for bed, washing her face, combing out her hair, putting away her clothes. Perhaps a minute after she put out the last light, I fell asleep.

Only to wake again an hour or two later, momentarily disoriented to find myself in a strange room filled with unfamiliar sounds and shadows. Memory quickly returned—oh yes, I was guarding Sheba's slumber while angels prowled the compound. And I had been so intent on avoiding those very same angels earlier in the evening that I had failed to eat a substantial dinner, with the result that hunger had roused me from sleep.

Long experience had taught me that if I didn't fill my stomach now, I would toss and turn for the rest of the night. Sighing, I pulled myself out of bed. After a quick check on Sheba, I crept out of the room and headed downstairs to the kitchen.

It was a big house and a lot of people lived there. More than once in my previous midnight forays, I had encountered someone in the kitchen ahead of me. Thaddeus was the one I came across most often, and we had shared some companionable late-night conversations over cold meat and warm milk. The housekeeper, who was twenty-five years older than I, and so restless that I sometimes thought she *never* slept, could also frequently be found eating a midnight meal. So I wasn't surprised, as I drew close to the kitchen, to see a fan of light spilling out from beneath the door.

I was surprised, as soon as I entered the room, to see who was there before me.

"Salome," the Archangel greeted me in his warmest voice. "I thought you must be here somewhere."

❧

For a moment I stood frozen on the threshold, staring at Raphael. He had lit only three or four candles, and their soft, buttery light lavished him with adoration. He absorbed that light and burnished it and exuded it back again, redoubled in intensity and tinged with gold. He was wearing practically nothing—snug leather trousers and his magnificent wings— and it was impossible to look at him and not be staggered by his sheer male gorgeousness. He was literally the most beautiful man I had ever seen.

And I quite simply hated him.

"Sorry—I didn't mean to intrude," I said, taking a step backward.

"Don't go," he said sharply, and I froze to the spot. He smiled and repeated his words in a more caressing tone. "Don't go. I would so much enjoy a chance to talk to you."

"*I* don't want to talk to *you*," I said, but I didn't move. It was hard to do anything else when Raphael issued a direct order. So I stayed.

He glanced around the kitchen as if assessing the worth of the whole compound from this one room. "So this is where you went to ground," he said. "Have you been in Jordana all this time? At this very farm? What a very bucolic lifestyle for such a cosmopolitan girl."

"I've been here the past ten years," I said.

"And before that?"

I shrugged. "Different places."

"I would have expected to find you in Luminaux," the Archangel went on. "Indeed, I *did* expect to find you there. I looked for you every time I was in the Blue City, but I always came up empty. But a farm? You never struck me as the agricultural sort."

"Maybe you never knew me as well as you thought," I answered.

He laughed at that, a low, indulgent sound. "Oh, I think I knew you very well indeed," he replied. "And the instant I saw that girl's face tonight—what's her name, by the way?"

"Sheba," I said, my throat suddenly tight. Of course he had recognized Sheba. I should have thought of that before now.

"The instant I saw Sheba's face, I knew you must be nearby," he continued. "Never did a girl look so much like her mother."

I took a short, swift breath. "She is my sister's child, not mine," I replied.

He looked unconvinced. "How old is she?"

"Seventeen."

"Yes, and seventeen years ago—I remember quite distinctly!—you were pregnant with an angel's child."

"It was eighteen years ago, and my baby died," I said flatly. "Don't you remember? A stillborn angel boy. I gave birth to him at Windy Point."

He tilted his head to one side. "Of course I remember. But I thought you managed to get pregnant a second time."

"No," I said, my voice barely audible. "Right after that, I gave up on angels altogether."

He responded with a light laugh. "And what a loss that was to all three angel holds!"

"I'm sure you could find plenty of other angel-seekers to take my place."

"Oh, dozens of them—hundreds of them," he agreed negligently. "But there was always something about you, Salome. A brilliance. A hard shine. I always thought you would have made a spectacular angel, if the god had thought to give you wings."

"From what I know of angels," I replied in a polite voice, "I am pleased that he chose to make me mortal instead."

Raphael laughed again. "So this Sheba—this niece, as you call her—she was your sister's child? Was I acquainted with your sister?"

"Sheba is not your daughter, if that's what you're asking," I said.

He looked amused. "Well, it would be helpful to know that in advance," he said. "In case, for instance, certain circumstances ever arose."

"If you ever try to take Sheba to your bed, I swear I will make you regret it."

Now he laughed even harder. "I don't think it's very wise of you to threaten the Archangel," he said.

"Sheba is going to stay clear of angels forever. She's not going to make the mistakes that I made."

"And that her mother made? Am I right in guessing that her father was an angel—even if that angel was not me?"

I was silent.

"So it's true," he said. "And your sister—what was her name? I simply cannot place her. Does she look like you?"

"She's dead."

"Very well, then, *did* she look like you?"

"Somewhat. Ann was more fair in coloring. A little shorter. Her eyes were brown."

"And was fair Ann an angel-seeker as well?"

I was silent for a long moment, but he waited with unshakable patience, obviously determined to learn the answer. "Ann wasn't an angel-seeker, haunting the holds to find a lover," I said at last. "As far as I know, she took only one angel to her bed. Sheba was his child."

"And the name of Ann's angelic paramour?"

I had to whisper. "Stephen."

Raphael threw his head back and laughed. The sound was so loud that I expected half the household to wake and come running to the kitchen. Little though I wanted to be caught having a private meeting with the Archangel, I thought I would relish the interruption. I wanted out of this conversation *now*.

"Oh, but that's rich," the Archangel exclaimed. "Your sister stole Stephen right from under your nose! And bore his daughter! If Sheba had been an angel child, your humiliation must surely have been complete."

"Trust me, Raphael," I said grimly, "it was complete nonetheless."

"We miss Stephen, at Windy Point," Raphael said.

I tried not to let my sudden sharp interest show on my face. I had had no news of Stephen for eighteen years. It had not occurred to me he might have relocated to some other hold. But I knew Raphael would withhold details if he thought I wanted them, so I pretended that I was not eager for every scrap of information he might let fall.

Raphael continued, "He left for Monteverde—oh, twelve or fifteen years ago. Practically an insult, Saul says. I can understand wanting to join Gabriel at the Eyrie, for there is some honor in being in the Archangel's entourage. But what is there to draw anyone to Monteverde?"

"It is pretty enough," I said, my voice indifferent. I had spent less time at Monteverde than at the other two angel holds, because I agreed with Raphael on this point. It was a much less exciting place, far from the exhilaration and commotion that swirled around any venue that the Archangel called home.

But I rather thought Stephen had had his fill of excitement and commotion. I sometimes thought he would have been glad to leave Samaria altogether, if such an option existed.

"It is pretty and dull and overrun with petitioners who find Monteverde entirely too easy to access," Raphael replied. "Any petty Manadavvi landowner with some imaginary grudge can stride up to the hold and demand Ariel's attention, and she has no choice but to listen politely. At least at Windy Point, we are safe from the intrusions of mortals. No one steps inside the hold without an angel's invitation."

Very true—Windy Point was one of the most inaccessible settlements in all of Samaria. The hold was nestled inside an inhospitable mountain peak; if anyone had ever climbed it on his own two feet, I had never heard the story. An angel must fly you up there if you wanted to get in—and an angel must fly you down if you wanted to get out. When I was younger, it had never occurred to me that the second situation might someday be more urgent than the first.

"You might have been a different kind of Archangel altogether if you had ruled from Monteverde instead of Windy Point," I said. "I don't think it would have harmed you any if you'd been forced to develop a common touch."

He seemed genuinely amused. "My dearest Salome, no accident of geography could ever have rendered me common," he replied. "And I always had as much *touch* as I needed."

Suddenly I was so weary I didn't think I could continue this edged conversation for another minute. If he was not going to talk about Stephen, and he was not going to promise to keep his distance from Sheba, there was nothing else Raphael could say that held any interest for me whatsoever. Stepping carefully, so I did not brush against those silky golden wings, I pushed farther into the kitchen and grabbed the food items that were closest to hand. A half loaf of bread and a handful of dried fruit. You would have thought the conversation had turned my stomach, but I was still hungry. I had long ago been forced to give up the luxury of squeamishness.

"I'm sure Thaddeus would tell you to make free of anything in the kitchen," I told him. "Breakfast is always served very early in the morning, so you won't have to linger long before setting off for Windy Point."

He was still smiling. "I hope we see you in the morning before we go. No doubt Saul would like to renew his acquaintance with you."

"No doubt he would," I said dryly. "Good night, Raphael."

"Good night, Salome. I have enjoyed our little visit."

He probably had, I reflected, as I escaped out the door and up the stairs, munching as I went.

If I had any control over the matter, it would be the last conversation I would ever have with the Archangel.

With *any* Archangel.

❦

In the morning, trying to be unobtrusive about it, I lurked in the kitchen and the gardens, once again avoiding the dining area where everyone else gathered to make a fuss over the angels one last time. There was a great deal of laughter and excited conversation over breakfast, interspersed with snatches of song as our visitors offered prayers and praise for the meal. The weather, as one would expect after angels had been called in specifically to control it, was glorious—full sun, deep-dyed blue sky, the faintest whisper of wind.

Perfect weather for flying. The sooner, the better.

Finally the meal dragged to a close, and essentially the

whole household emptied onto the front lawns to see the angels off. I crept around the side of the house and stood in the shadows, impatiently waiting for the angels to take wing and actually *leave* this place. I was pleased to note that Sheba was behaving extremely well this morning, standing a little apart with Eve and the older women, smiling at the visitors but not looking devastated at the thought they were about to depart. Ruth, on the other hand, was clinging to Hiram's arm, practically forcing him to drag her through the mud as he strode to the middle of the field, looking for enough room to launch into flight. She was weeping; her face was blotched with what had to be a couple hours' worth of tears. Neri, though she displayed a bit more decorum, also ran after the angels, calling out some final farewell. Saul turned to her and made a laughing reply, but he did not slow down or stop.

Raphael didn't even seem to notice that half a dozen women trailed behind him, inches from the feathers sliding so sinuously over the matted grass. He simply marched on a little faster, achieving a half run. The great wings spread, then began to flutter, then drove down hard in a swift, powerful spike. Suddenly he was airborne. For a moment, the sun was filtered through his golden wings and the whole world took on a delicious brightness; then he rose higher, and the sky was once again a stiff and empty blue. Shapes circled around him as Hiram and Saul flung themselves aloft, and the three angels quickly fell into a triangular flying pattern.

"Good-bye! Good-bye! Come back to us!" the girls cried out, waving even more furiously and wiping tears from their cheeks.

The angels flew higher, then performed a showy maneuver, sweeping around in formation and diving toward the ground again, merely to bedazzle the mortals watching. But they plummeted so rapidly and skimmed so close to the lawn that a few people shrieked and most of them scattered, ducking their heads and covering their eyes. I heard the windy, ruffled sound of their wings beating in perfect time.

When they lifted themselves skyward again, one of them had acquired a burden. Saul had snatched Neri up in his arms and was carrying her with him, back to Windy Point.

Three

The weather continued exceptionally fine for the next two weeks. Like everyone else, I made excuses to get out of the kitchen, into the gardens, or even all the way to the nearest field, merely to inhale that rich, dense, fertile *green* smell of growing things. Untroubled by clouds, the sun was exuberantly warm—uncomfortably so at times—but no one complained of the heat. No one complained about the aggressive, oversize insects that burst out of the dried mudslicks and feasted on livestock and humans alike. The rain had been chased away. What else mattered?

Neri's dramatic departure had been a source of endless speculation for the first week after the angels' visit, and I supposed it would continue to be a topic among the younger girls for the rest of the year. On the part of the older women, sentiment was almost evenly divided between shock and envy, though I had the sense that even some of those who professed shock secretly experienced a little envy. To have snared the attention of an angel so completely that he could not bear to leave you behind! To have been claimed by an angel in such a public fashion! Surely Saul was infatuated with our Neri. Surely he would shower her with all sorts of gifts and lavish upon her an intense and poetic affection.

It was impossible to live in our society and not be aware

of the fact that angels were notoriously inconstant lovers, and no one, not even Neri's mother, voiced the hope that Saul had found a soul mate whom he would cherish for the rest of his life. But surely he would treat her well, for a time at least, and she would live in idle luxury among the angels at Windy Point. Perhaps she would have the supreme felicity of bearing an angel child, an event so rare and so longed for that to accomplish it would elevate Neri's status forever.

I said nothing during all these discussions. But I knew that Saul did not love Neri, that he would not treat her well, and that if she managed to get pregnant, she was far more likely to die in childbirth than to bear a living angel infant.

I thought it probable that none of us would ever see Neri again, and if we did, we would hardly recognize her because she would be so changed. Beaten down and used up and nervous and hopeless and disappointed and ashamed.

That was how most angel-seekers ended up, and those who spent any time in Windy Point were the most broken-down and wrung out of all.

I was glad when the common conversation in the kitchen began to turn toward the festival in Laban, which was now only a week away. Hope Danfrees and her family were not the only neighbors who were planning to attend. It turned out that Thaddeus's whole family would be going, and he had made it known that any of the farmhands were welcome to take a short holiday as long as enough people were left behind to care for the crops. Maybe a dozen of the laborers and kitchen staff had decided to undertake the half-day trek to Laban, and now there was a great deal of jockeying for a place in one of the carts and wagons that would be pressed into service. David had already secured Sheba's promise to ride with him. He was one of the few young men I trusted, and so I would not insist on sitting in the wagon with them for that whole long ride, but would accompany Hope as I had originally planned. That would leave room for Ruth and Hara—and perhaps a couple of their young men—to join David and Sheba. All in all, it was shaping up to be a most agreeable outing. Even I was looking forward to it.

"Do you suppose there will be dancing at the festival?" Hara asked one afternoon as nine of us worked in the kitchen on baking day. Someone had asked this question every day for the past five.

"*Surely* there will be dancing," a girl named Adriel replied, as someone had replied every day. "There's that big central square in Laban. Surely they'll turn it into a dance floor."

"I'm going to buy red ribbon," Sheba said. "Narrow ribbon and wide ribbon and ruched ribbon. And I'm going to make a white dress and cover it with red bows."

"I'm going to find a bakery," Lazarene said. "I want one of those sweet cakes with the creamy filling."

"I want to buy a necklace," someone else said.

"I'm going to get scented cream. Look at my skin—you'd think I was harvesting crops with my bare hands."

"Do you suppose Jansai merchants will be in Laban?"

"Do you suppose there will be Edori traders?"

"Do you think any angels will come?"

I looked up at that last question, not sure if Ruth or Adriel had been the one to ask. Laban was not all that far from Windy Point. I didn't know why it hadn't occurred to me before that angels might fly down from the mountaintop to enjoy the festival.

"Maybe there will be *dozens* of angels in Laban," someone else said.

"Maybe Neri will be with them."

So then, of course, the conversation returned to our missing friend. *I wonder what Neri is wearing today. Do you suppose Saul has bought her rings and necklaces and beautiful new dresses? I wonder what Neri is eating. I bet Neri doesn't have to work in the kitchen, cutting up vegetables and frying the meat! Maybe Neri is reclining in a chair, and Saul is singing to her, and someone is brushing out her hair, and someone else is rubbing lotion onto her hands and feet. . . .*

I don't know what came over me, but suddenly I couldn't stand it anymore. I had been sitting at the huge center table, rolling out pie dough, but now I came to my feet and swept the whole room with one irritated glance.

"You think it is so romantic to take an angel as your lover," I said. "You imagine being caught up in an angel's arms and carried all the way to Windy Point. Have you ever been at the angel hold? Have you ever been picked up and flown halfway across the province? Do you know what it's like? No?"

I stepped up to Adriel and, grabbing a handful of her long brown hair, I whipped it around her eyes and face. "When you fly with an angel, he clutches you tightly against his chest because he would not want you to fall several thousand feet to your death. He's holding you so close that it's hard to breathe—but you're afraid to protest because you don't want him to let you go. He flies so high above the land that you're utterly freezing. You can't feel your toes and your face is streaked with tears and you can't wipe your nose because you can't get a hand free, and you know you have never looked so ugly in your life. But you don't care, because you're so terrified you can scarcely think. You can't look down or you would start screaming. The world is so far away and the wings holding you aloft are so fragile. You cannot imagine that you will survive the flight."

I moved away from Adriel and came to a halt in front of Ruth. "But you do. You land at Windy Point and you collect your thoughts and you look around. This is an angel hold! It must be a place of wealth and luxury and comfort and ease! But no one comes to greet you or show you to a room. No one tells you where the kitchens are or when the meals might be served. You're an angel-seeker and everyone here despises you." I smoothed Ruth's cheeks as if I was applying rouge; I straightened her shirt as if helping her dress. "You must fend for yourself. You must try to find a protector among the angels or a friend among the mortals. You must try to please the cooks, so they will be willing to feed you, and work in the laundry so that you have a way to clean your clothes. You must learn how to live among these people."

I spun around to point at Hara. "But you're thinking, 'I'm a pretty young girl! There will be plenty of angels who like me, who want to take me to their beds.' And maybe that will be true." I bent over to murmur in Hara's ear, though I spoke loudly enough for everyone else to hear. She sat frozen in her pink-and-blond state, clearly unnerved by my performance. "But perhaps you've never slept with a man before, and you're not sure how it goes," I said, my mouth so close to her hair I was practically kissing it. "Perhaps your angel lover might ask you to perform an act that you find degrading—or painful—or frightening. Can you refuse him? Are you strong enough to push him away if he insists? Will anybody help you if you free yourself from his arms and go running out into the hold in the middle of the night?"

I straightened up and glanced around the room again. All the women were staring at me with varying degrees of horror, depending on how good their own imaginations were—or how comprehensive their memories.

"Don't think the angelica will give you aid," I said. "They say that Raphael's wife is rarely seen in the halls of Windy Point these days. Long ago she withdrew to her own suites, as far from the Archangel as she could manage. Was she revolted by the acts he asked her to commit? Did she feel betrayed when he began importing angel-seekers the very week that he married her and brought her home? Does she hate him? Fear him? Love him still? No one knows. Leah never comes out."

I spread my hands. "But you are thinking, 'I do not need the angelica's help. I will give any angel my body, any way he wants to take it. I can be happy at Windy Point.' And maybe you can. If you can learn to endure the wind." Now I flung my hands in the air. "All day, all night, there is never a silent moment at the hold. It seems like the rocks are groaning or sobbing or begging for mercy. In a storm, the whole place howls as if it holds the soul of every creature that has died in Samaria, and each last one is in unending torment. Some people have gone mad before they have been there a week. Some people will do anything to escape those voices. Now and then desperate men and women have flung themselves off the top of the mountain, just to escape the sound of the wind."

I started and looked behind me, as if someone had asked me a question. "Why did they jump? Because there's no other way off the mountain—unless an angel will take you. And sometimes, I'm sorry to say, the angels of Windy Point find they have more interesting ways to occupy their time than ferrying weeping young girls to and from the hold."

I took three steps and I was standing right where I had been heading this whole time—in front of Sheba. She watched me with a carefully neutral expression, but I could read her face and its subtle blend of humor and irony. She knew, maybe all of them knew, that this entire performance had been for her benefit. I put my hands on either side of her face and tilted her head up so we could stare at each other.

"'But Salome,' I can hear you thinking," I went on. "'All of these hazards, all of these travails, will surely be worth it if only I can bear an angel child. And then I shall live in comfort and ease for the rest of my life, honored everywhere I go by angels and mortals alike.'"

"I should like to have an angel baby," Sheba said, her face utterly calm, her voice serene.

I dropped my hands and glanced around the room, but I stayed where I was. "Do any of you know a woman who has had an angel child?" I asked. I could tell by the startled expressions on their faces that none of them did. "Do you know what happens to girls who get pregnant by angel lovers? A very high percentage of them miscarry, because angel blood mixes badly with ours. Nine times out of ten, if the pregnancy goes full term, the child that is born will be mortal—of no use to anyone, or no more use than any other child. And, believe me, your angel lover will have no interest in helping you figure out what to do with the baby who is suddenly demanding all your time."

I did one slow, complete pivot, making sure I met the eyes of every young girl in the room—each one still young enough to be fertile, stupid enough to dream. "And if the child in your womb is angelic? If you have been fortunate enough to conceive the most precious bit of life there is? Why, you have won the prize. You have achieved the pinnacle. You are among the luckiest women in Samaria." I glanced down at Sheba. "You are also likely to be dead soon. At least one out of three women die giving birth to angel babies. And if the healers have to choose between saving the baby's life and saving the mother's—well, you ought to be able to guess which one will live through the night."

I took off my apron and laid it across the back of the empty chair next to Sheba. "You'll pardon me if *I* don't spend my energy hoping there will be angels at the festival," I said. "It wouldn't make me unhappy if I never saw an angel again for the rest of my life."

～

As it happened, of course, Laban was full of angels. I spotted the first one when we were still a few miles out from town, riding in the Danfrees' comfortable carriage. I paused in the middle of a question I was asking Hope, and I stared out the window at the lyrically beautiful sight of an angel swooping out of the sky like a messenger from Jovah himself.

"Do I think what?" Hope prompted me when I had been silent too long.

I dragged my gaze back to the interior of the carriage, though it was a moment before I could focus again on her face. "I've forgotten what I was going to ask," I said blankly.

She ducked her head to see what had caught my attention outside. Three more angels were circling overhead, canting their wings in preparation for a landing. She looked back at me with a slight smile. "Do I think we will have an interesting time of it in Laban?" she said. "Oh yes. I think we might."

The wagon carrying Sheba and the others had already arrived at the inn where I had booked us a room, and Sheba was waiting primly outside, a small pile of luggage at her feet. The expression on her face was cherubic; it was clear she wanted me to think she was going to behave with the utmost maturity for this visit.

"David and the others have already left for the fair, but I said I had to wait for you," she said.

"How very wise," I said dryly. "Let me pay for our room and freshen up, and then we can go find your friends."

"Shall we plan to meet back here for dinner?" Hope asked.

"An excellent idea. I'm sure I'll need the company of an adult by then."

A few minutes later, Sheba and I were hurrying off to see the fair. I have to confess that even I was quickly infected with the festive atmosphere that energized all of Laban, normally a rather sedate town where sober individuals engaged in ordinary commerce. But today the streets were thronged with small boys and harried mothers, flirtatious young girls and well-dressed young men. Flags and banners flew from every home and small shop; the scents of spicy cooking made the slightest breeze tantalizing. The air was filled with excited conversation, trills of song, bursts of laughter, and the random noisy bustle of people having a good time.

The bulk of the fair was set up in the center of town, spilling along one main avenue and four cross streets. *"Oh!"* Sheba exclaimed as we rounded a corner to see it all laid out before us. There were the broad, colorful tents of the Jansai traders selling any item you might desire, from food to jewelry. There were the clusters of smiling, dark-haired Edori who seemed to be equally divided among those who had goods to sell and those who merely wanted to visit with their friends. I noticed that the Jansai and the Edori had set up wagons as far from each other as possible—there was no love lost between those two groups, and indeed a great deal of hatred and suspicion.

Farmers had driven their carts to the middle of the fair and were selling big, fat tomatoes and bushels of peaches. Merchants from Luminaux offered the finest crafts imaginable, from delicate silver flutes to porcelain dishes painted with gold. Bakers were handing out pastries; vintners were pouring glasses of wine. Everything held an instant, exotic appeal.

"I don't even know where to begin looking," Sheba said.

I laughed and couldn't keep from patting her shoulder. This was nothing—this was a tawdry little street fair—compared to the opulence you might expect to see on a daily basis in Semorrah or Luminaux or even Velora. But Sheba was a country girl whose pleasures had always been simple ones. I had made certain of that.

"I know you have your own money, but I'll buy you a present today—anything you pick out," I said. I knew I didn't have to give her a price limit; Sheba was much too sensible to ask for something she knew I couldn't afford, and too canny to sulk about it.

She gave me a swift sideways smile. "You should buy a present for yourself, too," she said. "You never indulge yourself with anything."

"Maybe I will, then, today. Let's start shopping."

We began with food, of course, and we munched on fried bread and baked apples while we wandered down the haphazard aisles. I was drawn to the bright scarves and bolts of cloth laid out at the Edori tents, and I couldn't resist buying a length of red fabric shot through with streaks of gold and purple. Sheba held a fold of it against my face before the vendor wrapped it up for me.

"These are the perfect colors for your skin," she said. "You should wear bright clothes more often."

She was lured by the trays of jewelry laid out in the Jansai booths, though she didn't like the traders themselves, and she actually pressed a little more closely to me while we picked through the heavy gold chains and the thin gold bracelets. I don't much like Jansai men, either—most of them are loud and overbearing and feel such contempt for women that the scorn practically rises off of them like a smell. Their own women cower unseen in tents and wagons, though sometimes you can glimpse their veiled faces peering out as if they long to take in more of the world.

"I want a bracelet, but I don't want to buy it from *him*," Sheba whispered, after we had considered and rejected a number of baubles.

"Then let's go see what the Semorran merchants have to offer," I said. The wares tended to be more expensive when they came from Semorrah, but the buying experience was much more enjoyable, and she ended up with a lovely gold bracelet hung with clattering charms. Ruth and Hara were at a booth nearby, and I did not object when Sheba wanted to run over and show them her new acquisition—and I did not refuse when she turned back and asked if she could spend the next few hours wandering the fair with them. She had been so good, and goodness is so often not rewarded. I waved and let her go.

And then I was alone at the fair.

I glanced at the sun. It was mid-afternoon, and I had plenty of time before I was to meet Hope for dinner. I found I was hungry again—something about roaming through the open air of the festival stirred up my appetite, or maybe it was just the sheer luxury of being able to eat a meal that I had not had to prepare with my own hands. I stopped at every booth selling any kind of food and took samples of everything, from meat to bread to sweets. It was all delicious.

I was near the northern edge of the fair, at the last cross street that held any booths, when I heard the singing. My hands resting on a pile of apples that I had been sorting through, I turned my head to listen to the effortless harmonies drifting down the alley.

"Angels," said the woman running the fruit stand. "They've been singing all day. I feel drunk with the music, and I'm not one who's ever cared much for singing. I guess I never heard angels before."

"I've heard them," I murmured. "But it's a fresh shock every time."

"Do you want that apple?" she asked.

I shook my head and put my empty hands in my pockets. "Maybe later," I said. "I'm going to listen to the singing."

It was easy to guess which building held the performers, since a crowd of people had spilled out of the door and into the street, listening raptly to the heavenly sounds. As gently as I could, I pushed my way through the mob till I was almost at the door—close enough to hear every note, not close enough to see inside. And then I stood there, jammed hip to shoulder with complete strangers, and let myself be claimed by music.

Right now, two women were offering a complicated duet—not holy music, not something that would be presented at the annual Gloria, but something serious and sublime nonetheless. The soprano line arched and ached over the dark, melancholy alto like lightning over a louring sky. It would not have surprised me if the air had darkened to storm just from the passion of their voices. But after a frenzied twining arpeggio of minor harmonies, their voices suddenly resolved into a triumphant major third, and everyone in the crowd around me gasped. I opened my eyes—it seemed I had shut them—fully expecting to see the street around me washed with brilliant sunshine. It took a moment for me to reorient myself to an ordinary sky and my place in the middle of a crowd. It was some comfort to see similar looks of confusion on the faces of the people around me.

The audience inside burst into deafening applause; those of us out in the street merely shifted our feet and tried to find more comfortable positions. No one made any move to leave. I imagined the two women making their way off of a temporary stage and new performers climbing a shaky set of steps. Inside the building, the quiet grew intense, and those of us outside fell silent as well, filled with greedy anticipation. I noticed that my face and shoulders strained toward the doorway and that my whole body was clenched with readiness. Everyone around me had much the same pose.

When the new voice rose in song, I gasped so hard you would have thought someone had punched me in the stomach.

That was Stephen singing.

His voice was a rich baritone, silky smooth; he held each note as if it could be weighed in carats. The first piece I had ever heard him sing was a requiem at the funeral of a woman I had not met, and I had sobbed through the entire number as if I had lost all hope of the god. For a long time, I had not wanted to hear him sing again because I didn't think I could bear the sadness, but then I heard him deliver a love song. I realized that his voice was meant to express deep emotion—any emotion—as long as it was passionate and heartfelt. In all the time I knew him, I never heard him sing a playful melody or a tavern ditty, but when he performed a sacred mass, you would fall to the ground praying, and your soul would make a trembling obeisance.

This afternoon he offered a song of thanksgiving, a gorgeous expression of contentment and well-being. I could see the people around me nodding their heads and smiling at each other. I could tell his voice was infusing them with a sense of serenity and hope, a belief that the world was wondrous and all dreams were within reach. Even I—who believed neither of these things, as a general rule—felt my spirits lift and my burdens lighten. Laban was a very good place and I was having a very good day. Nothing impossible awaited me. Life was a treasure trove of joys.

When his voice reached its dramatic conclusion and abruptly ceased, I felt as if I'd been slapped. My head snapped back and my bright mood vanished. Once again, I saw my own emotions mirrored in the expressions of the people around me. But I doubted any of them felt a sense of letdown and betrayal as keen as my own.

I had to see Stephen's face.

Apologizing in an undervoice, but moving with a great deal of determination, I started elbowing through the throng, pushing my way into the crowded building. A few people elbowed back, and some refused to give way, but I managed to inch up the stairs and through the dense cluster of people packed into the back of the room. "Excuse me—please let me through—I'm sorry. Please let me get by," I murmured.

I had made it a few feet into the interior of the building, and I was deep in a knot of unyielding strangers, when Stephen began singing again. This time his deep, steady voice anchored a quartet of performers. I heard the pale-oak tenor, the black-satin alto, and the crystalline soprano lay their individual architectures over his flawlessly planed foundation. I found myself smiling again. Suddenly good-natured, the people around me agreeably made room when I pressed forward, trying to get closer. I pushed through one more tangle of people and found myself standing behind the back row of chairs, with a clear, unobstructed view of the stage.

My eyes went instantly to Stephen. His tall, slender body was so familiar; those narrow white wings made a compact silhouette behind his body as if they had been folded down to the smallest possible shape. There had always been such intensity to Stephen. It had always seemed as though his muscles were corded, his hands were clenched, his wings were quivering with readiness. He had always appeared to be on the verge of—something. Speech. Flight. Anger. Laughter. Declaration. Renunciation. Whenever I was with him, I always found myself leaning forward just a little. Just as everyone in this crowd leaned forward, listening to the angels sing.

My first thought was that he looked no different than he had when I'd met him twenty years ago. But as I stood there, hungrily staring, I gradually realized that that wasn't true. His curly brown hair still fell almost to his shoulders, but it was a little thinner, a little darker. He was still slim, but he had filled out more; his body had a man's weight now, not a boy's. His expression was more set, more severe. If I were closer, I was sure I would see a few permanent lines carved down his cheeks or edging his eyes.

He was my age, of course, or close to it—a year my junior, which I had never let him forget. I was the sophisticated young woman who could estimate the worth of a jewel merely by cupping it in her hand; I had bedded my first angel when I was sixteen. His father had sent him from Monteverde to Windy Point so he could gain a little sophistication of his own by serving with the Archangel-elect. He wasn't a virgin when he arrived, but he might as well have been. He understood so little about the games between men and women.

He learned them all rapidly and very well.

I wondered how many women he had loved in the years

since I had seen him last. I wondered how quickly he had lost his soulfulness, his sweetness, his sincerity. Was he by now as jaded as Raphael, as insensitive as Saul? Would I recognize his heart as instantly as I had recognized his face?

I studied him as he sang. He stood a little apart from the other performers, all of whom looked to be Sheba's age or even younger. He seemed to be watching them, as if they were children climbing the branches of a tree and he was afraid they would fall. As if he was standing directly beneath them, his hands already half lifted to catch them when they tumbled down. Perhaps this was their first public performance and he was guiding them through it.

Perhaps one of them was a son or a daughter, and what he was showing was not concern, but love.

I put a hand to my throat as if to hold back the sound of weeping.

It was impossible that such a small movement across such a large room filled with so many people could have caught his attention. And yet something turned his gaze my way. I saw him recognize me and then freeze, immobile. His eyes bored into mine; he actually missed a note of the music. The soprano sent him one quick, expressive glance of astonishment, while the tenor faltered and then manfully caught up. The alto, rapt in her own luscious melody line, didn't seem to notice.

It was only half a measure, and then Stephen's voice steadied, underpinning the whole complex composition again. The soprano gained the courage to fling her voice up half an octave, and the song finished up on a wildly exuberant flare of eighth notes. The audience erupted into applause, and most of those lucky enough to have chairs surged to their feet, whistling and cheering.

The whole time, Stephen did not take his eyes from mine.

There were calls for an encore, and the younger angels seemed willing, but it was clear Stephen wanted to get off the stage immediately. Still watching me, he motioned to someone out of my sight line, and a heavyset young man climbed the stairs to take his place. Stephen barely waited for this re-formed quartet to begin a new piece—something lively and up-tempo—before he exited the stage with a single jump, spreading his wings just enough to cushion his landing. I was certain that he would instantly find the nearest exit—and that he would be looking for me outside.

Part of me wanted to hide here among these strangers or slip out a side door and run with all the speed I could muster back to the safe haven of the inn.

Most of me wanted to claw and punch my way out of this room so I could find my way to Stephen's side and fling myself into his arms.

I followed the second plan of escape, though I tried very hard not to hurt anyone as I urgently broke through the crowd. "I'm going to be sick," I threatened, holding one hand to my mouth and one to my stomach, and this worked pretty well to clear a path through the mob. Finally I was at the door, I was down the stairs, I was dashing around the side of the building—

And there was Stephen, waiting for me.

This close, I could see the changes wrought by time. The curly hair definitely was not quite as thick; the face had gained an ineradicable knowledge of human nature. But the intensity was still there in the watchful expression, the slightly hunched shoulders. He looked, as always, to be poised on the balls of his feet, ready to leap into the air at a moment's notice.

I tried not to guess what similarities, what differences, he saw in my own face, my own body.

"Salome," he said.

I could not think what to answer—even his name wouldn't come to my lips. But before he could speak again there was a muffled shriek behind me and the sound of footsteps pattering closer. I could only guess that a few women who had clustered outside the building to hear the singing had just realized that an angel was practically in their midst. I could have laughed—I could have cried. All this time without a chance to speak to Stephen and now we would be surrounded by giggling girls and panting women, eager to stroke a wingfeather with their fingertips.

I saw Stephen's gaze go briefly behind me; his mouth tightened in the slightest display of irritation. Then he took three running steps in my direction, scooped me into his arms, and flung himself into the brilliant summer sky.

Four

I had lied to the girls back at the farm, of course. It is a magical experience to be carried in an angel's arms. Or at least it is if the angel is thoughtful, considerate, and remotely interested in your well-being.

He cradles you against his chest as if you were precious beyond description. The heat from his body—so much warmer than that of an ordinary man—fills you with a sense of well-being and protects you from the chill wind of the upper heavens. And you are *flying*—you are coasting above the world in a fluid, gliding motion that is simultaneously dizzying and exhilarating. You realize you have never before felt so deliriously alive. You realize you never again want to come back to the ground.

~

Stephen flew for maybe ten minutes, far enough to take us some distance beyond the confines of Laban, close enough that I could walk back if I had to. He circled to land in some random spot marked only by a stand of trees in an otherwise grassy stretch of land. He came down so gently that I barely marked the transition between divine flight and prosaic standing.

The minute he was on the ground, he set me on my feet,

released me, and stepped back as if he suddenly remembered that he did not want to touch me.

We stood there a few moments, merely staring at each other. I realized that I had not profitably employed my time during the flight formulating anything I could say to him.

I tried his name. "Stephen." But that just led to another long moment of silence.

Finally he spoke. "I had given up on the idea that I would ever see you again."

"Did you *want* to see me again?" I asked, before I bothered to wonder if I would like his answer.

He nodded, very slowly, as if not certain the answer was yes. "I had questions I wanted to ask."

I almost laughed. No doubt he did. "Well, ask them," I said. "Eighteen years ago, I might not have answered, but now—" I made a helpless gesture. "It seems pointless to keep any secrets."

"Have you been well?" he asked. "Have you been safe and healthy and adequately cared for?"

I stared. Those questions were not even on the list of queries I would have expected him to prepare. "Well enough," I said. "As safe and healthy as anyone is, I suppose."

"You were so frail," he said, "after the baby was born."

I caught my breath. Of course, he had been at Windy Point when I delivered that stillborn child. He had not come to see me, but any number of people could have given him hourly reports on my condition. "Within a month, I was well enough to travel," I said.

"I know," he said. "You left while I was taking a message to Monteverde. And no one knew where you had gone."

"To be perfectly candid," I said, "I have to say I'm surprised that you even bothered to inquire after my whereabouts."

For the first time, he glanced away from me, as if taking one long last look at something in the past. "It was badly done of me," he said, his voice very subdued, "to be so wrapped up in my own anger that I did not bother to notice how deeply you were hurt."

"If anyone should be making apologies for that time, it's me," I replied swiftly. "Generous as you are, you can't possibly believe that you can be blamed for anything that happened."

He shrugged, and his tightly held wings lifted and settled behind his back. "I could have tried harder to understand what mattered to you and why you did—everything you did."

"I abandoned a man who cared for me so I could become the bedmate of a more powerful man," I said baldly. "There is nothing there to understand but ambition."

He was still looking away from me. "I think perhaps you did not realize," he said, "how much I truly loved you."

I fell silent again, surprised. He was right, of course. I had adored Stephen, everything about him—his serious face, his earnest conversation, his passionate lovemaking. When I was with him, I felt such a blaze of internal happiness that at times I thought my skin would catch fire. But I hadn't believed he had loved me in the same way.

Oh, I knew he was fond of me. He didn't just show me affection, he spoke of it openly. But I was an angel-seeker. I had been living among angels for four years when I met Stephen. I knew very well what kinds of relationships were possible between angel men and mortal girls. Few angels bother to marry, and those who do are seldom faithful. It is so important that they produce new angel offspring, and it is so rare that they do, that the very culture of Samaria encourages them to be promiscuous. No girl who cannot bring a live angel infant to term expects to have any emotional hold on one of those magnificent creatures. I understood that rule; I was willing to abide by it. I had not had any reason to believe that, in Stephen's case, it did not hold true.

Now he looked at me again, his dark eyes darker with an old pain. "That is what I blame myself for," he said. "Not making sure you understood my feelings."

I made a small, fatalistic gesture with one hand. "Well, you should lay down that burden of guilt," I said. "The girl I was back then did not deserve any man's love. I was so flattered by Raphael's attention that I'm not sure anything you could have said would have kept me away from him. I wanted to bear an angel baby, and I wanted it to be the Archangel's child. I was so blinded by thoughts of my glorious future that it was hard for me to see any other riches that might have been laid out, waiting for me to sweep them up."

"I was so sorry to learn that your child was stillborn," Ste-

phen said. "I knew how hopeful you were that this time—"
Now he was the one to make a gesture that served to complete
his sentence.

I nodded. I had miscarried three times before—twice with
Stephen's children. I had been optimistic once I made it safely
past the third month, elated once I passed the sixth month. I
was certain that the child inside me was angelic, and so were
the healers at the hold. Those last few months, as my belly
distended and I began to suffer uncommon aches, one healer
or another was at my side almost constantly. I knew those
women didn't care about me; I knew they would be happy
to consign me to death if they could just coax a living angel
child from my womb. They fed me special concoctions; they
massaged my stomach; they forbade me to walk more than six
feet from my bed.

All to no avail. My son died before he could be born. I
saw the thin membranes of his wings wrapped around his tiny
body before they carried him from the room.

"It was a bitter day," I said.

"I would have thought," he said, and then hesitated and
tried again. "It had seemed to me—Raphael is careless of the
people around him, and yet in your case—"

I guessed what he was trying to say. "You did not expect
him to cast me from the hold mere weeks after I suffered such
a traumatic event," I said.

Stephen nodded. "I always thought he was fond of you, in
a rather careless way."

"He didn't throw me out," I said. "I chose to leave."

Stephen watched me, his dark eyes suddenly narrowed.
"That's what Raphael told me when I came back from Monteverde," he said. "But that seemed completely inconsistent
with everything I knew about you."

I smiled somewhat sourly. "What angel-seeker voluntarily
leaves the hold?" I said. "What angel-seeker ever gives up
hope that the *next* lover, the *next* baby, will be the one she has
waited for all this time?"

"You had seemed so determined to get what you wanted,"
he said. "I thought you could hardly fail."

"It turned out that what I wanted carried a price too high
for me to pay."

If possible, his expression grew even more intent. "What price?"

Now I was the one to look away. This was a story I had never told a soul, and I was not about to repeat it to Stephen now. "Something Raphael asked me to do," I said. "And I realized I could not do it."

"What was it?"

I shook my head. "If I were to say it out loud," I said, "I think the god might strike me dead."

Stephen took a long breath. I was sure he was trying to conceive of an action so heinous that it would have repulsed even someone as morally questionable as I had been—but I doubted he would ever figure it out on his own. "He didn't seem very happy that you were gone," he said now.

"Did he look for me?" I asked.

Stephen shook his head. "Not that I'm aware of. At least, none of the people at the places *I* went, trying to find you, mentioned that the Archangel had been there first."

Even after all these years, it was almost unbearably sweet to learn that he had sought me out. I spared a moment to wonder how my life would have been different if he had actually found me, but the images were so painful that I had to quickly close them out of my mind. "What places did you try?" I asked.

"I went to Velora, of course, and Luminaux and Semorrah. I remembered the names of some of your friends—women who had left Windy Point a year or two earlier—and I found three of them. But none of them knew where you were. I even went back to Monteverde, in case you had arrived there after I left, but you hadn't."

"And you asked my sister," I said in an even voice.

He nodded, showing not the faintest trace of self-consciousness. "I went to her last because I couldn't believe you would have taken shelter with her. You had told me often enough how strained your relationship was, but I thought that perhaps in such a stressful time, you would have found her your only haven." He shrugged. "But you weren't there and she said she hadn't seen you. I kept looking, but with less and less hope." He fixed his eyes on mine again. "I still cannot believe I found you here today."

I was finding it a little hard to breathe. How many nights had I tortured myself, imagining how quickly Stephen must have been attracted to Ann to take her as a lover the very day he met her? Sometimes I was able to convince myself that he brought her to his bed merely because she looked enough like me to satisfy him in the dark. More often I remembered her fair skin, her silky blond hair, her grace and her elegance, and I thought he had been drawn to her because she was, in so many ways, my exact opposite. But it had never occurred to me that the encounter would mean so little to him that he would gloss over it as if it had not even happened.

"I did not expect to find *you* in Laban, either," I said. "I was told you lived now in Monteverde. That's a pretty long way to come merely to attend a small-town festival."

He smiled slightly. "Ariel sent me to Windy Point with a message for Raphael," he said. "Enough of the other angels were going to Laban that I thought it might be enjoyable. I always think it is good to perform in these small venues, for it is rare that common men and women get a chance to hear the angels singing."

I had recovered my poise, or mostly. "Why did you leave Windy Point?" I asked. "And go to Monteverde, of all places?"

He was silent a moment. "I found—there were things about Raphael—I disagreed too often with the way he ran the hold," he said finally. It was clear he was editing out all kinds of calamitous detail. "To stay would have made me complicit in some of his behaviors. I do not want to claim that I am more virtuous than the next man—but I am not capable of living the way Raphael lives."

This raised my eyebrows practically to my hairline. "I always thought Raphael had the capacity to be utterly dissolute," I said. "I always thought that if he had been a mortal man, blessed with the same good looks and a certain amount of property, he would have sown bastards across the countryside and finished every night in a drunken stupor. But I believed that the very office of Archangel would have forced him to a higher standard. He is so much in the public eye. Angels from all holds are in and out of Windy Point on a daily basis. He could not possibly be as corrupt as he had the potential to be."

Stephen actually seemed relieved to hear me put the case so bluntly, for he was nodding energetically. "Yes—so you would think—but he found ways early on to separate the public business of the hold from the private. There are parts of Windy Point that visitors rarely see. And thus there are activities that occur in Windy Point—well. I can only say that if Gabriel and Ariel knew about them, I think they would petition the god to relieve Raphael of his responsibility before his term officially ended."

"Those are grave charges," I said.

Stephen nodded. "But I think you know the man well enough not to be shocked."

"Everything I hear about Gabriel leads me to believe he will be a better Archangel in every sense."

Stephen nodded again. "He is young, but he has a great deal of presence and self-assurance. I know that Ariel admires him greatly. Some angels will tell you that he is arrogant, and others will complain that his standards of behavior are so high no one can be expected to meet them. I say, after Raphael, no Archangel could be too righteous or too demanding. I plan to be at the Gloria and sing with all my heart the year that Gabriel is installed in that office."

"That will be an event worth celebrating," I agreed.

Suddenly Stephen fixed me with his intense gaze again. It was as if, while we discussed Raphael's flaws, he had forgotten that more personal matters lay between us, but now he had remembered. "And will you go to the Gloria on that day?" he asked.

"I doubt it. I haven't been to one in years."

"You haven't told me yet. Where are you living? What have you been doing? Why are you in Laban?"

"I came to Laban for the festival," I said.

He almost smiled. "Why are you in this part of Samaria," he said, speaking deliberately, "and under what conditions do you live?"

"I'm living at a large farm about forty miles from here—a big complex run by a wealthy landowner. About fifty people live there, and every one of us is needed to keep the place running. I mostly work in the kitchen, but at harvest, sometimes all of us are in the fields."

"I can't say this is a setting I would ever have expected to find you in."

Now I smiled. "No, nor the kind of place I would have expected to come to rest," I said. "But I find I like the work. I like the rhythms of the seasons. I like the thought that my labor contributes to something tangible and meaningful. Something that sustains life."

It sounded embarrassingly naïve and melodramatic, but Stephen was only nodding. "Yes—I can understand that—it is easier sometimes to get through the days if you are convinced they have a purpose. How long have you been there?"

"Ten years."

"And how long do you propose to stay?"

I had long ago perfected the art of watching someone very closely without seeming to be paying much attention at all. "As long as Sheba needs me to provide a home for her."

"Who's Sheba?"

"My niece. Ann's daughter. She's seventeen."

His brows dipped in a slight frown. "Why are you raising her?"

"Ann died fourteen years ago of a lung infection, and there was no one else to take Sheba."

"I'm sorry to hear that," he said, but the response was one of those automatic expressions of sympathy; he didn't seem remotely moved. "Did you reconcile with your sister before she died?"

I gave a short laugh. "No. In fact, I would say our relationship deteriorated after Sheba was born."

"Was there a reason?"

"Well," I said, my voice almost breezy, "she told me that the man who had fathered her child was you."

He simply stared at me.

I elaborated. "She said that when you came looking for me, you were satisfied to find her instead. She said you stayed with her a week, promising when you left to return often—but you never kept that promise. She said she wrote to tell you of the baby's birth, but you never replied."

"None of that is true," he said, finally finding his voice. "Not a word of it."

I could feel my spirits soaring, for what seemed the first

time in seventeen years. I had never known Stephen to lie, whereas Ann had lied all the time. But I had believed her about Stephen. He had left behind a bracelet, patterned with the Windy Point jewels, an item that I had seen on his wrist a hundred times. He had obviously been to her house. Why wouldn't he have slept with her?

"I told her that angels never cared about their mortal offspring," I went on. "I told her that she now knew what it was like to live an angel-seeker's life, and that she should be glad she learned her lesson in a few months, instead of years."

"I never went to bed with her," he said, his voice insistent. "I was in her house perhaps two hours before I left again. I never came back because I had no reason to believe that *you* would ever be at that house again."

"I thought she was telling the truth," I said simply.

He came a step nearer, though he was already quite close. "And all this time, that's what you have thought of me?" he demanded. "That I would betray you with your sister—a woman I knew that you despised?"

"I had betrayed you with a man you have come to hate," I said. "I suppose it seemed like justice."

"I have never believed in a justice so severe," he said, sounding almost angry. "You did not understand me at all if that is what you believed."

I bowed my head. "I left Windy Point thinking I did not understand anyone," I said. "I had been wrong about so many things. I so easily could have been wrong about you."

He lifted his hands to lay them on my shoulders. I felt the heat of his skin through my thin shirt; I felt the tension of his body in the convulsive grip of his fingers. "I was angry when you went to Raphael's bed," he admitted. "I was devastated when you disappeared. I have spent the last eighteen years trying to convince myself it would be better if I never saw you again. But nothing has ever made me so sad as learning that all this time, you have believed me capable of being so cruel."

I lifted my own hands to place them on either side of his face. Along his jaw, I felt the faintest edge of roughness from his whiskers, though his cheeks were smooth as a baby's. "I deserve your anger," I said. "But don't waste your time being sad for me. I don't deserve your compassion."

"I can't help it," he said, stubborn and sincere as always. His arms drew me slowly against his body. "I have never been able to bear the idea that you might be unhappy. I can't bear the idea that anything I might have done could have given you a moment's pain."

"You never loved my sister," I said. "Just hearing those words washes all the pain away."

His arms gathered me against his body; his wings wrapped around us both, enfolding us in a cocoon of saturated white. I rested my head against his chest and heard the thunderous hammering of his heart. My arms went around his back, my palms flat against his warm skin, and I felt feathers brush my hands with a whispering touch.

Sweet Jovah singing, if I could stand—just like this—for the rest of my life, I would be unutterably happy.

"I do not know," he said, and I heard his voice both above me and beneath me, rumbling against my ear, "that it will be possible for me to let you go again."

I laughed shakily and clung more tightly. "Oh, it is very exciting to meet with an old lover again, and all sorts of crazy feelings are stirred up," I said in a teasing way. "But then you start to remember her annoying habits—the way she gobbles her food or how she snorts when she laughs—and it turns out you didn't really miss her all that much. In fact, you start wishing she would go away again very soon."

He pulled back just enough to frown down at me. "What I remember now is that you would never let me be serious."

I stretched up enough to give him a quick kiss on the mouth. Just to get it over with—that first kiss after a long estrangement, which can otherwise be so important and so disappointing. "What I remember is that you were always much too serious for your own good."

"But I mean what I say," he said. "I do not want to fly out of Laban and fly out of your life."

There was a time I would have said, "Then take me with you to Monteverde!" and blissfully cut every other tie I had formed. I wouldn't have minded if I harmed anyone I left behind; I wouldn't have cared if my headlong action resulted in me being left alone and adrift when my angel protector grew tired of me. I never used to think about consequences or other people's feelings. Back then, I scarcely thought at all.

"I have never been able to imagine a time that you would be back in my life, even temporarily," I said quietly. "You have no idea how thrilled and hopeful I am that such a thing might occur. But I must behave rationally and I must think of others besides myself. I cannot abandon Sheba, and I do not want to abandon the farm. And so much time has passed! We may find that the emotions we feel this hour cannot be sustained for another year or even another day. Can we proceed slowly to figure out what we should do next?"

Now he was the one to plant a swift kiss on my mouth. "*Cautious*—it is not a word I ever expected to pair with *Salome*," he said. "I do not believe that what I am feeling now will quickly fade. But I admit that we face obstacles. And I am willing to work around them with a certain amount of care."

"You will create a frenzy if you come to visit me at the farm," I said. "Just a few weeks ago, angels arrived at the hold to perform a weather intercession, and all our young girls went mad with desire. One of them even left with the angels when they departed. I assume she is still at Windy Point." I shook my head. If she was not, then Neri's fate was probably even more disastrous than I had described.

I felt Stephen grow tense. "Angels were visiting the place where you live?" he asked stiffly. "Which ones?"

"Hiram, Saul, and the Archangel," I said steadily.

His arms turned to iron, but he did not fling me aside. "And did you have conversation with Raphael?"

"I tried to avoid it," I said, "but, yes. He seemed amused to find me in a menial situation, earning my living with such mundane work. He's the one who told me you had left Windy Point."

He did not answer, but he looked so wretched that I had to try to reassure him. "Stephen. I hate Raphael. If I knew that I would never have to see him again, I would thank Jovah without ceasing. I know it is my own fault if you don't believe me, but I never loved him. He dazzled me and I wanted the glory I thought I could have if he kept me near, but long before I left

Windy Point eighteen years ago I had come to despise him. The only emotions I felt when I saw him at the farm were contempt and revulsion. And a certain amount of fear."

He looked down, a little shamefaced. "You think I'm a jealous fool."

I lifted my hand to pat his cheek again. "I think it is astonishing that you could care enough to be jealous over *me*."

"Raphael took what I wanted most," he said quietly, "and threw it away."

"Then let us make sure he never has a chance to destroy anything else we value."

"I still love you, Salome."

"Oh, Stephen," I whispered, "I love you so much that it hurts my heart."

❧

We spent the next two hours on that lonely, uninhabited, ordinary stretch of ground, building ourselves a small square of paradise. The sun was hot enough to be uncomfortable, so we moved under the shade of one of the trees. Arms wrapped around each other and wings sheltering us from the slightest wind, we talked, we kissed, we confessed, we forgave. You would think both of us were a little too old for flinging aside inhibitions in a relatively public place, but we even stripped off our clothes and made love there in that blessed and almost holy spot.

I could not believe how completely the bitterness of eighteen years dissipated to be replaced by incandescent happiness. I was like a tarnished silver goblet polished to a new shine. There were no marks on me; you would not have believed I had ever been dull and neglected. From the things he said, Stephen was going through much the same transformation. Certainly, just by looking at him, I could see the way delight reshaped his solemn face. It was dizzying to think I was the one who had such power to change him.

"In a week, then, I will come to the farm to see you," he said once we had resumed our clothes and were sitting up, closely and comfortably embraced.

"More likely ten days," I said. He was being completely unrealistic about how long it would take to fly to Monteverde—

where he owed Ariel a message—and back to this corner of the world.

"You had better prepare Sheba and all those other silly girls for my arrival! Let them know that I am coming to see *you*."

"Sheba won't be so surprised—she knows there is something interesting in my past—but everyone else will be astonished. They think I am so straitlaced and a little prim."

"Perhaps Sheba would like to come live at Monteverde," he suggested.

"Perhaps she would, but I am not bringing her anywhere near an angel hold," I retorted. "I need to see her married to a dull, respectable man who will worship her and keep her in comfort. She doesn't realize it yet, but that is the best life any woman could hope for."

"She might want to make her own decision about that."

"She can make whatever decision she wants as long as it doesn't include angels."

He didn't answer that, but I could feel the skepticism in his silence. He didn't know Sheba, but I suppose he remembered me at a youthful age, and he knew full well that I had not cared about anyone's opinion but my own.

"I look forward to meeting her," he said, "in a week."

I laughed. "Or ten days."

He sighed and rose to his feet, pulling me up beside him. "If I am to return so quickly, I must be on my way now," he said. "I hate to leave you so soon after having found you again, and yet—"

"I am not afraid that you will not come back for me," I said. "That makes it easier for me to see you go."

Still, it was hard. We lingered another ten minutes in that tiny grove, another twenty. When he finally caught me up in his arms and took wing, I could tell that he dawdled on the flight, and we circled Laban more than once while we spoke another set of good-byes. I did not particularly want to have to explain my situation to any of my traveling companions, so I had Stephen put me down on the very edge of town, where fewer people were likely to see us. More farewells, more quick and hungry kisses, and then he tore himself away.

"Leave now or never leave," he said, backing away from me. "I will return as soon as I possibly can."

I watched him fling himself aloft. I stood there a full ten minutes, my hand up to shade my eyes, watching his narrow shape dwindle to the size of a bird, to a speck, to nothing.

Except that my body remembered every kiss, every touch, I might have thought I had imagined him. Except that my heart was so light it practically lifted me to my toes, I would have thought the whole day a dream.

~

Sheba hurried into our shared inn room, explanations tumbling from her mouth before she had even closed the door. "And then Adriel wanted to show me a dress she was thinking of buying, but it was *so* expensive, and I said we should try to bargain. And the merchant—he was Jansai, and I didn't like him at all—told us we insulted him with the price we offered, so we left his booth and found another, where they were much nicer, but I didn't realize how long we were gone, and I hope you weren't worried."

"Hope said she had seen you with the other girls not half an hour ago, so I knew you were all right," I said. "Have you made yourself sick eating from the vendors' booths, or do you want to have dinner? I'm meeting Hope and Joseph in an hour."

"Of course I want to have dinner with you!" she exclaimed. I knew she would prefer to go off with her friends again, but she figured she would do penance by joining me for the meal and being so sweet that I would lose any remaining anger. At times, her thoughts were so transparent I could hardly keep from laughing. "Do I have time to change my clothes? A drunkard spilled wine all over my dress."

About thirty minutes later, a small group of us sat at a pretty little restaurant with outdoor seating and festive lighting. Hope, Joseph, their two sons, Sheba, and I were joined by a few others from Thaddeus's farm, including Hara and David. The younger members of our party spent the whole meal flirting with each other, while Hope and Joseph and I talked more rationally about how we had passed our days.

In my case, of course, many details were omitted.

"Did you hear the angels?" Hope asked at one point. "Utterly divine! I just stood there in the middle of the street with my mouth hanging open."

"I did hear them," I admitted. "I never expect to be moved by their voices as much as I always am."

"I can't say I agree with all of Raphael's policies, but Jovah's bones! The man has a voice," said Joseph.

I looked up sharply at that. "The Archangel is here in Laban?" I said. "He wasn't among the angels that *I* saw."

"I believe they were performing at several venues," Hope answered.

I glanced at Sheba, but she and Hara were busy teasing Hope's older son, using one of their own combs to style his hair in a different fashion and laughing immoderately at the results. "I wonder if he might have news of Neri," I said in a low voice.

"Who—oh, the girl from your farm," Hope said. "Well, I don't know that I would have the courage to approach him to ask."

"No," I said. "I'm certain I don't."

I was not surprised when, at the end of the meal, Sheba turned to me and prettily asked if she could go to the dance that had been scheduled for the evening. I had seen the raw wood dance floor being laid and sanded in the center of town; I had been certain Sheba would want to attend.

"Please say yes, Aunt Salome," she said. She only called me *aunt* when she wanted to melt my heart. "I promise I won't talk to anyone I don't know."

"I'll go with her, and I won't let her out of my sight," David spoke up.

"We'll watch out for her," said Hope's older son. He glanced at Hara. "For *all* our girls," he added.

I wasn't too concerned about the possibilities for trouble at the dance, to tell the truth. Angels' wings made it so difficult for them to participate in such an activity that they rarely attempted it, and Raphael always avoided any pastime that might make him look ridiculous. In fact, Sheba would probably be far safer on the dance floor tonight than in almost any other location in Laban.

"Well, I will come with you for at least a little while," I said, as if allowing myself to be convinced. "I will see how respectable this crowd is. But you must come back to the inn with me if I don't like how people are behaving."

"I will."

"And in any case, you must be back in our room by midnight."

"I will be, I promise."

Hope's husband was already pulling out his money. "Then let's pay our bill and go," he said.

&

As I expected, the energy level at the makeshift outdoor dance arena was very high and the average age of the couples on the floor was about nineteen. The music—provided by a quartet of fiddlers and flautists so good they had to be from Luminaux—was exuberant, and the mood was infectiously happy.

"Even I would be tempted to go out there, if someone would be willing to have such an old bag as a partner," Hope murmured to me.

David instantly offered his arm. "You could dance with me," he said.

Hope laughed, charmed and delighted. I smiled. It was for just such easy courtesies that I found David so likable.

"Then let's dance," Hope said.

Hara and Sheba quickly paired up with the Danfrees boys, and I was left standing beside Joseph.

"I hope you aren't too disappointed," he said. "But ever since I broke my foot five years ago, I find it painful to dance. Not that I was ever too interested in it before," he added.

"Not disappointed at all," I said. "I'd rather watch."

I stayed about an hour, long enough to see Sheba rotate through four partners, all of them young men that I knew. Even the many strangers on the floor did not alarm me, for they all looked like hardworking farm boys happy to be away from the fields for a night and eager to make a good impression on local girls. I saw a few Edori in the crowd, as brightly dressed and lighthearted as any of the farmhands, but I had no objection to Edori, either. They were wanderers—a little feckless, a touch irresponsible—but generally peaceable and honest people, and I would never expect them to offer harm to a stranger.

There were no Jansai at the dance. And no angels. No one I would view with suspicion or alarm.

Once Hope and I were satisfied that our charges were in no danger, she and her husband and I made our way back to the inn. I was comfortably exhausted, and Hope yawned with every other footstep.

"When do you leave for the Eyrie?" I asked through a yawn of my own.

"The day after tomorrow," Joseph answered. "I figure it will take us about a week to get there, if we don't push the horses too hard."

"When are you leaving for the farm?" Hope asked.

"Tomorrow around noon. There will be plenty to do by the time we get home."

Hope sighed. "I don't even want to *think* about the work that will pile up while we're traveling, even though the boys are going back home instead of on to Velora. We'll be gone nearly three weeks!"

"You'll love every minute of it," I said. "Buy yourself something pretty in Velora."

We separated to our individual rooms, and I was in bed scarcely ten minutes after I shut the door. Not asleep, however—though I felt like I was dreaming, as if I might have been dreaming this entire day.

Stephen had found me. Stephen still loved me. Stephen was back in my life.

What had I done to deserve, at such a point in my existence, such felicity, such joy? How could someone so flawed be heaped with such riches? Why had the god placed his finger on my heart—why had he spoken my name?

I was not used to praying. I had not often turned to Jovah, either to seek comfort or beg forgiveness. But tonight I whispered my fervent thanks and promised I would never take my good fortune for granted. And then I snuggled deeper into my pillow and spent the night dreaming about my angel lover.

～

I slept late, but Sheba slept later. She only mumbled an incoherent reply when I asked her if she was interested in breakfast, so I left her alone and went down to the inn's taproom to see what was on hand. Hope was there by herself, since her sons were also recovering from a late night and Joseph had gone to see about the horses. After our meal, we sallied out to investigate what new wonders might be offered in Laban on the second day of the festival. Naturally, we ended up back in the market area, sorting through jewels and trinkets and fabrics.

"I know I will want to spend money in Velora, but I can't resist this cloth. It's so utterly *blue*," Hope said.

"Buy it. Or you will be thinking about it the rest of your life," I advised. "Which is the very reason I'm going to purchase these red gloves. Completely impractical! But I love them."

I would have shopped happily with Hope for the rest of the day, but I knew the wagons would be leaving for the farm within the next couple of hours, and I might need to roust Sheba out of bed. Hope returned to the inn with me and went off to show Joseph her latest purchases. I opened the door to my own room, talking before I was even inside.

"Time to get up and get dressed, sleepy girl," I said cheerfully.

But I was speaking to myself.

No Sheba drowsed in the bed or stood by the vanity, combing out her hair. My first thought was that she must be downstairs getting breakfast, but then I was struck by the quality of *emptiness* in the room. None of her shoes were lying in the middle of the floor, where I had tripped over them a dozen times. None of her dresses thrown over the back of a chair. Her suitcase was missing from the foot of her bed.

I kept staring around blankly. I had a hard time understanding that Sheba was *gone*. Why would she leave? Where would she go?

She had clearly planned her departure carefully and deliberately, slipping out with all her possessions during the short time I was out. Giving me no hint of what she might be intending. Wherever she had gone, it was obviously someplace that she knew would earn my violent disapproval.

Even as I had the thought, my eyes fell on an object she had left lying on her pillow. My stomach cramped with sudden horror. My skin grew cold.

It was a bracelet, a thick, smooth silver band set with an unbroken string of rubies. Rubies to signify the angel was from Windy Point.

This particular pattern to identify the Archangel himself.

Sheba had run away with Raphael.

Five

After all, I knew exactly what I must do.

Perhaps I had been planning for this moment for half my life—not even knowing it—coming up with a strategy for how I would rescue Sheba from Windy Point. Certainly the goal that had guided my existence for the past fourteen years had been keeping Sheba safe, and in my mind, she could never be in greater danger than she would be if she threw her lot in with angels. To be more specific, the most dangerous decision she could ever make would be placing herself at the mercy of Raphael.

All this time, I must have expected it to happen. Or feared it so greatly that I already knew what my next move would be.

So calmly I could hardly believe it possible, I went in search of the inn's proprietor and asked for paper and ink. Back in my room, I wrote out a simple letter in a single draft and sealed it with wax from one of the candles in the wall sconce. I bundled all my own belongings into the battered bag that I had owned since I first left home at the age of sixteen. There were still a few items rattling around on the bottom that I had never bothered to take out. A comb missing half its teeth, a hair ribbon I could still use in dire emergency, old toiletries, dried-up cosmetics. I locked the empty room behind me and stepped down the hall to knock on Hope's door.

Perhaps my expression wasn't quite as tranquil as I believed, because the instant she saw me, Hope drew me into the room and demanded to know what was wrong.

"Sheba has left with Raphael," I said.

"No! Salome, that's dreadful news! Are you certain? Did anyone see them go?"

Joseph, who had been standing across the room, strode over. "Do you want me to make inquiries?"

I shook my head. "It's not necessary. She left me a message."

"What are you going to do?" Hope asked.

"Is there anything *to* do?" Joseph said more practically. "Assuming she went willingly—"

"I believe she did." Sheba was a very smart girl. If she had been taken from the room by force, she would have found a way to let me know.

Joseph shrugged. "Then she has made her choice, and neither she nor Raphael will welcome your interference."

"If she had left with any other angel, I might sit back. I might say, 'Let her decide how she will spend or waste her life.' But not Raphael. I cannot let him have her."

Hope gave me a sharp look. "That's a strange thing to say. What do you know about the Archangel that should worry us?"

I shook my head and proffered my sealed note. "I know you are going to the Eyrie to speak with Gabriel," I said. "Unless I show up in Velora when you do and take back my letter, can you give this to him?"

Hope took it from me willingly enough, but her face showed even more astonishment and curiosity. "Of course, but— Salome—where are you going? What are you planning?"

"What's in the letter?" Joseph wanted to know.

I shook my head again, a small, despairing smile shaping my lips. "News that I think the next Archangel should have, maybe. And maybe not. I am going to Windy Point to ask Raphael to release my niece. If he does, I will have him fly me to Velora, and I will take my letter from your hand. If he doesn't—then I will stay at Windy Point and Gabriel will know what I have written. It will be up to Raphael."

"We'll be staying at my brother's house. His name is Adam Danfrees," Joseph said.

"I'll write down the address for you," Hope said, hurrying across the room.

"Then I will head straight to Adam's house when I arrive," I said. "If I arrive."

In a minute, Hope came back and pressed a scrap of paper in my hand. "How will you get to Windy Point? Do you want us to drive you there?"

I shook my head. "I want you to go to Velora with my message. I will find some means of transportation."

Hope was still watching me. "Are you in danger? Should I insist on accompanying you while Joseph goes on to Velora?"

Would I be in danger? That was an interesting question. I honestly didn't know the answer. "I'll be fine," I said. "I hope to see you at Adam's house within the week."

I picked up my suitcase and left the room, while Hope called farewells after me. Downstairs in the innyard, I found two of the four wagons that had come to Laban from Thaddeus's farm. The horses were already hitched and some of the other workers had thrown their belongings in the back.

Hara and Adriel were crowding close to David, who stood at the head of his team, feeding apples to the horses. The young women were giggling and flirting; it was clear they intended to ride back to the farm in his vehicle.

"Girls, I need you to deliver a message to Thaddeus for me," I said. "I must go after Sheba, and I don't know how long I'll be gone."

Naturally, that elicited cries from the girls and a sudden intentness from David. "Go after Sheba," he repeated. "Where did she go?"

"To Windy Point," I said baldly. "And I want to fetch her back."

The girls squealed again, although this time their voices were tinged with envy. David's expression turned grim. "Windy Point," he said.

"If anyone comes to the farm looking for me," I added, "tell him where I've gone."

Oh, Jovah only knew what Stephen would think if he arrived at the compound to find I had run back to Windy Point the instant he left me. He would be furious—he would be disgusted—he would feel betrayed, again, again, again. But, assuming he had spoken the truth and he really intended to come for me the minute he could leave Monteverde, he would almost certainly be at the farm before I could get back from Velora.

If I ever made it to Velora. If I was not able to blackmail Raphael into tossing Sheba aside, I would never leave Windy Point.

Hara was staring at me. "Who would come looking for you?" she said, honestly puzzled. I had never received visitors the whole time Sheba and I had lived there. I had told everyone that the rest of my family was dead. Of course, that didn't answer the question about why I had no friends, but no one had been rude enough to ask it out loud.

"There is an angel named Stephen," I said. "He and I have—business—to discuss. I believe he will come looking for me within the next two weeks. Please make sure he knows where I've gone. Please make sure he knows that I have gone after my niece. I wouldn't want him to think that I had left for any trivial reason."

Hara nodded, but she still looked so dumbfounded that I didn't think I could rely on her to convey accurate information to anyone. I turned to David. "Will *you* make sure Thaddeus is informed of my whereabouts?" I asked him. "And if Stephen comes looking for me, will you tell him my story?"

David appeared to come to a quick decision. "No," he said. "I'm going with you to Windy Point."

"What?" Adriel cried.

"We're riding back with you!" Hara exclaimed. "All our things are in the wagon!"

"Well, you'll just have to go in one of the other carts," David said. "There's plenty of room."

"I would welcome your company, but you don't have to take me there," I said.

He gave the horses one last pat and strode around to the back of the wagon, where he started unloading the girls' suitcases. I saw that they had also accumulated a large number of parcels, no doubt filled with items purchased at the fair. Hara and Adriel trailed behind him, bleating their dismay, but he ignored them completely. Once all their possessions were neatly stacked in the yard, he faced me.

"When can you leave?"

"I'm ready now."

He picked up my bag and threw it in the back of the wagon. "Then let's go."

~

It was a three-day trip from Laban to Windy Point. David and I accomplished much of it in silence. Strangely, this led me to like him even more. I watched him covertly as he guided the horses. His face was thoughtful and determined, but not furrowed in rage or bitterness. Despite the fact that he was clearly eager to get to our destination, he never pushed the horses too hard or expressed frustration when bad roads or slow-moving travelers forced us to slacken our pace. He spoke to me with unfailing courtesy and always made sure I was comfortable before we set out in the mornings. In fact, he reinforced every favorable impression I had ever had of him. This was the kind of man—if not, in fact, *the* man—that I had always hoped Sheba would be wise enough to marry.

I said as much to him on the second day. We were leaving the very small roadside inn where we had spent the night, me in the only room available and David in the barn, sleeping in the wagon. I don't think he had given a second's thought to what kind of accommodations we might seek on the road; I doubted he had more than a few coins to his name. But I was flush with money. I had hoarded my salary for the past ten years and I could have afforded almost any room in all of Samaria for as long as I wished to stay. I paid for our food, I paid for our beds, and I had the feeling my solvency impressed David almost as much as his maturity impressed me.

"What I regret most about Sheba's ill-advised action," I said abruptly, after we had traveled two hours without speaking, "is that it will change how you view her. She is young to be thinking of marriage, but I always hoped she would think about you when the time came. And now I am very much afraid that you will no longer think of her when you're looking for a wife."

He glanced at me. It seemed to me that his gray eyes were confident and wise. "One of the things that always drew me to Sheba was her—her brightness. The intensity with which she lived life, with which she *desired* things. She wants glamour and passion and excitement. She thinks she'll get it with the angels. You think she's ruined her life. What you don't understand is that she hasn't changed. She's no different from the person I've always loved. I can't hate her for being so true to her soul."

"That's generous," I said in a subdued voice.

He shrugged. "That's just how I feel."

We continued on for a few moments in silence. "I don't think she understands what awaits her at Windy Point," I said at last. "If she had chosen Monteverde or even the Eyrie—I might not have gone after her. But Windy Point is different. Raphael is different. I can't let her stay there."

He nodded. "Do you have any idea how you will get into Windy Point? Isn't it at the top of a mountain?"

"Oh," I said, "I've always been able to find my way into an angel hold. Don't you worry about that."

~

It can't be said often enough: Windy Point isn't like the other holds. Not just because it is in such an inhospitable spot— the Eyrie is also in a remote location—but because it seems to thrive on its inaccessibility. There is no friendly, bustling town like Velora nestled at the foot of the mountain, ready to accommodate travelers and provide services to the angels. Oh, people do congregate there at the foothills. There are a few impermanent-looking shacks where you can find shelter for the night and buy necessary goods, but it's not like there's a thriving independent city where any reasonable person would want to spend any time. A few Jansai caravans are usually drawn up at the base of the mountains—petitioners from across the region are usually camped out, waiting for an angel to appear and address their concerns—and young women are always there by the dozens. Pretty, polished, determined, and foolish young women.

Angel-seekers, hoping someone will fly them up to the hold.

What you don't see all that often, here at the base of the mountain, is angels. Raphael has always been a little cavalier about his duties to the people of Jordana, the province for which, theoretically, Windy Point is responsible. Petitioners from all over Jordana come to the hold with one request or another. Sometimes they have disputes they want the angels to adjudicate, but more often they are looking for the kind of assistance only angels can provide. They want angels to come to their homesteads and pray for rain, or for the cessation of rain; they want angels to pray for seeds or medicines, which—when the appropriate song is performed—come pelting to the ground with the force of hail. In other words, they want the angels to intercede with the god on their behalf.

The angels from Monteverde and the Eyrie constantly fly out to ask the god for weather or drugs or grain. On any given day, those holds might be half empty. And at the Eyrie, or so I have been told, Gabriel encourages his angels to routinely fly over the open land, peering down from above, looking out for signs of trouble both subtle and overt. Is there flooding? Is there fire? Have residents of some small farming community raised a plague flag, which is the sign that the mortals below are in dire need of assistance? I would guess Ariel sends the Monteverde angels out quite often in such a manner as well.

But not Raphael. The god alone knows how he spends his time, since he gives so little of it to his people.

"We need to find a place to stay or a place to camp," I said to David as we arrived at the windswept and barren excuse for a town. "We might be here a few days before I am able to get to the hold."

He surveyed the collection of carts and carriages and buildings huddled in the shadow of the mountain. "Camping might be the better option, though I suppose you'll find that uncomfortable."

I gave him a grim smile. "You'll find that my standards are flexible."

We found a spot on fairly level ground, a stone's throw from a few Edori tents. I knew from past experience that there were public wells in the middle of the "town," so I fetched water while David unhitched the horses and looked for firewood.

I took a circuitous route through the pitched tents and the makeshift buildings, and I strolled down the muddy road that served as the main street for this disreputable place, and I looked hard at every girl I saw. I may have passed a dozen of them, all very attractive, some fair, some dark, some who couldn't have been more than sixteen, others camped on the outskirts of thirty. Most were buxom, but a few were slim as baby birches and wore their fragility like dyed exotic clothing.

What kinds of girls would the angels find most appealing?

My eye was caught by a young woman who might have been three or four years older than Sheba. She had rich auburn hair, thick and curly and falling past her waist. Her eyes were dark green, and her pale face was beautiful in an elegant, icy way. Among the blondes and brunettes she was strikingly different; I thought she would catch any angel's eye.

I filled our water bottles at one of the wells, then retraced my steps. The redhead was standing outside the doorway of one of the few existing structures, gazing moodily up at the mountaintop. It seemed she had enough money, or enough charm, to secure herself a room here in a place where there were very few rooms to rent. Another point in her favor. She was willing to invest resources to obtain her desired result.

I stopped right in front of her and said, "I can help you get an angel lover."

She instantly transferred her attention to me, assessing me for lunacy or genuine useful potential. No pretense about her—no shocked protestation that she had no interest in such a thing. She just said, "How?"

I waved in the general direction of David's cart. "I have manna seed among my possessions."

Her eyes sharpened, but her expression became skeptical. Everyone—or, at least, every angel-seeker—knew that ground-up manna seed was an aphrodisiac. If you fed it to the man you desired, he would instantly become smitten with you. But manna seed was extremely rare these days, so much of it gone to making love potions that none was left to sow new plants. I supposed in time there would be no manna left at all.

"Where did you get it?" she asked. "And how much would it cost me?"

"I bought it years ago in Luminaux when I thought I might have use for it. And it would cost you only a favor."

"What favor?"

I gestured at the mountain hulking over us, jagged and unfriendly and just now darkening with the onset of night. "I want to go to Windy Point."

She made a little sound, halfway between a laugh and a sneer. "So do we all. But I have been here four days, waiting for an angel to fly me up to the hold, and not one has come down off the mountain."

Four days. Even by Raphael's standards, that was lax. "Then surely an angel will appear in a day or two," I said. "You want to be ready."

"How do I know that you really have the seed?"

"I'll show it to you. Will you recognize it?"

She nodded. Of course she would. "When will you give it to me?"

"When we are both inside Windy Point."

She made an impatient motion. "Not intending any rudeness, but what would persuade any angels to welcome *you* to a hold?"

I tried not to laugh. It was a fair question. "Tell them I did you a kindness on the road. Tell them I am an accomplished cook. Tell them I will work hard for no wages, that all I care about is being around angels. Make up any story you like. But I have manna seed, and if you want it, you have to get me into Windy Point."

"I want it," she said, "if that's what you really have."

She accompanied me back to our campsite, where David eyed her with silent disapproval. He had taken a couple of tarps and rigged a tent over the back of the wagon, and it actually looked rather inviting. He'd also started a fire and laid out the meat and bread we had bought at the inn we'd left this morning. I found myself hoping some enterprising Jansai or Edori had food items for sale, or pretty soon we were going to go hungry.

"Who's she?" David asked.

I looked at the young woman, realizing I had never asked her name. "Demaris," she supplied.

"She's going to help me get into the hold," I said.

He warmed up a little at that. "Is she having dinner with us?" he asked.

I looked at Demaris, a question in my eyes, but she shook

her head. "I've already paid for room and board. I want to get my money's worth."

"Let me show you the seeds," I said. I climbed into the wagon, under the tarp, and rooted around in my luggage for the wooden box at the very bottom of the bag—one of those items I had never bothered to toss out, even once my traveling days were mostly behind me. Sweet Jovah singing, I could remember a day when I hoarded these hard white grains as if they were diamonds. I had baked them into breads; I had ground them up and sprinkled them like salt over steaming dinner plates. Some people doubt their efficacy, but I had always had good luck with manna seeds. Every angel I shared them with became my lover, at least for a night or two. More than that you couldn't ask of a potion.

I had even given some to Raphael once, though it was at his request and he watched me stir the white dust into his glass of wine. He had been particularly ardent that night, and both of us remarked upon it, though we never tried the experiment again.

I had never fed the drugs to Stephen.

I shook a couple of grains into my hand and climbed out of the wagon to show Demaris. David stood to one side, frowning, as Demaris inspected the seeds, rolling them between her fingertips and sniffing at them delicately.

"How much do you have?" she asked.

"About a hundred grains," I said. "Have you ever tried manna before?"

She shook her head.

"You shouldn't use more than ten grains on any one person," I said. "If a man doesn't react to that amount, he won't react at all, so don't waste them trying to increase the dosage. Just try them on someone else."

"How many will you give me?"

I shrugged. "All of them."

"You don't want to keep any for yourself?"

I couldn't keep from laughing. "No. Jovah's bones. I've had enough of trying to better my life through the man I could catch by whatever means necessary. Here's a secret: It never made my life better. My life didn't improve until *I* started making sure I got what I needed."

She gave a faint, disdainful shrug. "Maybe you didn't catch the right man."

"And maybe the kind of man who can be caught isn't the kind of man anyone with any sense would want."

"If you see angels come down from the mountain," she said, "come find me. I won't have time to go looking for you."

I nodded. "I'll do that."

She didn't linger; she had no interest in us. David and I ate in near silence, until we began discussing the state of our provisions and the best way to restock them. I turned over some of my cash to him and told him to bargain with anyone who had food to sell. I wouldn't need money while I was in the hold, but it would be a different story once I arrived at Velora.

If I made it to Velora.

First I had to make it to Windy Point.

~

It was two days before the angels came, and then there was a whole flock of them, fluttering down like great snowy birds. I snatched up my bag and ran for town. Everyone else was on the move, too, the dozens of us who had camped here patiently for days, everyone eager to secure an interview. I wove between clusters of farmers and groups of Jansai, detoured around the individual angel-seekers, and found Demaris pacing in front of the building where she had rented a room.

"Have you talked to any angels?" I panted.

"Not yet. But at least three of them saw me and made a point of smiling."

"They'll be back," I said. "They'll deal with the petitioners first and then start picking through the girls."

She turned to face me, hands spread in a gesture that invited inspection. "What do you think? How do I look?"

I suggested she put on a bright scarf in purple or red—something flowing and colorful, something that would attract attention. I told her to wear her hair forward over her shoulders and muss it a little bit. Raphael had always liked long hair; most angels did. Other than that, not much needed enhancement. Demaris was a striking young woman.

We drifted toward the center of that little town—all the

angel-seekers did—and soon there was a ring of pretty girls posing casually around a makeshift conference table set up right on the main dirt road. Angels sat in specially made chairs, with cutaway backs designed to support their spines without troubling their wings, while mortals took turns standing before them and airing their grievances. Twice while we watched, angels took wing, going off to handle some more immediate problem.

That still left about a dozen angels.

It took nearly the whole day for the angels to meet with all the petitioners. The sky was ever so faintly tinged with red when the last farmer nodded and stepped away. Almost as one, the angels came to their feet, joking and talking with each other. Almost as one, the angel-seekers surged forward, smiles on their lips, seduction in their hearts.

I wondered what Demaris would do to set herself apart, to catch an angel's roving eye, but it seemed she had already done the trick. Two young angels whom I did not recognize—in their twenties, perhaps, both of them wickedly gorgeous—came straight toward her and laughingly competed for her attention.

"Do I have to pick just one of you?" she said, splitting a smile between them. "I don't think I can choose."

"*I'll* share if *he'll* share," said the one who was taller and darker.

"I've always been considered a generous man," said the other.

Demaris pouted. "But I have to ask a favor. I have a friend who wants nothing so much as to see an angel hold. She said she would work, she would clean, she would do *anything*, if only she could get inside Windy Point."

The dark one glanced in my direction, wholly uninterested. "How important to you is this friend?"

Demaris gave him a slow smile. "Well," she purred, "she taught me some—skills—that I think might end up seeming very important to *you*. So I think *you're* the one who owes her a favor."

Both men laughed raucously at that, eager and delighted. "Doesn't matter to me," said the shorter one. "I'll carry her up to the mountain if you want to fly with Matthew."

Demaris picked up her flowered canvas bag and held out her other arm. "That sounds perfect."

And just like that, I was in an angel's arms, flying up to Windy Point.

Six

I wandered the corridors of Windy Point for an hour, trying to find Sheba.

For the most part, the hold was exactly as I remembered. The gray stone walls seemed to have been hewn directly out of the bones of the mountain; here and there you could imagine you still saw the original fault lines carved by axe or chisel. The corridors, which were gloomy and dark, snaked and twisted around in no easily comprehensible plan. Newcomers invariably got lost, and there were stories of people who had starved to death trying to find their way back to a familiar room, though I had always suspected those tales were apocryphal.

And the wind. Jovah defend me, the *wind*.

It moaned up from the floors, hissed down from the ceilings. Even the big interior rooms of the hold seemed linked to narrow passageways that rattled and whined and screeched with wind. The sounds were inescapable, night or day. Some people claimed that, after they had lived at the hold long enough, they grew used to the wind—or stopped noticing it— or began to like its mistuned music. I always assumed those people were lying.

Nonetheless, eighteen years ago, I had been familiar enough with these groaning passages to find my way easily from one part of the hold to another. I knew where the kitchens were located, where the laundry rooms could be found; I knew the hidden passageways that led to Raphael's private chambers and the back stairwells that climbed to the small rooms where servants and angel-seekers slept. Every time I came to a key turning, I would pause, consider, and make a choice. So far, I had been right every time.

But I still hadn't found Sheba.

I first tried the kitchen, where harassed cooks and sullen girls worked to clean away remnants of the evening meal. I snatched up some bread and cheese, which earned me a burning glance from the woman I took to be the head cook, and crammed it in my mouth while I looked around. But Sheba wasn't there.

She wasn't in the laundry area, the huge steaming vat of a room where workers were busy around the clock washing clothes and linens for the residents of the hold.

I made my way with some stealth to the common rooms, particularly the huge dining hall with its high chandeliers and endless array of tables. Dinner was long past, but at least twenty people remained, drinking wine, laughing immoderately, and nuzzling whatever partner they had picked out for the night. I stayed well back, clinging to the shadows along the walls, trying to determine if Sheba was one of the girls wrapped in the arms of a drunken angel. She wasn't, and I was unutterably relieved.

I moved on.

Not until I reached the cramped upper corridors did I actually speak to anyone. I passed the open door of one of those tiny rooms and heard two women inside bitterly arguing about someone called Jacob.

"Excuse me," I said, peering in at their startled faces. "I'm looking for a girl named Sheba. Dark haired, about my height. Is she here?"

"What do you want with her?" one of the girls asked.

"I have a message for her. It's very important."

The other girl shrugged. "She sleeps in the room down the hall. The door with the big bare spot in the paint."

I felt my heart beat a little faster. "Is she there now?"

A hunch of the shoulders. "I don't know."

"Thank you."

But she wasn't in the room, which was so small it might originally have been designed for storage. A quick look through the possessions strewn around and I knew I was in the right place, for I recognized Sheba's shoes and jewelry.

But if she was not here, and she was not in any of the common areas, she was no doubt in bed with some angel.

Even I did not have the courage to stalk through these hallways and burst into angels' bedrooms at night, when most of them were probably engaged in some kind of sexual activity. With a sigh, I made room for my own suitcase on the floor next to Sheba's, and I lay down on the bed. Not expecting to be able to close my eyes, I fell asleep within minutes. Even the wind could not keep me awake for long.

❦

When I opened my eyes, Sheba was standing against the wall, staring at me. I made a little sound and scrambled to my feet, pushing my tangled hair back behind my ears. I wasn't sure what time it was—there were no windows in this room—but by the heavy, exhausted way I felt, I guessed it to be an hour or two past midnight.

"Sheba," I said.

I don't know what I expected her to say when she first laid eyes on me. I had been so focused on getting here, on finding her, on wresting her out of Raphael's cruel hands, that I had not bothered to wonder whether or not Sheba wanted to be rescued. Certainly if any of *my* fond relatives had come to Windy Point twenty years ago to try to convince me to leave, I would have laughed in their faces.

But Sheba was not laughing. Her face was so set that I could not read it, but she did not look horrified or contemptuous or angry or amused. She watched me a moment in utter silence, and then she said, "I knew you would come for me."

"I know you think the life of an angel-seeker is glamorous and exciting," I said, wishing I had given more thought to what I would say in this particular speech, "but it's not. It's degrading and ugly and powerless and short. I want you to come home with me."

"I want to come home," she said, still in that careful, neutral voice. "But Raphael won't let me."

I felt a clutch of fear. "You asked him already? You told him you wanted to leave?"

She nodded. "After my very first night with him. He was—" She paused, shook her head, and went on. "I wasn't a virgin, of course; I'm sure you knew that. But he—I found that I did not enjoy his company." She shrugged, conveying a wealth of information, from a deep sense of revulsion to a lack of self-pity. "That did not seem to trouble him."

"Raphael is a very depraved man."

"So I told him I wanted to go home. And he laughed. And he said someday an angel might have time to carry me down from the hold, but it wouldn't be any day soon."

"We'll leave tomorrow," I promised.

She went on as if I hadn't spoken. "And I knew you would come for me, but I also knew it wouldn't do any good. Raphael likes having people in his power. He will like having you in his power as well."

"I can deal with Raphael," I said. "Get some sleep now, and pack your things in the morning. We'll leave as soon as I've had a chance to talk to him."

Now some of her unnatural calm began to crack. I saw her eyes shine with tears, and her hands clench together, though she tried to hold on to her composed expression. "I wish that was true," she said, her voice hardly above a whisper. "But—"

In a single step, I was close enough to gather her into an embrace. She rested her head against my shoulder and began sobbing in my arms, something she had not done since she was eleven or twelve years old. "Don't worry, baby. Don't worry," I murmured into her ear. "Aunt Salome will save you from the angels."

❧

It was important to look good. To scrub off the grime of travel and wash my hair and put on the one clean dress that I had managed to save all during the trip from Laban. I didn't want to be *attractive* for Raphael—that wasn't it—but I did not want to seem strained and desperate. I needed the advantage of self-confidence, and I had always secured that by appearing my best.

I found I remembered precisely how to get to Raphael's private quarters.

I waited until nearly noon to seek him out. He was a notoriously late sleeper and he snarled through the early hours of the day. But once he had had a shave and a meal, he regained his urbanity and his self-possession. I wanted him to listen to me, and for that I needed him awake, alert, and sane.

There was the main door to his suite, of course, accessed from the front hallway. Depending on his mood or his activities, he sometimes declined to open this door, no matter how long a visitor knocked or called. But there was a secondary entrance, reached through a warren of back corridors, that fed directly to his bedroom. That door had rarely been locked back when I lived at Windy Point, and it was not locked this morning.

I stepped in and looked quickly around. A tangle of blankets on the bed, a confusion of clothing on the floor. Raphael wasn't immediately visible, but through the open door that connected to a small sitting room, I heard someone moving. I took a deep breath and strode through.

Raphael was standing in the middle of the room, scanning a piece of paper. He was half dressed and barefoot, but his well-muscled body glistened as if he had just stepped from a bath. His damp golden hair was just beginning to regain its curl; his wings were fluffed up behind him as if they had been newly washed and hung out in the sunshine to dry. It was hard for me to imagine a more beautiful man.

"Good morning, Raphael," I said.

He spun around to see who had addressed him, but the instant he recognized me, his expression changed from astonishment to delight.

"Salome!" he exclaimed. "But I have been expecting you for days!"

"I apologize for arriving so late," I said. "But I wasted time at the base of the mountain, waiting for angel transport."

He made a dismissive gesture. "Really, there is so much activity going on within the hold that it's hard to remember about the petitioners gathered below," he said.

"And you have so little interest in them."

He grinned. "Because other people are so much more interesting."

I wouldn't let him goad me. "Yes, indeed, Sheba is a fascinating girl," I said in a calm voice, "but it's time for her to leave Windy Point."

"I'm not so sure about that," he said. His face was filled with merriment. "I am very much enjoying her company."

"How odd," I said. "She has not enjoyed yours at all."

He laughed. "Oh, but the longer she stays here, the more accustomed to me she will become," he said. "It always takes a little time to understand someone else's habits and preferences."

"She's leaving today," I said. "And so am I. You or one of your angels will fly us off the mountaintop within the hour."

"No, you see, you're wrong about that," he said, his voice quite genial. "I like Sheba. And I rather like you. I say you shall *both* stay—until I am tired of you—which I think will not be for quite some time."

I watched him a moment in silence. My heart was beating very fast, but I still felt remarkably calm. I had known back in Laban that our conversation would go something like this. What kind of man holds a woman against her will? How could the Archangel be that kind of man? We must all hope Gabriel was nothing like Raphael or the whole of Samaria could fall to ruin in the next twenty years.

"The last time I was in Windy Point," I said, "you were a few short months away from your wedding day."

I had caught his attention. A sharp, arrested expression edged the laughter from his face. "Indeed I was."

I strolled deeper into the room, still not close enough for him to touch me. "The god had selected a Jansai girl named Leah to be your bride. You had met her briefly, but you didn't even know what she looked like, because of course her face was heavily veiled, as is the face of every Jansai woman."

"Yet her father had assured me she was beautiful, and if you've met her, you know he spoke the truth."

"Oh, I've met the woman you married," I said.

There was a short silence.

"She has been a fine angelica," he said at last. His eyes were narrowed. I wouldn't say he was worried, but he wasn't pleased.

"And yet you were not looking forward to your marriage,"

I said. "In fact, you told me you wished you could marry me instead."

He forced a laugh. "All angel-seekers pray that their angel lovers will offer to marry them. Are you sure you didn't dream such a conversation?"

I went on as if he had not spoken. "In fact," I said, "you told me you *would* marry me. If I was willing to make a few sacrifices. Give up my family. Give up my friends. Change my name to Leah. Pretend to be another woman altogether."

Now his expression was ugly. "As I recall, you expressed a certain contempt for my generous offer."

"I didn't mind the part about giving up every other aspect of my life. I'd have done it, and gladly, to be your bride. But the part where you would have to murder Leah so I could take her place—I admit, that bothered me a little."

He shrugged. "I still think it would have been an excellent plan! No one but a few of her sisters had ever seen her face. Who would know the difference?" He shrugged again. "But you refused and fled the hold, so I married my Jansai bride after all."

"That's the thing," I said. "You didn't. That woman who calls herself Leah and pretends to be your wife—her name was Sarah. She was an angel-seeker in Velora when I met her twenty years ago. Greatly changed by now, after a lifetime suffering at your side, but I know her. You killed that Jansai girl, after all."

"She was strong-willed and uncooperative and imagined she could tame me," Raphael said. "I knew I could not endure a month of her company, let alone twenty years. Putting her aside was the best decision I ever made."

"I think Gabriel would be very interested in knowing that the Archangel is a murderer."

Now his tawny eyes narrowed with menace. He came nearer and his golden wings began a nervous sweeping, back and forth, coming close enough to brush my toes before folding back. "I think *you* will never be the one to tell Gabriel such a story," he said in a dulcet voice. "Silly Salome, don't you realize you have just given me another reason to never set you free of Windy Point?"

"A letter is even now on its way to the Eyrie," I said. "In

the care of a friend. If I'm not there in—I think it is two days now—he will hand it over to the Archangel-elect. You may keep me here if you like, but Gabriel will arrive very soon, asking questions."

Now his handsome face was suffused with fury. He grabbed my shoulders in a grip so painful I had to swallow a cry. "You're lying," he said.

I stared up at him, letting all my hatred show. "I'm not," I said. "I have waited years to tell this story. I'm glad the time has finally come."

His hands tightened; he shook me, hard, and his angry face blurred before my eyes. For a moment, I thought my life was in real danger, but then he flung me from him so roughly that I stumbled against a chair and almost fell to the floor. I grabbed the back of the chair and steadied myself, taking a long breath.

He had his back to me now, but his wings quivered with indignation. "If I let you and your pathetic niece leave the hold," he said in a cold voice, "will you keep your silence?"

"Yes," I said.

He glanced at me over his shoulder. "I have no reason to trust you."

"I have kept silence so far," I said.

"And I have always wondered why."

"Perhaps I didn't think people would believe me."

"Somehow, I doubt that was your reason."

I shrugged. "I thought such knowledge would do more harm than good if it was loose in the world. The Archangel is a murderer! The man the god has raised up to the highest post is the man to be despised above all others! I thought it would cause such turmoil and chaos that Samaria might never recover."

He sneered. "And yet, when it serves your purposes, you are willing to expose me."

"Oh yes," I said. "To protect Sheba, I would beg the god for thunderbolts. I would bring the mountains down. I would destroy you—or anyone who tried to harm her."

"Too bad your own child died," he said. "What a mother you would have been."

"Thank the sweet god that my own son was born dead," I

replied in a steady voice. "So that I don't have to live with the knowledge that I brought a child of *yours* into the world."

Maybe I had gone too far. He whipped around and took a hasty step toward me, as if he wanted to seize me again and this time do real damage, but there was a sudden urgent pounding at the door.

"Raphael!" a man called furiously. "Raphael, let me in!"

We both recognized the newcomer's voice at the same time. I gasped; Raphael looked first angry and then amused. "And how did you ensnare *Stephen* in your net a second time?" he demanded.

I didn't answer. It now sounded like Stephen was kicking at the door in an attempt to break it down, and he continued to call Raphael's name. The Archangel crossed the room in three strides and threw the door open. Stephen practically tumbled inside.

"Enough!" Raphael thundered. "She is here, she is unharmed, and you will please me greatly if you remove her from my sight with all speed."

Stephen caught his balance and whirled around to locate me. "Are you all right? Has he hurt you?"

"How did you get here so quickly?" I demanded, running across the room to fling my arms around him. His skin was warm and slick with sweat. He must have flown at a blistering pace, mad with fear the whole time.

His arms squeezed me close, and his wings ruffled around me, betraying his agitation. "I didn't have to go all the way to Monteverde. I stopped for the night at Semorrah and Ariel was there. I arrived at the farm this morning—but you weren't there—"

"And they told you I had come to Windy Point, and you thought the very worst of me—"

He lifted his head to glare at Raphael. "They told me you had gone after your niece, and I thought the very worst of *him*," he said.

"How touching," Raphael said with a sneer. "I am moved by your affection for each other and mortified by your contempt for me. I shall repent my sins and pray to the god for forgiveness—if only you will leave. Both of you. *All* of you. Grab your niece and go."

Stephen released me and pivoted to face Raphael. He had pushed me behind him and made a little cage for me out of his wings, to protect me, I think. I could read his fury in the tension of his back. "You shall answer for the harm you have done to Salome," he said coldly.

"Actually, if you'd only been here five minutes earlier, you'd have learned she could inflict a great deal more harm on me than I could on her," Raphael said. "I believe you'll find that she doesn't want to be avenged. She just wants to leave this place."

I put both my hands on Stephen's waist and urged him gently toward the door. "Yes," I said. "I just want to find Sheba and go."

I felt Stephen's muscles bunch in protest; he planted his feet and would not budge. "I want to go *now*," I said.

"He is cruel and destructive, and it is wrong that he is never called to account," Stephen said.

"Someday the god will strike him down, but I don't want to be lingering still at Windy Point when that day comes," I said gently. "Stephen. Please take me away from here."

A moment longer he resisted, and then I felt his whole body loosen. Not speaking another word to the Archangel, Stephen stalked out the door and I followed him. Once we were in the hallway, I ducked out of the shelter of his wings and hurried to catch up with him, grabbing his hand and holding it tightly to my chest.

He glanced down at me. "What do you need to gather up before you can leave?"

"Sheba. And my clothes, I suppose, though I don't really care about them."

"Where is she?"

"In her room, I hope."

Now I took the lead and he followed. Over my shoulder I asked, "When did you get to Thaddeus's farm? What did you think when you found I was here? I was so afraid that you would be too angry with me to understand why I had to come."

"I arrived there this morning, very early. The moment I touched down, two girls came running out of the house asking, 'Are you Stephen? Are you Stephen?' I found it hard to believe you had been telling all your friends about me during the few days we had been separated, so I instantly suspected you had been called away and forced to leave a message for me." He touched me on the back, either to reassure me or to prove to himself that I was real. "Not for a second did I believe you had come to Windy Point to pursue a relationship with the Archangel."

I sighed with relief. "I was so worried about what you might think. I was more worried about what to say to you than what to say to Raphael."

"And what *did* you say to him?"

I shook my head. "I promised I would not repeat it if he would let us go."

There was a short silence. We continued winding through the hallways as fast as I could remember the turns. "Then I will not ask again," Stephen said at last.

In another five minutes, we were in the cramped corridor where the angel-seekers lived. Five or six girls clustered in the hallway outside Sheba's door, murmuring in excitement. One of them caught sight of me and exclaimed, "There she is!" It was a moment before I recognized her.

"Neri!" I said. She was so changed! Her straight brown hair had been cut and curled; her plain face had been artfully made up. She was wearing a dress so low-cut that Lazarene would have ordered her out of the kitchen—or off the farm altogether. "We have been so concerned about you! Are you all right?"

She laughed. "Oh, *quite* all right! I have become particularly close to half a dozen angels, and even the Archangel knows my name."

Sheba stepped out of her room, all our luggage in her hands. Her eyes went from me to Stephen. "Can we go? Who's this? He's not a Windy Point angel."

"I used to be. My name is Stephen," he introduced himself.

Neri took a step closer to him. "Hello, Stephen," she cooed. All the other girls smiled or waved or batted their eyes at him. He did not even appear to notice.

"He's a friend of mine from quite some time ago," I said. "He's going to take us off the mountain."

"Now?" Sheba demanded.

"If you're ready."

"Let's go."

I turned to follow her down the hall, hesitated, and looked back at Neri. "You can come with us, if you like," I said. "Stephen will return for you. You don't have to stay."

She laughed. "I *want* to stay, Salome, I assure you. Even more so once Sheba is gone! The Archangel will have time for other girls now."

I tried to hide my shudder. Glancing around at the other women in the hall, I said, "Any of you? Stephen will be happy to come back for everyone who wants to leave." He hadn't actually said so, of course, but I knew he would. Any angel-seeker torn from Raphael's arms would be a slap in the Archangel's face, and Stephen really wanted to administer a blow or two.

But the other girls all shook their heads. One or two looked wistful, I thought, as if thinking about the lives they used to lead before they came to Windy Point. The others looked determined, even eager. Like Neri, they saw Sheba's departure as a fresh opportunity for themselves.

"None of them will want to leave," Sheba said. "Come on. Let's go." She started moving forward again, but glanced back once at Stephen, who was behind me. His height and his wingspan made it a little tricky for him to pass through the narrow hallway, but he wasn't letting this slow him down any. Sheba asked him, "Can you carry both of us all the way back to the farm?"

"Yes," he said.

"But he doesn't have to," I said. "David is on the ground below with a wagon, waiting for you."

Sheba came to a dead stop and both Stephen and I nearly crashed into her. "*David.* Oh, no, no—I can't bear to face him," she said. She looked like she was about to start crying again. "He must think the worst of me—I deserve to have him think the worst of me—"

This reminded me so much of what I had said to Stephen a few short days ago! In a quiet voice, I said, "He deserves to hear your apologies. He deserves your thanks. He brought me here. He made it possible for me to rescue you. You owe him a chance to tell you how he feels."

"But, Aunt Salome—"

"And, anyway, I'm not going back to the farm, not just yet," I added. "I have to be in Velora as soon as possible, and I want Stephen to take me there."

"Velora! But I need you!" Sheba wailed.

"And I will be back with you as soon as I can," I said. "But I made a promise and I have to keep it, and it must be kept in Velora." I glanced back at Stephen. "At least—will you take me there? Today?"

He nodded, the faintest trace of amusement on his serious face. "Although it is not a trip that is easily accomplished in a day."

"If I am there by tomorrow evening, all should be well."

"That I think I can manage," he said.

I gave Sheba a little push. "Then let's go."

It took us another fifteen minutes to navigate the twisted corridors of the hold. Gusts of wind greeted us at every step, and the trapped breezes hooted and soughed through the passageways like demonic spirits. We also encountered mortals and angels along every turn. A few of them nodded or spoke to Sheba; a couple of the angels seemed startled to encounter Stephen and stared at him or said his name. Neither Sheba nor Stephen bothered to reply, and we were finally, finally, at the outer chamber with the wide gate that opened onto empty sky. The place where angels landed and took off when coming to or going from Windy Point.

"This young man David is waiting at the base?" Stephen asked, putting one arm around my waist and one around Sheba's.

"Yes," I said. "Just carry us down."

He tightened his hold and flung himself off the mountain. For a moment we plummeted through the sunny air, and I heard Sheba's smothered cry of fear, but in a moment his beating wings slowed our descent. We landed smoothly; Sheba and I instantly found our feet. She was still looking around unbelievingly, as if dazed to find herself free of Windy Point, when we heard someone shout her name and saw David racing toward us. I saw her face crumple with tears, and then she was running toward him with her arms outflung.

"I think you need not worry about whether they will be able to forgive each other," Stephen remarked.

"Although forgiving is not easy, and forgetting is often impossible," I said.

"What's important is to be willing to try," he replied.

I nodded, still watching Sheba. David had gathered her in a tight embrace and she was weeping into his shoulder. I knew she was capable of sophisticated pretense, but I believed that, at this moment, the emotions she showed were real. After all, Sheba was not as much like me as I had feared. She had learned so much more quickly than I had what things in life had value and what things were so worthless they should be thrown aside. If she still wasn't quite sure what dreams to pursue, she saw clearly what dreams were false and bitter. I had such hopes for her. The rest of her life could be so bright.

"Tell her good-bye, then let's take off for Velora," Stephen said. "I want to get you there by your deadline."

I smiled up at him and twined my arms around his neck. "Thank you for taking such good care of me," I said. "Thank you for not asking questions."

He smiled and kissed the top of my head. His arms went around my waist and his wings draped themselves over my shoulders. I nestled against him, sheltered and content. "I want to be done with this part," he said. "I want to get you *to* Velora so I can bring you *home* from Velora. And then I think we can begin again."

"You can take me where you like," I said, murmuring the words against his chest, "but I'm already home."

Blood

One

Finally the train stopped. Kerk stared out the window, as he had for the last four days, but there was less to see here in the underground city terminal than there had been along their entire route through Geldricht. People waved and shouted, men pushed carts, women urged their children out of harm's way, and all the purposeful chaos took place under high artificial lights insufficient to illuminate the cavernous interior of the station.

He kept staring anyway. So many of those people were blueskins. More than he had ever seen together in one place in his entire life. He had been told the whole city was full of the indigo—far more blueskins than gulden like himself—but he had had a hard time making his mind form the images. He wondered how long it would be before he could stop staring at them.

"Kerk," said a deep voice. He turned swiftly to see Brolt already on his feet, pulling luggage down from the wall racks, filling the small compartment with his height and bulk. "Watch Tess and the children. Don't let them stray."

Reminded of a sense of duty, Kerk jumped up, too. He was almost as big as Brolt, and over the four days of the trip they had found that at least one of them had better be seated if anyone else was going to have room to maneuver through the semiprivate room. "Everyone come with me," Kerk said, waving Tess and the three children ahead of him toward the exit. "And nobody take a step until I say so."

Tess and the girls hurried to obey, but Makk gave him an insolent look and sauntered out as slowly as he could, just to prove he was no man's underling. Kerk managed to hold back a smile. Makk was a few months shy of his twelfth birthday and well aware that he would soon be considered a man by gulden standards. He had spent most of the last year trying out his independence.

"One of my nephews should be here with a car," Brolt told Kerk as he hauled down another suitcase. "Find him and wait for me there. I will hire a cart and meet you."

Kerk nodded and followed the others out the train door and into the vast, echoing station. Despite the fact that she had been here before and he had not, Tess watched him, waiting for his instructions. Makk was looking around with interest, his attention wholly caught by a knot of young blueskin boys crouching around some entertainment on the pavement of the station. Maybe a game, maybe an insect, Kerk thought.

He addressed his stepmother formally. "Let us walk quickly through this crowded place," he said in the delicate, nuanced goldtongue that shaded every word with an extra meaning. "If the lady Tess would be brave enough to lead us toward the doors where her nephews are waiting, I will ensure that no harm comes to her or her children."

They were hardly likely to be in danger here at the station, but the point was clear: *You lead, I'll follow, and we will all be fine.* Nothing could be stated so directly, however.

Tess nodded. "Girls, stay behind me," she said to her daughters. She gazed a moment at her son, who was still fascinated by the strangers.

"Makk," Kerk said sharply, and the boy's head whipped around. "Walk beside your mother and guide us out. Do your duty."

Makk scowled but obediently fell in step beside Tess, and they were finally moving away from the great mounded silhouette of the train. Soon enough they were in a warmer, better-lit space bustling with commerce. Kerk saw food stalls and book vendors and news monitors and ticket sellers and great arched doorways that seemed to lead out to the street.

And people. Mobs of people. Indigo with their deep blue skin, golden-hued gulden, the occasional white-skinned albino. Even Makk was a little intimidated by the sheer numbers. On the pretense of helping his mother keep her balance on the slick stone floor, he edged closer to her and took her arm. Kerk laid one hand on each of the girls before him. They were seven and nine, easily distracted, easily lost, and no moment's inattention on his part would allow them to slip away.

Finally they were out one of the great doors—and, yes, there was a long, sleek car awaiting them, with one of Brolt's nephews leaning against the fender. "Hax!" Makk exclaimed and hurried over to greet his cousin. Hax mimed a punch to the boy's chin, then grabbed him by both shoulders and made him stand still.

"Look at you! Getting some of your height at last," he said. "You'll be a man soon, I think."

"And then I'll be able to beat you in a fight," Makk boasted.

Hax laughed and let him go. "I don't think so," he said.

Hax turned more respectfully to greet Tess, and made a great show of helping her and the girls into the car. Naturally, he situated them on the backward-facing seats. The rows that faced forward would be reserved for the men. Makk continued chatting cheerfully, though Hax clearly was paying little attention. Hax had done no more than glance and nod at Kerk. Not disrespectful, not antagonistic, but not warm, either. Kerk was not a blood relation, after all. None of Brolt's family owed him anything but civility.

It was ten minutes before Brolt arrived, followed by a luggage cart being pushed by a young gulden man. Another ten minutes before Hax had greeted his uncle, the suitcases had been stowed away, and the men had climbed inside the car. Hax sat in front to drive, and Makk clamored to sit beside him, and with a nod, Brolt gave his permission.

Once they were settled in, Brolt leaned forward to take Tess's hands, and she smiled at him. "Here we are, my husband," she said. "Soon we will be living in a new home in a new city. Our life is filled with such impossible joys."

"Any new opportunity is made sweeter when it is shared with someone loved and respected," Brolt replied.

The car moved away from the station and into traffic. Kerk resumed his staring out the window. The city was nothing like the towns that sparkled across Geldricht, full of color and beauty. Here, the buildings were more varied and surprising— some quite tall, some short, most of them severely constructed of formal stone in blacks and whites and grays. Where were the flags and fountains and flowerpots? Where were the bright roof tiles, the gaily decorated walls? Who could live in a place so dismal?

You wanted to come to the city, Kerk reminded himself. *Brolt told you he would make provisions for you back on Gold Mountain. But you wanted to come.*

He watched the tall buildings flatten out, the neighborhoods change. Now they were in an even stranger landscape of low redbrick houses and narrow lawns planted with unfamiliar grasses. He remembered now; Brolt had explained that the three different races worked together more or less harmoniously in the commercial districts of the city, but that they tended to live apart from each other in enclaves that reflected their cultural preferences. The few individuals Kerk saw on the street here had pale skin and odd, white hair. This must be an albino district.

They passed through more neighborhoods, the skyline gradually changing again. Brolt was pointing out sights and explaining traffic routes to Tess and the girls, who kept demanding to know when they were going to be *home*, at their *own* house. Kerk found himself getting more and more discouraged as the length of the journey made it clear to him how big the city really was, how complex.

How would he ever locate one person amid the thousands who lived here? How would he ever find his mother?

❧

The city house was not nearly as large as the home that Brolt maintained in Geldricht, but it was spacious and pleasing nonetheless. Kerk knew that Tess's visits here during the past year had been largely to furnish the city house, and her taste was evident everywhere in the bright colors, comfortable sofas, chiming fountains, and subtle scents. While Hax and Brolt wrestled the luggage in from the car, Tess led the rest of them on a tour through the fifteen rooms spread over three stories. Kerk was not surprised to learn that Hax and his brother lived here in their own suites; a man would naturally offer accommodations to any of his brother's sons who did not have households of their own. He was pleased to see that his own rooms were just as good as the nephews', with thick blue carpeting and a gaily patterned coverlet that Tess herself had certainly picked out.

The only rooms they did not inspect were the kitchen, which Tess reserved as her own domain, and Brolt's *hoechter*, a small private study that no one was allowed to enter without an invitation.

"What do you think, my son?" Tess asked Makk as they ended up in a large common room filled with overstuffed chairs and couches. "Can you be happy in the home your father and I have made for you away from the city of your birth?"

Makk opened his mouth to make one of the sarcastic comments that he was so fond of these days, but then he caught Kerk's warning look. He visibly changed his mind and spoke respectfully instead. "My lady mother has gone to a great deal of effort to create a place of comfort and beauty," he said formally. "I believe we shall all be quite happy here."

The next few weeks were full of adjustments. Because the house was smaller than the sprawling home on Gold Mountain, they were always tripping over each other. The food markets were missing many essential gulden ingredients, so Tess constantly had to exercise creativity as she planned her menus. The seven-year-old fell ill with some virus and cried for three days, while the nine-year-old missed her cousins and cried for other reasons. Makk did not like his new school and came home twice bearing the marks of fights with other boys.

"You must win your battles," was all Brolt told him. Kerk spent a couple hours working out with Makk in a small unfinished room in the basement next to the heating and water filtration systems. Kerk knew all about being the boy who was picked on because he was new or because his father was dead;

he had turned into quite a brawler, particularly once he started bulking up. A man must fight honorably or be forever branded unworthy; but still, there were some tricks that could be used fairly that helped ensure the encounter would go your way.

The third time Makk came home bruised and bloodied, he was smiling. He never lost another fight, and he began to like school a little better.

Kerk sometimes felt he was in a different kind of battle altogether, being pummeled on a daily basis by new sights, new thoughts, new experiences. He wouldn't cry, like the girls, but he wasn't sure he should fight back, like Makk. He just tried to keep his balance as the city landed one blow after another.

They were not killing blows, he thought. They were more like the slap of irritated affection that a man might land on a brother's face. *Why aren't you paying attention? See what you have been missing?*

Almost at once, he loved the city, despite its tall, formal buildings and its lack of color. He loved its energy, the constant pulse of excitement that ran through it like an overstimulated heartbeat. He loved the Centrifuge, a huge circular traffic tunnel that connected all the major districts. He loved the staggering variety of food—the restaurants that were open to any patron of whatever race—the news channels that broadcast from streetside monitors at every hour of the day. He loved the foreign, unfamiliar jumble of blueskins and gulden and albinos all existing side by side, mostly ignoring each other, occasionally challenging each other, sometimes sharing a joke or a meal or a cheer at a sporting event.

He loved living in a place where the rules were different. He had not fared so badly by gulden rules, but only because he had been lucky. He never forgot that, if not for Tess's determination and Brolt's kindness, he would be dead.

But even a fatherless man like Kerk could make his own way in the city.

Even a man like Kerk might find what he was searching for.

Two

Brolt was pleased with Kerk. The big gulden man sat at his desk, looking over Kerk's report analyzing the company's sales for the past three months. Brolt's skin was a dark gold, almost a bronze; his hair was a deep auburn just now coarsening to gray. Brolt exercised faithfully every morning. Kerk was pretty sure the older man could still wrestle him to the ground in four falls out of five.

"So you think we would be more efficient to sell to the three or four top houses rather than distribute to all of the vendors we have used in the past," Brolt said.

Kerk nodded. "That's what the numbers say to me." Kerk liked numbers; he always had. They made more sense than people did, as a general rule. "If you import from fewer sources and sell to fewer outlets, your savings in terms of transportation and logistics will be significant."

Brolt nodded. Brolt traded for electronic components with three countries across the ocean and sold them to factories in Geldricht and the city. The fact that his city business had grown so lucrative had prompted the move from Gold Mountain. "I had suspected as much," Brolt said. "But only a fool does business with a single man. For what if that man is a cheater? Or what if that man dies? Then the fool has no income at all."

"You're correct," Kerk said. They were using bluetongue,

a language that allowed more directness, and both of them were speaking plainly. At any rate, more plainly than usual. "And even though the profit margin is higher when you deal with blueskin corporations, you wouldn't want to cut off all your dealings with gulden companies. That would make you unpopular with the merchants on Gold Mountain." He hitched his chair closer and tapped on the folder he had given Brolt. It had taken him days to run the analysis. "But you could consolidate. If you chose, say, two gulden outlets and two blueskin outlets, you could reduce your supply-chain costs by thirty percent. You could then discount your offerings to the four outlets you chose—but only if they increased the amounts they order from you. I believe this would not only improve your profits, but the profits for your clients as well."

"I will study your reports," Brolt promised, switching to the more formal goldtongue. "But I commend you for your hard work and your good mind. I am pleased to have you on my payroll and in my family."

Kerk bowed his head. "Brolt Barzhan is kind." To use a man's full name was to give him the greatest honor.

Brolt smiled. "And Kerk Socast is faithful," he replied. "You have been working very hard since the move from Gold Mountain, and I'm sure you have not had much opportunity to visit the city where you now make your home. Take a couple of days and roam the streets. I think you will like what you see."

Kerk lowered his head in another respectful bow. "Thank you, Brolt Barzhan. I will happily do so."

He knew exactly where he wanted to go.

⌒

Brolt's offices were deep in the commercial district that clustered around the Centrifuge stop labeled North Zero. It was an easy walk through the hazy autumn sunshine to the arched stone gate that led into the tunnels of the Centrifuge. Maybe fifteen ringcars were idle inside the tunnel, awaiting riders at this slow time of the day. Kerk stepped into the first one and strapped himself in before carefully pulling away from the landing and into the lower lane of slow traffic. Hax and his brother had willingly, if unenthusiastically, taught Kerk how to operate the ringcars, but he wasn't quite up to their levels of speed or self-confidence and he preferred not to fly during the heaviest traffic hours. He accelerated a little as he followed the honey-colored walls curving endlessly to the left. Two cars swooped by overhead, buzzing quickly out of sight. The North One gate blinked by.

Kerk kept flying until he arrived at West Zero, then he carefully maneuvered the car over to the apron and stepped out. There was only one other ringcar waiting at this gate; clearly not a popular stop. Kerk had to hope there would be transport available when he was ready to go home.

He emerged from the darkness of the tunnel into a sere and broken landscape. Here, the afternoon sunlight was harsh, mercilessly playing across the whole squalid scene. The low buildings were all squat and devoid of beauty; some were starting to crumble and others looked like they had been deliberately defaced. The few patches of lawn or park acreage could scarcely muster the energy to nourish scrubby brown grass or the occasional misshapen tree, mostly bare at this time of year, and Kerk could not spot a flower bed or a fountain anywhere in his line of sight. A few blocks over, a handful of boys were playing an energetic game of baltreck, and he could hear the distinctive reverberation of the ball hitting one of the metal cones. He saw women quickly stepping down the street, shepherding girls before them or carrying limp bags of insufficient groceries. The whole place shrieked of poverty and despair.

Kerk couldn't imagine that anyone would prefer to live here instead of Gold Mountain.

He couldn't imagine how he would find one person huddled somewhere inside one of these dispirited houses.

But he was here now; he would try. He chose a direction at random and strode down the badly paved street, exuding a supercilious confidence completely at odds with his inner unease. He had learned very early to cultivate that air of self-assurance that most gulden men acquired practically as a birthright. They were lords in their households, demanding unquestioning obedience from all their dependents; they were aggressive negotiators in the business world, quick to capitalize on anyone else's weakness. A gulden man who showed fear or indecision risked losing everything that mattered to him.

The street continued on for a few blocks before ending in a tumbledown collection of broken playground equipment, a few twisted metal bars and a shattered ramp that might once have been a slide. Children were still playing in and around the ruins, laughing and shrieking, chasing each other around fallen rods and chains. Two gulden women sat together on a tilted bench, watching the children. Or, no, watching Kerk, their eyes wide and alarmed. Wondering, no doubt, who he was, why he had come to this part of town, what trouble he might bring.

He gazed at each of them coolly, too proud to show that their worried scrutiny made him want to crawl back down the street. One of them looked to be close to his own age—mid-twenties—while the other one was older, forty-five or so. She had golden-brown skin and soft brown hair pulled back in an unflattering bun. Her skin was lined with too much grief seen too early.

The right age to be his mother. The right hair color. The right expression. But the wrong face, the wrong shape. It was not the woman he wanted.

A moment longer he kept his eyes on them, just so they would not think they had routed him, then he turned smartly and strode back the way he had come. In front of the Centrifuge gate, he hesitated, then turned to look in first one direction and then the other. Where should he go next? How could he possibly find the person he sought?

A voice behind him asked almost the same question in the coldest possible voice. "What are you looking for here in the Lost City?"

He spun around to see that a blueskin woman had emerged from the Centrifuge gate and was staring at him with every bit as much cool arrogance as he had mustered for the gulden women. He had never been this close to a blueskin woman before and he couldn't help staring. Her skin was a deep cobalt, a color so rich it was almost tactile; her glossy black hair was shoulder-length and simply styled, though the clip holding it back on one side was surely pure gold. Likewise, her clothes were of plain design but expensive materials, and diamonds glittered casually around both her wrists. None of these clues was necessary to tell him she was one of the high-caste indigo women; her haughty tone and confident stance instantly conveyed that message.

When he did not answer, she went on in the same tone. "Gulden men are not welcome here in the women's ghetto."

Only then did he realize that she addressed him in perfectly conjugated goldtongue, though she did not even attempt the proper subservient tone. Just to be difficult, he replied in the indigo language. "I understand this is a place where gulden live, so I cannot imagine blueskin women are any more welcome than I am."

Her thin, elegant eyebrows rose—at the reply or at the choice of language, he couldn't be sure. She answered in her own native tongue. "I at least offer the residents no threat of violence," she said.

"Neither do I," he said swiftly.

She surveyed him deliberately, her black eyes taking in his confrontational stance, his broad shoulders, the hands that he had balled into fists. "You do not look," she said, "like a harmless man."

He narrowed his eyes and took a step closer. "If I am dangerous," he said, his voice soft, "you are careless to put yourself in my path."

Her hands had been hanging down at her sides, but now she lifted her right arm and revealed a neat weapon: a can of volatile chemical spray designed to incapacitate an assailant from a short distance. "I am never careless," she replied.

He laughed and twisted his left hand so he could show her a weapon of his own: a dagger quickly shaken out from a sheath on his forearm. "I can fling this so fast and so accurately that it would be buried in your heart before you could react," he told her scornfully. "And I would wager I've had more experience than you've had winning a fight one-to-one."

For some reason, that didn't seem to frighten her; she looked intrigued instead. "Then why haven't you knocked me down already?"

"I didn't come here to hurt you," he said shortly. "I didn't come here to hurt anybody."

"Well, you still haven't answered my question," she said,

and now she sounded more exasperated than haughty. "Why *did* you come here? Because most gulden men just show up in the Lost City to bring grief."

He lowered his hand and looked around him, once again taking in the ugly street, the uglier buildings. "That's what you call this place? The Lost City? The name certainly seems to fit."

She was still watching him. "To some women, it is paradise," she said steadily. "Compared to where they have been."

Now his chin came up in defiance. She should not be allowed to insult Gold Mountain. "Geldricht is a place of great beauty and strict order," he said. "A woman living in Geldricht knows where she belongs and—"

"And who she belongs to," the woman interrupted.

Kerk scowled. "And what shape her life is supposed to hold. A woman who comes to the city and finds herself on this misbegotten street—" He swept his arm to indicate the whole sad neighborhood crouched apprehensively before them. "Has traded beauty for ugliness, certainty for insecurity, plenty for—for what looks like starvation."

"Slavery for freedom," the woman returned calmly. "That's why women run away from Gold Mountain. To be free. To choose their own lives. To escape cruel husbands and fathers. There may be very little here in the ghetto, but there are no daily beatings, no forced conjugal relations that are scarcely better than rape—"

He was so shocked he almost gaped at her; he had never heard anyone, man or woman, utter the word *rape* aloud. "You know nothing about life on Gold Mountain," he said furiously.

"I have befriended countless runaway gulden wives," she replied. "I know enough."

They stared at each other another moment without speaking. His face, he knew, showed hostility, but her expression had turned curious. She was the one to finally break the silence. "Why are you here?" she asked again. When he didn't answer, she added, "I might be able to help you. If I decide I want to."

"I don't need your help," he said.

"Well," she said, "I think you do."

He glanced about irritably. "Where is your husband or your brother?" he demanded. "Why are you out by yourself without a man to protect you and speak on your behalf?"

She made no attempt to restrain her laughter, and Kerk scowled again. "An indigo woman doesn't require any man's escort or interference," she said. "If you have been in the city long enough to learn the language, you must surely have realized *that*."

"I learned bluetongue back on Gold Mountain," he said stiffly. "I am employed in a Geldricht firm that trades with Inrhio, and so I learned the language of the Inrhio people. Why do *you* know goldtongue?"

"I have an unconventional aunt," she replied. "And I am inquisitive."

"And why are *you* here?"

She glanced around, as if to remind herself exactly where she was standing. "I have an unconventional aunt," she repeated. "And I am a little unconventional myself. I liked the idea of aiding impoverished women with whatever resources I could command. Which," she added, although he had not been planning to ask, "include a certain amount of wealth, a passion for justice, and a stubbornness that makes my mother despair."

"Aid them how?" he demanded.

"Train them. Help them find jobs. Help them find places to live. Help them educate their children so the next generation of gulden will be completely free of any debt to Gold Mountain."

No gulden will ever be completely free of debt to Gold Mountain, Kerk thought. "That seems like a great deal for one woman to accomplish," he said, his voice edged with sarcasm.

She actually grinned. "I didn't say I was doing it by myself."

Then he began to realize the magnitude of what she had just said. He fixed her with an unwavering stare. "So then," he said, "if a gulden woman has come to this Lost Ghetto—"

"Lost City," she murmured.

"You might know where she is now?"

Her answering stare was just as unblinking. "I might," she said. "Who are you looking for? A runaway wife?"

As if any ambitious gulden would be willing to marry his daughter off to a fatherless man like Kerk. He shook his head. "My mother."

Three

They sat in the window seat of a small café just off the North Three gate and talked for an hour. This was the restaurant closest to the Lost City, the woman explained to him, a quiet and rather run-down place where people just one step above real poverty could come for a meal or a drink. The other patrons were a mix of all three races, though gulden predominated. Not the kind of gulden Kerk was familiar with from Gold Mountain. These were tired men and fierce women who by turns ignored each other and watched each other and did not follow any of the complicated protocols that governed relations between the sexes back in Geldricht.

How did a man know how to treat a woman if he did not follow the rules that everybody understood?

Although clearly this blueskin woman didn't know any of the rules and wouldn't have abided by them if she did.

She had insisted on being the one to drive the ringcar almost all the way around the Centrifuge to North Three, the gate right before West Zero. During the flight, she had asked for his name and given him her own: "Jalciana, but a lot of people call me Jalci." Even the diminutive was much more flamboyant than the meek names bestowed on gulden women, and Kerk repeated it to himself several times just because it was so new. He had to admit she was excellent at piloting the small craft through the curving tunnels, though she drove much faster than he had dared thus far—and with much less caution. He could not imagine Tess even attempting to take the controls in one of these vehicles.

Or approaching a strange man on the street and demanding to know his business.

Or taking refreshments with a strange man in a public place and paying for her own beverage.

Or turning to her companion and demanding, "Tell me your story."

Kerk sipped at his drink, which was hot and aromatic and like nothing he'd ever had on Gold Mountain. "My mother left my father seventeen years ago and came to the city with my baby sister. There has been no word of her since. I thought, since I was here, I would seek her out." He shrugged. No more to say.

Jalci, it seemed, thought there was plenty more for him to relate. "Seventeen years ago? How old were you?"

"Seven."

"That would be a hard age to lose your mother. How well do you remember her?"

Kerk took another swallow. "What is this drink?"

"Mocha," she said impatiently. "How well do you remember your mother?"

"Her face, very clearly. Her voice, as if I heard it speaking yesterday. I have a few memories that are detailed and specific, like the day we sat on the floor together, building houses from toy bricks. But much of the rest of it is lost."

"What was your impression of her? Was she happy, sad, afraid, rebellious? Was she loving or was she cold?"

Kerk had never tried to resolve his hazy memories into such defined terms. "She was quiet," he said at last. "She rarely spoke when my father was in the room. I don't think she was rebellious. I remember how surprised everyone was to find out she had gone."

"Why did she leave your father? The usual reasons, I suppose?"

He gave her a cold look. "What would those be, in your opinion?"

She waved a hand. "Cruelty, abuse, starvation. Was your father a mean man?"

Kerk narrowed his eyes and did not answer. A gulden man did not disparage his father, not to anyone, even if his father was dead. Kerk would never speak a word of his father's rages, his screaming fits, the beatings he had administered to his wife and his son.

"I gather he was," Jalci said shrewdly. "And maybe he got meaner once your sister was born. Maybe he was disappointed that his second child was a girl, not a boy."

Kerk considered that. "Every man wants sons," he said at last.

Jalci leaned her elbow on the table and rested her chin in her hand. "Was your sister in danger from him, do you think?" Jalci said. "Did he maybe threaten to kill her, and that's why your mother ran away?"

Kerk shrugged. "She was just a baby. Not even a person." But he thought Jalci might be right. His father's fury had seemed to double once the infant girl was in the house. One of Kerk's very specific memories involved his mother shrieking in terror after his father had jerked the baby from her arms and flung the little girl across the room. But the baby hadn't been hurt—or, at any rate, she had been robust enough to wail at the top of her little lungs.

Which, as Kerk recalled, had just infuriated his father more.

He firmly turned off the rest of that memory.

Jalci was staring at him. "Just because she's a baby doesn't mean she's not a *person*," she said.

He shrugged. "Perhaps things are different in Inrhio," he said. "In Geldricht, children do not have any legal status until they are twelve. Until they reach that age, their father can terminate them—"

"*Murder* them," Jalci interrupted.

"And be considered within his rights."

"I thought Chay Zanlan had outlawed that practice," she said.

At first he was surprised to hear Chay Zanlan's name on a blueskin's lips. But this indigo, obviously, knew much more about Geldricht than he knew about Inrhio, and she had clearly made it a point to learn who governed Gold Mountain and what some of his policies were. "Chay Zanlan has discouraged that practice," Kerk replied, "but it continues on, even in the wealthiest gulden households, and no one is astonished or outraged. It is just the way things are."

"And *the way things are* in Geldricht is the reason women escape to the city every chance they get," Jalci said with heat. "I am hardly surprised to learn that women run away from Gold Mountain. I am more surprised to learn that any of them *stay*."

"It is not so easy to leave," Kerk said quietly. Even for a young man who could travel alone, speak to strangers, carry his own money, and negotiate his own terms, it was not easy to leave. If a man left the household he had been born into— or adopted into—who would have him? If he went to the city, what would he do? Where would he live? What place could he find? People might chafe at the restrictions of life in Geldricht, but everyone had a defined place; everyone knew who had responsibilities and who had allegiances. It was the perfect life as long as everyone performed as expected, as honor demanded.

Of course, some people behaved without honor. . . .

"No," Jalci echoed. "It is not easy to leave Gold Mountain. But your mother did it, seventeen years ago. You think she came here and took haven in the city? You never heard from her again?"

"No."

"Did your father? Or any of her relatives—her father, her brother, her mother?"

Kerk shook his head. "If they did, they did not mention it to me."

Her chin was back in the palm of her hand and she was watching him again. Her dark eyes were amazingly dense; they were difficult to look away from. "So what happened to you after she left?" Jalci asked in a soft voice. "Did your father turn his rage onto his seven-year-old son?"

Yes—sometimes—brutal beatings that had left a couple of scars that Kerk would carry his whole life. But for the most part, his father had left him alone, being completely uninterested in his son's existence. Kerk remembered how much he had longed to hurry time along until his twelfth birthday. How much he had wanted to be a man so that his father would notice him. "A gulden man rarely concerns himself with children," he answered, his voice starchy again. "He has other matters to occupy his time."

Jalci rolled her eyes. "Gulden men deserve to be smacked in the head, but that's a conversation for a different day," she said. "I'm still trying to figure out what happened to *you*. You're the least forthcoming person I've ever met."

"I have no particular reason to be sharing stories with a blueskin woman," he said.

"You do if you want my help," she reminded him. "Does your father know you're here in the city, looking for your mother?"

"My father is dead."

"When did he die?"

"When I was ten."

That made her raise her eyebrows and straighten in her chair. If she had spent much time with gulden women—as it seemed she had—she would quickly understand how precarious his life had become at that point. "A ten-year-old with no father or mother, living on Gold Mountain," she said. "It's a wonder you're still alive. Who took you in? Did you go to an uncle or a cousin?"

"I stayed with Tess," he said.

She looked bewildered. "Who's Tess?"

"The woman my father married after my mother disappeared."

"So she's your stepmother."

"Yes."

"And what's *she* like?"

Kerk permitted himself a smile. All his thoughts of Tess were good ones. There was not a single bad memory from any of the years they had spent together. He and Jalci had been speaking in bluetongue, but the nuanced, roundabout gulden language was best for speaking of a gulden woman. "She knows that softness can be the greatest source of strength. She knows that kindness is an investment that pays back a thousandfold. She knows how to bend and bend without coming close to breaking. She is cherished because she makes every-one around her feel cherished first."

Jalci digested this. "So you like her," she said in bluetongue.

Kerk nodded and resumed her language. "Very much."

"So your father married this Tess woman when you were, say, eight or nine. Did they have any children together?"

"No."

"Was this a disappointment to your father?"

Disappointment was hardly a big enough word to cover it. "Yes."

"But Tess didn't run away from Gold Mountain. Maybe he wasn't as cruel to her as he had been to your mother," Jalci guessed.

Kerk didn't answer. But he thought Jalci was wrong.

"So then your father died and—how did he die?"

"A fever. Everyone in the household was very ill, but the rest of us recovered."

"And there you were, a ten-year-old nonperson and your stepmother. If I understand things correctly, even widows aren't allowed any independence in Geldricht. Some male from her family would have to assume responsibility for her, yes? So where did she end up? And why was she allowed to bring you with her?"

"She returned to her father's house. She was allowed to bring me with her because her father is very wealthy and he already housed a dozen cousins and nephews. He never spoke to me that I recall, but he did not mind that I was there."

"That must have been an interesting time for you," Jalci said. "I've seen young gulden boys fight for pride and posi-tion. You must have been taunted and picked on a lot."

"I was able to defend myself," Kerk said modestly. In truth, he had acquired formidable fighting skills in Tess's father's household. From his father, he had learned how to endure pain without whimpering, and those jeering young boys had not been able to inflict nearly the level of punishment his father had meted out on his most casual day. And while any boy who defied his father risked literal death, it was expected that he would respond aggressively when his opponents were his own age, or close to it. Kerk had learned to fight back, and fight back hard. Pretty soon, the sons and nephews and cousins decided to leave him alone.

Jalci was openly appraising him, noting the breadth of his shoulders and the muscles of his arms. "I'll just bet you *did* defend yourself," she muttered. "So then what happened? Do you still live with Tess's father?"

"Tess remarried. A man named Brolt Barzhan." He had been trying to limit his answers to strictly accurate responses to her questions, but at this point he couldn't help adding, "A good man. The best Gold Mountain has to offer."

"Well, I'm glad to hear that, finally!" Jalci exclaimed. "So far, your life has sounded very grim indeed. And Brolt didn't mind that Tess brought this ten-year-old nonperson along with her into the marriage?"

Kerk couldn't hold back the tiniest of smiles. "Tess's father pressured her for some time to marry, but she kept finding excuses to delay," he said. "Her father presented two—perhaps it was three—potential grooms to her, but none of them suited her."

"Tess's father sounds more patient than the average gulden man," Jalci observed.

"Tess's father loves his daughter," Kerk said. "By the time he found a husband who was agreeable to Tess, I had turned twelve."

Jalci practically bounced in her chair and clapped her hands together. "Oh, clever Tess!" she exclaimed. "And she did that on purpose?"

"We did not discuss her marriage prospects," Kerk said coldly.

Jalci rolled her eyes again. "I'm sure you didn't. But I am going to assume that wise-kind-strong Tess knew exactly what she was doing when she didn't take a husband until after her stepson was considered a grown man. I think I like her very much."

"I'm sure that would please her," Kerk said sardonically.

Jalci grinned. "So this Brolt married Tess, you came along, no one was mean to you anymore, and—then what? You were raised in the household like a son?"

"Not exactly," Kerk said. "I have been treated with great

fairness, and I have been given a position in the family firm, and Brolt Barzhan respects my contributions. It is possible that I might retain this position the rest of my life."

She was listening closely, so she heard the unspoken half of that sentence. "And it's possible that you might not," she said. "Do Tess and Brolt have children?"

"Three. A son and two daughters."

"How old is the son?"

"Eleven years and eight months."

Jalci raised those fine eyebrows again. "So in four months, when this son is officially a man, what happens to you?"

Kerk had wondered that every day since Makk had been born. "My life becomes very interesting."

Jalci flung her hands out. "But here you are in the city," she said, her dark eyes snapping with excitement. "In the city, a gulden man can take a job that does not depend on his father's position or his uncle's goodwill. An indigo woman can flout her grandmother and refuse to marry the very nice but very boring man her mother has picked out for her. In the city, people can be responsible for themselves. They can make their own mistakes and figure out their own rules."

"It sounds like a lonely existence," Kerk said.

Jalci laughed, somewhat taken aback. "You have not been so lucky in your family that I would think you would want to cling to it."

He was surprised to hear himself speak the words. "Family is the only thing I have ever wanted," he said. "I didn't hope to leave it behind in the city. I hoped to find it."

Jalci had dropped her chin in her hand again, but now she seemed to be considering her own life. "I've spent much of *my* time trying to get free of family," she said. "Much is expected of an indigo heiress, you know! All the land that will fall to her once her grandmother passes it on—all the responsibilities that come with it—all the social connections she is expected to maintain, the duties she must perform. My grandmother can spend a solid *week* with me and never stop lecturing me about proper behavior, essential land management, the bloodlines of the Higher Hundred, and how *instantly* she wants me to produce a daughter. She never once will ask what I'm thinking or feeling or what I desire from my life. And my mother's just as bad, except a little more subtle about it. There are days I feel like I will start shrieking and never be able to stop."

Frankly, Kerk didn't think it sounded like a bad life at all. Frankly, he was not that interested. But she might be able to help him, and so he tried to be polite. "And what *do* you desire from your life?"

"I haven't entirely figured that out," she admitted. "But I know I want it to mean something. I know I want to do work that matters, that puts good into the world in some fashion."

"Maintaining property and watching over a family is meaningful work," he said.

"I want to do something more immediate," she said. "That's one of the reasons I started volunteering at the Lost City. I thought I could be of some use."

"How did you get interested in the Lost City in the first place?"

"Through Aunt Kitrini." Jalci waved a hand. "Well, technically she's not my aunt, but it's too hard to try to explain the relationship. She's this incredible activist who has volunteered at the Lost City for years. She's the one who taught me how to speak goldtongue. She's my idol."

Kerk had no idea what to say in response to that. "She sounds most inspiring."

Jalci laughed. "And you don't care at all," she said. "You just want to find your mother."

He looked at her. "Yes."

Jalci got to her feet. "Then let's go looking."

Four

A very short trip on the Centrifuge took them back to West Zero. Jalci strode confidently down one of the tumble-down streets, and Kerk fell in step beside her. She pointed to a few of the buildings as they passed. One had been pur-chased outright by a donor Jalci had courted; newcomers to the Lost City could live there free of charge for up to a year. Another housed a women's cooperative where residents could exchange food and other goods.

"Nothing ever goes to waste," Jalci said proudly. "And lots of restaurants and clothing stores in the city donate their left-overs and unused items to the co-op, so there's always fresh merchandise."

It looked like a horrible way to live, Kerk thought. He said nothing.

They eventually arrived at a sort of compound, a few mod-erately well-maintained buildings that appeared to be an office building, a school, and maybe a warehouse. There were chil-dren playing in the schoolyard and women bustling between doorways—all of them gulden, though it took Kerk a minute to realize why they didn't look like any of the guldwomen he knew. They were all dressed in drab, nondescript clothing, beige and olive and brown, colors that washed out their skin tones and did nothing to enhance their features. Why had they left behind the bright colors so favored by women on Gold Mountain? Why did they no longer put ribbons in their hair and brush cosmetics on their faces? Were they trying to turn invisible here in the city, to completely escape the attention of the gulden men? Or were they just trying to reject every outward symbol of their former lives? *When I was a gulden chattel, I dressed in red to please my husband. But now I am a free woman, and I will dress in the colors of the earth to please myself. . . .*

Kerk shook his head. His goal had always been to be *more* gulden, to steep himself in the culture, not to strip it away. He could understand leaving Geldricht behind physically, but not emotionally. He had always wanted to get closer, not farther away.

"I warn you," Jalci said as she pulled open the main door in the building that looked like administrative offices. "Del isn't very friendly."

In fact, everyone they encountered in the hallways looked downright hostile. Kerk tried to keep his arms down, his muscles lax; he tried to make his expression tranquil. But it was difficult when everyone who saw him gasped or glared or turned away as if afraid he would go berserk and smash all of them against the walls.

Del turned out to be a small woman bent into an even smaller shape by the pressures of age. Her skin was paler than that of the average gulden, and her hair was pure white. She gave the impression of having been left outside so long she had been bleached to a husk by the unforgiving sun.

But she mustered enough energy to jump to her feet when Kerk followed Jalci into her office. "Jalciani Candachi!" she exclaimed. "How dare you bring a gulden man into a place of safety for gulden women? How could you be so careless and so cruel? We have trusted you, and you have betrayed us all!"

She was speaking bluetongue, obviously believing that Kerk would not understand her words. He stepped forward and answered her in the same language, trying to keep his voice soft and nonthreatening. "She has done me a great kindness by bringing me here, and I will not dishonor her by offering any threat or incivility," he said. "Please do me the courtesy of listening to my story—and do Jalciana Candachi the courtesy of believing she would never bring harm to her friends."

Del's head had snapped up at his first words, and she listened to him in cold silence. But at least she had stopped scolding. "Who are you?" she asked when he had finished speaking. "What do you want?"

She had continued employing bluetongue, which was the language for plain speaking, so he answered in the same language. "My mother left Gold Mountain seventeen years ago, and I was hoping to find her here."

Del was unimpressed. "So you can beat her into a grave to avenge the insult to your father?"

"My father is dead," Kerk replied.

"Dead fathers sometimes require the hardest vengeance."

"I will speak no word against my father, but no part of my quest relates to him," Kerk said.

"An abandoned son might very well seek vengeance on his own behalf."

Kerk held on to his temper. This difficult, defiant old woman held too much power in her hands, and Kerk knew better than to offend any individual with power. He switched to goldtongue. "A seven-year-old boy knows little of the world beyond the doors of his own household," he said in that careful, indirect singsong. "He knows little beyond what his mother says to him at night, what his father teaches him by day. What is he to understand once his mother is no longer there to tell him stories? What should he try to glean from his father's silences? Whispers tell him what the true story might be. His own mind puts the puzzle pieces together when he is old enough to understand the ways of the world. A woman might leave her husband for many reasons. These would not concern a boy. All a boy knows is that he loved his mother and that she is gone. All the man knows is that she is somewhere still, and perhaps he can find her. Does that tale offer any threat to you? Does that tale offer any threat to her?"

"Gulden men have lied before this," Del said flatly in bluetongue.

Kerk watched her steadily but still without menace. "And do gulden women only speak the truth?" he said softly. "Are they without flaws and errors?"

Del snorted. "I have no reason to trust you," she said, but for the first time she seemed to relax. At any rate, she seated herself behind her spindly desk again, and Jalci and Kerk took chairs facing her. "Most gulden men who find their way to the Lost City trail violence behind them like a brightly woven flag."

"What can I do to prove to you that my intentions are peaceful?" he asked.

"Nothing," Del said. "I will never tell you your mother's whereabouts."

"Del!" Jalci exclaimed just as Kerk jumped to his feet.

"Then I will take no more of your time," he growled, spinning toward the door.

Del's voice stopped him. "But I might help you," she said.

Kerk turned around more slowly to face her. It was becoming harder and harder to hold his temper in check, particularly since he was not used to placating women. Del was being deliberately obstructive; perhaps she was trying to provoke him into a rage, trying to prove her very point about the untrustworthiness of gulden men. He kept his voice even. "I would welcome any aid you would be willing to give me," he said.

"I will see if I can find your mother for you," she said. "And I will ask her if she is willing to be reunited with you. If she is, I will set up a meeting. If she is not, I will not speak another word to you."

"That's fair," Jalci said, before Kerk could answer. "That's perfect. Thank you, Del."

Kerk inclined his head ever so slightly. "The lady Del is most generous to a stranger," he said formally in gold-tongue. "I will strive to prove to her that her faith in me is not misplaced."

"I hope you are able to perform such a feat," she answered in the same language. "I would like to meet a gulden man who was worthy of my respect."

Kerk inclined his head again and did not reply. Del spoke in bluetongue again, a little more briskly. "But I'm not certain I'll be able to help you, even with the best will in the world," she said. "Seventeen years ago, this charity did not exist. There might be no records and no memories that go back far enough to contain your mother's arrival."

"Then how will you find her?" Jalci asked.

Del permitted herself a small smile. "Someone will know someone who knows this woman's story," she said. "There cannot be a guldwoman in the entire city I cannot find." She addressed Kerk. "What is her name?"

"Bree Socast," he said.

Del tilted her head to one side, seeming to test the name against an internal data bank, but coming up without a match. "And her father's name, in case she no longer wanted to be known by her husband's? And her mother's?"

"Velder and Cahbrist," Kerk replied. He thought Del looked surprised that he could answer so readily. He was pretty sure Makk didn't know his mother's mother's surname; few gulden boys would. But Kerk had tried to immerse himself in family history. He could have offered names from many more generations back, if Del had asked for them.

Del shook her head. "None of these sound familiar. But someone will recognize one of these names. In fact, Ria might."

"Oh, yes, Ria knows everyone," Jalci said, on her feet at once. "Is she here today? Let's go ask her."

They made a strange procession out of the office and down the hallways again. The small, stooped old guldwoman led the way and was greeted with universal respect by the younger women they passed. Jalci, following after Del, elicited a mix of friendly, curious, and measuring stares; in this setting, her cobalt skin and night-black hair marked her as utterly alien. Kerk, bringing up the rear, towered over all of them and came in for most of the attention. As before, it was largely hostile, but the fact that Del was tolerating him made some of the women eye him more with speculation than hatred.

He supposed that was an improvement.

Leaving the building, they headed toward a sprawling one-story structure that looked like it might have been hastily assembled by a dozen crews all working from different sets of architectural plans. Probably built piecemeal by volunteers, Kerk guessed, and lucky to still be standing.

"It's a community center," Jalci informed him, though he had not asked. "We hold some adult education classes here for the women, but mostly it's used for activities for the gulden boys." She shook her head. "It's really not enough to keep them occupied. Especially the teenagers. They don't like living in the Lost City, but most of them are afraid to go back to Gold Mountain, and they aren't old enough to find jobs in the city. We arrange sports tournaments and all kinds of classes—but even so, not that many of the boys spend their time here."

As soon as Kerk stepped inside, he could see why. The place seemed smaller on the inside than the outside, with cramped corridors and low ceilings and the sweaty smell common to gymnasiums. Down a hallway to his left he could hear the shouts and echoes of a baltreck game in progress; from his right came the sounds of women's voices raised in high-pitched laughter.

"Ria is no doubt with the women in the cooking class," Del said. "Wait for me here."

"I'll go look in on the game," Kerk said, and started toward the gym. No surprise, Jalci followed close on his heels.

"I've watched them play plenty of times, but I confess I have no idea how they keep score," she said.

He grunted in amusement. "That's what Tess says."

He pulled open a swinging door and they stepped inside the gym, which was a little more welcoming than the outer corridors. The ceiling was high and graced with skylights; the walls were covered in bright oranges, yellows, and reds. The space was a little too small to be a regulation baltreck field, but the correct lines and zones had been painted in place, and the metal scoring cones looked to be properly positioned. About twenty young gulden men, all between the ages of twelve and eighteen, were scrambling around on the polished floor, battling each other for possession of three rubberized balls. Two youthful referees stood on opposite sides of the playing field, shouting just as much as the players. A few spectators lounged against the walls, calling out encouragement or derision. Two of the balls simultaneously landed in scoring cones on opposite sides of the floor, and the noise for a moment was deafening. Half the players cheered, and the other half shouted that a penalty had been overlooked.

"I mean, what is even *happening* here?" Jalci demanded.

Kerk grinned. "There are four teams on the floor at the same time. Each team is trying to get possession of all three balls. If you have two or more balls, you can score by throwing them into the cones, but of course the other teams are defending the cones. If you only get one ball in, you don't get any points. If one of the other teams takes away one of the balls *and* has the third ball in its possession, it can try to make a quick score before the other defenders realize that they have now become the offensive team. If—"

She flung up a hand. "Stop. I'm already lost."

"Well, it's not that hard," he said. "But it moves fast."

"And it's *stupid*," she said.

He merely shrugged and watched the action. Unlike school-based and pro leagues in Geldricht, these players didn't have matching uniforms, so it took him a while to sort them into teams. Apparently they were divided by who was wearing any item of clothing that could be considered to fall in the same color category. One team consisted of a boy with a dark red shirt, a boy with a crimson headband, a young man who had tied a woman's red scarf around his stomach, and two players who had split a pair of red socks between them. The level of talent varied wildly, as was to be expected, and clearly no one had bothered to spend much time honing defensive skills, so the scoring was pretty high. So was the level of energy. A couple of fights broke out in just the few minutes Kerk and Jalci stood there watching, but they involved nothing more than a couple of shoves and a few insults before play resumed again.

"It seems like a very violent game," Jalci observed.

"Even more so at the professional level," Kerk replied. "Fun, though."

"Do you play?"

He nodded but did not answer.

One player, who looked to be about fifteen, was far superior to all the rest. He was thin and slightly built, a little shorter than average, but unbelievably fast and uncannily able to read the action on the floor. Anytime his team had possession of the third ball, he instantly tried to strip one of the other two game balls from the opposing teams, and managed it three times while Kerk watched. And his ball went straight into the metal cone each time, even when his teammates weren't able to capitalize on the steal.

"That boy is really good," Kerk said.

"Which one? They're all moving so fast I can't tell them apart."

"The boy with the red hair, wearing the yellow shirt."

"The short one?"

"Yes. Keep your eyes on him. He's going to take the ball from the big player with the blue headband. There—and then he'll score—*there*. Did you see that?"

"How did you know what he was going to do?"

Kerk shook his head. "It's just how the game is played."

"I bet you're really good at this, aren't you?" she asked.

He shrugged.

A few of the players had noticed them as they came in, and the longer they stood there watching, the more attention they drew. At first he thought the players were all looking at Jalci, the blueskin who did not belong, but then he realized that *he* was the draw. *He* was the unfamiliar sight: a grown gulden man in top physical condition in a place ruled by women. Slowly, the action on the field began to shift; more and more plays were executed around the cones nearest to Kerk. A few of the younger boys were practically staring at him; a few of the older ones made elaborate, acrobatic passes and scoring throws, almost as if they were showing off. He and Jalci had been watching for fifteen minutes before a referee called a time-out, and a few of the players at Kerk's end of the playing floor clustered together just inside the painted boundaries, their eyes on him. Waiting for him to speak. Wondering if he would be willing to acknowledge them, fatherless boys who had no claims on anyone.

He gave a decisive nod. "Good game," he said. "Looks like the yellow team is going to win."

That was enough of an invitation for the younger boys, though most of the older ones hung back. Within seconds, Kerk was surrounded by about twelve of the players, all vying for his attention.

"Yellow always wins," one of them said. "At least, when Quint's playing."

"Did you see his pass to Shoev?"

"Helten made that pass."

"He did not! I mean the pass where Quint scored."

"Did you see the last score? All three balls in the cones, all at once!"

"Do you go to the pro games?"

"Do you know any of the players?"

"Do you play?"

"Do you want to play?"

Kerk held his hands up to stave off the questions, and they mostly fell silent, still grinning, still watching him. "I've played a little," he said.

"Do you want to play now? You can be on the red team. They need help."

He pointed at his hard-soled shoes, not designed for running and jumping. "I'd fall on my face."

"We could lend you shoes. There's a whole box of them. They're used and they stink but there's probably some in your size."

He smiled a little. "I didn't come here to play baltreck."

"But you *could* play, couldn't you? You know *how* to play, don't you?"

"Sure," he said, and let a little arrogance come into his voice, the tone they would expect from him, so much their superior by age and size and position in the world. "I'm pretty good at it."

Again, they clamored for him to join them, to put on a pair of borrowed shoes and tie a red band around his arm.

"Oh, why don't you do it?" Jalci said. "You can see it would make them happy."

"How would it make them happy for me to humiliate them with my advanced skills?" he said. But he was grinning, and the boys hooted and pointed at him, then renewed their pleas for him to join them on the court.

"If I could get your attention for a moment," said a dry voice behind him, and Kerk realized Del had stepped into the gymnasium while he wasn't watching the door.

"Your pardon," he said, pivoting to face her. "Do you have news for me?"

Before she could answer, the red-haired boy named Quint spoke up. "Stupid old bitch to come interrupting men. Go back to your filthy office and let us play."

Without even thinking about it, Kerk spun back around and

grabbed Quint in a headlock, doubling the boy over till he yelped with pain. "You will apologize to the lady Del," he said in a calm but implacable voice. "I am embarrassed to hear such rudeness from the mouth of a gulden man."

Quint grunted and tried to wriggle free, but Kerk's hold on him was unbreakable. "She's just a *woman*!" the boy gasped out.

"She is a woman who spends every hour of her day making sure you are clothed and fed and safe," Kerk said. "But even if she never lifted a finger to ease your way, you owe her courtesy as you owe courtesy to every living soul. A man who shows dishonor to anyone, no matter how insignificant, proves he is without honor himself. Is that the kind of man you are? Dishonorable?"

There was dead silence in the gym. The entire mass of players had drifted to this end of the court and every gaze was fixed on Kerk's face. He didn't look up from the back of Quint's head, but he could tell they were all stunned and a little excited. He wondered if some of them might break through the crowd and come to Quint's defense, in which case the situation might get dicey fast, but none of them moved. None of them spoke. They just watched Kerk and seemed to suspend their breathing.

Quint made a little sound that might have been a whimper. "I just want to play baltreck," he whined.

"And we will all play as soon as you apologize," Kerk said. He heard the little murmur that went through the other boys as they assimilated his words. *He said we will all play! The guldman will join us to play baltreck!*

"Apologize, you gilder prick," one of the older players called out, and the rest of the boys laughed.

Kerk lifted his eyes briefly to scan the crowd. "And that's the last time I want any of you to say *that* particular word," he said coldly. *Gilder* was the highest insult that could be leveled against a gulden, and Kerk had heard it often enough, directed at himself.

He could feel Quint's thin ribs expand as the boy took a deep breath. "I apologize to the lady Del," he said formally. "I spoke rudely. I hope she will forgive me and never have cause to be pained by my disrespect again."

"I will hope the same thing," Del said shortly. "You are forgiven."

Kerk loosed his hold on Quint, and the boy instantly swung around to face him. His expression was eager. "And you'll play with us?"

"I will, for a little while," Kerk said. "But I must first ask the lady Del a question. Go find shoes that will fit me." He kicked off his hard-soled shoes and Quint scooped them up. He and three companions ran across the gym to a box that apparently held cast-off gear and other donated items.

Kerk returned his attention to Del. "Do you have any news for me?"

She was eyeing him with an expression that was hard to read, but Kerk thought he could decipher it nonetheless. She was impressed at how he had handled the boys but not about to say so outright. "No," she replied. "But Ria is willing to make inquiries. If you come back in three days, I might have information for you."

He gave that studied nod that signaled great respect. "Thank you. You are most kind. I will return then and see what you have to tell me."

"Are you really going to play baltreck with these boys?" Jalci demanded.

Quint was racing back across the floor, waving a pair of truly disreputable shoes over his head. "I am," he said. "You don't have to stay and watch."

"Oh, I wouldn't miss this for any amount of money," she said. "Especially now that you've *explained* the game to me."

He laughed. Two minutes later, he had donned the shoes, stepped onto the playing court, and redivided the teams to compensate for the way his presence would skew the balance of skill. One of the referees shouted, "Go!" and the game was on.

It was ridiculously easy for Kerk to steal balls and make scores, especially when even the opposing players seemed utterly delighted with every move he made. Pretty soon he began passing to his teammates, trying to demonstrate the value of unselfish play, and then he was stopping the game to explain to the other teams what they were doing wrong.

"Defending against a score is just as good as making another point," he told them. "Quint, you try to knock in a ball while I guard against you. Everybody else watch."

It was clear that the concept of defense was almost entirely new to them, but they were quick to catch on, especially when Kerk made them run through a few exercises designed to keep the ball from the opponents' hands. In fact, they were a little *too* enthusiastic; when the third fight broke out, Kerk called a halt to the whole demonstration.

"Enough for today," he said, untying his borrowed shoes and slipping his own back on. "Practice what I've taught you, and you'll see how much you all improve."

They clustered around him again, scrawny, smelly, excited boys so socially impoverished they thought *Kerk* was someone to idolize. He could hardly sort out their words as they all questioned him at once. *Will you come back? Hey, did you see me make that final shot? When are you coming here again? Is it a foul if I shove someone in the shoulder? Can you come back? What happens if two balls go out of bounds at once? Are you coming back?*

"I'll be here again in three days," he said at last.

"Will you play with us again?" Virtually every boy asked some version of that question, all at the same time.

He hesitated only a moment. "I'll bring my own shoes," he said.

One of them loosed a victory yell, and then they all dashed back onto the playing floor. The game had resumed with even more ferocity when Kerk finally stepped out the gym door into the hallway.

Jalci was right beside him as they headed outside. The air had cooled considerably as the sun started to sink; Kerk felt an actual chill as the sweat evaporated from his body. He set a pretty good pace just to stay warm, but Jalci kept up easily.

He thought he had a fair measure of her personality by now, so he was surprised when she didn't immediately begin pestering him with questions and observations. They had walked about five minutes without speaking before he glanced down to see a pensive look on her face.

"Jalciana Candachi does not seem like the kind of woman who spends even such a short stretch of time in silence," he finally said in formal goldtongue.

"I'm afraid to say anything!" she exclaimed in the indigo language. "Or you'll try to strangle me, like you did poor Quint!"

He laughed. "He deserved it. And he did not resent it. A boy like Quint needs discipline. The less he gets, the worse he'll be."

"I must say, all those boys seemed infinitely improved by even short contact with a grown gulden man for whom they could feel respect."

This time his laugh was a little bitter. "If they knew more of the world, they might view me in a different light."

"Will you really play with them when you come back?"

He nodded. "I said I would."

"Would you come back again after that—and play with them again?"

"If Del has no answer for me in three days, I will return again. And again."

"Would you come back even if you had already learned everything Del had to share?"

He hesitated.

Jalci pressed on. "You saw how much those boys loved having you among them! You could—you could coach them in baltreck! Just by being around them, you could show them how a gulden man behaves. I don't think any one of them has ever before been lectured about honor by a guldman. They don't know how they're supposed to behave. But if you—"

"I am an ordinary man, with a lower place than most," he interrupted. "I have no father of my own and little enough I could offer anyone else."

"And they have nothing," she said. "They have no one except mothers they are beginning to despise and a community they are dying to leave behind. They don't know how to behave in the gulden world. You could show them."

"It feels like it would be lying," he said, "to hold myself up as a model for anyone."

"It feels like it would be generous," she said, "to share yourself even if you have very little."

That shut him up; that was a very good argument to use with a guldman. They walked another block in silence. The arched gate to the Centrifuge was taking shape ahead of them in the gathering dark.

"I will come back in three days," he said at last. "After that, I will decide."

"I'll come back in three days, too," she said instantly. He had to admit he was not surprised; he had already pictured her there in the gymnasium, watching and cheering and wondering about him.

Or maybe he was the one wondering about her.

There was only a single ringcar waiting at the gate. "I suppose you're going to West One?" she said. "We can share the car. I'll drop you off."

They said nothing during the short ride until Jalci pulled over to the landing to let Kerk out. When he reached for the door, she put a hand on his arm to hold him in place. Her touch was so warm he thought he could feel the blue of her fingers against his paler skin.

"How can I get in touch with you if I need to?" she said. She must have read the question on his face, for she quickly added, "In case Del finds out something about your mother right away. I'd want to let you know as soon as I can."

"I work in Brolt Barzhan's firm near the North Zero gate," he answered. "You can send a note there."

She nodded, but she did not drop her hand. Her dark eyes were scanning him, trying to look inside him. He thought he must seem as foreign to her as she did to him—although, after this long day, she was a little less alien. Almost comprehensible. "I'm glad I found you when you came to the Lost City today," she said softly in goldtongue. "You have given me a great deal to think about, Kerk Socast. I hope that you do not walk out of my life again too soon."

Goldtongue was really the only language for such delicate sentiments. "For whatever period of time you walk through my life, Jalciana Candachi, I am certain the days will be made colorful and full of music," he said carefully. "I am already grateful for the textures you have introduced to my days."

Smiling, she released him. "See you soon," she said in bluetongue. He had scarcely made it safely out of the car before she took off from the landing, again at a reckless speed. He stood on the stone apron and watched her ringcar until it was out of sight.

❧

That night, after dinner was over and Tess had put the girls to bed, Kerk made his way to his stepmother's room. Brolt was still in his *hoechter* and Makk was finishing up schoolwork; this was always the best time of day to seek out Tess for a private conversation.

She smiled at Kerk when he knocked at her open door, and gestured for him to sit beside her on the purple sofa that she had imported from Gold Mountain. It had always been her favorite piece of furniture and she had been unwilling to leave it behind.

"Come tell me about your day," she said as he settled next to her. "My husband tells me you earned a holiday from work. How did you spend it?"

She was relaxed, but he was not. He sat stiffly beside her and folded his hands tightly together. "I might have a tale to tell the lady Tess that I am not yet ready to tell anyone else in the household," he said.

She nodded, her face instantly sobering to the narrow, thoughtful expression that meant she would give his every word her utmost attention. "Now and then we all have something on our minds that we are not ready to share with the world," she said. "I can be your confidante."

So she was willing to keep a secret from Brolt. Well, it wouldn't be the first time. "The lady Tess has been closer to me than a mother," he said, staring at his hands. "And yet, somewhere in this city is the woman who bore me, twenty-four years ago. I find that my heart is not content to know she is so close and still outside my reach."

Tess was silent so long that he glanced up at her face, afraid he had hurt or offended her. But what he saw in her expression was compassion—and a certain amount of worry. For him. "A woman who leaves a son behind is not always eager to have him find her," she said softly. "Prepare your heart for some bruising if it goes on this quest."

"My heart is already bruised," he said. "The lady Tess is the one who kept it from actually breaking, but even she could not protect it altogether."

"And there are those who believe gulden men do not even have hearts," she said in a soft, teasing voice.

He smiled painfully. "This heart beats with borrowed

blood," he said. "I cannot help but wonder what my mother's heartbeat sounds like. All this time later, and I think I have forgotten what once I surely knew."

Tess reached for him, so he unclenched his folded fingers. She took hold of his left hand and laid her left wrist across his, so that their pulses fluttered against each other, a mistimed but pleasing counterpoint. "It is not the same blood, but it flows from me to you nonetheless," she said quietly. "There are ties stronger than those woven around mother and son. You will not be able to break them, no matter what quest you set out on."

"I do not want to break them," he said. "But I must go looking."

She put her free hand up to touch his face. "If I had lost you, I would want you to come looking for me," she said. "Bring back to me any news you find. Whatever it is, I will be waiting to hear it."

"Whatever it is," he said, "you are the one I will trust to keep it safe."

Five

Three days later, Kerk was back at the charity bank in the Lost City, making his way to Del's office through another hostile gauntlet of gulden women. He had not heard from Jalci during these three days, but she was awaiting him in Del's office, along with the white-haired old woman. Jalci smiled when he stepped in; Del did not.

He nodded at both of them and addressed the guldwoman. "I have come to see if the lady Del has any news for me," he said.

Del shook her head. "Ria is still making inquiries," she said. "So far she has found no trace of your mother, but she is still investigating."

"Should I come back in another three days?" he asked.

Del watched him a moment and then waved him to the empty seat beside Jalci. "You may come back as often as you like, as long as you cause no trouble," she said, abruptly switching to bluetongue. "But I think it's best if you prepare yourself for the notion that you might not find what you're looking for."

He gazed at her steadily and did not answer. He could feel Jalci's eyes on his face. Reluctantly, Del continued, "You say your mother came here seventeen years ago, but in fact, all you know for certain is that she left Gold Mountain. She might not have made it all the way to the city. The trip is difficult today for a gulden woman on her own, and it was perilous back then. More than one woman died on the journey." When he still did not answer, she offered an even more unwelcome possibility. "And even if she made it safely to the city, she might not have survived very long. It is rare now, but gulden men still arrive from Geldricht to seek out their missing wives. Whole families have been slaughtered by angry husbands and fathers. Was your father capable of such violence?"

Unquestionably, yes. And Kerk's father had often left Geldricht for weeks at a time, pursuing business interests in the city and overseas. If he had killed his errant wife and infant daughter, he had not bothered mentioning it to his son—or his second wife. Kerk was certain Tess would have given him this news if she'd had it.

But it might not be true. There was no proof. Just because Bree Socast had not been found yet did not mean she was dead.

"I have no wish to speculate about my father's possible actions," Kerk said, his voice cold to cover his pain. "It would please me if you and your friends would continue to search for my mother. I am not yet ready to concede that she is lost."

Del nodded slowly. "Then we will keep looking."

Kerk heard Jalci inhale a deep gust of air, almost as if she had been holding her breath ever since he stepped in the room. "Well, since we don't have any definitive news, let's go play baltreck," she said brightly.

He looked at her, allowing himself to be distracted, allowing himself to be amused. "Yes, let *us* go play," he said. "I'm sure you have mastered the sport in the short time since I saw you last."

She laughed. "Well, I watched the game for *hours* on the monitors over the last two nights," she said. "And I'm a passable athlete, you know—I probably *could* play as well as some of these ghetto kids. If I could figure out the rules."

"They would not welcome you on the court," he said.

She made a face at him. "I know that, stupid. I just want to watch. Del, you want to come?"

"I have plenty to occupy me here," the old woman said dryly. "But I hope you both enjoy yourselves."

Two hours later, Kerk had to say that he, at least, had

obeyed Del's injunction. He couldn't speak for Jalci, but he'd had a splendid time. The boys had been wildly excited to see him again, and he had had to be very stern to get them calm enough to pay attention, but they'd had a fruitful session of coaching followed by a fast-paced game. It was clear they'd all been practicing madly since he'd been here last, because the level of play had gone up almost across the board. Quint alone had improved substantially; he even managed to make a pass around Kerk's outstretched hands and scored twice on what should have been impossible shots. Kerk tried to be sparing with his praise, but he could not help shouting out approbation at the second electrifying goal. Even some of the defenders cheered.

"Here are more exercises you can practice in the next few days," he told them once the game was over. They watched him with famished attention; he imagined that every move he made was imprinting on their memories to be constantly replayed. "If you had extra equipment, more of you could practice at the same time."

Someone laughed and said, "I think Helten stole one of these balls from a store in the city."

"I didn't *steal* it. It was lying in a park."

Kerk ignored this exchange. "And, if you want, you can play a version of baltreck with only four players. Scoring is harder, but it gives you a workout on both offense and defense."

None of them had ever tried to play on such minimal teams before, so he called out Quint and Shoev and Helten, the three best players, and joined them on the court to demonstrate the abbreviated version of the game. He couldn't help showing off a little; four-man play heavily favored the best athlete, and baltreck was Kerk's game. Everyone on the sidelines was yelling as he made score after score. Even young men who had not been on the teams were watching—even a few women. Kerk made a final shot, which rattled with a satisfying clatter in the metal cone, and risked a quick look at the spectators. Jalci was cheering just as loudly as everyone else.

"That's all I can show you for today," he said, jogging off the court and reaching for his duffel bag. He had come prepared this afternoon, bringing gym clothes as well as appropriate shoes.

As expected, the boys wailed loudly when they realized he was leaving, but they quieted soon enough when he promised he would return. "Three days from now," he said, though Del had not specified such an interval this time. He would have liked to shower before changing back into his clothes, but the gymnasium didn't offer many amenities. In what passed for a locker room, he was able to strip to the waist and scrub off the worst of the sweat before getting dressed again and heading out the front door.

Jalci, of course, was waiting for him outside, and they walked toward the Centrifuge through a slowly layering dark. It was colder than yesterday and the threat of winter hung glumly overhead.

"Are you as good at baltreck as you seem to be, or is it just that I'm not very knowledgeable about the game?" she asked, once the last trailing boys had dropped behind them.

Kerk laughed. "A man does not boast of his accomplishments," he said.

"So you are. Could you have played in one of the professional leagues?"

"Maybe," he said.

She appraised him. "And why did you choose not to? From what I can tell, the players lead pretty sweet lives. A little adulation might be just the thing a fatherless boy would need to make him forget his lousy childhood."

He shrugged. "Maybe," he said again.

"I think I want a better answer than that," she said.

They were at the Centrifuge by now. There were three cars clustered at the gate, but, without even discussing it, they both headed to the first car in line. "It's complicated," he said.

"There's a new restaurant off of East Two that's been getting raves," she said. "Owned by an albino couple, but the chef's gulden, and half the patrons are indigo. Let me treat you to dinner and you can tell me some of your secrets."

"I don't tell anyone my secrets," he said, amused. "That's how they stay secret."

She had settled into the driver's seat and barely waited for him to close the door before she zoomed away from the landing. "Then tell me whatever you feel like sharing."

❦

The restaurant was a strange but pleasing place, Kerk thought. The main dining room was low-ceilinged and paneled with material that looked like seaweed or some kind of dried greenery; the muted lighting filtered out from behind translucent shades of watered pastel. The chef might have been gulden, but the items on the menu were eclectic, borrowing spices from Inrhio and countries across the ocean. The clientele was decidedly mixed, and the atmosphere was both relaxed and a little jazzed, as if the customers were excited to be in a place that they liked very much.

Kerk agreed with Jalci's plan to order and share a variety of items, though such an idea would never have occurred to him on his own. He declined to sample any alcoholic beverages, though. More and more these days, he was feeling as though he needed to keep his wits about him. It seemed like it would be too easy for him to be thrown off balance.

"So why didn't you try out for a professional baltreck team?" she asked, once they were settled at their table and had given the waiter their order.

"There's a pretty small window of time for going pro," he answered. "Most teams recruit seventeen- and eighteen-year-olds. By the time you're twenty, you've passed your peak and it's rare that a team will even give you a chance."

Jalci sipped at the drink that *she* had not been too cautious to order. It was lime green and bubbly, and Kerk thought it looked lethal. "So what was happening to you when you were seventeen?"

"Tess's third child was born and Tess was very sick," he said.

Jalci's eyes widened. "And you stayed in the house to care for her?"

He shrugged. "There were nurses to do that, and women from her family. I wasn't needed in the sickroom." Though he'd spent plenty of time there, mostly at night, reading to Tess when she couldn't sleep or just watching her face when she could. "I was of more use to Brolt Barzhan, for I had been working in the company for five years already and there were tasks I could do for him that eased his way."

"Well, I hope they appreciated your sacrifice!" she exclaimed.

Kerk wasn't sure Brolt had ever known of his dreams to be a professional player. Kerk had never been the confiding type. Until he met Jalci, anyway. "It was not a sacrifice," he said quietly. "It is what any son of the house would have done. I was glad to be able to repay, in some small way, the generosity they had always shown to me."

"But how long was she sick?" Jalci asked. "I mean, it couldn't have been for years, could it? Surely there would have been time for you to go pro after she recovered."

"By then, I had lost the inclination."

"By then, you were thinking that you didn't want anyone you loved to die while you were someplace else," Jalci said shrewdly. "So you didn't want to leave."

Kerk shrugged again. "Maybe."

Their food arrived, aromatic with unfamiliar scents, and they spent the next fifteen minutes tasting each dish and comparing their reactions. Kerk had formed the opinion that most blueskins had delicate palates and unimaginative preferences in food, but Jalci tried everything and liked everything, even the extraordinarily spicy meat dish that Kerk could barely tolerate. She did gulp down an entire glass of water after she'd finished it, though.

"I wouldn't want to eat that every day," she said, "but it's very good."

She got distracted while they split a couple of desserts, both too sweet for Kerk's taste; her eyes kept going past him to a spot in the middle of the restaurant.

"What are you looking at?" he asked finally.

"There's a young couple sitting a few tables behind you," she said in a low voice. "Mixed race. She's gulden and he's blueskin. I don't mean to be staring, but that's such an unusual sight."

"There's you and me," he said dryly.

"Yes, but they appear to be *together*," she said. "Married, maybe. They've got a baby."

That almost did make him slew around in his chair. "Really? I didn't think that ever happened."

"Well, it almost never does," she said. "I think that less than one percent of the babies born in the city last year were to interracial couples." She grinned. "I read that somewhere. I can't remember why it stuck in my head."

Casually he repositioned his chair so he could glance behind him to get a glimpse of the parents. They were young, neither of them over twenty by his guess, and they looked exhausted. The woman's gold skin seemed a little dingy around the eyes, as if she hadn't slept for about a week, but her blond hair frizzed around her face with a great deal of manic curl, and her weary smile was wide and genuine. The blueskin boy had night-black hair and the coarse features that Kerk associated with mid- or low-caste families, but he, too, was smiling. The baby sat in its mother's lap and looked around with plain astonishment at the world. Its skin was a blue as dark as Jalci's but its hair was a tightly curled yellow. The contrast was startling and seductive.

"There's a child who is not going to have an easy time in either world," Kerk remarked.

Jalci nodded. "Just what I was thinking. They'll never be able to live in Inrhio or Geldricht. They'll have to stay in the city forever. I wonder if his mother has disowned him."

Kerk didn't even have to wonder. "Her father has certainly cast her off," he said, sitting forward in his chair again. "Unless she has no father. Unless she grew up in the Lost City. Even then, gulden men who see her in the street might feel free to express how much they disapprove of her choice."

Jalci's face was solemn. "Really? They might hurt her? The indigo might harass him, but I don't think it would go any further than that."

"And what would they say to you," he said softly, "if they saw you out in public with a gulden man?"

Her head came up at that and her dark eyes gleamed. He imagined defiance was an old habit of hers. "I am from one of the Higher Hundred families, and only my female relatives may presume to comment on my behavior," she said.

"And sometimes you like shocking them," he said.

"That's not why I'm here with you," she said instantly. "We're friends."

"We don't know each other well enough to be friends," he said.

She put her head to one side. "Very well, then, you interest me," she answered. "I would *like* to be your friend. But I'm not sure you ever let anyone get close enough for the word to apply."

That was so true that he immediately stiffened up. "There are many borders separating us, Jalciana Candachi," he said. "We have crossed a few of them, but I imagine the rest are impassable."

"Then why are *you* out in public with *me*?" she demanded. "Since you don't particularly want to shock anyone? In fact, the less attention you draw to yourself, the happier you are."

Which was also true, and made him turn even more remote. "Because you can be of use to me," he said coolly. "For the same reason I would accept a dinner invitation from one of the blueskin men who does business with Brolt Barzhan."

That hurt her a little; her eyes darkened and her pretty face tightened. He was immediately sorry, but he didn't have an apology in him. Nor did he have a good answer for the original question, and it made him uneasy that it had even been asked. Why *was* he out in this public place with a blueskin heiress whom he had no reason to want to know? What would Tess think if she saw them? What would Brolt say?

"I will strive to be as useful as possible, then," she said, her voice as chilly as his. "I would not want you to complain of your treatment at the hands of a blueshi."

He was shocked that she would use the word, which was as filthy an insult to the indigo as *gilder* was to the gulden. "You shouldn't talk that way," he said sternly. "If you dishonor yourself, others will dishonor you as well."

For some reason, that made her laugh; the hurt look went away. "Very well, then," she said, "I will draw on my reserves of self-respect and try to overlook the fact that you are trying very hard *not* to be nice to me. Even though I think you want to be."

He didn't have to try to find an answer to that because she was suddenly on her feet. He spun in his chair to watch her go over and speak to the interracial couple, who had gathered all their paraphernalia and were just about to leave the restaurant. He didn't hear what she said, but she reached down to touch the baby on the cheek, and her words made the young parents beam with pride. They headed out the door; Jalci stepped up to the bar to place another order. When she returned to the table, she was carrying drinks for each of them.

"Just taste it," she said. "A few sips. I think you'll like it."

He complied, but two swallows were enough to convince him that his head would be spinning if he had any more. "It's very good. What is it?"

"A kind of wine made from fruit that can only be found in northern Inrhio. Very expensive. My grandmother grows acres of the stuff."

He couldn't resist one more swallow. The wine tasted like wild berries and black soil and fermented exaltation and money. "What did you say to those people before they left?" he asked.

"I told them I thought their baby was adorable." The surprise on his face must have been hilarious, or the wine had gone instantly to her head, because she threw her head back and laughed. "It was something to say," she added. "It gave me a chance to approach them and let them know I approved of them. You can hardly walk up to complete strangers and say, 'Good for you! You've risked banishment and brutality and ostracism just to be together, and I applaud your choice! You're in the vanguard of social change, and even though it's hard on *you*, the generations that come after you will have an easier time of it because you were brave enough to fall in love.' So instead I told them I liked their baby. It means the same thing, but it's more socially acceptable."

He took a much longer pull on the wine this time; he felt a flutter at his elbows and knees and knew that it wouldn't take much more for him to get drunk. A certain recklessness overtook him, or maybe he was drunk already, inebriated on something other than a high-proof indigo vintage. He finished off the wine and set the glass down with a snap. "You intrigue me, Jalciana Candachi," he said. "Even though I wish you didn't."

She laughed at him again. "I know I do, Kerk Socast," she replied, "and I'm going to make sure it stays that way for a long time."

Six

O ver the next three weeks, Kerk visited the Lost City seven times. Each time, he first stopped in Del's office to inquire after news of his mother; each time, she told him she had no answers for him.

On his fifth trip, he asked her if she was lying. Not as bluntly as that, of course. Speaking in goldtongue, he said, "I like to think the lady Del believes that my visits to the Lost City have been beneficial to its residents."

"Indeed, Kerk Socast, the time you have invested in the young men of this neighborhood has paid back more handsomely than I could have imagined. I freely admit I was not pleased with you the day you first arrived, but now I am glad every time I see your face at my door."

"It has become my plan," he said, "to return to the Lost City at intervals for the foreseeable future. To continue teaching the baltreck teams until I have no more to teach them."

"That is welcome news," Del said.

This was the tricky part. He spoke slowly. "You need not fear that any news you have to give me about my mother would change my mind. Even if I learn my mother is dead, I will return to the Lost City as I have promised."

There was a good deal of comprehension on her face. But she, too, replied in the most roundabout fashion. "I like to think

I would not stoop to abusing a man's trust in such a way," she said. "I like to think I would not withhold information simply because it was advantageous to me to know something that someone else did not."

He stood up. "Then I will come again in a few days, and perhaps you will have an answer for me, and perhaps you will not. And whatever you tell me, I will return again a few days after that."

"Then I will see you again at that time," she said.

Most days, when Kerk coached the boys, Jalci was in the gymnasium watching. In the middle of that third week, she had a surprise for him: dozens of shirts of all different sizes in four different colors.

"Not quite team uniforms," she said cheerfully. "But better than socks and headbands."

"Where did you get these?" he asked as the boys ripped open packaging and argued over who would wear what colors.

She waved a hand. "One of my donors runs a clothing store. I talked about the value of sports in teaching teamwork and pride. Most of these were extras from bad dye runs. He was just as glad to get rid of them."

Kerk was watching the boys parade around the gym floor, seeming to stand taller and shoot more accurately once they were properly attired. "This was a great kindness, Jalciana Candachi."

"I've been thinking," she said.

He glanced down at her, smiling faintly. "I have come to feel a certain disquiet whenever you open a conversation with those words," he said.

She gave him a look of utter innocence. "I can't imagine why you would say that."

"What have you been thinking about?"

"Most of the schools within the city have baltreck teams," she said. "Gulden *and* indigo schools. They play championship games in the spring. It might be possible to have your boys play one of the school teams. I could help arrange that."

He just looked at her, keeping his face blank. What had startled him most in that sentence was the phrase *your boys*. These lost children were not, by any measure, his. He was not responsible for them; he had no hand in their destiny; he did not even *want* to be considered their surrogate father, not in the smallest, remotest fashion.

That was not the part of her comment he addressed.

"There's no team here," he said. "Just people playing."

"Aren't there eight men on a baltreck team?" she persisted. So she had been investing some time in getting to know the game. "Plus three alternates? You have at least five players who are actually gifted. With a few months of coaching—"

"They would still not be good enough to make a decent showing of themselves against skilled players from an organized team," Kerk said. "And they would not want to play if they would be humiliated."

She was listening carefully. "You mean, if they wouldn't win."

He smiled. "No gulden man likes to lose at any contest, that's true, but in this case I said what I meant. If they could play a game they had a *chance* at winning, I would be willing, but I don't think such a chance exists."

"But if you continue coaching them—"

"I do not believe my skills are good enough to put them on a level with other teams."

She frowned and then shrugged. "Well, think about it from time to time," she said. "Maybe you'll change your mind."

No gulden woman would have said such a thing to a gulden man; no gulden woman would have thought she could continue to wheedle and plead and come up with fresh arguments and wear down the patience of her husband or father or son. But then, as had been clear from the very first day, Jalciana Candachi had no intention of behaving like a gulden woman.

"Maybe," Kerk said, and slipped onto the polished floor to resume his coaching.

~

Four days after that conversation with Jalci, Makk came home from school with complex forms for Brolt to fill out. The boy's birthday was less than three months away; the school had to arrange for the transfer of responsibility from the father to the young man. Makk and Brolt disappeared together into Brolt's *hoechter*, no doubt laying out the course of Makk's future. Kerk spent the evening in the women's quarters, playing games with Tess and the girls and trying not to let his mind fret too much over his own future. More than once, he caught Tess's troubled gaze on his face, but he did not share his uneasiness with her and she was not bold enough to introduce the topic.

The following night, Kerk made his own appearance at the *hoechter* door, knocking respectfully. Brolt was relaxing in a deep, comfortable chair, reading what looked like a historical novel, but he smiled as he looked up and saw Kerk.

"Come in," he invited. "I keep thinking this book will begin to catch my interest, but so far it has not, so I would much rather have a conversation than try to read."

Kerk stepped inside and spoke formally. "The conversation I would like to have is of a serious nature, and perhaps my father-who-is-not would prefer to concentrate only on lighter topics at the end of a busy day."

Brolt's face sharpened but he did not look alarmed or dismayed. "Indeed, no, I am alert enough for important debate," he said. "Close the door so that we are not disturbed."

A moment later, Kerk was sitting across from Brolt in one of those well-padded chairs, wondering where to start. Goldtongue had never seemed so abstract—but circumlocution had never seemed more necessary.

"It is hard to believe," he said at last, "that in eleven weeks, Makk will become a man. I remember when he was a baby, sleeping in his mother's arms. I remember how small his fingers were when they caught at his father's hands."

"It is strange indeed," Brolt agreed. "I myself have aged only by a year or two. How can Makk have aged by twelve?"

They both laughed at that, though Kerk's laugh was a little sad. "When Makk becomes a man," Kerk went on, "he will no doubt wish to participate in his father's business. His father has built a successful, honorable company where any man would be proud to work."

"He does wish it," Brolt said. "We have discussed the areas where he might profitably begin his training. He will be a man, it is true, but still a very young one. There is much he will need to learn, and it will take a great deal of time."

"Your nephews both continue to be employed in your firm as well," Kerk said.

Brolt nodded. "They are good workers and loyal to the business."

"Perhaps Brolt Brazhan is more blessed than a man could want," Kerk said softly. "Perhaps he has an excess of young men for whom he feels he must find a place in his company. Perhaps he is hoping that one of the young men under his care might look for a situation elsewhere."

Kerk wanted to drop his eyes as he said the words, a sign of both humility and respect, but instead he kept them on Brolt's face, to show fearlessness and strength. Brolt's return gaze never wavered as he closely listened and carefully answered.

"I have long been proud of my ability to provide for so many members of my family," Brolt replied. "If I had ten sons, I could feed them all. If I had twenty nephews, all of them could find a place in my house and in my business. I am not overburdened with young men. I have places for them all and am happy to be able to provide for them."

Kerk felt a rush of relief so powerful it almost made him sway in his chair, but he still did not drop his eyes. "Brolt Barzhan is a generous man. No wonder his household is vigorous and full," he said.

"And Makk Barzhan will be a generous one as well," Brolt said. "In the normal course of events, as you know, a man dies and his sons take over his properties. I am unfortunate in that I have only one son, but fortunate in that his notions align so closely with mine. He, too, values the contributions of his cousins and his stepbrother. He would be loath to see any of them leave the company once it comes under his control. He told me so just yesterday, without any prompting on my part. I do not think there will ever be a time, Kerk Socast, when you will find yourself thrown into the world without any semblance of family at your back."

Kerk took a sharp breath, for that was more direct speaking than goldtongue usually allowed. "I did not mean to cast doubts on how well the Barzhans guard their ties of family," he said.

Brolt smiled and leaned over to briefly rest his big hand

on Kerk's shoulder. "And you did not," he said. "You spoke up just as you should, and that took courage. For my part, I needed no courage at all! I was merely required to be benign and munificent."

Kerk allowed himself a laugh, though it was a small one. "Perhaps for a man like yourself, such a conversation was easy," he said. "I am not so certain that a mean-spirited individual would have answered as you did."

Still smiling, Brolt dropped his hand and leaned back in his chair. "But I confess, I thought you might be coming to my *hoechter* with a different sort of question," the older man said.

Kerk gave him an inquiring look. "What question might that be?"

"It has not escaped my notice that you have spent a great deal of your time away from the business and away from the house," Brolt said. "Clearly, there are other enterprises that have captured your attention. What does a man of your age find so fascinating? I ask myself. There seem to be two possible answers. One, it might be a woman."

"A woman!" Kerk exclaimed, so surprised that Brolt laughed out loud.

"When I was your age, I might not have been eager to marry, but I was eager to know more about women," Brolt said cheerfully. "It seems logical to suppose that some of your time has been spent with a member of the opposite sex."

"No," Kerk said decisively—and then, as Jalci's image rose unbidden in his mind, "Well, yes. But not the kind of woman you mean. That is—she's not—I don't think of her as—It's hard to explain," he ended lamely.

Brolt was smiling even more broadly. "I see," he said. "Then perhaps I needn't even ask if the second situation might apply."

"What would that other situation be?" Kerk asked a little desperately. He was still thinking of Jalci. Well, of course, she *was* a woman. A fascinating, unpredictable, chaotic, restless thunderstorm of a woman, but not someone you *thought* of as a woman. Not the kind of person you imagined sharing your house with, sharing your bed with, sharing your life with. Not *that* kind of woman.

"A man your age might be thinking of how to free himself

from the influence of his father and his other male relatives," Brolt said. "You came here tonight and offered to leave if I had no more use for you. Perhaps you were trying to tell me that there is other work you want to do at some other company."

"I would not say such a thing," Kerk said. "That would be disloyal."

Brolt shrugged. "Now and then, a son must leave the family business, or no new businesses would be formed," he said. "It is not disloyal for a son to move on, as long as the new place he finds is honorable and efficiently run. I would smooth your way if you wished to leave for another company. I would do more. I would back an enterprise you wished to found on your own, provided I was convinced it was a sound financial investment."

Now Kerk straightened in his chair, truly surprised. This was a mark of favor that he had never expected. "Brolt Barzhan is openhanded indeed," he said. "I have no words to express my gratitude."

Brolt smiled. "But should I conclude that no such business idea has germinated in your head? Should I understand that all your abstraction has been caused by a woman—even if she is one you cannot explain? Or is there, indeed, a business proposition you would like to discuss with me—if not now, at some point in the future?"

Kerk sank back against the chair, studying Brolt's face. This man had taught Kerk everything he knew about honor, everything he understood about family; this man had shown Kerk how a good man was supposed to live. And yet this man had the unconscious sense of entitlement common to any privileged gulden man who had lived in a society constructed to adore him. Brolt did not know from experience what it meant to live as an outsider, a dependent, or a castoff. Honorable as he was, Brolt might not understand what Kerk had to say next.

"I have spent my recent days in an activity that I am not sure you will approve of," Kerk said finally, speaking slowly and as plainly as he could in goldtongue. "I wish you would hear my entire story before you judge."

Once again, Brolt's face grew serious and composed. "I will," he said.

"There is a place in the city where gulden women go,"

Kerk said, "when they have left the protection of their husbands and fathers in Geldricht. Let us not discuss their reasons for leaving or how despicable their actions might be. When they come to the city, sometimes they come alone. Sometimes they come accompanied by their children. Some of those children are boys."

Kerk paused a moment before proceeding. "Young gulden men who grow up in the city apart from their fathers' influence are young gulden men who are completely lost. They understand nothing about honor. They do not know how to show respect. They do not know how a family works, how a man protects those who are under his roof, how a woman cares for the hearts of those who are within her circle. And yet they live, and they grow, and they will soon go out in the world, where I think they will do nothing but wreak havoc."

"I would think the same," Brolt murmured.

"I had occasion to visit this ghetto in the city where women live and young men grow up fatherless," Kerk said. "Some of those young men have had so little direction that they looked to *me* for guidance. Since that first visit, I have spent many days in the ghetto, teaching those men what I know. I do not lecture them, you understand, for what young man will sit still to be told how to behave? Instead I have chosen to coach them in baltreck, and in that way to model the behavior that is expected of a gulden man. I don't know that they have learned as much as I would have wished, but they have learned more than they knew before."

Now he looked up at Brolt, whose face was solemn but closed, giving away none of his thoughts. "Part of me wishes there is more I could do for them. And part of me wants to leave them behind and never return. Am I not endorsing their runaway mothers if I stay to teach them? Am I not in some sense betraying Gold Mountain if I stay?" He spread his hands. "I do not know any of the answers. Brolt Barzhan is wise. Perhaps he can explain to me what I should do next."

It was a long moment before Brolt replied, and Kerk felt his stomach twist with anxiety. He had just been offered a lifelong place in the Barzhan firm; he had just been offered funding for his dreams, if he happened to have any. Would both those offers now be rescinded?

"I think you should not ask if you are betraying Gold Mountain, but ask instead if Gold Mountain has betrayed these boys," Brolt answered finally. "The way of Geldricht is precisely defined and beautifully functional until it fails completely. I love to look at my family and see generations of strong men and beloved women, all connected by pride and honor. But I do not have to look far to see cruel men and abused women, both of them shaped by and trapped within an unforgiving society. I wish no woman had ever felt the need to run away from Gold Mountain. But I think it is the fault of Gold Mountain that they did."

Kerk caught his breath. This was more philosophical than Brolt's typical conversation, and a little harder for Kerk to follow. But Brolt was not angry with him, that much was clear, and Kerk could begin to relax.

Brolt went on. "Should you continue to model the proper behavior for these boys? Indeed you should. Is there more you can do? Perhaps there might be. Are they capable of working? Can they be trusted with responsibility? There are jobs available in the city for willing hands. I am not looking for more sons, but I could use more workers."

Kerk just stared at him. At no time when he imagined this conversation had he expected Brolt to speak those words. "There are one or two who show remarkable discipline and a will to improve," he said. "Investing in them would be a risk, even so."

"I know how to minimize risks," Brolt said.

"I had not even thought of trying to find employment for them," Kerk said. "My greatest ambition has been to see them play together as a team. Jalci even thinks they could take the court against school baltreck leagues, but I am not so sure they will ever be skilled enough for that."

He had not meant to say the name, and, of course, Brolt instantly caught it. "Jalci?" he said, smiling broadly. "Does she serve on your coaching staff? Is she the reason you are so often gone from home? Is she one of the runaway wives now living in the ghetto?"

"She's a blueskin heiress who volunteers in the Lost City," Kerk said baldly. "Hardly the sort of woman you would be proud to see me befriend."

That silenced Brolt completely. For the first time during this conversation, the older man seemed wholly at a loss.

"And now you know the worst of it," Kerk said. "But despite the color of her skin, I believe she is an honorable woman. What she wants is to put more good into the world than existed before she was present. That is a noble goal for gulden *or* indigo."

"Indeed it is," Brolt said, his face and voice once again neutral. "I know you confide in the lady Tess from time to time. Is she aware of this most unlikely friendship you have managed to strike up?" Kerk imagined the rest of the sentence. *And why hasn't she informed me of this disastrous turn of events?*

"No," Kerk said. "She knows I have been to the Lost City. She does not know how often, nor how I spend my time when I am there."

"I myself have done business with blueskins, and found them, at times, reasonable and intelligent and not without honor," Brolt said. "I suppose your new friend might fall within that same category. But anything other than friendship—"

"I know."

"Would be scandalous in the extreme."

"I know."

"And very difficult to tolerate."

"I realize that. It is strange to me that I even consider her a friend. I have not viewed her in any other light."

"Might I know the full name of this blueskin woman who has so dangerously befriended a member of my family?"

"Jalciana Candachi."

"Candachi?" Brolt exclaimed. "Is she any relation to Anton Solvano's daughter?"

Kerk was confused. "Who? I don't know. She's mentioned her aunt Kitrini a few times, but—"

Now Brolt was staring at him, but his wide smile was back. "She is from the family of Kitrini Candachi? How is it that you have managed to find, among all the indigo in the city, the only one for whom the gulden can feel a genuine affection?"

"I know nothing of Kitrini Candachi," Kerk muttered.

"She is a great favorite of Chay Zanlan. They had a grave disagreement ten years ago, but they have reforged their relationship. The Candachi name will open more doors in Chay Zanlan's palace than the Barzhan name ever could."

"Then you're not angry that I have met her?"

Brolt watched him awhile before answering, smiling slightly. "I am thinking that of all the surprising news you have brought me this evening, this is the most surprising—and the most welcome. And yet none of it was unwelcome. You have long been an honorable man, Kerk Socast, but tonight you have proved to me that you are much more than honorable. You are enterprising—you are committed to kindness—and you are lucky. Such a man is an asset anywhere he goes. I am happier than ever that the family you call your own is mine."

Seven

Although they never explicitly made plans, Jalci and Kerk had fallen into the habit of leaving the Lost City together after a coaching session and heading to some small, intimate restaurant where the races were allowed to mingle without harassment. The day after Kerk's revelatory conversation with Brolt, Jalci took him to a rather more upscale place than they had frequented so far. It was near the East Three gate, practically back in the commercial district, and decidedly more biased toward indigo than gulden. Kerk counted only seven guldmen eating at any of the tables, and none of the items on the menu would have been served on Gold Mountain.

Jalci was oblivious. "You ought to try this dish with wine sauce. It's a specialty of the restaurant and it's *so good*. Oh, and we'll have to order some of the spiced nut bread. The only person who's ever made it better is my grandmother, and she says she'll give me the recipe if I ever get married. Which is almost enough incentive to let my mother matchmake for me after all."

"I can't tell what would be good, so just tell me what to order," Kerk said. He realized he would never ask a gulden woman to direct his choices that way—in fact, if he were here with Tess, he'd be picking the items she should eat—but, as always, life with Jalci didn't conform to what he considered ordinary rules.

"Well, let me figure out what *I* want first, and then we'll get something completely different and share."

Once the waiter had taken their orders and brought them a plate of spiced nut bread—which was even better than Jalci had led him to expect—Kerk said, "So tell me more about your aunt Kitrini."

Jalci widened her dark eyes. "What made you think of her?"

"I had a conversation with my stepfather last night. He asked where I have been spending my time lately. I told him."

"Oh, I hope he wasn't angry with you!" Jalci exclaimed.

"He surprised me by seeming to approve of what I have been doing."

She eyed him. "And if he had been displeased? What would you have done then?"

"It would have been more difficult," he said quietly, "but I would have continued to come to the Lost City. But to have gone against Brolt's stated wishes would have caused a rift between us, and such rifts tend to grow instead of mending."

"So. You told him about coaching the team and—" She tilted her head to one side. "And you must have told him about me."

He smiled very slightly, just to tease her. "I barely mentioned your name. But he recognized it right away, and he asked me if you were related to Kitrini Candachi."

"I'm hardly surprised he knew her name. He might even have met her, if he's ever gone to the palace to see Chay Zanlan, because Kitrini practically grew up there," she replied. "Kitrini's always said that Chay Zanlan was like a second father to her." Jalci thought it over for a moment and added, "Kit and Chay had a terrible falling-out a few years ago, but they've patched things up. When Chay Zanlan comes to the city, he often stays with Kitrini and Uncle Nolan. She's probably the reason relations between the races are as good as they are today. There are indigo politicians who hate her—and they *despise* Uncle Nolan, but that's a whole different story—but she's on every board and committee that has anything to do with indigo-gulden collaborations."

"How did a blueskin woman become so close to Chay Zanlan?"

"Her father and grandfather were sociologists who lived in Geldricht for years. They were activists who fought for gulden rights in the city—*very* unpopular in their day, but now all the schoolchildren learn about the Solvanos, who laid the groundwork for peace between races." She cut a piece of bread, took a small bite, and let her face show a brief look of ecstasy. "Have you tried this yet? It's like eating autumn. I can't believe your stepfather didn't ask you any more questions about *me*."

The quick change of topic would have taken him off guard except he had been waiting for it. "He did, but I said very little. The conversation would not have been awkward at all except he had just asked me if I was leaving the house so often to seek the company of a woman."

"And you said, 'Jalci's not a woman!'" Jalci said. "Don't deny it. I know you did."

His slight smile was back. "Indigo females do not conform to the mold that gulden consider womanly," he said.

She was indignant. "Oh, so just the *fact* that I'm indigo would have reassured your stepfather? 'No gulden man could find a blueskin woman attractive, therefore I don't need to worry about how much time Kerk spends with this Candachi woman.'"

"I think he might have been slightly more alarmed than that," Kerk said, "but not much."

"*Hmpfh,*" she said and tossed her hair. He couldn't tell if she was actually miffed or merely pretending.

"I cannot imagine you have said much more about *me* to your mother," he said.

She laughed out loud. "Oh, I've been much more forthcoming, although I have to admit my motives weren't pure. My mother has been needling me to have dinner with this *relentlessly* boring man who has been living in the city for two months. I have known him my whole life and never managed to have a conversation with him that did not revolve around his dietary restrictions. So I told her I was not going to marry Stuver, I wasn't even going to have dinner with him, and that if she didn't leave me alone, I would make a disastrous runaway marriage with my current flame, whom she would consider appallingly inadequate. Even so, she was excited by the idea that I might be dating someone until I told her you were a gulden man. Then she practically fainted. I actually had to grab her and guide her over to the sofa or I think she would have fallen on her face."

For a long moment, Kerk just looked at her. "You told your mother you were dating a gulden man? That you were considering marrying him?"

She laughed again, a little more nervously. "Well. Yes. But only to upset her."

But just to speak the words—even for a disreputable reason—meant Jalci had considered the idea at some point. That she had looked at Kerk and seen him, if only in the most speculative fashion, as a potential mate, and not just some random individual collection of bones and body parts. It was almost beyond his ability to fathom. They were so different, so far apart, that falling in love with Jalci would seem as alien as falling in love with a sea creature or a land plant, tragic and ridiculous and impossible all at the same time.

And yet . . .

"I didn't mean to horrify you," she said, when the silence had stretched on too long. "I'm really not eyeing you as a possible husband. I'm never even sure you're going to allow me to be your friend for one more day. But in case you were wondering, yeah, I think you're cute. I think you're sexy. All those muscles and that intimidating stare. Yes, that one." Now she was laughing, though he thought she was still speaking the truth. "But trust me, I don't expect you to return the compliment. I know I'm not the kind of girl who makes an impression on a man like you. So don't get all worried about it."

It seemed probable, if he didn't answer, that she would just keep talking this way for the remainder of the meal. "You *are* attractive, Jalciana Candachi," he said formally. "I imagine your mother has no difficulty at all finding men who would be overjoyed at the chance to marry you. If I appear stunned, it is not because I find the notion distasteful, but because my mind has not, so far, turned in this direction."

"Yeah, well, once you think of it, it becomes difficult to think of anything else," she said, flashing him a brilliant smile.

She actually seemed much less uncomfortable than Kerk felt—though he had to admit that part of his discomfort was actually excitement.

How strange, to think of an indigo girl admiring him.

How alluring, to think of *this* indigo girl attracted to him . . .

"I believe I will be able to school my thoughts," he said.

She burst out laughing again. "Oh, you probably will. Look, what excellent timing! Here's our food. Now we can talk about something else."

He would have expected the rest of the conversation to be strained and halting, but in fact, they were both in high spirits, laughing at comments that were not particularly funny, sharing observations about their fellow diners, sharing food. She insisted he taste her wine, and so he drank from her glass; she touched his hand more than once to catch his attention; he called her by name more times than he could count. They were pleased with each other and amused by each other and drawn to each other, though Kerk, at least, would not examine that last thought too closely. It was, in many ways, the best two hours they'd spent together since they had met more than a month ago.

"Damn! It's so late!" she exclaimed after one quick, unwary look at her watch. "Your stepfather will *really* begin wondering about how you spend your time if you don't get home fast."

"I might need to begin inventing excuses," he replied. They had already paid their bill—some time ago—and so they just shrugged on their coats and headed out.

She paused with one hand on the door. He was so close behind her that his arm brushed against her shoulder. "You'd do that? Lie to Brolt? About me?"

He smiled down at her. "I am not in the habit of lying," he said. "But I have sometimes found it useful to fail to provide all the truth."

"I'll keep that in mind," she said with a laugh, pushing the door open. "Because I *hate* it when people withhold information from me."

"I've noticed that," he said, following her out into the chilly dark. "That's why I find it so entertaining to tell you only part of a story."

She laughed again and turned around to answer him. But before she could speak, rough hands pushed her to one side; two burly bodies shoved themselves between her and Kerk.

"You *dare* to touch the hand of an indigo goddess," someone hissed in Kerk's ear, and he felt a hard blow land against his kidney from behind.

Without conscious thought, he sent his body into motion. A tight whirl, and he had rammed a hard fist across the faces of the two men in front of him, whipped a steely forearm against the throat of the attacker in back. Another spin, another series of punches, plus a ferocious kick that brought one of the men to the sidewalk with a wailing howl. The two who were still on their feet came boring in with renewed purpose, yelling and brandishing makeshift weapons—an umbrella in one case, a piece of street junk in the other. Kerk shook his dagger into his hand and backed against the restaurant wall, falling into a crouch. His eyes were burning, his blood was racing, and he was prepared to unleash any level of force.

Astonishingly, Jalci jumped in front of him, her own hand upraised, her own weapon out. She really thought that ridiculous bottle of chemical spray would stop a determined assailant. "Step away from both of us," she ordered in a cold, clear voice. "*Back away!* Now. I'm embarrassed that indigo men would behave so offensively."

The man on the ground was still sniveling in pain, but the other two shifted position, uncertain and still angry. "Gilder trash," one of them snarled.

"Blueshi bastard," Jalci shot back. "The man is here at *my* invitation. Doing work on *my* behalf. How dare *you* interfere with a woman's business?"

"He's too familiar," the snarling man said.

"At least he's not stupid," was her contemptuous reply. "At least he behaves with the dignity of a man."

"I can't stand up," whined the assailant on the ground. "Help me. I think he broke my leg."

Jalci looked down at him and toed him none too gently. "You deserve to have your leg broken. You deserve to have every bone in your body broken." She returned her angry gaze to his companions, who were backing away a little, starting to look sheepish. "Take your friend and go. Be glad I don't ask who your families are so I can report your behavior to your mothers."

"*Hela*, we will leave when this gilder man is safely gone," said the one who hadn't spoken till now.

"You will leave now," Jalci replied fiercely. "Or—no—stay where you are and *I* will leave, so that I no longer incite you to reckless and misguided behavior."

Without even looking behind her, Jalci reached back and grabbed Kerk's wrist. She kept her hard gaze on the blueskin men, who still looked mutinous but a little more subdued. "Stay where you are," she repeated, and drew Kerk along the sidewalk in the general direction of the Centrifuge. She didn't glance back once as she hurried him away from the restaurant, around the corner, and out of sight of the indigo vigilantes.

They continued at a pretty rapid pace for another few blocks. Kerk listened closely to make sure they were not being followed, but within a couple of turns he was certain that the blueskin men had obeyed Jalci's orders. Nonetheless, he kept his dagger in his hand. No telling how many blueskins had witnessed the altercation and might agree with the general sentiment. No telling when he might find himself in a real fight that even Jalci's indigo arrogance couldn't defuse.

It was full dark now, and cold, and the streets were relatively empty, though they passed dozens of shops and restaurants filled with people of all races. They were only a block or two from the Centrifuge gate when Jalci abruptly stopped and drew Kerk into the flimsy shelter of a shallow doorway that seemed to lead to some kind of commercial establishment. Not a restaurant, at any rate; its high plate-glass windows revealed only an empty darkness inside.

"I'm sorry," she said. She had not yet dropped her hold on his arm.

"For which part of the encounter?" he asked.

She peered up at him, but he doubted she could see much of his expression. Her face, so much darker than his own, was almost completely lost in the shadows. "I am sorry that they were stupid and officious enough to *care* that I was having dinner with a gulden man," she said, rattling the words off as if to get out as many as possible before he interrupted. "I am sorry that they attacked you and insulted you. But most of all, I am sorry that it had to appear as if I was protecting you. I'm sorry I couldn't let you defend yourself. I know you are proud, and that you must be mortified to be shielded by a woman. But, Kerk, I could not let you fight them. City justice still favors the indigo, and if you had actually hurt those wretched boys, you'd have been in jail before the night was out. I *couldn't* let that happen. Kerk, if you had cut one of them—if you had killed one of them—"

"I am impressed that you think I could have done that much damage when there were three of them and one of me," he said in a clipped voice.

She shook him by the arm she still clung to. "I *know* you could have! The only reason all three of those men aren't dead right now is because you aren't the kind of man who kills at random!"

"And because I learned long before this that I cannot give myself the luxury of succumbing to rage," he said.

She dropped her hand then, but did not step back. Did not indicate in any way that she was afraid of standing so close to a man she believed could commit three murders with a few swipes of his hands. "You're furious," she said in a low voice. "I don't blame you. I'm so sorry. But please, please, don't be angry at me. I wasn't defending you against indigo men. I was protecting you from the indigo system—and no gulden knife has ever won a fight in *that* battle."

"I *am* angry," he acknowledged. "But not at you, Jalciana Candachi. I knew what you did as you did it. It is why I allowed you to speak in my defense. I put my trust in you instead of in my own instincts. But it goes very much against my nature to allow someone else to fight a battle on my behalf. Had one of those men spoken the slightest insult to you, I don't believe I could have kept myself from ripping out his throat."

She took a deep breath, shuddering a little. "I thought you were going to do it anyway," she said. "I could feel you coiled behind me. I was so afraid."

She had been touching him all night, but now, for the first time, he deliberately put a hand out and laid it against the side of her head. His fingers felt her hair, silky black against his skin; his palm rested against the smooth heat of her cheek. "You showed no fear, Jalci Candachi," he said. "You showed courage, and quick wits, and wise judgment. I am proud to be defended by such a noble companion."

They stood that way for a long time, his hand against her skin, her body only inches from his, the chill air seeming to snap with a sizzling current. She didn't move and yet he could sense her battling an intense inward pressure that bent her in his direction, as if she would collapse against him and mold herself to his chest. As for himself, he held his body utterly rigid, utterly still, neither leaning forward nor pulling away, unwilling to back off from the emotion swirling through him, unwilling to give in.

Jalci spoke after what seemed a flayed hour of nerves and resistance. "If you're not going to kiss me," she said in a voice barely above a whisper, "I suppose we'd better go home."

"Then we'd better go home," he said. But he still did not drop his hand.

She reached up then, tentatively, touching those ink-dark fingertips to his cheek, his chin. "I can't get over your *face*," she said in a marveling voice. "Your color. I always thought gulden men were pasty and sort of—unfinished looking. But I love the textures of your skin. I love the way it seems as if it's lit from underneath. I keep thinking that if I touch you, it will be like I'm holding a candle under my hand—my bones and veins will light up and grow transparent."

"The color of your skin seems to register on me with an actual heat," he replied. "So perhaps you are the candle, after all, and I am the thing that is going to burn up."

She laid her palm gently across his mouth, brushing it infinitesimally back and forth as if to test the grain of a particularly delicate satin. "You are too cool to burn," she murmured. "From the very beginning, you have been indifferent to my particular brand of fire."

"I am gratified that that has appeared to be the case," he said.

Footsteps on the nearby sidewalk sounded shockingly loud; a woman's laugh floated toward them in the still air. Kerk and Jalci leapt apart as if an axe had sliced down between them, but they were still staring at each other as a cluster of blueskin women clattered by, hurrying toward the Centrifuge.

"More reminders that we are not alone in the world," Jalci

said. She sounded as if she was smiling, but she also sounded as if it took some effort.

"And that we both have other places to be," Kerk said. "Time, indeed, to go home."

For the first time since he had known her, they departed in separate ringcars, Jalci cheerily waving good-bye as she sent her vehicle lunging into the thin late-evening traffic. Kerk drove more slowly, keeping to the bottom lane, terrified of miscalculating speed or distance or reaction time and causing a pileup in the tunnels. He had already made a seriously dangerous mistake in judgment; it seemed only too possible that he would err again.

Eight

When Kerk returned to the Lost City three days later, he was completely in command of himself again and not even worried about the little thrill he might feel the first time he laid eyes on Jalci. He knew, if she did not, that their relationship—however exciting it might be—could never progress beyond its current stage. He would not be tempted into more light flirtations; he would not let her take his hand or joke about marriage or continue to toy with the heart of a gulden man. He would be rational; he would be cool; he would treat her with the same courteous remoteness he offered to the lady Del.

He would do none of those things, for she was not there.

She was visiting with her mother, who had come to the city unexpectedly, Del told him. She might not be back at the charity bank for four or five days. Kerk nodded, as if the information was of limited interest to him, and then he inquired after his mother. When Del reported that she had no news, he nodded again. It was hard to know which of Del's announcements had disappointed him more.

At the gym, he put the boys through a particularly grueling training session. At home that evening, he invited Makk to a game of choisin, and they played till late that night, ending in a draw. At work over the next few days, Kerk attacked his as-

signments with such absorption that Brolt twice had to remind
him to go home when it was almost the dinner hour. But in this
way, the time passed; the days seemed full instead of empty.

When Kerk made his way back to Del's office three days
later, he had convinced himself that Jalci would not be there.
No doubt her mother was still in town, requiring Jalci's atten-
dance, reminding Jalci of all the reasons she should not make
alliances with gulden men.

So it was something of a shock to see Jalci's face the minute
he stepped inside Del's office. He thought he was successful at
hiding his leap of happiness, which was powerful enough to
skew his balance for a moment. He was pretty sure he kept his
voice cool as he said, "Del told me your mother was in town.
Has she found a husband for you yet?"

She laughed, but he thought the sound was forced. "No, but
not for lack of trying. She went home this morning, discouraged by her lack of success."

"No doubt she'll be back soon with the same agenda."

"No doubt."

After this exchange of pleasantries, Kerk turned and gave
Del a brief nod. "Good afternoon, lady Del. Do you have
news of my mother for me?"

"I do," she said.

The unadorned, unexpected reply froze him where he
stood, but he managed to keep the neutral expression on his
face. "I am glad to hear it," he replied. "Can you give me details? Is she alive? Will she see me?"

"She will see you, and she is here," Del replied. "She is
waiting for you in the park out back."

The "park" was a square of badly tended grass and a few
haphazard trees interspersed with crumbling stone benches.
Though recent nights had been freezing, the autumn afternoon
was invitingly warm, perfect for sitting outside for an hour.

"I will go to her, then," he said.

"Kerk," Jalci said, her voice laced with concern. "Wait."

He glanced at her, still letting nothing show in his expression. Not hope, not joy, not wild excitement. Not fear. "I have
already waited," he said.

"Can I come with you?"

She was trying to warn him without speaking a word. He

kept his eyes on hers but shook his head. "I am prepared," he said to reassure her. "I do not need assistance to take this meeting."

Del pointed vaguely behind her. "Out back," she repeated.

He nodded and left the room, almost blindly blundering down hallways to the creaking door that led to the park. The stunted trees were almost completely bare, the grass was ragged and brown, and three of the four benches were empty.

On the fourth one sat a gulden woman, facing the door, watching for him. She didn't move when he stepped through the door, didn't leap to her feet, didn't cover her mouth with her hands to press back almost uncontainable joy. He stood still for a moment, allowing her to study him, studying her in turn. The shape of her face was as he remembered, though softened by time; the thick brown hair was shorter. She was dressed in plain, unremarkable clothes instead of the deep blues and rich reds she had worn on Gold Mountain, and her hands were folded tightly in her lap.

He would have picked her out from a hundred gulden women, from a thousand. If he closed his eyes when she began to speak, he would sway toward her voice like a child toward safety.

But he would not close his eyes.

Slowly he crossed the final twenty yards to her side, reminding himself to breathe. He came to a halt in front of her and inclined his head in the most respectful of bows.

"I believe you are the lady Bree," he said, and he was proud to hear that his voice did not tremble. "I am your son."

"Kerk," she said. "Take a seat beside me and we will talk."

He perched next to her on the bench, and for a moment they merely stared at each other. On her face he read rough work and harsh disappointments, minor triumphs, fierce dignity, and a hard-won peace. He had no idea what she read on his.

"The lady Del tells me you have been looking for me over the past several weeks," she said.

"In my heart I have been looking for you for seventeen years," he replied.

"I have not been eager to be found," she said.

"Perhaps the lady Del has assured you that I am a good man who will offer you no harm."

"Perhaps she has said that, but it is not an assurance that can be offered about any gulden man."

"I believe it can," he said quietly, "though perhaps not about any of the men you have known."

"Does your father know you have been looking for me?"

"My father is dead," he said. He was certain Del had shared this information, along with the news that Kerk could be trusted, or Bree would not be sitting here right now. Still, the words needed to be said; no doubt she could not hear them often enough to be satisfied.

"I am glad to hear it," she replied.

There was a moment of silence. "So tell me what you will of your life in the city," he said. "It could not have been easy for you to come here with no family to help you—"

"With every hand turned against me, and a baby at my breast," she interrupted. "No, it was not easy. There were days neither of us had food, nights we slept on benches like this one because there was no other bed. There were weeks I had nothing but rage in my stomach and despair in my heart. But I never once wished myself back on Gold Mountain, living the life I had left behind."

He gestured. "You look as if you have found your place here. You look fed and cared for and out of danger."

"I found work and a place to live and a gradual measure of safety," she said. "I cling to these things like a miser clings to his money."

"No one is asking you to give them up."

"Your very presence here asks something of me."

"I already have what I have wanted for so long. My mother beside me, her face before me, her voice in my ear."

The expression on her face, which had been briefly roused to belligerence, smoothed again to blankness. "What of your own life, once I was gone?" she asked.

"My father married a woman named Tess Dushay," he said.

His mother frowned. "I think I knew her," she said. "A pleasant woman, younger than me. Did she treat you with kindness?"

"Unfailingly."

"And when your father died?"

"Tess went to Brolt Barzhan as his bride and I was raised in their household alongside their children. I am not his son, but Brolt Barzhan has told me I will always be treated as if I am his by blood."

"So you have found your place as well," she said.

He nodded. "And now that place appears to be in the city. My stepfather has moved his family from Geldricht, and I believe this is where he intends us all to stay."

The look she gave him bolted him to the bench. Her dark-green eyes had always been brimming with emotions she was afraid to express, but now she looked ready to speak. "Do not think," she said, "that you and I will meet fondly and often now that we have both found homes in the city."

She was using the most precise language the circuitous goldtongue would allow; it was clear she did not want him to misunderstand her. "I have formed no expectations at all," he said quietly. "But I did hope, having found you once, that I would not lose you again."

"I was married to your father for ten years," she said, as if he had asked her a question and this was the answer. "Out of those ten years, there might have been a dozen weeks when he did not bother to strike my face or beat my back or abuse my body in whatever fashion pleased him. My mother did not understand why I complained to her—this was how she had been treated for the entire time of her marriage. When I begged my father for assistance, he carried me back to my husband's house and took his turn beside your father, raining blows upon my head. I had no happiness at all in those ten years except what I took from being with my children. When my son was first laid in my arms, I thought I understood why I had been forced to suffer so much. I thought that every joy must have a price, and my price was so steep because my joy was without bounds."

He was too moved to know how to answer, but she gave him no time to construct a reply. "When my daughter was laid in my arms," she continued, "I thought my heart would shatter into pieces. So much love I had for her! And at the same time, so much fear. She was so tiny and so delicate. How could I raise her to be strong enough to endure what I had endured? How could I be cruel enough to prepare her for a world that offered her no hope of anything except violence and pain? How could I love her, and feed her, and comb her yellow hair, and someday turn her over to a gulden man?"

"You left because my father hurt her," Kerk said.

Her voice was hammered steel. "I left because *you* hurt her," she said.

He felt his entire body chill with shock.

"*You* came to the nursery where she lay," she continued in an implacable voice. "*You* stood over her, pinching her face and her little fingers, making her shriek, bruising that beautiful skin. I came running into the room to see what was making her scream, and I found *you* torturing your baby sister. Who knows what you would have done to her if I had not heard her crying? I left Gold Mountain because of *you*."

Kerk could not speak. Horror had paralyzed him; revulsion had stopped his heart.

"I left a week later, knowing both of us could die upon the journey," she said. "But that risk seemed smaller than raising my child in a house full of gulden men."

"I'm sorry," he whispered. He could barely get the words past his strangled throat. "I have no memory of such behavior. I just remember a small girl, and my father's anger, and the desperation on your face. It is as if I'm watching a scene filled with other people, but I am nowhere in it. If I did such things—"

"I never loved you after that day," she said flatly. "I have not wondered once what became of you. I do not care now. I am only here to tell you to stop looking for me. There is nothing either of us has to give that the other one would want."

"I would want forgiveness," he said, barely breathing the words. "But there is nothing else I would ask of you."

Bree Socast came to her feet. "I do not have even that much to offer," she said. "Your search has ended. Let me go."

She didn't wait for an answer; she just walked away. Kerk thought she headed in the direction of the Centrifuge, not bothering to stop first in the main building and speak a farewell to Del. He couldn't be sure; he wasn't watching. He had buried his face in his hands and was trying with all his energy to keep his body from disintegrating into poisonous molecules of pain. He thought it was possible he would die of a broken heart on that very bench.

A shadow, a rustle, a warm shape settling beside him. He didn't have the strength to look up or strike out, and he certainly didn't have the ability to speak. But it was no surprise at all to hear Jalci's voice, subdued and wracked with pity.

"Oh, Kerk, I'm so sorry," she whispered. "What did she say to you?"

He shook his head to indicate he could not answer. A gulden man did not show weakness to a woman; he did not turn to a woman for help. A gulden man must display strength at all times. He could not break down; he could not weep.

Kerk kept his face nestled in his hands and let the tears wash through his fingers. His breath was ragged and insufficient. He was showing weakness before an indigo woman and he couldn't stop himself and he didn't care.

She shifted beside him on the bench and put her arms around him, rocking him against her and brushing her lips against his exposed cheek. "She was so strange, when she spoke to us in Del's office," Jalci whispered in bluetongue. "So *cold*. I knew she was not interested in a reunion with you, but she must have done something worse than simply reject you. Kerk, what did she say? Tell me. You know I won't stop asking until you tell me everything."

"She said—she said—that she found me hurting my baby sister," he gasped out. "That she left Gold Mountain because of *me.*"

"That gilder bitch!" Jalci exclaimed.

He was so astonished that he looked up, not caring that she would see his face ruined with tears. "Don't call her that."

But Jalci was furious. "Why would she *say* something like that? Only to wound you. Only because she wanted to be cruel."

He was bewildered. "But I am the one who was cruel."

"You were seven years old! You were jealous and confused and you didn't understand why this new creature was in the house, sucking up all your mother's love."

"That excuses nothing."

"What did you do to your sister? Did you throw her down the steps? Try to suffocate her?"

"I—I pinched her and made her cry."

"That's *it*? Kerk, I *terrorized* my younger sisters! I crept into their rooms at night and pretended I was a monster come to devour them. I made them eat insects. I told Surabeti that she wasn't really my mother's daughter, that we had found her in the woods one day and decided to take her in. She believed that for a whole *year*."

He stared at her, forgetting for a moment to cry. "That's horrible," he said.

"I know! I feel dreadful about it now, but I was simply awful when I was a little girl. All children are savages. Don't you know that?"

"But to physically harm a young child, a baby—"

"Well, that's bad, of course, but it was your mother's job to tell you that," Jalci said firmly. "How does anyone learn the right behavior? They copy it from their parents—or, since your parents didn't provide the best example, from their stepparents and their teachers and the other adults they admire. You aren't *born* knowing that you shouldn't hurt people. You aren't *born* knowing that you have to be kind and that you have to forgive and you have to laugh. Your mother should have *taught* you that what you did was wrong. But she didn't. She abandoned you instead. She's the one at fault, Kerk. Not you. Never you."

He continued to stare at her, feeling the tears drying on his cheeks. He had never seen anyone so sincere, so convinced, so determined to believe in him. Her arms were still around him; she still leaned against him, and he could feel the heat of her body everywhere it touched his. "I don't understand why you think I'm a good man," he said at last.

She smiled. "And I don't understand how you could think you're not."

He sighed and leaned against the back of the bench, careful not to displace her arms. She settled beside him and rested her cheek against his shoulder. "I don't know how I go forward from this," he said. "I don't know how to readjust the way I think about what I want."

"She has not been in your life for seventeen years," Jalci said. "You have already filled it with other things."

"Some of those things have been accidental," he said.

"Well, that's true for everybody! Do you think I was walking along one day, thinking, 'Hey, wouldn't it be fun to meet a gulden man? I bet we'd be best friends within a month.' It never crossed my mind."

"And I did not expect to find so much of my time dedicated to the Lost City—"

She lifted her head. "Well, I hope you're not thinking of walking away *now*," she said. "Because of what happened with your mother."

He shook his head. "No. It's just that I will have to acknowledge that I come here for a different reason than the one that brought me here to begin with."

"That's been true for a long time," she said. "You just didn't realize it."

He looked at her for a moment. "It is not just because I enjoy coaching the boys."

She gave him a radiant smile. "I know. It's because you want to see *me*."

His answering smile was rather bleak. "Now that my search is over, I have to think about the things that have happened because of the search. And you are the thing that is most precious and most complicated. I do not want to lose that, but I do not know how long either of us can sustain the friendship we have now."

"Oh, but, Kerk, I have the most wonderful news!" she exclaimed. She had released him so she could clap her hands together like a little girl. She was practically bouncing where she sat. "You know I have spent the last three days with my family—my aunts and my cousins and my uncles—and I thought it would be utterly dreary, but it *wasn't*. My aunt Bella spent an hour talking business with me, and she went on and on about how she wanted to expand her import business, and she was looking at electronics, and everyone told her the man she needed to meet with was Brolt Barzhan, but so far she had not been able to arrange an introduction—"

He was dumbfounded. "You can't be serious."

"I *am*! And I casually mentioned that I had met his adopted son, and that I thought you had some influence with him—"

"Hardly that."

"And she was very excited, and she asked if I thought you

might be willing to *come to the house* someday and meet her! She lives in my grandmother's city house; we could go there any day you were free—"

"I would first want to ask Brolt if he is interested in expanding his indigo accounts, because we have determined that we should cut back on distribution—"

"Who *cares* if he's interested? In fact, it's better if he's not! Because then she'll have to invite you to her house again and again, trying to make you like her, and you'll be very haughty, and she'll tell my mother that she wants me to be nice to you, and then no one at all will mind that we're—that we're friends," she ended lamely.

He smiled at her. And then, because he missed the warmth of her touch, he reached out and took both of her hands in his. The gesture pleased her; she instantly returned the pressure of his fingers. "You're right. That would be best," he agreed, mock-solemn. "We must do everything in our power to keep Brolt Barzhan from making a deal with your aunt Bella."

She brought his hands up and lightly kissed his knuckles, then nursed their folded hands against her chest. Her dark eyes searched his face. "So I have made you smile," she said. "Does that mean you will be all right? Does that mean you have already let the healing start?"

"I don't know the answer to either of those questions," he said honestly. "I'm not sure I have the strength to go to the gymnasium today. I would make a poor coach this afternoon, and the players would sense it. Maybe I'll come back tomorrow. One way or the other, I *will* come back. You may tell the lady Del that, if she is worried. You may tell the boys."

"Because you realize how important it is that they see how a gulden man is supposed to behave," she said. "Because you can teach them what your parents failed to teach you."

"Yes," he said. And then he smiled. "And because I enjoy the game."

She laughed and let him go and accompanied him halfway to the Centrifuge before waving a cheery good-bye and turning back to the charity bank. He knew she was worried about him, though she pretended not to be, and he appreciated both the worry and the pretense. His brief lift of spirits had faded before he had settled into the ringcar, and his heart was heavy as he made the short drive home. It was not yet dark, which seemed strange. He thought midnight must have fallen on the whole world while his mother spoke of the blackness in his soul.

Brolt's house hummed with activity as Makk and the girls argued in the common room and Tess busied herself in the kitchen making dinner. Brolt and his nephews were still at work and might not be home for another hour or more. Moving slowly, because this was a route he rarely took, Kerk headed down the hallway to the kitchen to where Tess was mixing ingredients over the stove.

"Kerk! You surprised me," she exclaimed, when he spoke her name. Then she looked at him more closely. "Kerk," she repeated in a quiet voice.

She didn't ask what was wrong. She merely turned off the stove, laid down her spoon, and dried her hands on a towel as she crossed the room. When she put her arms around him, he started crying again, weeping into her hair. He had never realized until this day that women possessed a certain kind of strength. He had never realized before how much he relied on it and how he would do anything to keep it in his life.

Nine

Brolt was not opposed to the idea of Kerk meeting Jalci's aunt. "She gave her name as Riabella Contego, so I did not realize there was the Candachi connection," he said two days later when Kerk had recovered his equilibrium enough to approach his stepfather with part of his story. "Even so, we must be prudent. We must be diligent. I have no reason to suppose that Kitrini Candachi is a particularly skilled businesswoman, and we cannot make deals with people just because we approve of their politics."

"I agree," Kerk said. "But we could begin researching her company."

Brolt nodded. "I think we should. And if she indeed is willing to meet you, I think you should accept her invitation."

"Then I will."

"But I am not yet ready to set foot inside the house of a blueskin woman."

"No," Kerk said. "I am not certain I am ready, either."

He sent a courier to Jalci, letting her know the first step of the negotiation was successfully completed, and received her reply within the hour. "Meet me tonight at Sorrietta," she wrote. "It's the new restaurant a block from North Zero with all the red awnings. We can talk. Give my name—I've already made reservations."

So a few hours later he made his way to the crowded, brightly lit building in the heart of the commercial district. As a waitress led him to Jalci's table, he glanced around, appraising the clientele. Mostly young, mostly fashionable, mostly wealthy. More indigo than gulden, though the servers seemed to be split evenly between the races and no one gave him more than a passing glance. He and Jalci were unlikely to be assaulted this night because no one liked to see a gulden man talking to an indigo woman.

He was studying his menu when someone pulled out one of the other chairs and dropped into it. But it wasn't Jalci. He gazed in some surprise at the young gulden woman sitting across from him. She looked to be about sixteen, with creamy, rich skin, smooth flaxen hair, and an expression of blossoming excitement.

"Perhaps you have made a mistake," he said civilly in goldtongue. "I do not believe this is your table."

"Kerk Socast?" she said.

He nodded, baffled.

"Jalci told me to find you."

"Did she give you a message? Is she going to be late?"

The girl was still staring at him as if she couldn't believe her luck. As if she had been promised the most delightful gift and, when it was delivered, it had exceeded all her expectations. "I'm Coe," she said in bluetongue. "I'm your sister."

He had to grab the table; the world titled that violently. "My sister," he breathed.

She laughed so happily he could almost see notes of music floating from her mouth. "Oh, I can't believe I've finally met you!" she cried. "We look alike, don't you think? Your hair's darker and you're bigger, of course, but your *face*. It's just like mine."

"My *sister*," he said again. He was starting to feel a strange bubble in his chest, like panic or fear, but it was neither of those emotions. It was lighter. Bigger. Closer to joy.

"I was in the house when Del told Mother about you, and I eavesdropped on the whole conversation," Coe said. "I figured out pretty quickly that she wasn't going to tell me about you—and she wasn't going to let *you* back into her life. So I went looking for Del the next day. And she introduced me to Jalci. And here I am."

"She wouldn't want you to know me," he said. "Our mother. She doesn't believe I'm a good man."

"Well, maybe you're not, but I want to find that out for myself," Coe said. "Anyway, Jalci and Del couldn't say enough nice things about you, so I think you can't be so bad." She grinned at him. "I have wanted to meet you for as long as I can remember. So *tell* me about yourself! Tell me everything! Where do you live? Who do you live with? What do you do? What do you *like*? Are you married? I can't even think of everything to ask."

"I am the most ordinary of men," he said.

But he told her his story anyway, interrupted dozens of times when she had a comment or another question. She was fascinated by the most mundane detail of Geldricht life, demanded the minutest accounting of his own existence. "What happened then?" she said a dozen times. "And what happened *then*?"

"But tell me about *you*," he said, when she finally stopped asking questions. "Growing up in the city like this—what was it like?"

"Well, I think the first few years were dreadful," she said candidly, "but I don't remember them. Mother still talks about that time with a kind of horror, and whenever things go badly she gets this—this—look of *fear* on her face. As if she's afraid she'll be dragged back to some charnel house or slave pit. But I can usually calm her down." Coe shrugged. "I've been working since I was twelve years old; I can speak three languages; I'm *really* good with money. I figure I'll always be able to find a job. I've been thinking about going back to school and learning more about business. I might want to open a restaurant. I might want to open a clothing store. Basically, I think I'll be able to do anything I want."

He shook his head, half admiring and half amazed. "No girl from Geldricht would ever speak that way," he said. "Tess's daughters wouldn't know what to make of you."

She tossed her blond hair. "Well, once they've lived in the city long enough, Tess's daughters might *start* thinking like that," she said. "Who wants to be dependent on a man for everything in her life? Who wants to hope that she'll be cherished and protected, when she can so easily take care of herself?"

He should have been shocked, but instead he was grinning. "You'll have trouble finding a husband if you talk that way," he teased.

"Maybe I won't look for a husband—a *gulden* husband," she said. "Maybe I'll find a blueskin man instead."

Even that wasn't as shocking as it should have been. Less than two months in the city, and Kerk had seen all of his familiar notions questioned and twisted and tossed aside. If he had grown up here, as Coe had, how different would he be now? If he stayed here the rest of his life, how different would he become?

"I hope you find room in your life for one gulden man," he said seriously. "I did not realize that, this whole time, you were the one I was looking for."

Her eyes widened. Not green like their mother's, but gray-blue, like Kerk's. "Of course I want to keep *you* around," she said. "I have to go to work now, but can I see you tomorrow? Can I see you every day? I don't think—I'm not sure that our mother will be able—"

"I do not believe she will want to see me again," he said quietly.

"And maybe I won't tell her that I've found you," Coe replied. "I don't know. I haven't decided yet. But, Kerk—you are part of my life from this day forward. You are my brother forever."

"Sister," he replied.

She jumped up then and he stood to accept her hug, as fresh and impulsive as a summer rainstorm. "Come back here tomorrow," she ordered, "and we'll figure out some kind of schedule for how we can meet." She kissed him on the cheek. "I've only just met you and I *adore* you," she said. She kissed him again, waved good-bye, and dashed out of the restaurant.

Bemused and a little battered, Kerk sank slowly back into his seat. She would take some getting used to, this gulden girl who had no trace of Gold Mountain in her veins. But she had captured his feeling exactly. He had only just met her, and he already adored her; he had already rearranged the furniture of his heart to accommodate Coe.

He looked up as someone approached and Jalci dropped into Coe's vacated seat. "That seemed to go extraordinarily well," she said, her face hopeful. "I was watching from across the room."

"How long have you been here?"

"I saw you walk in."

"Why didn't you come over and say hello?"

She smiled at him warmly. "Maybe next time," she said. "But I wanted you to meet her this first time by yourself. Did you like her?"

"She's—" He shook his head. "She's so happy. She's so beautiful. It's hard to believe she's a part of *me*. And yet I had this sense, when she was sitting here. That we belonged to each other in a way that I cannot explain."

"That's how it's supposed to be with family," Jalci said. "So many times it's not. But when it is—well, you understand what people mean when they talk about blood ties."

"That's what you have with your family," he said.

She nodded. "That's why I'm a wealthy girl."

"This is one more thing I have to thank you for," he said. "Finding my sister."

She laughed and leaned back in her chair. "Good," she said. "I guess you'll be in my debt forever."

He laughed back at her. "Perhaps there is some way I can begin to repay."

"For starters, you can join me next week," she said. "Aunt Bella wants to have a very small dinner party. Maybe twenty people. She'd like you to attend. Aunt Bella is very progressive—you wouldn't be the only gulden there. No one will talk trade, of course, but everyone present will be in business of some kind. You could make a lot of contacts on Brolt Barzhan's behalf."

Kerk nodded serenely. He had often been Brolt's deputy at business meetings in Geldricht, and he knew the kind of conversation that was expected. "I will wear formal attire and make my face very stern," he said, assuming his most mask-like expression. "I will listen, and nod, and offer very few observations, but I will be extremely polite. I do not think you will have cause to be embarrassed by my behavior."

Jalci laughed again, impulsively reaching out to take his hands where they lay on the table. "Oh, I don't think I will have cause to be the least little bit sorry I have found you," she said. "You will intimidate everyone—and fascinate everyone—and cause everyone to start whispering about what wild thing I might try next. Kerk Socast, I can't wait to see their faces when I take you home."

Gold

One

Finally Orlain stopped. I looked around in disbelief.

We had been traveling for two days, first on horseback through the green countryside of Auburn, then on foot along the overgrown pathways through Faelyn Wood. I was tired, I was hungry, I was afraid, my feet hurt, and I'd spent the last half hour thinking about grabbing a fallen tree limb and hitting Orlain on the back of the head as hard as I possibly could.

There was nothing in the current scenery to make me change my mind.

"Where *are* we?" I demanded. I tried to make my voice regal, but even I could tell it came out whiny instead. "This looks *nothing* like Alora."

In fact, it looked exactly like the last ten miles of forest we had traveled through, so dense with interlaced tree branches that the sunlight trickled through like sand between tightly squeezed fingers. Actually, even that was an exaggeration. It was close to sunset; within a half hour, we would have no light left in the woods at all.

Orlain gave me a quick grin. He was about five inches taller than I was, and so even when he wasn't actually laughing at me, he always seemed to be looking down at me with amusement. It infuriated me even more. "You've never been to Alora," he replied. "You have no idea what it looks like."

"Well, it doesn't look like *this*," I said instantly. "There's more to it than *trees*."

"Alora's somewhere on the other side of the Faelyn River," he said, pointing straight ahead of us. "But we won't make the river by nightfall, and even if we could, the Faelyn River's a spooky place to camp. I want to cross in the morning, when we can see what's around us."

"But I thought we'd get to Alora *tonight*," I said, my voice rising. "I thought I'd stay at Uncle Jaxon's house tonight, and sleep on a real bed, and eat real food. You *promised* you'd get me there in two days."

"I didn't," he answered. "I said I'd try."

"I hate you," I said and burst into tears.

"So you've told me before," he replied, not a trace of sympathy in his voice. "I'll gather some wood. You just sit here and cry."

He dropped his pack, tethered both of our horses to a tree, and *left* me! All alone in the forest!

I sank to the ground and completely gave myself over to tears. Truth to tell, it wasn't the first time I'd wept during the hasty, scrambling journey. I had been crying bitterly yesterday morning when we rode out from Castle Auburn. I didn't want to go, and it had taken my father's unyielding insistence and my mother's unmistakable alarm to persuade me that this was the best course of action. Rebel troops from Tregonia had been only a half day's march from the castle; my mother and father were hoping to avert war, but Dirkson of Tregonia was clearly armed for it. Just as clearly, Dirkson hoped to secure one of three things in his assault on the king's court: the keys to the castle, my younger brother, or me.

Keesen had been bundled up and shipped off to Cotteswold, where my mother still had family, and which was so far from Tregonia that it seemed unlikely Dirkson could ever track him down. *I* had been sent in the opposite direction, toward another destination that Dirkson would be unlikely to find: the hidden, magical kingdom of Alora.

In its own way, Alora would be more dangerous to me than Dirkson of Tregonia. But at least I would be unlikely to die there, even if I never returned.

I could hear Orlain's footsteps crunching through the undergrowth as he came back, and I made some effort to pull myself together. Not because I cared what he thought of me, of course. But I was disappointed in myself. I usually didn't act like a petulant little girl who hadn't gotten her own way. Even around Orlain, who tended to bring out the worst in me for some unfathomable reason, I usually did not behave so badly. I sniffled and made myself stop crying.

Orlain dumped an armload of branches right beside me on the ground. "Remember how to make a fire?" he asked. He had shown me last night.

"No," I said, trying not to sound sullen.

"Then I'll start the fire while you unpack the gear. If you unsaddle the horses, you can spread one of the blankets on the ground and sit on that."

See, this was one of the things I simply *hated* about Orlain. It didn't seem to occur to him that a crown princess should not have to unsaddle the horses or gather up the cooking implements or fetch the water or bury the trash. Mind you, I was willing to do my share of these camp chores—though I flatly refused to dig the privy—but the fact that he *expected* me to galled me no end.

All of the other men at court considered me a delicate flower, delightful, gamine, precious. *I* knew I was competent, capable, and inclined to take charge, but I loved to be considered waifish and adorable. Any other man from Castle Auburn would have spent this whole journey fussing over me, helping me on and off the horse, inquiring about my comfort, praising my bravery. Orlain wanted me to cook.

The fact that I *could* cook, and fairly well, did not make his attitude even marginally more acceptable.

On the other hand, I probably wouldn't have trusted any other man from the castle to take me so far away from home, down such chancy roads, and deliver me safely to my destination.

Where I would not, in fact, be safe.

Scrubbing my fingers across my cheeks to clear away the last of the tears, I stood up and approached the horses. I was wearing some of my brother's clothes—not just because they were eminently more practical for desperate flight than my usual elaborate dresses, but because Dirkson would be watching for a fleeing woman—and I found them very comfortable indeed. A little baggy in back. Not entirely flattering. Not that Orlain cared in the slightest how I looked.

I unsaddled the horses with some efficiency—my uncle Roderick had taught me that skill—and paused to pat their noses and give each of them a treat. Then I lugged the heavy packs to the circle that Orlain had already trampled out under the live canopy of the oaks. Blankets down, metal pans laid out, fruit and dried meat pulled from the side pouches. I nibbled on an apple while Orlain coaxed the fire to light. I had seen him give the same cajoling attention to a starving feral dog terrified of coming close enough to take a bite of food from his hands.

He'd tamed the dog. Kept him, too. No surprise the fire gained confidence under his hands and started frisking around the kindling.

Orlain sat back on his heels and gazed at me across the fire. "Hungry?" he said.

I nodded. "But there's not much food left. One loaf of bread and a couple of strips of dried meat. Some fruit."

"I can probably catch fish tomorrow in the river."

"I don't like fish," I said.

He burst out laughing. "No, I don't suppose you do. You can have the rest of our provisions, then, and I'll just forage for myself."

I frowned. "But you'll have to have food to make the trip *back*," I pointed out. "We can't eat all of it on the way."

He grinned. Firelight picked out the blond streaks in his otherwise unremarkable brown hair. He had a broad face, wide features, and an invariably cheerful expression. More than once I had wished he wouldn't go out of his way to make me want to kill him. More than once I had wished that he actually liked me.

But because he didn't, I often put some effort into making sure he *really* didn't like me.

"Is the princess worried that the guard might starve upon the road?" he inquired. "I hadn't expected such solicitude! I thought she was only concerned for her own needs and comforts."

"Normally that would be the case," I shot back. "But I want

you to survive so you can get back to Castle Auburn and help my parents defend the throne."

"Well, then," he said. "I shall eat as heartily as I can." He gestured in my direction. "Hand me the bread. Throw that meat in the pan and add a little water. We can make a somewhat tastier meal than we managed last night."

We ate very fast in almost total silence. When the last drop of sauce had been wiped up with the last crust of bread, Orlain handed me his plate and utensils.

"I suppose you'd prefer cleanup duty?" he asked politely.

The other choice, I had learned last night, was digging—for various reasons. "Yes," I said with a modicum of dignity.

"Try not to use all the water," he advised. "We'll be at the Faelyn River in the morning, but we don't want to be completely dry till then."

In another half hour, we had completed our camp and were once more seated on the blankets on either side of the fire. Now there was nothing to do except stare at the flames and try not to quarrel. And worry.

"What do you suppose is happening back at the castle?" I asked in a low voice, after we had passed some time without talking. "Is Dirkson's army there yet? Has there been any fighting? Has anyone—has anyone been *killed*?"

Orlain shrugged. "No way of knowing," he said. "So no point in thinking about it."

"I can't think about anything else," I said.

"Your father has troops coming from all seven of the other provinces," Orlain said. "More than enough to hold rebel forces at bay."

"Six of the other provinces," I said in a subdued voice. "Goff of Chillain has sent soldiers to Dirkson."

"Ah," Orlain said. I couldn't tell by his tone of voice if he'd known that already but just hadn't mentioned it, or if it came as news.

"Why would anybody want to throw my father off the throne?" I burst out. "He's the best king of the past seventy-five years!"

"And how would you know that?" Orlain asked lazily. "You've only been alive for seventeen."

"It's what everybody says," I replied. "*Including* people who are seventy-five years old."

"He *is* a good king," Orlain admitted. "And even if I didn't know that by my own observation, I'd think so because that's what my uncle Roderick says."

"He's my uncle Roderick, too," I snapped.

Orlain grinned. "So he is," he said. "I always forget."

Despite this strange connection, Orlain and I are *not* related by blood, a fact for which I am everlastingly grateful. It works this way: My mother's sister fell in love far below her station, and married an ordinary guardsman named Roderick. Well, Roderick is not so ordinary, in my opinion. He's thoughtful and smart and loyal—and good-looking for someone who's so old—and I never mind it when he teases me because it's always clear that he likes me anyway. Orlain is Roderick's brother's son. So Roderick's brothers own farms and work the land. His in-laws sit on the throne. He straddles the divide with more grace than most men would show, I think, but he doesn't have to do it often. He and my aunt rarely come to Castle Auburn, preferring to spend their time on the estates that she inherited from my great-uncle Jaxon when she married.

"But some people don't care whether or not a good man sits on the throne," Orlain was saying. "They're only interested in power for themselves."

"Dirkson claims he's fighting on behalf of the illegitimate prince," I said.

Orlain shrugged. "And who's to say he's telling the truth?" he asked. "Who's to say he wasn't just lucky enough to find some red-haired boy in the street and decide to make trouble?"

"My father has met him," I answered. "He said the young man looked like Bryan. He said he could understand why people might be willing to fight for him." A chill passed over me, and I hitched myself closer to the fire.

"I wouldn't trouble myself quite so much, if I were you," Orlain said, his voice unwontedly kind. "There are two things people value more than any other, and those are prosperity and stability. King Kentley has brought both of these to the realm, and his subjects know it. A new prince might be exciting, but he trails trouble and uncertainty along behind him, and that's a bad bargain. And Dirkson is not so popular himself that people will warm to the idea of installing him in the castle to guide a new king on his way."

"Goff of Chillain seems to like Dirkson well enough," I said, my voice muffled as I spoke into my updrawn knees.

"Goff's a political man," Orlain said. "He's sparring for power and concessions. If your father offers him something he wants, he'll take his armies and head home."

"Like what? What could my father give him?"

Orlain was smiling again, an edge of mockery in the expression. "Well, now, what might an ambitious man want? A closer connection to the throne? Goff's got a son about your age, doesn't he? Maybe he won't be coming to Auburn brandishing a sword. Maybe he'll come waving a marriage contract."

"Goff's son is fourteen and *hideous*," I replied. "The last time I saw him, he was half a head shorter than I was and his face was covered with blemishes and he was trying to put a spider down my dress. *No one* will ever marry him."

Orlain shrugged. "All men at some point were short and pimply and fond of insects," he said. "They grow up."

"I'm not marrying him," I said firmly. "I'm marrying for love. My mother promised me I could, since *she* did."

"Oh?" he asked. "And have you picked out the lucky fellow?"

I hunched my shoulders, irritable that I was even having this conversation with someone as insensitive as Orlain. You didn't talk about love with a stupid guardsman. You talked about love with your girlfriends and your aunt and sometimes your mother, when she wasn't lecturing you about some slight imperfection in your behavior. "No," I said shortly.

"Maybe I could help you look," he suggested. "Are you set on someone noble? Because those aren't the sorts that come my way often. But if all you're interested in is a tall man who doesn't play with spiders, well, I know a few of those."

"He must be handsome and funny and intelligent and brave," I burst out, goaded past endurance. "He doesn't have to be noble, but he has to have an elegance of mind. And he will love me. He'll shield me from the wind if it's blowing and from the wet if it's raining. He'll—he'll make great sacrifices to attain me, and he won't care if those sacrifices put him in danger. It wouldn't matter to him if I wasn't a princess. He would love me just as much if I was a tavern girl. And he will never say an unkind word to me for as long as he lives."

There was a short silence after I finished up my list of attributes. "Well," Orlain said, "I'm surprised it's taken you this long to find him."

I turned away from him with what would have been a flounce if I'd been wearing the proper clothes. *Why* did I allow Orlain to nettle me this way? "So, no, I don't think you can help me look," I said over my shoulder. "I don't think you'd be able to recognize such a man."

There was nothing much left to say and no energy to say it, anyway. Within a few minutes, Orlain and I had gotten ready for bed as best as we could—which meant we'd each taken a turn visiting the privy, we'd banked the fire, we'd pulled off our boots, and we'd arranged ourselves under our thin covers. Camping out in the wild, I had discovered, did not offer amenities such as nightshirts and pillows.

"Sleep well, Princess," Orlain said softly once we were settled in on opposite sides of the fire.

I did not bother to answer.

Exhausted though I was, I did not fall asleep right away. I couldn't stop wondering what was happening back at the castle. It was true that six of the eight provinces had sent armies to help defend my father's right to the throne, but spies had raced back three days ago to report that Dirkson's army was even bigger than we had anticipated. He seemed to have conscripted every able-bodied man of Tregonia between the ages of fourteen and sixty-four to fight for his cause. Dirkson was old, nearly as old as my grandfather Matthew, but still vigorous enough to lead his own troops. Beside him, so our spies had said, rode the redheaded young man called Brandon. Born twenty years ago to a lady-in-waiting who had visited Castle Auburn in the company of Dirkson's daughter Megan. Possibly Prince Bryan's illegitimate son.

There were still stories about the wild, wayward Prince Bryan, who had died so suddenly at the hands of an unknown assassin. My father had inherited the throne because he was Bryan's cousin. While I was convinced that my father—who just *radiated* competence—was an admirable king, I couldn't help thinking of Bryan as a tragic figure. I had spent some time studying the portraits of him that could be found in strategic places throughout the castle. If he was half as handsome as the artists had made him look, he must have been a swooningly beautiful man.

His most distinctive feature, of course, was his red hair. And Dirkson of Tregonia had produced a claimant to the throne whose hair was a corresponding color. Although, as I had heard Grandfather Matthew say, "If every redheaded bastard born to the eight provinces is going to lay claim to the throne, we'll be fighting battles for the next twenty years."

My father had responded, in a very wry voice, "The chances are good that Bryan could have sired every one of them, don't you think? He very well could have bedded this young woman, since she came to the castle more than once in Megan of Tregonia's train. The boy that Dirkson is promoting is the right age. He has the right look. He may very well be Bryan's son."

"It doesn't matter," Matthew had flatly replied. "There is a legitimate king on the throne, who has produced legitimate heirs. The Ouvrelet line continues. There is no throne open to this pretender."

I had to confess that, if it had not been *my* family that was under siege, I might have found the young pretender a glamorous figure. It was highly romantic to think of the true prince being sequestered in Tregonia all these years till he was old enough to ride out and claim his throne. As it was, however, I found it very easy to be immune to the charm of his situation. My brother, Keesen, only twelve years old, had looked so young and small and frightened when my mother kissed him three more times and then helped him into the coach that would carry him to safety. I might be the only one who knew that Keesen still had nightmares sometimes, for he would creep to my room whenever he was too afraid to sleep alone. I might be the only one who knew that he was not always the energetic, laughing, rambunctious boy who raced through the castle and upended platters in the kitchen and tore through the gardens, trailing havoc behind him. I had seen him cry as recently as a month ago, when one of the dogs had to be put down.

I could not imagine how he would manage so far from

home with no one he loved nearby. I could not imagine how he would get through the scary dreams if I was not nearby.

I couldn't believe my mother and father separated us. "But he's so young," I had said to my mother over and over. "Who will watch out for him?"

"We will send a whole troop with him," she said.

"But who will *take care* of him?"

"Your grandmother is very fond of him; you know that. Well, as fond as she is of anyone."

"Let me go with him."

She had put her arms around me and rested her smooth cheek against mine. "We can't risk it," she whispered. "We have to separate you. If the worst happens—if Dirkson finds your brother—we have to make sure one of you is safe—"

"Then let him come with me to Alora," I begged.

She was silent for a moment. Then, "We can't risk it," she repeated on a sigh. "I am almost as afraid of sending you to Alora as I am of sending Keesen to Cotteswold. And yet I am certain that, whatever else happens to you there, you will at least survive."

"I won't fall under the spell of the aliora," I promised her.

She kissed my cheek and pulled away. "Oh, yes, you will," she said. "Everybody does. You have no idea how seductive the aliora are. And yet I think Jaxon and Rowena will keep you safe. I think they both understand how important it is that you come back to us."

The only aliora I had ever met was Jaxon's wife, Rowena, and I had to admit that there *was* something mesmerizing about her. She looked human—almost—although thinner and somehow more ethereal. I would not have been surprised to learn her bones were made of cattails or sea glass, her skin from pressed rose petals. She did not seem to walk through the world so much as float through it; I had yet to see a footprint that her shoe had left behind. When she was nearby, it was impossible to be interested in anyone else's conversation.

If all the aliora were like Aunt Rowena, Alora would truly be an enticing place.

Years and years ago, hunters caught and enslaved the aliora, selling them to aristocratic households for vast sums, but that practice had been stopped before I was born. Stories still persisted, however, that the aliora lured humans to Alora and never let them go home. The humans never *wanted* to go home—that's what the stories said. Alora was a place of such richness, warmth, and enchantment that once a man crossed its hidden boundaries he was ensorcelled; he was content. He was never seen again.

Jaxon was the only man who seemed to possess the knack of moving between worlds, and even he rarely emerged from that magical place. My mother and my aunt had devised a system of communicating with him by leaving messages in a cairn on one side of the Faelyn River. Now and then these messages would say *Come visit us*, and he would make his way to Castle Auburn or his old estates, where my aunt now lived. He never stayed for long. It was clear that the desire to return to Alora was like a gnawing hunger inside him, an urgent imperative that would not let him settle comfortably anywhere else. He was less restless when he was accompanied by Rowena, but only a little.

No one else who had ever entered Alora had crossed the Faelyn River again.

Oh, there were talismans you could use to try to keep yourself safe from the fascination of the aliora, and my mother had loaded me down with all of them. First and foremost, of course, was the application of a little gold. Metal of all kinds was anathema to the aliora, but gold was the worst. It burned their skin—it had actually been known to leave scars behind, as evidenced by two small marks on Aunt Rowena's cheeks. If you wore gold on your person, an aliora would be afraid to touch you.

So naturally, I was practically dripping in gold. I wore a bracelet on each wrist, narrow hoop earrings, and a wide, flat necklace. The necklace had been soldered on—at great risk to the skin on the back of my neck, may I say—because my mother had insisted.

"I won't take it off," I told her at least a dozen times.

"You think you won't," she said. "But I can guarantee you that you won't be in Alora longer than a day before someone encourages you to remove your jewelry. I just want to make sure you can't take all of it off."

She had also made up dozens of potions for me and poured

them in tiny glass bottles stoppered with cork. "Drink one every day," she told me. "Even when you don't want to. Promise me, Zara."

I had held up one of the little vials and shook it till the amber liquid inside frothed to bubbles. My mother had trained as a wisewoman when she was my age, and she still knew more about drugs and herbs than the castle apothecary. She didn't flaunt this knowledge much, because people weren't always comfortable thinking of the queen as some kind of roadside witch, but her skill had come in handy more than once when Keesen and I were ill.

"What's in it?" I asked, because she had taught me what medicines went into some of the very simplest potions.

"Domestic spices, mostly," she said. "Cinnamon, clove, and a touch of ginger. Things to make you remember what you love about home."

I eyed the little bottle, where the bubbles had already disappeared. "There's more in here than spices," I said.

She smiled. "Well, I might have added one or two other herbs. Nothing to trouble you. But drink one every day."

I counted. There were thirty bottles. "What if I have drunk them all and I am still in Alora?" I asked.

She looked very sober. "I will mix up another batch and send them to you. We will send news as often as we can."

"What if there is terrible news?" I whispered.

She hugged me very tightly. "Then you must be very strong."

Is it any wonder I wept as we rode from Castle Auburn?

Is it any wonder I cried myself to sleep?

Two

Morning slipped in among the eternal shadows of Faelyn Wood and knelt beside our fire, fanning it to fresh life. Or, no, I supposed that was Orlain feeding more sticks into the blaze and rattling the metal plates with unnecessary force.

"I'm *awake*," I snapped and pulled myself to a sitting position. You always think sleep is going to refresh you, but it is amazing how dreadful you feel when you wake up after lying on the ground all night. At least it was summer and the ground wasn't stiff with ice. I told myself there was something to be grateful for, at least.

"Freshen up," Orlain said. "I'll have breakfast ready in five minutes, and we can be on our way in twenty."

Fine with me. I didn't want to linger anyway.

In less than a half hour, we were back on the trail, leading our horses through the endless gloomy miles of Faelyn Wood. I can't tell you how my heart lifted when I finally saw ahead of us a broad band of sunlight that signaled a break in the trees. I could also catch the rushing rumble of tumbling water, a sound that grew louder the closer we got to the edge of the forest.

Orlain looked back at me with what passed for a smile. "Hear that? There's a waterfall not too far from where we're going to cross. I'd take you to see it, for it's truly spectacular, but I think it's better to get you to Alora as soon as possible."

I nodded and said, "I don't even have the energy to *demand* that you take me there *right now*."

He laughed, and for a few moments we traveled on in good spirits. My mood quickly turned apprehensive, however, when I got my first glimpse of the Faelyn River. "It's *blue*," I said stupidly, staring at the swift water that leapt and jostled by with joyous abandon. "How can it be that color?"

"They say that Alora is so close to the river that the current here is enchanted," Orlain replied. "The water tastes the same, I know. But I always wonder if I'm drinking magic when I scoop some out and take a sip."

I looked doubtfully from the fresh blue river and back at Orlain. "Is it safe to drink?"

He smiled. "It better be. We're all out of water."

"But—"

"Anyway, you silly girl, what do you think you're going to be drinking the whole time you're in Alora?"

"Don't call me silly," I said.

I could see the words hovering on his lips. *Then don't behave foolishly.* But he didn't say them. "Come on. Let's fill our water bottles and then cross."

We knelt beside that strange sapphire river and filled all our containers, pausing to lap up a few mouthfuls from our cupped hands and splash water on our faces. The morning was already warm and the cool moisture felt heavenly. I could not resist skimming my heel through the water and covering Orlain with a light spray. He turned to me, laughing, but his eyes conveyed a warning.

"Do that again and I'll throw you in," he threatened. "Don't think I won't just because your father's king."

Impossible to resist such a challenge. This time I splashed him with one big gout of water. "You wouldn't," I said.

Or started to say, since all I produced was a squeak as he scrambled to his feet, snatched me into his arms, and bounced into the racing water. I was shrieking and kicking and laughing and trying to get free and trying to cling to him as he waded deeper into the river. "Orlain! Orlain! Don't you dare!" I cried. The water was up to his waist by now and both of us were drenched just from the spouts thrown up around his body. His grip loosened and he made one hard quarter turn as if to fling me from him, and I squealed and wrapped my arms even more securely around his neck. But he didn't let me go. His hold tightened at the last minute and he charged forward onto the other bank, water streaming from both of us as he staggered up the incline. We were both breathless and laughing as he came to a halt, still holding me close to his chest.

"I thought you were going to throw me into the river," I said impudently.

"I should have," he said.

"Maybe you have some respect for royalty after all."

"I doubt it."

"Maybe you have some respect for *me*."

I expected that to elicit the same reply. *I doubt it.* But he just gazed down at me a moment without speaking. The laughter still illuminated his wide face, leaving it warm and open, but his smile had disappeared. For a moment I was struck by the thought that he was much handsomer than our uncle Roderick.

"I wish you were staying in Alora, too," I said in a low voice. "I'm a little afraid to be going by myself."

"I would," he said, "but every sword is needed at the castle. You'll be safe here."

I took a deep breath. "My mother is worried," I said. "What if I fall under the spell of the aliora? What if I never want to come home?"

"You'll come home anyway," he said. "I'll come get you."

"What if they won't let you into Alora?"

"I'll find my way."

"What if I tell you I won't go back with you?"

Now his smile returned, smaller, sweeter. "I'll grab you and throw you over my shoulder and haul you out of the forest no matter how much you scream and kick."

"You said you'd throw me into the river, but you didn't do that," I pointed out.

"That time I only threatened. This time I promise."

"And a promise is better than a threat?"

"Always," he said.

"Then I believe you," I said.

I don't know if he would have answered. I don't know if he would have kissed me. I thought he might—he looked like he wanted to—and I was trying to make my expression as soulful as possible, so that he would realize a kiss would be welcome. But suddenly there was a shout from a distance and the sound of boots striding through the undergrowth.

"Zara!" someone called out.

Orlain dropped my feet none too gently to the ground. "Uncle Jaxon!" I cried as I spun around to see him.

He was barreling out of the forest, a big man with wild dark hair and a full beard. His arms were already outstretched to hug me, so I ran toward him to be enfolded in a welcome embrace. Jaxon was a burly man; his hugs always had a lot of heft to them, and he was not above lifting a girl off her feet and squeezing her so tightly she couldn't breathe.

"Zara!" he exclaimed again, releasing me just enough so that he could peer down at me. "Lord, I can't believe how much you look like your mother. Those dark eyes and those dark curls. And that expression. Nothing but mischief in that girl from sunup till sundown."

I giggled because "mischief" wasn't something I associated with my mother. At least, it wasn't ever something she encouraged in *me*. Maybe she was strict with me because she remembered what she had been like at seventeen. "How did you know I was going to be here today?" I asked.

"Your father has sent messages over the past couple of weeks," Jaxon replied, pointing. I half turned to see the small stone cairn on this side of the river. "We weren't sure when you'd arrive, but we've been watching for you."

"I'm to stay in Alora until it's safe for me to come home," I said.

He nodded. "What's the news back at the castle?"

"Dirkson's army was half a day away when we left two days ago," I said, my flush of happiness quickly dying. "I don't know what's happened since."

"Well, I don't have much interest in the affairs of men these days, but I remember Dirkson of Tregonia well enough to hope he does not succeed in this venture," Jaxon replied. "And I would be loath to see any son of Bryan's on the throne if the boy was half as stupid and willful as his father."

"Jaxon!" I exclaimed.

My great-uncle shook his head. "He was a bad man." He

shrugged. "Dead now, and no reason to mourn." He smiled again and patted me on the shoulder. "So! Are you ready to come to Alora to live? Rowena has your room all ready."

Orlain spoke for the first time. "Ready to come to Alora to *visit*," he corrected.

Jaxon laughed and turned his appraising look on my escort. "That's what I meant," he assured him. "You're Roderick's nephew, aren't you? I think I've encountered you at Halsing Manor when I was visiting my niece."

"I am. You have."

Jaxon shook his hand and seemed far more pleased with Orlain than Orlain seemed with him. "Thank you for taking such good care of Zara on the trip here. We will watch out for her from now on."

It was clearly a dismissal, but Orlain held his ground. "Her mother has asked that I serve as her envoy from time to time, bringing news to the princess," he said.

"Excellent," Jaxon said heartily. "You can leave messages in the cairn. Someone checks it every couple of days."

"I will not want to leave a message," Orlain said calmly. "I will wish to speak with Zara directly."

I had to think about it for a moment. Was that the first time during this whole trip that Orlain had used my name instead of calling me *princess*? Maybe.

Orlain was still speaking. "How will I accomplish that? Will you take me deeper into the forest so that I know where the boundaries of Alora lie? Is there a landmark I can look for that will let me know I am close?"

Jaxon eyed him consideringly. "You could always wait beside the cairn until someone spots you and brings Zara to see you," he suggested.

"I would rather have more direct access," Orlain replied.

"Landmarks are rare here in the forest," Jaxon said. "It would be hard to describe our route to you."

"Then I will have to travel with you today so I can find Alora when I return."

"The aliora have not always had a happy history with men," Jaxon said in a regretful voice. "They are not eager to lead humans to their doorways."

"I'm sure they're not," Orlain replied. "I will try not to intrude upon their solitude. I am not interested in Alora or its residents. All I care about is Zara and her well-being."

Jaxon burst out laughing. "If you spent half a day with the aliora, you *would* be interested in them!" he said. "Come with us, then, just to the edge of the kingdom. I am afraid I cannot invite you any nearer than that."

Orlain nodded. "Let me check on the horses and get the princess's bundles." He paused to give me a brief, very serious look. "Wait for me while I cross the river and come back."

I nodded dumbly. I had stood mute during this whole exchange, amazed at the animosity bubbling beneath their civil words. Or maybe the animosity was just coming from Orlain, who had as good as said out loud that he didn't trust Uncle Jaxon.

That was almost as astonishing as the idea that Orlain cared enough about *me* to bother distrusting Jaxon at all.

Orlain plunged back into the river, moving easily against the punishing current. Jaxon glanced down at me and winked.

"What do you say? Shall we run off while he's still in the water?"

I wasn't entirely certain he was joking. "All my things are with the horses," I said.

"Everything you need you can find in Alora," he said.

Not my potions, I thought. Not the note that Keesen had thrust into my hands right before he climbed into the coach. *I love you Zara* was all it said in Keesen's broad, almost illegible writing. "My life is so strange already," I said in a soft voice. "I will need some familiar things around me."

"And even the familiar seems strange in Alora," Jaxon said. "We'll wait for him."

Orlain was back with all speed, my saddlebags over his shoulder, and we set out once more into the forest. The woods were just as dark and shadowy on this side of the Faelyn River, but the gloom didn't seem so deep. Maybe that was due to the proximity of Alora's magic. Maybe it was due to my excitement at finally coming to the end of the journey. Maybe it was due to the fact that I couldn't stop thinking about Orlain. Who had held me so tightly as we crossed the river and who had argued with my uncle Jaxon on my behalf.

Was it possible he didn't hate me after all?

Because, of course, I had been in love with Orlain for years.

If there were landmarks to be seen along our journey, none of them was visible to me. I couldn't tell how Jaxon was finding his way through the untracked acres of forest, and I couldn't believe Orlain would ever be able to retrace our route. But now and then Jaxon would point to something—a tree with a particular bend, perhaps, or a vine hung with brilliant red blossoms—and Orlain would nod and we would all keep walking.

We had been hiking through the forest for about an hour when Jaxon came to an abrupt halt. "What most men don't understand about Alora is how changeable its boundaries are," he said. "They are not defined with a river or a chasm or a stone fence, as human borders are. You cannot measure them precisely with a surveyor's tools or find them with a compass. They shift. At some point you are within them and at some point without. But here is where that moving line begins."

Orlain looked around, as if impressing on his memory the precise placement of the trees, the peculiar slant of the sun, at this very spot. "Then this is where I will come when I have news to share with Zara," he said. He handed my saddlebags to Jaxon, who slung them over his left shoulder.

I risked a quick look at Orlain. I felt suddenly shy with him, which infuriated me and made me awkward at the same time. "When will you be back?" I asked.

"I will try to come ten days from now," he said.

"You'll lose a couple of days each way just on travel," Jaxon observed.

Orlain nodded. "I know. Otherwise I would come back once a week. If I am here every ten days, I will be able to spend a week at the castle before I set out again."

"I'll look for you then," I said. I resumed my soulful expression and held out my hand to him, a sweet, brave princess bestowing her favor on a faithful knight. "Thank you so much for your care in bringing me here to Alora."

He took my hand in one of his. He made a fist with his other hand and touched it gently to his forehead, a mark of great respect. "Don't cause your uncle any trouble," he said with a grin. "Don't make him sorry he took you in."

I was so annoyed I jerked my hand away. "Don't get lost on your way back home," I huffed.

Orlain nodded a farewell at Jaxon, then turned on his heel and strode back through the forest toward the river. I only watched him from the corner of my eye, but I saw that he did not once look back.

"Interesting young man," Jaxon commented.

I hunched a shoulder. "Do you think so? I find him very ordinary."

Jaxon laughed. "Well, there are a few young men in Alora who might help you forget him."

"I don't need help *forgetting* him," I said. I was tired of talking about Orlain. "So where's Alora? How do we get in?"

Jaxon resettled the strap over his shoulder and took my hand. "We step this way—we wait for a strange shiver across our skin. No? Then we take a few steps in this direction, and wait a moment. Nothing. Then we walk forward with our eyes half shut, as if waiting to feel spiderwebs brush across our cheeks."

He moved slowly but determinedly in each direction as he spoke, tugging me behind him. I had to admit my whole body was tingling with anticipation, but apparently it wasn't quite the sensation I would feel when we finally did cross into Alora.

"Then you look around to see if the air seems to hold a sparkle. Look—see? That patch of sunlight sifting down. It's brighter than it should be, don't you think?"

Indeed, it was almost incandescent. Jaxon increased his pace as he pulled me toward the eerily glowing shaft of sun; I approached with a touch of trepidation. It was so vivid, so alive with color, I thought it might sear my skin. But Jaxon and I stepped together through the dazzle, and I suffered no ill effect except a sudden wash of warmth across my bare cheeks.

"And now we are in Alora," he said.

❧

Impossible to describe Alora.

It was not a town or a village the way I knew them, yet there were clusters of buildings marking either side of what could have been a road. But these were not houses or castles or other familiar structures, not like the buildings of men. There was a room, perhaps, set out under a wide fanning branch of some exotic tree. Perhaps there was a ladder of sorts, straight bars of wood tied to a broad trunk, and twenty feet above the ground a low platform nestled in the branches. Now and then I saw free-standing structures, haphazard piles of wood and stone that might be divided into two levels—but they had few walls and nothing that resembled a roof. I could peer into most rooms as we passed and gather an impression of soft pillows, wide mats, transparent curtains fluttering around open bowers.

Aliora were everywhere.

They gathered at the side of the road to watch us pass, hung down from the tree branches to stare as we went by. They were all narrow-faced and spindly-thin, with unnervingly long arms and legs. Their faces were gentle, curious, smiling, and every-where they stood, an evanescent glow built up around them. It was as if moonlight had mated with a weeping willow and tried to produce a human shape.

And they hummed. Or sang. Or chattered. Some kind of low, joyous sound bubbled out of them, not any kind of speech that I could understand, but surely a form of communication. It leapt ahead of us on the road, a kind of anticipation, and buzzed behind us once we'd passed, no doubt in speculation. *A human girl has come to visit us in Alora,* they might have been saying. *How strange she looks. And yet how familiar . . .*

I pressed closer to Jaxon. He glanced down with a grin.

"Nothing quite like it, hey?" he said. "I've been to all eight provinces and traveled some distance across the ocean and never come across any place that filled me with the shivers the way Alora does."

"Everybody's staring at me," I said in a low voice.

"It's not often they've seen a human woman. All of the hunters who have stumbled across Alora have been men."

"So I'm the *only* girl who's ever been here?"

"I wouldn't say that," Jaxon replied a little vaguely. I re-membered the stories of human babies stolen by the aliora and raised here among their fey brethren. If the tales were true, might I encounter some of those kidnapped children? Would they even look human to me after years of captivity?

I wanted to take Jaxon's hand again, but I didn't. "My

mother says they might invite me to stay with them," I said. "Forever."

His laugh boomed out. "No doubt they will. The aliora will be delighted with you."

"But they won't *make* me stay," I added, trying to keep the anxiety out of my voice.

He glanced down again. "No aliora ever held a human against his or her will," he said firmly. "Men and women who settle in Alora stay because they want to."

"That's all right, then," I said, relieved.

He grinned once more. "But after a few days here, you might want to."

"No," I said. "I'll be going home. As soon as it's safe."

We had been strolling through the unconventional dwellings of Alora for about thirty minutes when Jaxon finally pointed. "Rowena's place," he said.

It was more like a building than anything we had passed so far, but even so it was less like a house than a gazebo, albeit a very large one. It was round and many-storied, and some portions had walls of stone and some portions had walls of wood, and some portions had no walls at all. The bottom floor seemed to be one big atrium decorated with living greenery. In the very center, a simple fountain sent up a spray of water that fell back into a shallow pool. Unlike the great fountain in the courtyard at Castle Auburn, this one did not appear to run through any kind of pumping mechanism, but to feed directly from some underground spring.

A handful of aliora bustled across this open floor, exchanging news and murmuring to each other in that strange, melodic language. A winding stairway gathered strength on the bottom level, then twisted upward toward leafy lofts overhead, growing thinner and less reliable as it rose. I could not tell how many stories were piled above this one. It seemed likely that the roof, if there was one, would be woven of starlight and netting and a few plaited leaves. I hoped my bedroom was not too close to the top.

"This doesn't seem like the kind of place people *live*," I said to Jaxon in a low voice.

"Not people," he said. "Aliora."

We had barely stepped inside the house—if you could

say you were *inside* such an open place—when Rowena herself came sweeping up to us. The few times I had seen her outside Alora, I had been struck by her beauty, for she had pearl-white skin and crow-black hair and such elegance of movement that her smallest gesture seemed choreographed. But here in Alora, she was astonishingly lovely, rich with radiance, bewitching.

"Zara!" she called, floating toward us with her hands outstretched. "It is so good to see you here."

Without thinking about it, I started forward to fling myself into her arms. But Jaxon caught me hard and hauled me back. "You cannot touch her," he said gruffly in my ear. "Not while your hands are covered with gold."

"Oh!" I said. I knew that, of course. It was why I was wearing the bracelets, after all. But such was the welcome on Rowena's face, such was the sudden desire to be enfolded in the embrace of an aliora, that I had forgotten. I stood awkwardly before the queen of the aliora, twisting my hands together.

"I'm sorry," I said. "My mother made me promise I would not remove any of my jewelry."

Rowena's returning smile was full of warmth and forgiveness. "It was the correct promise for her to require," she assured me. "I love Alora and cannot understand why anyone would choose to live anywhere else, but you have a home and responsibilities elsewhere. You must resist us with all your might." She was laughing when she said this, as if joking, but I rather thought she was speaking the truth.

"I wish I could hug you," I said truthfully.

Very carefully, making sure no part of her hand made contact with my necklace or my earrings, Rowena reached out and brushed her fingertips across my cheeks. It felt as though raindrops or perhaps honeysuckle nectar made a fresh track along my skin. "I feel as if I am hugging you," she said in a soft voice. "I cannot express how deeply I want to welcome you to my home."

"Let's get her settled in," Jaxon said practically. "Are you hungry, Zara? It's been a long journey, I know."

"Starving," I said. "But then, I usually am."

"I'll see about lunch," Rowena said. She laid one hand quickly on Jaxon's arm, as if she couldn't help herself; one quick possessive touch, and then she turned away. "You take her up to her room."

I followed Jaxon up those haphazard stairs. They started out as stone, and gradually gave way to wood, and then eventually it seemed as if we were just stepping from one springy tree branch to another, still winding upward. I would guess I was on what corresponded to the third story before Jaxon led me down something you could hardly call a hallway—it was more like a rope bridge stretched above the ground, and it swayed when we put our weight on it. I was relieved when the room he showed me to actually seemed to deserve that designation. It had a floor of wooden planking, a couple of real walls, and something that looked enough like a bed to probably *be* a bed, though it was low to the floor and covered with moss instead of a blanket. Or something very similar to moss, at any rate.

"Oh, this is so charming!" I exclaimed.

"A little different from the castle," he said. "You'll find all the washing up is done down on the ground level in a little area built around a pool. But once you're used to everything, it all makes sense. I hope you'll be comfortable here. It's strange, but it's wonderful."

I smiled at him. "That's how it seems so far."

"And the longer you're here," he added, "the less strange it will feel, and the more wonderful."

Lunch at Rowena's house was more like an outdoor picnic. We sat on logs and boulders in the open air while tree branches seemed to shake down alternating particles of sun and shadow. The food was wholly unfamiliar—slices of something that might have been bread, except it tasted like ground nuts; some kind of rough paste that was sweet as straight honey; chopped fruits that were foreign and utterly delicious. We ate off of plates made of wood and implements carved from bone. There was not a scrap of metal in the whole kingdom, from what I could tell, except for the tiny steel hooks on my trousers and the gold lying flat against my flesh.

People came and went while we ate. I couldn't tell if they were friends or servants; I couldn't tell if they were visiting or performing chores. Most of them paused to stare at me and exchange observations with Rowena, but they spoke in that musical, clicking speech that I could not understand.

"But I just realized!" I exclaimed as our meal came to a close. "If I can't speak their language and they can't speak mine, I won't be able to talk to anyone in Alora except the two of you!"

"There are fifty or so aliora who know human speech," Rowena said. "You may meet some of them while you're here."

"Why did they bother to learn my language?" I asked.

I saw Rowena and Jaxon trade glances. He looked away, but she answered. "Because they lived for a time in the world of men."

Now I understood. "Oh!" I said. "When they were—when they were slaves."

"A long time ago," Rowena said. "There have been no hunters tracking down aliora since well before you were born."

I pulled myself up into my most majestic pose. "On behalf of all humans, I apologize for those shameless depredations."

Rowena reached over and, careful not to touch my bracelets, brushed her fingertips across the back of my hand. Again, I felt as if dew or nectar had dropped upon my skin. "Your apology is accepted. Let us hope there will forever be harmony between our races."

Jaxon was on his feet. "There's so much more to show her," he said. "Let me give her a tour of Alora."

We spent the rest of the day exploring, although I by no means saw the whole of the kingdom. Truth to tell, I never got an exact sense of its size and limits, its population, its industries. All that really became clear was that this place where I had come to rest—the village of sorts that had grown up around Rowena's house—was as close to a capital city as the kingdom claimed. I had the impression that Alora itself unrolled for miles through the forest, along tracks even more overgrown than the one we had followed from the border. I would not have been surprised to learn that the aliora who made their homes deep within the woods existed almost like wild animals, burrowing underground or digging into broad tree trunks, clothing themselves, if they dressed at all, in trousers made of bark and skirts made of braided grasses. Rowena and the aliora who lived near her had adopted some of the conventions and mannerisms of men— perhaps because these trappings appealed to them and perhaps because they had needed some measure of sophistication to understand how to combat the hunters who came calling. But most of the aliora, or so I surmised, were so shy and untamed that Rowena's little village would be as alien to them as it was to me—though for different reasons.

"But I don't understand what the aliora *do* all day," I said to Jaxon once we had completed the tour. There had been no shops, no restaurants, no blacksmithing forges, no weavers or millers or soldiers. None of the common occupations I would have considered essential for civilization.

He found this amusing. "And what do *you* do all day, might I ask? You're not spinning wool or baking bread, either."

I lifted my chin. "I'm a princess, learning to be a queen," I said.

"You dress, you talk, you eat, perhaps you sew," he said, counting off the activities on his fingers. "You flirt, you dance. Aliora do all those things."

"But—" Explaining trade and interconnected commerce was hardly one of my skills, but I felt certain something crucial was missing. "People must be productive in *some* fashion. I mean, someone has to grow the food. And make the clothes. And build the houses. Or they would go around naked and hungry with no place to sleep."

"The necessary work gets done," he said. "But so little is necessary. Aliora, unlike humans, are content to exist. They are peaceful and serene, restful and joyous. There is none of that drive to compete, to dominate, to achieve, to improve. Merely, they are. It can be a blissful way of life."

"It sounds boring," I muttered.

"I'll wager you change your mind within a week," he said. "Perhaps within a day."

❧

I had not changed my mind by the end of that day. All the walking—combined with the excitement of finding Alora to begin with, combined with the sleeplessness that had marked my previous night—made me tired. I yawned through an early dinner with Rowena and Jaxon, then sought my room.

The moss-covered bed was sinfully comfortable, and I snuggled into the soft pillows with a sigh of sheer contentment. One wall of my bedroom was completely open to the elements, except for the loose weave of thin branches that formed a green-and-brown grillwork. I could smell summer drifting in; I could taste starlight. The light breeze was scented with mysterious perfumes.

Before I closed my eyes, the last thing I did was pull out one of the vials my mother had given me. Uncorking it, I took a sniff. Just as she had said, cinnamon and clove, and perhaps a touch of orange peel. I tilted the bottle back and downed the concoction in one swallow. It was sweeter than I had thought it would be, so good I almost opened a second bottle just to recapture the taste on my tongue. For a moment, my memory conjured up detailed images of my mother, my father, my brother. I had one sharp, swift impression of the silhouette of Castle Auburn as viewed from the courtyard right at sunset. I remembered my maid's south-country accent, the sleek feel of my horse's withers beneath my hand, the smell of a wax candle in the instant the flame had been snuffed out.

I thought of Orlain and the look on his face when he carried me out of the river.

I closed my eyes and fell asleep before the moon had even risen. Otherwise, I'm sure I would have seen it peeking into my room through those half-formed walls.

Three

In the morning, I bathed myself in water that was scarcely more civilized than a woodland pool, and barely more sheltered, either. Rowena assured me that I would have complete privacy if I wanted it—which I did—but nonetheless, I washed and dressed as quickly as I could just in case any aliora stumbled through the circular hedge that was meant to shelter me from the sight of strangers. I was not sure how well I would like such an arrangement in the dead of winter; I was far from sure I liked it even in summer.

I put on a dress Rowena had given me, since my own wardrobe was limited. Green and sleeveless, it might have been stitched together from broadleaves and gossamer; it felt airy and peculiar against my skin, particularly where the hem swirled about my ankles. But I liked it. I felt like I was clothed in the forest itself.

Breakfast consisted of more foods I couldn't identify, except for an exceptionally sweet red fruit called dayig. "I *love* this," I exclaimed, helping myself to more than my fair portion. "This is my mother's favorite fruit, though it is rare to get it at the castle. We spent a week at Faelyn Market once, and I ate it every day."

Jaxon chuckled. "Well, you asked yesterday how aliora spend their time. A few of them harvest dayig and sell it to farmers who live near the forest. Not for money, of course—the aliora have no need for coins. But sometimes they trade for products they cannot make themselves."

"Just let me know what kinds of products those might be," I said, cutting up my third piece of fruit. I was careful to pry out all the white seeds inside, for they're a very mild poison that will make you throw up if you eat enough of them. "I'll come back to the forest myself and make some of those trades."

"We hope you will come back to the forest anyway, whether or not you have something to barter," Rowena said in her musical voice. "We would love to have you visit often."

"What shall we do today?" I asked Jaxon, a hint of challenge in my voice. He had practically told me that I would fall under Alora's spell so quickly that I would be content to lounge around under the interlaced branches, moonstruck and misty-eyed. But back at the castle, I was used to keeping busy. I didn't think I had it in me to merely sit and dream.

"Do you like to sew?" Rowena inquired. "Cressida and some of her girls have finished dyeing a new lot of cloth and they're about to start making dresses. Would you like to sew one of your own?"

I was an adequate seamstress, though usually too restless to sit still long enough to set a dainty stitch. But I was intrigued by the idea of working with that delicate, cobwebby Aloran cloth and making something I could bring back home with me.

"Oh, may I? I would love that! Who's Cressida?" I exclaimed in quick succession.

Rowena smiled at my enthusiasm. "An aliora who was fond of your mother," she said. "I think she is curious to get to know you."

That's never good—to meet someone who knew your mother—because how can you ever compare to a memory? You won't look as pretty or be as charming or offer such witty and insightful comments. I sighed, and Jaxon laughed.

"Yes, you've quite a legacy to live up to," he said. "Your mother *and* your aunt. Both quite remarkable, each in her own way." He stood up and held his hand out to me. "Come along. I think you'll like Cressida."

～

I did, of course. Cressida was tall and thin, even by aliora standards, and even more ethereal looking. Her hair was short and untended, and her face, while tranquil, showed evidence of suffering. I wasn't sure how to explain it. She was the first aliora I'd met whom I would describe as familiar with the concept of sadness.

"Princess," she greeted me, coming forward with her hands outstretched. The smile routed the sadness, or mostly.

"Watch out for her gold," Jaxon said sharply, but Cressida didn't pause. She merely showed care as she placed her palms against my cheeks and bent down to kiss the top of my head.

I felt a moment's blissful serenity. I was whole and cleansed, at peace, home from long wanderings.

She pulled away and for an instant I was as bereft as an orphaned infant.

"Princess," she repeated, smiling down at me while I tried to adjust my thinking. *You have no idea how seductive the aliora are,* my mother had said. I was beginning to get an inkling. "How delightful to welcome you to Alora."

"How delightful to be here," I managed. I was still feeling as if she had abandoned me merely by dropping her hands.

"Zara has expressed an interest in being productive while we harbor her in Alora," Jaxon said. "Rowena offered you as a diversion. Can you accommodate another worker?"

"Of course," Cressida said. "Come with me, Princess. We shall make you a beautiful gown out of the bounty of the forest."

❧

Soon enough I was cutting and basting a dress from the strangest cloth I had ever seen. It was red as ripe raspberries, thin as lace, a light, rippling fabric that spilled like rainwater over my hands. I couldn't detect the weave at all; it was more like fine paper, pressed from a slurry of raw materials. When I held it up to determine where to cut, it draped across my body like dampened silk.

It might actually be indecent to wear a dress like this, but, oh, I was going to make it anyway.

Cressida had taken me to a work site that was little more than a clearing along the side of the road. Planks were set up as tables under a broad canopy, and near them sat trunks of fabric, baskets of thread and needles, and boxes of accessories like ribbons and buttons. Three other aliora were already in place, stitching at their billows of fabric, giggling with each other as they worked, eyeing me with curiosity that was nicely tempered by welcome. Not one of them, as far as I could tell, spoke a language I could understand.

The needles, I quickly learned, were shaped from bone and not nearly as easy to ply as the metal ones I used back home. In fact, I snapped two of them in half before I got the trick of holding them. The red fabric was oddly forgiving, not only hiding my uneven stitches but seeming to heal any holes I made by pushing the needle through with too much vigor.

In about an hour of sewing, I hadn't quite gotten bored yet, when the girls around me started fluttering and giggling. I looked up to see a cohort of young men striding by in the direction of Rowena's house, laughing together over some unexplained joke. Most of them were helping carry an assortment of logs and branches—items scavenged from the forest floor, I was guessing, since none of them was carrying an axe.

Well, of course not. None of them could abide the touch of metal.

When they spotted the girls, of one accord they tossed down their burdens and came splashing through the grass to join us under our canopy. I suppose Cressida introduced me—at any rate, she pointed in my direction and uttered some incomprehensible syllables—for everyone turned to appraise me and offer some version of a smile.

One of the young men broke off from the others and came to kneel beside me. "So you're Princess Zara!" he exclaimed. "Jaxon said we should be expecting you."

I stared down at him. He was slim and white-haired and gave an impression of springiness; I had the fanciful notion that he had just transmogrified from a birch. His eyes were black as soil and his smile was bright as noon. "You speak my language," I said stupidly.

He laughed. "I do. I learned it from Jaxon Halsing and some of the other humans who have come to live among us. I have a great curiosity about the world of men, even though I know the land beyond our borders is dangerous to folk like me."

"I would like to think aliora could travel through the region and encounter no harm," I said. "But it has only been twenty years since they were captured in the forest and sold in Faelyn Market. You are better off to stay where you are."

"Particularly if the best of the eight provinces comes here to visit *me*," he replied.

I smiled. "You mean me? I'm not sure I would say I am even the best of Auburn."

"Then Auburn and the other seven provinces must be magnificent indeed," he said. "And I will be tempted to set out and see them all."

This was flirting; this was the first thing in Alora that actually seemed familiar to me. I pressed my hand to my heart. "Oh, you mustn't be so rash," I said. "I take back what I said before. I am the very crown jewel that Auburn has to offer. You would never meet another young lady as attractive or as accomplished as I am."

He laughed and, shaking back his white-blond hair, he settled more comfortably on his heels. "I am Royven," he said. "Rowena is my mother."

I could feel my eyes grow huge. "And Jaxon is your father? Are we cousins?" Or relatives in some complicated fashion that I could not quite determine at the moment.

"No, no, my father died before my mother married your uncle."

I inspected him more closely. His face was baby-smooth; I couldn't remember if aliora ever needed to shave, but this one certainly never had. "I would have guessed you were my age or younger," I said. "But I know they were married before I was born."

"Aliora age differently from humans," Royven replied. "I have been alive for twenty-seven years, but I might live to be two hundred. I am a man, but I am still considered young."

"Two hundred years!" I exclaimed. "It's rare for a human to live past seventy-five."

Royven raised his eyebrows. They were as pale as his hair, expressive and nicely shaped. "A human who resides in Alora might live twice as long. There are tales of men and women who wandered across the borders and chose to stay, and whose lives extended to a hundred and fifty years."

I couldn't decide if such an idea was abhorrent or attractive. "I wouldn't mind living so long," I said cautiously, "if I was healthy and strong. But if I were as old and bent over and crabby as the apothecary's mother, who is always complaining about her aches and pains, I don't believe I would enjoy those extra years."

Royven smiled again. "Ah, but there is no pain and sickness in Alora, didn't you know? Age comes like a faithful friend and guides you a little farther along a familiar trail. You grow thinner, perhaps—you lose a little strength. You sleep longer in the mornings and nap in the afternoons. Then one day your afternoon nap comes only a few minutes after you rise from your nighttime slumbers, and after that you do not bother to wake again. In Alora, neither death nor old age is a thing to fear."

Until Dirkson of Tregonia started displaying hostility, death had pretty much never crossed my mind, and I certainly hadn't wasted much energy thinking about what kind of horrors old age might hold. "Well, that sounds very peaceful," I said.

"Wouldn't that be a reason to want to live in Alora for the rest of your life?" he asked.

Cressida spoke sharply. "Royven," she said. "No more of such talk."

I looked blankly between them. I was still trying to come to grips with the notion that I might someday age and die. It hadn't occurred to me that Royven might be deliberately trying to paint a picture of Alora that was so alluring I wouldn't want to leave.

Maybe the aliora were seductive in ways that I hadn't considered yet. Maybe it wasn't just their touch, their serenity, that was so beguiling. Maybe they were not just hoping I would be bewitched by the peaceful beauty of the kingdom. Maybe they would actively try to convince me to stay.

Not Cressida, however. She stood over Royven, her arms crossed, her sad face drawn into a frown. "Zara has no intention of lingering in Alora one minute longer than she must," Cressida said. "We should not hope she wishes to."

Royven came to his feet and placed a hand on Cressida's arm as if to reassure her. Among humans, such casual affection was rare, unless you were with a blood relation. But I had noticed that the aliora touched each other all the time. "I only said what I was thinking," Royven said.

"You should not think such things around Zara," she replied.

He smiled at her winningly. "How can I not?" he said. "Wouldn't it be delightful if she chose to stay here the rest of her life?"

"Don't be alarmed," I said to Cressida. "My heart is back at Castle Auburn. I couldn't live here without my heart."

"I lived in Auburn a long time without mine," she replied.

Royven gave her a warm hug. "Be at peace," he said against her cheek. "Everything will unfold as it should."

It occurred to me to wonder if Royven's idea of what *should* be matched my own. But then he turned and smiled at me, and I forgot to worry about it. "Maybe I'll see you at dinner tonight," he said, then skipped off to join his companions.

I looked after him for a while before resuming work on my new gown. I have to say, sewing had lost its appeal somehow. I made only a few more stitches before I laid aside the cloth and went to look for other entertainment.

❧

Royven indeed joined us for dinner that night, as did the former hunter Jed Cortay. In some respects, Jed was a physical match for Jaxon, because they were both burly men with full beards and the hearty self-sufficiency of the born outdoorsman. Jed was rougher-edged than Jaxon, though, not a nobleman as Jaxon had been. I imagined him growing up in some small cottage with six or seven siblings underfoot, fighting for attention and extra scraps of food. But none of that showed in his face now. He was smiling and gentle; his speech was unfailingly courteous. He showed Rowena a painting he had completed on the curved inner surface of an eggshell. The egg was so huge I could hardly conceive of what kind of bird had produced it, and I spent more time fretting over that mystery than admiring the delicacy that had been required to produce such a fine work of art on such a fragile surface.

Then I spent a little time wondering about the potency of the magic that could turn an uncouth, unlettered country man into a quiet, compliant artist whose smile was so perpetual that, at times, I expected him to drool.

"You look like someone with weighty issues on her mind," Royven said to me at one point late in the meal.

I managed a smile—a much less fatuous one than Jed's, may I say. "I am thinking about my family and wondering if they are well," I said. It was only partially a lie; thoughts of Keesen and my parents were always just at the back of my mind. "I wish I knew how the war was progressing."

"Try not to fret," Royven said softly. "Events will occur as they will, and you cannot control them. Even if you know what's happening, you cannot change them."

"I still want to know," I said.

"Your friend Orlain will come with news in a few more days," Jaxon promised.

"Nine days," I said. "A great deal can happen during that time."

Still, I did not want my edgy mood to taint their own tranquility, so I made an effort to be cheerful for the remainder of the meal. And it was an effort—I was glad when it was time for all of us to scatter to our rooms. As soon as I had seated myself on my bed, I opened the case with the twenty-nine potions remaining, and I quickly picked one and downed the contents.

The prosaic, familiar scents briefly made me intensely homesick, and for a moment I curled up on my bed and cried. But soon enough, the philter had its intended effect. It cheered me up; it drew the happier images to the surface of my mind like some kind of wicking material that acted upon memory. With that taste in my mouth, I could not be sad. Everything I cherished seemed still within reach.

But it was starting to be clear to me that I was not immune to the spell of Alora—indeed, if someone like Jed Cortay could be made over by forest magic, anyone was susceptible. I would have to carefully guard against its pervasive sweetness; I would have to remember that I belonged in the world of men.

Orlain would remind me, when he returned. I separated out eight more vials and arranged them on the round, flat stone that served as my nightstand. When I had finished off these eight bottles, Orlain would be back. It would be easy to lose a sense of time here in Alora, I suspected, but these bottles would help me keep track. My mind would be clear, no matter how long I stayed.

~

Royven was waiting for me at the breakfast table—or the cleared patch of ground that served as the breakfast table here. His hair was so bright that for a moment I mistook him for a patch of sunlight.

"Your uncle says you require entertainment," he said. "Will you let me supervise your activities?"

I laughed. "I don't know that entertainment is what I want so much as activity," I said. "I am willing to be useful as long as I am occupied."

"We'll go through the forest to gather food," he said. He gestured at my clothing, another of those soft, mossy dresses that Rowena had conjured up for me upon my arrival. "You might want to wear something more practical."

So I changed into one of the outfits I had borrowed from Keesen and put on my sturdy walking boots. Royven, I noticed when I returned downstairs, wore shoes that looked more like slippers, soft as pith or linen. I expected that he would bruise his insoles if we did much clambering over rocks and fallen trees.

"Alora is completely sustained by the forest," he told me as we set off into the dappled woods. "It supplies our food, our shelter, the materials we use for clothing. You will often see aliora down by the Faelyn River, but that is only because we love the fast current. There is plenty of water to be found inside the woods."

"How many aliora are there?" I asked. We were hardly ten minutes from Rowena's tree house and I was already hopelessly lost. Clearly I could not deviate from the main pathway if I was ever wandering through Alora on my own.

"It's hard to be certain," he said. "A few thousand, my mother thinks. There are some who live so deep in the woods that even she has never seen them."

"That's not very many." I replied. "Are they—are you— is there any fear that someday there won't be any left?" *Any chance you might all die off?* Exactly how did you phrase a question like that?

"That's always a fear," he said quietly. "It is one of the reasons my mother was so determined to stop the humans from stealing aliora. There are so few of us already. We could not afford to lose one more."

"No," I said. "Well, now that my father is king, it will never again be acceptable for men to enslave aliora." I did not mention the thought that instantly presented itself. *What if Brandon becomes king? Might the young upstart prince have a different perspective?* I shook my head to chase the thought away. Awful for too many reasons to contemplate what might happen if the pretender took the throne.

We had come across a pretty big deadfall in the woods and there was no easy way around it. "Looks like we'll have to climb over," Royven said. Nimble as a wild cat, he scaled the first few tumbled logs, then turned around to offer me help up. I had almost laid my palm in his when he suddenly snatched his hand away.

"Gold," he said, when I looked at him in astonishment. "I could feel its heat."

A different kind of heat rose in my cheeks at my thoughtlessness. "I'm so sorry. I forgot."

"Can you make it up and across without my help?"

"I think so. Let me try."

Much less gracefully than Royven, I crawled and clambered up the mound of fallen branches, then back down the other side. I acquired a few scratches on the way, including one that welled with blood, but nothing to be concerned about.

Royven was pointing. "There's a stand of dayig trees not too far ahead of us. That's what we're aiming for."

"Dayig," I repeated. "Then I don't care how many cuts and bruises I get!"

Still, this deep in the forest, pushing through the undergrowth was like breaking through hip-deep snow—treacherous, heavy going laced with hidden hazards. I took an unsteady step and felt a loose branch snap under my foot, and my arms started flailing as I went down.

"Zara!" Royven called, and made an instinctive grab. Then

he howled and flung my hand away, nursing his arm to his chest while I plopped down straight on my bottom.

I leapt up again as soon as I caught my balance. "I'm sorry, I'm sorry. You shouldn't have reached for me," I cried. "Are you all right? Did you burn your skin?"

He had put his hand against his mouth and was licking his scalded fingers. "I'll get a blister, I think. Don't worry about it," he said.

"You just have to remember not to touch me," I said in a scolding voice.

He smiled. "But what if I want to touch you?" he teased.

"Now is not the time to be flirting," I said.

"Any time is the time to be flirting," he returned with a laugh. "But seriously, if I see you slipping down, I can't *not* try to help you. And if you were to break your leg or twist your ankle, I'd have to carry you back, gold or no."

"Surely I won't break my leg," I said. I glanced around. "How dangerous *is* this forest?"

"But you might fall again," he said. "If you were to take off your gold—just your bracelets—at least I could hold your hand and help you up."

I thought about that for a moment. I wasn't supposed to remove any of my gold, for any reason whatsoever, even while I slept or bathed. But it would just be the jewelry on my hands. I wouldn't remove the earrings, of course, and I *couldn't* take off the necklace. And I could always slip the bracelets back on once we were safely back at Rowena's.

"I'll put them in my pockets," I decided. "That way I can at least take your hand if I need to."

I unsnapped the bracelets and tucked them in the front pocket of my trousers. Royven held out his hand again and I laid mine in his. He made a great show of bowing, just like a human courtier, and kissing my fingers.

I almost swooned from the sensation. This was a sharper bliss than the drunken contentment I had felt so far when an aliora touched me. This was more like . . . fever. But a deliriously exciting fever.

I laughed shakily as I pulled free of his hold. "Somehow I don't feel like you're rescuing me from the consequences of a fall," I said.

He laughed back at me. In the light-spattered forest, with his dark eyes and white hair, he looked like a patch of scenery suddenly gone mobile. "Just expressing my happiness at having you to myself for the day."

"Let's go pick some dayig," I said.

The tree branches were heavy with the big ripe fruit, red as a persimmon but shaped more like a pear. Proving he had operated with some foresight after all, Royven produced a couple of large cloth bags, and we each started tugging pieces off the trees and storing them in the sacks. We stopped maybe five times to slice open a particularly plump dayig, scrape out the seeds, and cram the pieces in our mouths so greedily that the juice ran down our chins. No dayig purchased in Faelyn Market had tasted half as good as that fresh fruit plucked directly from the tree.

"If you lived in Alora, you could eat dayig every day," Royven said in a coaxing voice.

This was so far from being subtle that I had to laugh. "Only when it's in season, I would think," I said. "Only a few months out of the year."

"There are other fruits that grow well into winter or ripen early in spring," he said. "Almost as good as dayig. Things you've never seen back at the castle because they cannot travel any distance before they bruise and shrivel."

"Maybe I'll get a chance to taste them, if I'm here that long," I said.

"I hope you do."

"No," I said, "I hope I'll be home before long."

He slanted a sideways look at me. "I keep thinking you'll forget," he said.

"Forget my *home*? Forget my *family*?"

"Forget that they're in danger. If you knew they were all safe, that war no longer threatened, could you let them fade a little? Could you be happy here?"

I put my hands on my hips. "You're not supposed to ask me that. You're not supposed to try to convince me to stay."

"But I'd like you to stay," he said whimsically. "Why shouldn't I say it out loud?"

I picked up my heavy bag, lumpy with its harvest, and turned to go. Except I couldn't precisely remember which direction led back to Rowena's. "You don't even know me," I said. "You have no reason to think you'd like me to live here forever."

"And how will I get to know you if you go back home too soon?"

It was almost like arguing with a child. I gave a rueful laugh and shook my head. "At any rate, it's time to go back to the place *you* call home," I said. "I have no idea how to get there, so please take the lead."

The forest was no less treacherous now that we were both weighed down with awkward burdens, and more than once I skidded on loose piles of twigs or he slipped on slick patches of mud. Twice he caught my hand to steady me across some insecure footing, and twice he released me. The third time I almost fell he had to haul me upright with more than a little force.

After that, he did not let go of my hand, and we completed the rest of the hike with our fingers interlaced. By the time we returned to Rowena's open cottage, it was hard for me to remember why it might be a good idea to let him go.

⌇

I was a little hazy during dinner, pleasantly weary from the exertions of the day, still replete with dayig, fuzzy with happiness. Jaxon laughed more loudly every time I yawned, and Rowena promised to forbid Royven to take me on any more exhausting excursions.

"I had a good time," I said through yet another yawn. I was just finishing up a dessert confection that looked like rose petals and tasted like molasses. "But I don't think I can stay awake much longer. Good night, everyone. I'll see you in the morning."

I practically floated up to my room, no longer disconcerted by the stairway made of tree branches or the corridor constructed of rope. I had changed into my nightshirt and curled up on my bed before I realized I had forgotten to drink my nightly potion. For a moment, my head comfortable against one of those deep pillows, I debated skipping the ritual—just until the morning!—but then I grumbled and sat up. I had promised my mother. One vial every night.

I reached for the nearest one and gulped it down. Only after

I swallowed it did I register that it carried a different taste from the first two—in fact, had it not been flavored with cinnamon, it might have carried no taste at all. It was just like my mother to mix up a range of concoctions, all a little different, each one suited for a different purpose—without warning me that she had done so. What would be the effect of this one? I wondered. What were the ingredients, and why had she thought I might need them?

I ran my tongue across the roof of my mouth, searching for clues to the tonic's composition in the faint residue left behind. The consistency was familiar—this was something I had sipped once before in my life—but it took me a few moments to place it. And then I was even more confused.

She had blended a love potion for me, but not the sort of draught that would make me tumble head over heels. This was the kind of brew that wakened your senses, heightened your awareness, revealed to you someone's true qualities. She had first made me a sample four years ago, when I couldn't stand to be in the same room with Keesen, when just the sound of his boisterous laugh made me clench my hands and hunch my shoulders in disgust.

"All girls your age hate their younger siblings, but you're the princess, and you don't have that luxury," she'd told me calmly as she'd handed me a glass half filled with liquid. We were in the sitting room attached to her bedroom, where she stored all kinds of interesting herbs, most of them securely locked away. "Drink this. You'll see him for the child he is and not the embarrassment you think he's become."

Still fuming, I'd done what she told me. Then I'd folded my arms across my chest and waited to prove to her that the potion didn't work on me because Keesen really *was* a loathsome child.

Moments later he careened into the room, chasing a frolicking black puppy that I had taken an instant dislike to the day Keesen brought it up from the stables. They skidded across the room and bounced off a low table, knocking three books and a brass paperweight to the floor. The dog barked and Keesen pounced on it, laughing uncontrollably. The dog was squirming in his arms, frantically licking his face. It was hard to tell which one had the most energy. Both of them were covered with mud, and their assorted footprints made a smeared track across my mother's freshly washed floor.

I watched them, my mouth half open so I could draw in air. My heart was so full of love that for a moment I couldn't speak.

"Zarabara!" Keesen cried—the nickname he'd had for me since he was a toddler, the name I absolutely abhorred. "Look, I taught him tricks! You want to see?"

And I laughed and dropped to my knees right there on the dirty floor and I said, "Yes, show me what he can do."

From that minute on, I adored him. Oh, there were days I wanted to hand him over to the castle guard for a quick and efficient death, but most of the time I loved him. If someone else teased or belittled him, I sprang to his defense. I even argued with my father once when I thought he was too harsh on Keesen—though, of course, arguing with my father was rarely worth the breath. And Keesen *had* borrowed the royal scepter to use as a bludgeon in a fight with the groom's oldest boy. But if I was nearby, no one else could harm or punish Keesen and get away with it.

I dropped the empty vial in a basket by the bed and lay back against the pillows, watching the night sky through the woven wall. Coincidentally, Orlain had been at the castle the day I swallowed that first love potion my mother had mixed for me. He had ridden in a week earlier with a formal letter from Roderick, recommending Orlain be accepted into the royal guard. I had known Orlain practically since I was born, of course, so I had been pleased enough to see him when he arrived, but a little ruffled, too. He never treated me with the excessive flattery I had grown used to from all the other young men at court; in fact, he always seemed to view me as a rather exasperating little sister. Much as I had viewed Keesen. In return, I treated him coolly, trying to prove by my remote courtesy that I was indifferent to his existence. For the most part, I had succeeded in persuading myself that that was true.

But the day I drank the potion, all that changed. Keesen had dragged me down to the stable to introduce me to his puppy's littermates, and Orlain had been there, talking horseflesh with the head groom. It was as if I had never seen Orlain before. It was as if I had never seen *any* young man before, and his height and body mass and rumbling voice struck me as almost godlike. I could hardly get my breath. I was so unnerved that I crawled into the empty stall where the puppies made their home and actually tried to avoid drawing Orlain's attention.

I had been crushed when he walked out of the stable without even bothering to greet me.

I recovered—somewhat—over the following days. At least, I could speak in the man's presence again, and eventually I resumed my pose of haughty indifference. But I never quite got over my bedazzlement. In my eyes, a faint glow of glamour still clung to Orlain. But I was never tempted to coo and sigh over him, since he never gave the slightest indication that he felt anything except affectionate derision for me. All in all, I was heartily sorry that I had had the misfortune to lay eyes on him so soon after swallowing my mother's brew.

I turned on my side and tucked my hands under my chin. I couldn't believe that my mother intended me to fall in love with Alora or any of its people. She had to know that this hidden kingdom possessed plenty of beguiling magic on its own. But she wanted me to discern some truth, see the reality of some person or some situation. I could only wonder what Alora would look like to me tomorrow, now that my eyes had been opened.

Four

In the morning I rolled out of bed, realized that I had never put my bracelets back on, rectified that omission, and dressed myself in a set of human clothes. I eyed the swaying rope bridge with a mix of annoyance and determination, and climbed down to the ground level wishing that the aliora had bothered to learn the basic carpentry skills that would have resulted in a proper stairway. At breakfast, I skipped the dayig and had a second helping of bread.

Royven eyed me uncertainly. "You're different this morning," he said at last.

"Am I?" I said. "I feel very much like myself. What kind of project do you have for me today? I have so much energy I must do something with it or my head will start steaming."

Jaxon burst out laughing. "So much for Alora putting its spell on you," he said. "Most humans drowse away their time here, but not Princess Zara."

I smiled prettily. "It's a quality I get from my mother," I said. Truer than he knew.

"Some of my friends are building a cottage," Royven said. "Do you feel like helping out with some hard physical labor?"

"Your idea of a *cottage* is half a wall and one or two weight-bearing beams," I retorted. "I wouldn't think such a construction would be all that taxing."

Royven came to his feet and held out his hand. "Then let's go join them."

I stood up without his aid, flashing my palm at him. "Gold again," I said. He looked so startled I had to laugh. I added, "It just felt right to put the pieces back on."

Rowena watched us all this time, smiling slightly. Whatever else looked different to me in the clarity provided by the potion, Rowena was unchanged. So beautiful that she was dangerous to look upon. If there were hazards in Alora, they were embodied in its queen. "Indeed, it is clearer every day why your mother felt safe sending you here to us," she said. "Go. Enjoy your day with Royven."

I did enjoy the day, though I hoped I never again had reason to try to complete a construction project with the aid of aliora laborers. What a hopelessly disorganized bunch! No wonder none of the structures in the kingdom had finished walls or tiled floors. It was a wonder any buildings were standing at all.

Royven's friends were the ones who had marched past the day I worked on my dress with Cressida's girls. Apparently that morning they had been gathering the materials they needed to build a house for a young couple who were expecting a baby. In addition to the logs and branches they'd collected, they'd rolled a few stones up from some gully and woven a couple long lengths of hemp and laid out half an acre of wide, flat leaves to plait into a roof. The young mother-to-be—thin as any other aliora except for her great round belly—had invested some time in procuring materials of her own: yards of fabric to serve as curtains to divide the rooms, stacks of baskets to hold household items, platters of food to serve the hungry workers.

There were, of course, no hammers, no saws, no nails.

It was clear from the beginning that whatever resulted from this effort, it would be nothing like an actual house.

Even so, everyone fell to work with a will. I was still filled with tremendous energy and, with such an untidy group, my natural tendency to order others about came to the fore. So I consulted the floor plan, divided the workers into teams, and directed the labor for the rest of the day. I don't flatter myself that I'm any kind of carpenter but I *do* think this particular cottage went up with more efficiency than most houses in Alora, and it looked more likely to survive a strong wind, too.

Once we were done, the soon-to-be parents held hands and darted through the rooms, laughing in delight, ducking around curtains, and checking the view from each of the windows (which were really incomplete walls). I couldn't understand what they said, of course, but it was easy enough to interpret. *Thank you so much for helping us build our home! We will be so happy here!*

They were in Alora. Of course they would be happy.

I was happy, too, but today, at least, I saw the place for what it really was. A strange, bewitched, drowsing kingdom, full of an insidious beauty. It was a little like quicksand—if you didn't keep moving, it would draw you remorselessly in. Once you abandoned yourself completely to its pull, it would never release you.

For some folk, I thought fairly, that would be just fine. I wouldn't blame them for wanting to merely exist, blissful and serene, suspended in a pool of unspoiled gorgeousness. Such a life had its definite attractions. But more was required of a princess of the realm. I did not want to spend the next fifty years smiling beatifically as I contemplated peace. I wanted my life to count for more than that.

"Are you going to *run* all the way back to my mother's house?" Royven asked, striving to catch up with me as I strode back toward Rowena's.

I laughed. "I might."

"Just watching you exhausts me sometimes," he said.

"Do you suppose you're the first person to ever say that to me?"

He sighed. "Probably the first person in Alora."

I bustled through dinner, took a brisk walk before bedtime, and charged up the idiosyncratic stairs. I even straightened my room before seeking my bed. Once tucked in, I pulled out another one of my mother's vials.

The fourth one. Six more bottles before it was time for Orlain to come back.

This one, like the first two, held clove and nutmeg and distilled memories. I lay back uneasily in bed, worry a needle in my heart. Was my brother safe? Were my parents under siege? Were all the things I loved already broken and scattered, or already sheltered and secure? I wasn't sure I could wait six more days to find out.

❦

But those six days slipped by more indolently than I had expected. There was still work to do for someone determined to keep busy, but there seemed to be less of it, and I felt less urgency to do it. I rejoined Cressida and her young seamstresses for two of those days, but unaccountably, I didn't quite finish my red dress. There weren't enough bone pins to hold the bottom edge in place, so I never got around to hemming it. I wanted to add a fall of lace at the throat, but none of the pieces in Cressida's basket pleased me, so I started to look for ribbon instead. I thought I might embroider a decorative design around the cuffs. I needed to put the buttons on the back. Someday I would finish these details. Certainly before I left Alora.

Similarly, Royven and I joined another crew of young men putting up a house for a newly married couple, but the work did not go as smoothly as before. The floor plan was more ambitious, so I let someone else step forward to direct operations. I spent a good hour with one of the prospective owners, transplanting forest shrubs along what would be the front walkway, should the walkway ever be laid in place. The whole lot of us spent three days laboring to raise the walls and level the floors, but even so, we hardly made any progress at all. I felt a little bad about it, but the young bride and groom seemed pleased with the shell we *had* managed to construct, and they walked around the site all three days with wide smiles on their narrow faces.

Royven and I spent one day simply roaming the forest. The plan had been to bring back more raw materials for the new house, but we abandoned that notion fairly early on when it turned out that I didn't have the strength to carry my end of a fallen tree farther than fifty yards. Instead, we started gathering herbs and flowers that grew wild throughout the woods— and what a bounty we harvested! Nariander and stiffelbane, siawort and orklewood, ingredients that my mother used every day in her concoctions. I even found a small patch of haein-wort, one of the rarest herbs of all, and I plucked half a dozen blossoms. My mother would be delighted.

Naturally, we had to clamber over deadfalls and splash through little streams many times during this expedition. I needed Royven's help so often to keep my balance that it was just simpler to leave my bracelets in my pockets.

"What are you going to do with all these roots and flowers that you have so industriously gathered up?" Royven asked as we finally wended our way back toward his mother's house. "Will you turn apothecary or midwife? Cure all our illnesses? Minister to our broken hearts?"

"I'll give them to my mother," I said. But who knew when I would see her again? And her stores of herbs might be running dangerously low if there had been much bloodshed near the castle. I added, "Maybe Orlain will take them back home with him."

"The inestimable Orlain," Royven said, for of course I had told him all about the guardsman. "I'm sure he will."

❧

In the morning, I headed straight toward the river, following the single road that wound through Alora toward the kingdom of men. I had been obliged to accept Royven's escort, because I knew I would be unable to find the way by myself, and Jaxon had claimed to be too busy to take me, although it was hard to guess what pressing business might occupy him. I wasn't quite sure what Orlain would think of Royven, but somehow I suspected that the two men would not like each other.

"You may feel strange as we cross the boundary," Royven warned me.

"A tingle. I remember from when Jaxon brought me here."

"Stranger than that," he said. He took my hand. "Are you ready? Straight through that patch of sun, and we'll be on the other side of the border."

I stepped forward eagerly, already looking for Orlain. But once I passed through the translucent bars of light, I staggered and had to take a moment to regain my balance. Royven squeezed my hand hard, or I might have fallen to the ground when my knees buckled. It was as if I had dragged myself to land after a long period afloat; I felt heavy, graceless, unmanageable. My head felt as if it had ballooned up behind my eyes, which remained small and slitted. My lungs clamped down, and my open mouth could not take in sufficient air.

"The sensations will pass in a moment," Royven assured me, still gripping my hand tightly. "You'll actually feel better if you keep walking."

It *seemed* like I would feel better if I slumped to the road and let the ground take my weight, but I nodded and forced myself to continue forward. Indeed, within a few paces, I had appreciably improved, although my bones were still leaden and heavy, and my eyes continued to burn.

"I don't see Orlain," I said, looking around. A rush of disappointment cleared the rest of the clutter from my head. Disappointment or fear. What could have delayed him? Orlain was the most dependable man in the country. He would not break a promise unless the situation was dire.

"He's probably waiting for you at the cairn," Royven said reassuringly.

"No—he told Jaxon he would come *here*. To the border."

"This place is very difficult to find," Royven said, still in a soothing voice. "He must have realized he would get lost, and he turned back. We will go to the river, and we'll find him there."

"Then let's hurry," I said, tugging on Royven's hand to make him move faster. I knew we had too far to go to run all the way, but I could hardly restrain myself from trying.

We had not proceeded half a mile before we saw, on the path ahead of us, a tall masculine shape striding toward us through the alternating patches of sun and shade. Even when he was completely in shadows, I recognized his silhouette, and then he stepped into a circle of light, and the sun made a brief halo of his hair.

"Orlain!" I cried, dropping Royven's hand.

"I'll wait here," the aliora said, but I didn't pay much attention. I was flying down the pathway, my arms outstretched, running toward Orlain.

I don't know what I was thinking—that he would take me in a crushing embrace, that he would catch my hands and clasp them to his heart, that he would call out my name and drop to his knees in a feudal bow. Instead he stood stock-still in the road, his arms crossed on his chest, and the first thing he said when I skidded to a halt in front of him was, "Where's your gold?"

It took a moment for me to understand what he meant. "What?"

"Your bracelets," he said impatiently. "Why aren't you wearing them?"

How had he discerned *that* in the imperfect lighting from a distance of twenty feet? "I've got my necklace on—see?" I said, pulling it out from under my collar. "And my earrings—"

He jerked his head to indicate the direction from which I'd come. No doubt he could see Royven lounging on the side of the road, waiting for me. "Well, a necklace and a pair of earrings don't seem to inhibit aliora from taking your hand," he bit out. "Don't you think that's a little dangerous? We'll ignore the part where it's a little too familiar. We'll just pretend that it's perfectly acceptable for a princess of Auburn to bestow her favors on anyone, no matter his rank or station."

At that I burst into tears.

"Why is it every time I see you, you're crying?" Orlain demanded.

"Maybe it's because you're so mean!" I wailed. I turned my back on him, desperately wiping at my cheeks, wishing with a bitterness I could actually taste that it had been anyone but Orlain sent to bring me news. How could I have been so eagerly looking forward to *his* visit?

"I don't intend to be mean," he said stiffly. "But you are very well aware of the attractive dangers that surround you in Alora, and you are equally aware of the measures that have been taken to shield you from them. And the first time I see you, it is obvious that you have cast off your talismans while blithely embracing—*literally* embracing—your foe."

"The aliora are not my enemies," I sobbed. "They have offered me shelter—and friendship—and—and they have not tried to hurt my feelings—"

"I'm sorry if I hurt your feelings," Orlain said, and he did actually sound a little contrite. "But you are so thoughtless— and you are so much at risk—"

I made a great effort and forced myself to stop crying. I was a princess of the realm. I would *not* let an unsympathetic guardsman turn me into a whining child. Without turning around to face him, I said, "The least you could do is tell me the news you have brought me, without making me ask for it."

"I didn't mean to—"

"The *news*, please?" I interrupted in a haughty voice.

After a short pause, during which I guessed he was contemplating and then deciding against an apology, he said, "Everyone you love is well. A courier from Cotteswold arrived the morning I was leaving, saying your brother is safe with your great-grandmother, and that no strangers have been seen in the village looking for him. Your parents are also unharmed."

"What of Dirkson and his armies?"

"They have camped some distance from the castle but they have not attempted to lay siege. Your father's forces are distinctly stronger—more soldiers answered his call than he anticipated. We speculate that Dirkson might be waiting for reinforcements from Chillain, or perhaps he is hoping to spur the countryside into an uprising. Our spies report that Brandon is very much in evidence, riding a roan horse up and down the army sidelines, showing off his red hair and his father's countenance."

"And people are coming to see him?"

"In significant numbers," Orlain admitted. "But they might be merely curious. We have not noticed that Dirkson's ranks of fighters have swelled appreciably since Brandon has paraded before the masses."

"So what happens now?" I asked. I was still speaking to the trees, since I still had my back to Orlain. My tears had dried, but I didn't want him to see the vulnerability that might remain on my face.

"Your father hopes to try diplomacy. He and Dirkson have sent envoys back and forth, negotiating for a time and place to meet. It is a delicate business, for neither one wants to put himself in danger. And yet if they do not talk, this stalemate could continue another week. Or even two."

"A stalemate is better than a war," I said.

"It is indeed," he agreed. "Many fewer bodies."

"But what could they negotiate *for*? Dirkson wants Brandon on the throne and my father will not relinquish it. There doesn't appear to be a middle ground."

"Your father has an exquisite bargaining chip," Orlain said, his voice neutral. "You."

For a moment I savored being called exquisite, and then I frowned at the forest. "What do you mean?"

"He could offer to merge your claims by marrying you to Brandon. It's what I would do if I were him."

I spun on one heel and punched Orlain hard in the stomach. I know I hurt him because he made a surprised grunting sound and his face went loose with shock. "Stop trying to marry me off in the name of politics," I said fiercely. "I understand that you consider me nothing more than an—an asset in my father's treasury. I understand that you have no feelings of your own. But it is cruel of you to assume that my father cares so little about my happiness. He loves me for myself, even though you find it hard to believe that anybody would."

Orlain said nothing, just stared down at me, his eyes dark with anger or some other powerful emotion. I thought it very likely that he wanted to pick me up and shake me till my head fell off, so I decided to give him the incentive. I hauled back my right arm to hit him again.

He grabbed my wrist before I could land another blow— and then caught my left hand when I brought it up swinging. I struggled in his hold, briefly considered kicking him, and settled with merely panting, "Let me go, you wretched man."

"Princess—stop—Zara, I apologize, all right?" he said, squeezing my hands and forcing my arms down so that the pressure brought me two steps closer. "Your father would never compel you to wed a bastard son of questionable parentage. Not even to keep peace in the realm."

"No," I said, "*you're* the only one who seems determined to marry me off to whoever is the first one to show up at the castle gates, looking for an alliance. Are you that eager to see me ride away from Auburn? Do I make you that miserable just by my existence?"

I didn't expect him to answer—what possible reply was there to such an accusation?—but his mouth tightened and he suddenly looked defeated. "No," he said quietly. "Not at all eager for you to go. Just bracing myself for the inevitable day when it comes. Finding ways to remind myself that it will come all too soon."

I stopped struggling in his hold and simply gaped at him.

The strangest expression crossed his face—almost a smile, almost an admission of guilt. "And there," he said. "That's enough ammunition for you to use against me for the rest of your life."

"You don't care if I marry anyone else," I said stupidly. "You don't even like me."

"There are days I don't," he agreed.

I stamped my foot. "Don't say things like that," I cried. "I'm trying to understand—"

"There's nothing *to* understand," he interrupted. "You're the princess. You may well be queen one day. I'm a respectable guardsman without a drop of noble blood in me. Good enough to captain your troops. Not good enough to hope for any other position in your life. And I *don't* hope for it. But I don't hate you, Zara. No doubt it would be easier if I did."

"But then—if I—but let me—" I stammered.

He shook his head, released my wrists, and moved back a pace. When I stepped forward, he flung up his hands to keep me in place. "Too many words already," he said. "But you shouldn't wonder at it when I get angry that you don't watch out for yourself. You are too precious to too many people. You must take care."

"Don't leave yet," I said.

"I must," he said. "Your parents are hungry for news of you."

"When will you be back?"

"In ten days. And ten days after that."

"I wish you would stay," I whispered.

His face shaped the barest memory of a smile. "Someone must be ready to rescue you from the consequences of Alora," he said. "And to do that, I think I must remain outside its borders."

"I will not succumb to Alora's magic," I said.

"I hope that's true," he replied. "Promise me you'll put your bracelets back on immediately."

"I promise," I said. I gulped down another plea for him to

stay and said, in the most regal voice I could summon, "And you swear to return in ten days."

"Princess, I swear." He briefly touched his fist to his forehead. "May the news be better by then."

I tried to think of something else to say. I tried to think of something else to ask that would make him admit he cared for me. None of the words would come. He waited for a moment, as if hoping I could frame the right question. Then he nodded and smartly turned around. He went striding back through the forest, away from Alora, away from me.

I watched him go, battling back tears. I might have stood there forever, convincing myself that I could still make out his straight shape through the rustling shadows, except Royven slipped up beside me and took my hand in his. I should have pulled away, I should have resisted his touch—I knew it—but my need for comfort was so great just then that I could not shake myself free. Indeed, I leaned against him, just the tiniest bit, and felt the rush of well-being that the slightest contact with an aliora brings.

"What was the news from Auburn?" he asked in a gentle voice.

"Little enough, but none of it bad," I said. "At the moment there appears to be a stalemate and some negotiation. Not true war, at least not yet."

"But the danger has not yet passed?"

"Oh, no."

"Then we have you for some time yet."

I gave him a reproachful look. "You should not be happy that *my* life continues so unsettled."

"I know I shouldn't," he said simply. "But I cannot help being a little glad at anything that keeps you nearby, no matter how briefly."

I should have been furious. I should have been insulted. For he as good as welcomed war if it meant I could not go home. But it was unbearably sweet to have someone want me—and admit he wanted me. I gave him a sad smile and, hand in hand, we once more crossed the living border of Alora, back into that sweet, treacherous land.

❧

Once we were at Rowena's, I immediately slipped my gold bracelets over my wrists. Just sliding them in place cleared my mind a little; I thought perhaps the gold was not only a barrier the aliora could not cross, but it was also a tether that connected the human mind to the everyday world. Wrapping the gold around my arms was a bit like sipping one of my mother's potions—designed to bring me back to a sense of myself.

Then I sat on the moss-covered bed for a half hour and tried to think. What had Orlain been trying to say—or rather, trying *not* to say? If he was constantly imagining me married off to someone else, did that mean he wished I would never marry? Did that mean he wished I could marry *him*? Did that mean he cared for me? If he loved me and I loved him, didn't that mean we could marry if we wanted to?

There was a reason to resist the wiles of Alora.

Of course, if Orlain knew that I was in love with him, he might very well *pretend* to be in love with me just to provide me with a reason to come home—where he would then gently tell me the truth. I didn't think he would mind breaking my heart if he thought it would serve the kingdom.

But if there was a chance it was true . . .

Everyone always forgets that my mother herself is only half noble. She does not have the respect for bloodlines that might be expected from a queen. I did not think she would be shocked at the notion that I might marry outside of the upper class. And my father—well, *he* had married my mother. He wouldn't be shocked, either.

I must keep my wits about me. I must be ready to force Orlain to naked honesty the next time he seeks me out in Alora. I must cling to my gold as if I were adrift on a pitching ocean, and the metal was all that kept me from drowning.

Five

The next day, I removed the bracelets just for an hour while Cressida showed me how to set a particular stitch, but I instantly resumed wearing them.

The day after that, I left the bracelets behind while Royven and I went wandering through the forest again. It was just so troublesome to try to keep them in my pockets and be forever worrying that I might drop them by some half-rotted tree stump or lose them in a woodland pool where we had stopped to drink the water. Of course I slipped them back on before dinner, but I almost wished I hadn't. Twice when I passed platters I accidentally burned someone's delicate flesh. I spent half the meal apologizing.

Three days after Orlain's visit, I removed the bracelets for good, because I could not learn how to dance with an aliora while my arms were wrapped in gold. Yes, they had *dancing* in Alora—my very favorite thing!—except the patterns were like nothing I had ever encountered in a proper ballroom. Royven and his friends took turns showing me the steps, which involved a lot of twirling and clasping hands and winding through forest trails lit only by the brilliance of a full moon. Imagine! Dancing outdoors at midnight! Well, of course I couldn't resist such an opportunity.

"You can wear your new red dress, if you finish it," Cressida suggested, so I invested the effort to tack the hem in place and attach the last buttons. It was ready just in time.

"How do you plan to wear your hair?" Rowena asked on the day of the full moon.

My hair was so dense with curls that styling it was always a challenge. At home in Auburn, there was a single maid who had a knack for coaxing it into some semblance of sleekness, but here in Alora I simply tied it back with a ribbon if I wanted to keep it out of my face.

"I hadn't given it any thought," I said.

She reached up to brush the heavier strands away from my face. "We could tuck in some red blossoms right above your ears—or here in back—I think I can do something quite striking if you're willing to let me try."

"Oh, yes, please do!" I exclaimed. So I followed her to the room she shared with Jaxon on the second floor—bigger than mine, but no more complete in terms of finished walls—and I sat on a stool that was little more than a tree stump covered with a plump pillow. She stood behind me and gathered my hair up in both hands.

And then smothered a cry and yanked her hands away.

"What—oh, my earrings—I'm sorry, I'm sorry," I exclaimed, hastily reaching up to unfasten the hoops and lay them in my lap. "Did you burn yourself? I'm *so* sorry."

Rowena was nursing her hand against her mouth. "That was clumsy of me," she murmured. "It's not like I haven't seen them every day for the past two weeks."

"I won't put them back in," I assured her. "But I can't take the necklace off. So be careful when you take hold of my hair again."

She was careful, and she produced a hairstyle that I simply loved. It was a mass of braids and curls and dripping trails of blossom. There were no mirrors in the house, of course, but a reflecting pool on the bottom story gave me back my face, all angles and shadows and dark tendrils of hair.

"I *love* it," I breathed. "I wish I could copy this look when I'm back at the castle."

"I'll sketch it for you," she promised me. "Your mother or one of your maids should be able to duplicate it easily enough."

Because of the necklace, I couldn't fling my arms around her, but I squeezed her hands in mine. "You've been so generous to me," I said. "I wish I knew what to do for you in return."

"Just be happy here," she said. "That's payment enough."

❧

It is almost impossible to describe the sight of aliora dancing by moonlight.

You think that the light is coming from above, milky and mysterious, sifting down through the dense forest to throw a muted sparkle across your pathway, across your eyes. Then you realize that the aliora themselves are glowing, that they are winding around the dark trees like a pale and aimless river, spilling in all directions. You think the moon itself is crooning to you, a hypnotic lullaby, until you realize it is the aliora singing or humming or merely calling out to each other their wordless, euphoric delight. One of them takes your hand—a young man you barely know—and he smiles at you and pulls you into the dance. You circle a tree; you circle each other; you step into the living stream of incandescent dancers and skip along some invisible forest trail. Perhaps there are nightbirds singing, perhaps the leaves overhead are soughing with a great bell-like clamor, but it seems as if music is welling up from the ambient air. Scents you never noticed before threaten to overwhelm you with their intensity—the odors of pine and cedar and some night-blooming flower—till the air is almost too rich for you to breathe. But of course you breathe it anyway, and it is more intoxicating than wine. Your blood fizzes through your veins and you are laughing, you are dancing, you are twirling madly through a luminous landscape, and you cannot remember what it ever felt like to be a human girl.

Someone has taken your hand again, and he draws you close to him. This is not part of the dance that you learned in all those days of careful lessons. His arms are around your back; yours are around his neck; you would be too giddy to stand there and smile up at him except you have leaned into him and your body rests oh so lightly against his. He is smiling but there is something mesmerizing in his intentness; you could not look away if you wanted to.

When he kisses you, all your senses tell you that time has completely stopped.

Yet time must still be running forward, because he kisses you forever.

~

I have no idea what might have happened if Cressida had not come across me where I stood deep in the forest, completely yielding to Royven's embrace.

"Zara! Royven!" she said sharply. Royven was startled enough to lift his head, but he did not release me. I was too dazed to jerk my head around or struggle to get free. I merely blinked at him, then glanced over my shoulder to see who had accosted us.

"Cressida," I said, and even to myself my voice sounded languorous. "Are you lost?"

"No," she said pointedly, "but I'm afraid *you* are."

Royven laughed softly. "I know exactly where we are."

"You are on the steep path to trouble," she said in a firm voice. She placed one hand on my shoulder and one on his, and pried us apart with no pretense of subtlety. Once we had reluctantly disengaged, she pushed him backward with a little force and took hold of my arm with a hard grip.

"*You* will come back with me right now," she said to me. "Royven will stay with the other dancers."

"I'll come back with you to my mother's house," he said, but Cressida once again gave him a little shove on the shoulder.

"You won't," she said. "I will take care of Zara tonight."

It seemed like too much trouble to argue. "Good night," I called back to Royven as Cressida guided me through the forest. Some distance away from us, I could see that white river of aliora still snaking through the forest; I could catch bits and pieces of their eerie song.

"I love the way the aliora dance," I told Cressida as she tugged me along.

"I'm not surprised," she said. "Few humans can resist us when our magic is at its strongest, as it is during the full moon."

"Why would anyone want to resist?" I asked.

She looked at me sharply. "Your place is not in Alora,"

she said. "Therefore, it is your responsibility to resist as stubbornly as you can."

"Castle Auburn seems so far from here," I said.

"It is a two-day ride," she said. "And a world away. But you will be returning to that world as soon as it can be made safe for you."

I stumbled over a tree root, impossible to see even by the faint glow of Cressida's skin. "Don't you want me to stay here?" I asked, a plaintive note in my voice. "Everyone else does."

"You don't belong here," she said gently.

"That doesn't seem to bother Royven or Rowena or Jaxon. Or me," I added as an afterthought. "Why does it bother you?"

"I wish you *could* stay in Alora and live among us, beloved and beautiful," she said in a soft voice. "If it were any other young human girl who had wandered across our borders, I would do everything in my power to convince her to stay. I myself invited your mother to come live with the aliora—I offered her my home; I told her I would take her in as my own daughter. If she stepped across those borders tonight, I would redeem those promises, and she would never want to leave."

"Then why shouldn't *I* want to stay?" I asked.

"Because your mother is *not* here, and because she needs you to go home to her," Cressida answered. "Because I owe your mother a debt too great to repay in a dozen lifetimes. I will not betray her by failing to look after you."

"You look after me *very* well, Cressida," I said warmly.

"And I intend to continue doing so."

I was surprised when she did not lead me back to Rowena's house. Instead, she escorted me to her own cottage, a much smaller place with the same whimsical, airy architecture.

"Safer here, for the night at least," she said, making up a bed for me on the ground floor. I could feel twigs and acorns through the thick pile of blankets. "Perhaps in the morning, your mind will be clearer."

"Perhaps," I said drowsily, "but don't expect miracles."

I stayed at Cressida's house for the next three days. It was very pleasant, though I missed my moss-covered bed and she was astir much earlier in the mornings than I was used to. She was something of an herbalist, it turned out, so we spent the days looking over her stores of dried plants and grazing through the forest to find fresh ones. In the evenings, she taught me recipes for cooking with dayig and other wild fruits. The spices were so rich they colored my vision; even my dreams were more vivid during the nights I slept at Cressida's house.

The fourth morning I was there, Royven arrived with my saddlebag over his shoulder. "If you're going to be living here from now on, perhaps you want the rest of your things," he said.

It was like opening a box of unexpected presents; I had forgotten what treasures lay inside. "Look at this pretty dress," I said, pulling out a simple blue gown. "Oh! And a hairbrush! *That's* something I've needed for days."

Small items were clinking together in the bottom of the bag, so I pulled out a padded pouch and looked inside. "I forgot about these," I said, extracting one of the small vials filled with honey-colored liquid.

Royven held out his hand and I passed it over. "What is it?" he asked.

"One of the potions my mother gave me. To remind me of home."

Royven unstoppered the bottle and sniffed at the contents. "It smells delicious."

"Go ahead and drink it. I don't think she'd mind."

He emptied the contents in two swallows. "It tastes like something you'd blend into a cake recipe," he said.

I giggled. "Maybe we should give them to Cressida next time she's cooking."

"Are you going to have one?" he asked.

"Maybe tonight," I said. "I think I'm supposed to drink them at bedtime."

But that night I was so tired that I fell asleep without swallowing a potion. In fact, I couldn't remember the last time I had actually thought to do so.

Royven was fascinated by the tiny bottles, though, and they were the first things he inquired about the next morning when he arrived. "Could I have another one?" he asked. "Do they all taste the same?"

"I think some are different," I said, sorting through the bottles to search for gradations of color and density. "Here—this one. It's got a lighter flavor."

Royven uncorked it and swallowed, his face showing as much concentration as a connoisseur trying a new vintage. "I don't like it as well," he said.

"Then have one of the others," I offered.

He laughed. "Maybe tomorrow. I'll drink them one at a time so I can savor them."

I titled my head to one side, watching him. "I think they're supposed to have some kind of effect," I said. "At least on humans. Has the potion done anything to you this morning? Made your vision dim or your memories sharp?"

"No—but *you* look different," he said, surveying me critically.

"In what way? I don't look uglier, I hope."

"No, but I'm not sure I can describe it." He held out his forearm to lay alongside mine, as if testing to see who had acquired the deeper tan. As always, his flesh held a faint phosphorescence. Against it, mine looked plain and a little dingy. "You look as if you're made of a different material. As if your bones and your blood are visible through your skin. Look at that—I can *see* your pulse. It's such a different rhythm from my own."

I frowned and put my hands behind my back. "That sounds gruesome," I said. "I wouldn't want to see anybody's bloody, icky insides."

He lifted his hand to touch my face. "It's not gruesome; it's marvelous," he said, a note of amazement in his voice. "Look at the color of your cheek! An aliora's skin is so pale, as if moonlight runs in her veins. But your skin is so rich and beautiful—there is so much life going on beneath your surface—I want some of it for my own—"

And he leaned forward and kissed me.

I swirled into heat and sensation; elation hammered at my heart. Forget breathing or thinking or even existing. This was death by rapture. I crowded closer, hungry for another kiss, desperate to feel his arms tighten around me, meld our two bodies into one—

He swore and released me so quickly that I nearly tumbled

headfirst into the dirt. "Zara!" he exclaimed and caught me before I fell. I was dizzy and stupid and confused.

"What—why did you—"

"Your necklace—I'm sorry—when I hugged you, it seared my skin."

I made an infuriated noise deep in my throat and tugged futilely at the loop of gold soldered around my throat. "I can't take it off," I said. "We'll just have to be careful when you're kissing me."

"You make me forget how to be careful," he said, exhaling on a laugh. "Is there nothing you can do? Can it be broken?"

The idea had never occurred to me. "I suppose—but it's awfully thick. I don't think I can yank it hard enough to break it."

"Maybe if you twisted it around a stick—"

In this open household, he didn't have to hunt far to find a short, straight branch. "Try this," he said. "But first—place some padding against your throat so you don't hurt yourself. Now wrap the necklace around the stick—and twist it—and twist it again—"

I registered the satisfying *snap* against my fingers the same instant I felt the necklace slacken against the back of my neck. Giggling, I tossed away the stick and lifted one dangling edge of the severed chain and slowly pulled it free. I held it up between us like a tiny glittering snake that had been summarily beheaded before it could do any damage in the garden.

"And now I suppose you can kiss me as long as you want," I whispered.

"Princess Zara."

Cressida's sharp voice made both of us spin around like guilty schoolchildren. I was so unnerved I dropped the necklace onto the grassy floor.

"Royven, back away. Zara, pick that up," Cressida ordered, her voice so stern that neither of us thought to disobey. I coiled the chain in my hand and watched her nervously.

"Refasten the necklace about your throat," she directed.

"I can't. It's broken."

"Then put on your bracelets and earrings and every other scrap of metal you own."

"They're—they're somewhere in Rowena's house," I said. "Royven didn't bring them when he brought everything else."

"I couldn't pick them up," he defended himself.

Cressida gave me a long, measuring stare. I could not tell if she was angry or sad, but she was certainly disappointed. "Then we will go together to Rowena's house, and you will resume your protections," she said. "And then you and I will walk through the boundaries of Alora and await the arrival of your young man."

I had to think a moment. "Orlain? He's coming here?"

"You told me he would visit you every tenth day, and tomorrow is the twentieth day you have been with us. If he can be depended upon, he will arrive tomorrow."

"I'll come with you," Royven said. "I know exactly where they're supposed to meet."

"You," she said, "will wait here and do your best to stay out of trouble."

It was as if Orlain had already arrived—to see me at my worst. Naturally I burst into tears.

～

Cressida and I made a cold camp beside the cairn on the Alora side of the Faelyn River. As soon as we had crossed the magical boundary, I had been weighed down with a black depression. My limbs were leaden; my head was so heavy that it kept tilting forward, almost toppling me to the ground. Cressida, who until now had been the most considerate companion, did not bother to slow down to accommodate my misery; she did not take my hand to offer comfort or reassurance. I stumbled after her, too breathless to complain, too weary to weep. And when we arrived at our destination, I made no effort to help her fetch water or otherwise set up camp. I just sat in a heap on a folded blanket and gave in to my suffering.

Cressida did not bother trying to convince me I would feel better in the morning, but she flavored my evening meal with one of my mother's potions. My spirits did rise after I'd swallowed the cinnamon-and-orange-scented concoction, but I wasn't actually happy. Who could be happy once outside the borders of Alora?

We slept side by side on the ground, the wild music of the Faelyn River providing a tumultuous counterpoint to our dreams. When I woke, the sun had cheered the whole landscape, Cressida had made breakfast—and Orlain had crossed the river to join us.

I scrambled to my feet, suddenly very conscious of my tousled hair, my crumpled clothing, and my missing necklace. "Orlain," I said breathlessly. "What's the news?"

"Tense," he said. He was frowning as he looked me over, and I was sure he didn't miss a detail of my disorderly state. "Goff of Chillain arrived four days ago and engaged in a skirmish with some of the castle forces. Losses were minimal, but tempers have frayed in the heat. Now the king's allies want to storm the rebel troops in a strong reprisal, although your father is still hoping for peaceful resolution. Young Brandon is still riding up and down at the head of Dirkson's army, hoping to lure deserters to his cause. At any day, the situation could deteriorate into all-out war. Why are you out here, sleeping by the river?"

I had been so intent on visualizing his description of the hostilities that I almost missed the swift change in subject. "It—I wasn't sure when you would arrive and I didn't want to miss you."

"You wouldn't have missed me," he said. "I wouldn't have left until I'd seen you."

Cressida spoke up bluntly. "She is falling under the spell of Alora," she said. "It is not safe for her to stay any longer. You must take her back with you."

"Cressida!" I exclaimed, outraged. This was the first time she'd mentioned such a plan to me.

Now Orlain gave her the same thorough inspection he had turned on me. He seemed to find *her* looks more prepossessing, though, because his face softened and he held out his hand. "I'm Orlain," he said. "A captain in the royal guard."

Cressida smiled and shook her head. "You'd better not allow me to touch you," she said. "You, too, could be bewitched by our magic."

He let his hand fall and a smile came to his own face. "I doubt it."

"Then I am the one who does not want to take chances," she said. "Take her home, or risk losing her forever."

"I'm not ready to leave yet!"

"I cannot take her," Orlain said quietly. "On my way here, I passed three sets of Tregonian troops, riding out to join Dirkson. If Zara were to be recognized—"

"Then return here with an escort at your back, and do not delay another ten days," Cressida said.

"If the troops engage in true battle, there is no safety for her at Castle Auburn, either," he replied. "I would rather she was alive and lost to us than—" He did not complete the sentence.

"I would not be *lost*," I said with exaggerated enunciation. It was very annoying to have people talk about me as if I were not present. "I would be in Alora and doing quite well! Anyone could come see me there."

Cressida turned on me suddenly. "Who would come visit you?" she said.

I was at a loss. "Well—anyone who wanted to."

"List them."

I gestured. "Orlain, of course."

"Who else?"

"My parents. My brother."

"What's your brother's name?"

I stared at her blankly.

"What does he look like?" she said.

"He's—he's—well, he's shorter than I am, of course, and he—" It was a struggle to call up his features, but they slowly came into focus as I concentrated. "His eyes are dark. His eyelashes are longer than mine, which is so unfair. He has a scar across his left eyebrow from where he hit himself with a wooden sword. And he—Keesen," I said abruptly. "That's his name."

Cressida glanced at Orlain. "You see?"

Orlain's expression was closed, impossible to read. "She's strong-willed," he said. "I have faith that she will not succumb."

"Give her a reason to remember her human life."

He gestured behind him, toward the leaping blue waters of the Faelyn River. "Everything she loves is at Castle Auburn. I don't believe she will truly let those memories cloud over and evaporate."

"She needs a stronger reason than that," Cressida said.

I was remembering the last conversation I'd had with Orlain, right at the enchanted border. I was remembering that he had almost confessed he loved me. "Orlain," I said shyly, putting my hand on his arm. "Come back with us to Alora. I know you are worried about my safety. Come with us and watch out for me there."

He glanced down at my hand and then slowly lifted his eyes to mine. His flesh had turned to iron under my touch. "My responsibilities take me back," he said flatly.

"Then return to me as soon as you can," I suggested. "We could live there together. There are no social classes in Alora—no distinctions. Everyone is the equal of everyone else."

"Princess," he said. "No magic is powerful enough to make me forget my place."

I heard Cressida's hiss of annoyance—clearly she had hoped he would speak more persuasively. I said, "Love is the most powerful magic of all."

I felt the muscles cord in his arm as his hand clenched to a fist. "It is," he agreed. "I think it will make me remember what you are determined to forget."

"I think I will remember it," I whispered, "if you kiss me."

He stood there for a long time, looking down at me, immobile as one of those great forest oaks that never tremble no matter what the tempest. Then slowly, as if he was one of those trees just now learning the mechanics of movement, he bent from the waist and gently brushed his lips across mine. I closed my eyes to savor the sensation, and he kissed me one more time, just as softly, holding the contact a second or two longer. When he lifted his head I opened my eyes and smiled up at him, suffused with a sparkling satisfaction.

"Where's your necklace?" he asked abruptly.

I dropped my hand from his and scowled. "It broke."

He raised his eyebrows and made no other comment, but his hands went up to the back of his neck, and I realized he was undoing the chain to a gold medallion he always wore. All the castle guards were given such medallions as soon as they were hired. "Put this on," he said.

He slipped it over my head and fastened the clasp. I felt the smooth disk of the pendant against my skin, warm from contact with his. I pressed my hand across it to absorb that faint heat. "But now you won't be safe if you cross into Alora," I protested.

"I'll bring some other talisman for protection."

"Come back as soon as you can," Cressida urged. "Don't wait another ten days."

"I'll try," he said. He bowed to me, very low, touching his hand against his forehead. "Princess," he said. "Do not quite forget."

Six

I moped around Cressida's house for the next two days, disinclined to search for more herbs, sew a new dress, learn another dance, or help another aliora construct a flawed and charming house. Sleeping was the only activity that held any appeal, and I loved to curl up on my pile of blankets in the middle of the floor and slumber the hours away. Usually I slept with Orlain's medallion under my cheek. Whenever I would finally wake, I could feel the flat round indentation in my skin.

On the third day, Royven arrived just as I sat up, yawning, from an afternoon nap. He tilted my chin up and inspected my face. "I didn't think that was possible," he said.

"What?"

"Humans never develop an antipathy to gold. But I think you are."

"Why do you think that?"

"Your cheek. It looks so red."

"I was sleeping on Orlain's medallion."

"Did it burn your skin? Does your face feel hotter where it touched you?"

I rubbed my fingers across the affected patch. "Maybe. Just a little."

"How about your bracelets? Are they burning your arms?"

I investigated the flesh along my wrists, which bore the reddened impressions of the metal circlets. "My arms were pressed against the bracelets while I was sleeping," I explained. I had to admit I was slightly uneasy, however. Now that Royven mentioned it, each piece of gold felt a little warm to the touch.

"Maybe that's all it is," he said, giving me a reassuring smile.

"I'll pay attention," I promised. "If it gets any worse—"

"Oh—I'm sure it won't," he said. "As I say, I've never met a human who couldn't handle gold. Jed Cortay has lived in Alora for twenty years, and no metal ever bothers *him*."

But it was hard to get the idea out of my head. That night, instead of sleeping with the medallion, I laid it carefully beside me on the ground, and I slipped it back on first thing in the morning. The bracelets, too. But I could feel them all through the day, chafing my skin. I pulled out the medallion and let it rest on top of my dress, but I could still feel its heat through the layer of silk. The bracelets felt so warm that I finally had to remove them altogether.

"I could make a pouch for you," Royven suggested. "A little bag you could slip over the medallion. That would help protect your skin. If you still want to wear the pendant."

"I do," I said firmly, though I was having a hard time remembering why. "Thank you. I would love that."

He wove a small bag out of lemongrass and orchids, and the wide, flat disk fit perfectly inside. Its coolness was an instant relief against my skin; soon I forgot I was even wearing the pendant.

A day later I forgot to put the pendant on.

"Let's go walking through the forest to see what we can find," Royven suggested.

I put my hand in his and said, "Let's."

We were gone most of the day, though we accomplished very little. Now and then I noticed a particularly beautiful flower or useful plant, and I plucked these to bring back to Cressida. A few times, Royven spotted sturdy or well-seasoned branches that met some construction need, and he bundled up about half a dozen of them and slung them over his shoulder. We held hands, of course, as we strolled through the woods, and now and then we paused to trade kisses. His lips burned as hot as gold. I closed my eyes and melted into his embrace.

It was late afternoon when we reluctantly retraced our steps to Cressida's house. She was waiting outside for us, more nervous and impatient than I had ever seen her.

"*There* you are," she exclaimed, coming between us with such force that our clasped hands loosened and fell. "Quickly— you must come with me to Rowena's."

I was tired and I had been looking forward to another nap. "What's wrong?" I asked through a yawn.

She took my arm and pulled me forward, not answering directly. "Come with me."

I glanced at Royven, who shrugged and fell in step behind us.

As we drew closer to Rowena's, I could see a small crowd gathered before the open house. The clattering, humming language of the aliora rose from this group in an orchestral cacophony that held a note of distress. I caught Jaxon's voice, louder than the rest, expostulating with someone, and Rowena's, low and soothing. With much less than her usual courtesy, Cressida tugged me through the assembled aliora until I was face-to-face with Rowena.

A young man stood before her, his back to me.

"Orlain," I breathed.

He heard my voice and jerked around to face me. "Princess," he said, stepping closer and taking both my hands in his. "The uprising has ended. I've come to take you home."

"What uprising?" I said.

His hands tightened on mine. "The mutinous armies led by Dirkson of Tregonia," he said, speaking slowly and distinctly. "They have been disbanded. There was another quick encounter between the rebels and the royals, and the counterfeit young prince Brandon behaved with utter cowardice. A handful of loyal men chased him off the field of battle, too afraid to even draw his sword. No one would follow such a despicable prince, and Dirkson could not hold his troops together. It is safe for you to return. Soldiers have already ridden for Cotteswold to fetch Keesen."

"Who is Keesen?" I said.

Now his grip was painful. "Your younger brother. You love him very much."

"It's been such a long time since I've seen him," I said.

"You'll be with him as soon as we get back to Castle Auburn."

"But I'm not going to Castle Auburn," I said. "I want to stay here."

"That's what I told you she would say!" Jaxon exclaimed. "She's happy in Alora."

"Her life is elsewhere," Orlain replied, not bothering to look at Jaxon. "And my duty is to return her to that life."

Rowena spoke up in her musical voice. "Shouldn't Zara be allowed to choose what she wants? We would never bind any human against her will, but we gladly extend a welcome to any who wish to stay. And even in this short time, all of us have grown fond of her. We wish her to remain with us."

Orlain was just watching me with an urgent intensity, as if willing some privileged knowledge of his own to be visible in his eyes. "You were born at Castle Auburn," he said. "Your first word was *princess*. Your bedroom is decorated with yellow roses and a painting of Bryan Ouvrelet that you stole from the south gallery. Your favorite cat is thirteen years old, blind in both eyes, and lame, but you will not allow anyone to advance the notion of putting him down. You love to waltz, and whenever you take the dance floor, all the young men of the kingdom stare after you, wishing they could be your partner. I kissed you the last time I saw you and you seemed to like it. If you come with me, I will kiss you again."

"I wish you *would* kiss me," I said. "But not if it means I have to leave Alora."

"No matter what I do," he said, "you must leave Alora."

Jaxon had lost his patience; he charged over and shouldered between us, making Orlain drop my hands. "She doesn't want to go with you. How plain can she make it?" my uncle blustered. He wrapped one arm around my shoulder and seemed to be protecting me from unwanted attention, but I was a little sorry. I liked the feel of my hands in Orlain's.

Orlain turned to face Rowena, his hands open and extended in a gesture of supplication. "I know you want to keep her," he said quietly. "I know you want to keep any human who wanders into your path. Let her go. I will remain in her place."

Rowena put her hand up, gentle as mist, and brushed it across his face. I saw him flinch and then tremble, but he did not pull away. "There is no need for such sacrifices," she murmured. "You need not be parted. Both of you may stay."

"At least one of us will be riding back toward Auburn before nightfall," Orlain said. I wondered how he could resist her touch. Most men would be too dazed to speak once Rowena trailed her fingertips across their skin.

"Then I am afraid it will be you," Rowena told him, dropping her hand. "Zara has made her choice."

I fidgeted in Jaxon's embrace. "Don't go just yet," I begged Orlain. "Stay the night at least. Maybe—maybe in the morning you will change your mind."

He turned to me again; his face was set. "Nothing will change my mind," he said. "I must leave—and now."

Wistful, I pulled free of Jaxon's arms. "Will you not kiss me good-bye anyway? Even though I will not leave with you?"

I was a little surprised but more delighted when he gave one decisive nod. "I will," he said. "But I must first wash away the dust of the road, for my journey was hasty, long, and dirty."

He lifted a small water bag to his mouth and drained the contents in a few quick swallows. Then he took two steps to my side, swept me into his arms, and laid a desperate, grieving kiss upon my mouth.

I tasted winter in his kiss, a season that never comes to Alora; his water bag must have been filled with the melt of a thousand snowflakes. I tasted a splash from the great fountain that plays incessantly in the courtyard of Castle Auburn. I tasted cider from Cotteswold, spun sugar from Faelyn. I tasted nectar from the rare red orchid that grows only in Chillain.

I tasted gold. Pounded and powdered and poured into a potion and transferred to my lips by a single sweet kiss.

I cried out and broke free, clapping my hands to my cheeks and staring around me in alarm. Orlain called my name— Jaxon and Royven and Rowena called my name—the gathered aliora chittered and cooed and reached for me with their attenuated fingers. I backed away from all of them, trembling with heat, flushed with memory. I felt as if I had been flung back into my body after a week of fever, as if I had reentered my own mind after a period of delirium.

I was the Princess Zara, my country had been at war, and my place was with my family.

"Orlain," I whispered. "Take me home."

—

There was an outcry, of course, and sweet pleadings from Royven and Rowena. Jaxon planted himself in front of me and took turns wheedling and arguing about how I should stay just another night and see how I felt about my decision in the morning. But Cressida had already bustled back to her place to gather up my clothes and trinkets, and Orlain wasn't taking any chances. He had produced another water bag filled with the selfsame elixir and bid me to drink the whole thing down. With every taste my past became clearer; with every swallow I grew more resolute.

"At least promise you will return to visit us—someday very soon," Royven was saying as Orlain and I set out on the path toward the Faelyn River. We were trailed by half a dozen aliora, but I figured none of them would actually cross the border.

I laughed. "That would be a terrible promise to make! Alora is a dangerous place to visit."

"You could come to us *armored* in gold," he suggested. "You could drink nothing but your mother's potions night and day."

"I am not strong enough to resist you—any of you," I said regretfully. "I do not think I would be safe from your blandishments if my very bones were made of gold."

"Though that's an idea," Orlain said. "You could seek out a surgeon who might replace a finger bone, say, with a shaft of metal. Then you could visit Alora with no risk at all."

"Somehow I don't think even that would keep me safe," I said.

As I expected, the aliora fell behind as we approached the boundary. I waved good-bye to all of them; the only one I dared to hug was Cressida, and even that might have been a mistake. Just that brief embrace filled me with an almost ir-resistible longing to scurry back across the border and drown in the sumptuous serenity of Alora.

She pushed me away when I started to cling. "Go. Try to cross the river before nightfall. Don't be too sad about what you've left behind. And tell your mother I have repaid some small part of my debt."

I had to brush away tears as I stepped back from her. "What debt?"

"She set me free. Now I have done the same for you."

"Princess," Orlain said. "We must go or we will be swim-ming the Faelyn River in darkness."

"Good-bye," I whispered—saying it to Cressida, to Royven, to Alora, to my alternate life, I didn't know. "I do not think I will ever be back again."

❧

Orlain and I traveled on in silence until we were almost at the river. I was such a mess of conflicting emotions that I hardly had the energy to walk, let alone speak. I knew without a sliver of doubt that I wanted to return to Auburn, be reunited with my family, take up the life I was meant to live—and yet it was hard, it was actually painful, to leave Alora behind. My heart felt as if it had developed a ragged crack that flinched with every beat. I did not think it would be mended soon; possibly it would never heal.

But I was glad when I caught the boisterous sound of the rushing river—glad to know that within a few minutes we would truly be back in the kingdom of men. Sunset was just beginning to layer peach and amethyst across the western ho-rizon. We had made this landmark none too soon.

I took a deep breath as we paused on the riverbank. The current looked formidably rapid.

Orlain glanced down at me, his expression quizzical. "Don't tell me a girl who's had all your adventures is afraid of getting wet," he said.

I stared right back at him, a challenge on my own face. The prospect of a confrontation with Orlain was chasing away some of my sadness, releasing a wash of adrenaline into my veins. "The last time we crossed this river together," I said, "you carried me in your arms. Don't tell me a man who's fought *your* particular battles has lost his chivalrous notions."

It was hard to tell in the fading light, but his face appeared to redden slightly. "Maybe I'm thinking some of those chivalrous notions have led me into trouble."

"So tell me," I said. "I assume my mother mixed up the brew that you carried in your water bags."

"Of course she did. I told her that I thought you might need a strong antidote to aliora magic."

"And did you discuss exactly how you thought you might induce me to taste her potion?"

"She thought you would take a sip of it, of course."

"*Did* she? She expected me to be standing around in Alora with an empty glass in my hand, merely waiting for someone to offer me a strange concoction?"

He eyed me uncertainly. "I don't know what she expected, but perhaps we could discuss it once we're across the river."

I stood my ground. "My mother is a skilled herbalist. She knows *exactly* how much halen root to grind up if a potion will be used to ease someone's pain and how much will be needed if it will just help someone fall asleep. She changes any formula depending on how much it will be diluted. She made that concoction so strong that a single drop would clear my mind. She knew you were going to bestow it upon me in the form of a kiss. So how did she know that?"

"I have often thought your mother knew things an ordinary woman would not."

"Did you tell her? Tell her you were going to kiss me? Tell her you *had* kissed me?"

"If you're asking me if she knew I loved you, I suppose the answer is yes," Orlain said, so deliberately that I could tell he had not actually capitulated; he was merely making a show of surrender so I could not have the satisfaction of defeating him. "That's the reason she sent me with you to Alora in the first place. She said that love was a talisman stronger than gold, that it could not be laid aside and it would not be diverted. She said she knew that I would be able to resist Alora because I would never be able to resist you."

I caught my breath. "Then why are you trying?" I said. "To resist me?"

Without warning, he scooped me up in his arms and waded into the bubbly blue waters. "It really would have been easier," he said, "to leave you in Alora."

"Or to throw me into the river. You didn't answer my question."

"It's a stupid question."

This was the Orlain I knew best, scoffing, teasing, pushing me away, all the while watching out for me to make sure no harm could come my way. I relaxed in his arms. I said, "Since you don't even *like* me, it's hard to understand how you could *love* me."

"Since you aren't lovable, it's truly a mystery."

"Maybe the best thing would be to have my father grant you property of your own," I mused. "Would you like land in Veledore by your father's family, or someplace in Auburn, closer to the castle? Or I suppose there might be an estate available near Uncle Roderick."

Orlain climbed out of the river with a great deal of unnecessary splashing, so that I was almost as wet as he was. Two horses tethered to nearby trees offered soft whinnies of welcome. "I don't want property," Orlain said. "I don't want anything. I'm a simple guardsman and happy with my life as it is."

"That's unfortunate for you," I said, "because your life is about to change."

He dropped me unceremoniously to my feet, but I noticed how his hands hovered near my shoulders until I had completely recovered my balance. How could I have ever failed to realize how closely he guarded me? It almost made me want to put myself in danger just to see what he would do to rescue me.

Put myself in danger *again*. To see how he rescued me *again*.

"I don't want to be your plaything," he said. "I don't want to be the man you take up because he intrigues you and cast aside because he bores you. I don't want to be a—a—summer novelty. It would be much simpler for me if you just let me go on the way I always have."

"I imagine it would be," I said cordially. "What makes you think I want your life to be simple?"

He stared down at me a moment in silence. Darkness was almost upon us, but I could see the expression on his face—a curious look of resignation crossed with faint excitement. And perhaps a bit of hope. "You're the most wretched girl," he said in a conversational tone. "I'm tempted to let you find your own way back to the castle."

I put a finger to my cheek. "Hmm. Why is it I don't believe you?"

He shook his head and turned away. "Time to make camp," he said over his shoulder. "Do you want to cook or do you want to dig?"

I laughed out loud. "Oh, I think I'll cook," I said. "Let me see. I may have a few of my mother's potions left. I think one or two of them might be love spells—should I flavor our meal with those?"

He was a dozen paces away, but he spun around to give me a sardonic look. "It hardly seems necessary," he said. "Though I would be willing to drink an antidote if you have it on hand."

"No, nothing like that in my supplies, I'm afraid," I said cheerfully.

"I'll just have to consult your mother, then. Maybe *she'll* be able to help me."

"Indeed, I'm sure she and my father will both have a lot to say," I said. "I quite look forward to seeing them again and telling them everything that's happened to me."

Orlain merely grunted and headed off into the shadows to gather up firewood. I approached the horses and started pulling items from the saddlebags. It had been a long, head-spinning day, and I was hungry and tired—and energized and exhilarated. It would require a fifteen-course banquet to adequately celebrate all the emotions I had been through in the past few hours, but I would settle for river water and camp food.

At least, I would for tonight. Things would be different once we arrived back at the castle. Once I had reassured myself that my family was safe, once I had heard Keesen's tales about Cotteswold, then I would work on securing my future. To my father, I would praise Orlain for his courage and steadfastness. With my mother, I would plot the best way to turn my plain guardsman into a fashionable young man—or at least a man of enough standing to court a princess.

Oh, yes, things would be very different once we got home.

Flame

One

Finally the pain stopped. Senneth cautiously sat up to see if movement would startle the headache loose again, but it only crouched at the back corner of her mind, a ravenous monster satiated for the moment.

She swung her legs over the side of the bed and contemplated standing up. At first she thought the effort would be beyond her, but the longer she maintained an upright position, the stronger she felt. Hungrier, too. She had lain there a full day, too blinded by misery to eat or speak. And now she was starving and just a little light-headed.

The aftereffects of too much magic. She had learned—in the most unpleasant fashion imaginable—that calling upon her power while she was in the grip of rage resulted in crippling migraines; but she hadn't been angry yesterday when she caused one after another of the small cottages to burn. She'd been sad. She'd been worried. She'd been expending a great deal of effort to control the fires. It seemed that such fierce concentration could wake that beastly pain almost as quickly as fury.

She pushed herself to her feet, decided that walking would not be beyond her, and crossed the room to make use of the amenities in one corner. After using half the water to cure her thirst and half to wash her face, she pulled on a shirt and trousers that seemed cleaner than everything else in her bag. Barefoot, she padded out the door, through the long corridor, and down the curved, elegant stairs to the front hallway. Through the windows lining either side of the carved door, she could see that yesterday's endless, wretched rain had turned to snow overnight. The slabs of gray slate that lined the foyer floor felt as cold and textured as river ice beneath her feet.

She liked the sensation. Her soles were so hot that river ice would melt beneath them, but the slate stayed solid and wintry against her skin.

She heard a rustle behind her and a woman's voice. "Senneth! You've finally woken up! How are you feeling?"

Summoning a smile, Senneth turned to greet her hostess. Evelyn was a small silver-haired woman with a big heart and a warm manner. In some complicated fashion, she was related both to Senneth's mother and Eloise Kianlever, the marlady of this part of the world. Still, Evelyn had only the faintest trappings of nobility—a small manor house and a general air of good breeding, as opposed to the magnificent castle and attitude of supercilious hauteur that were the birthrights of most Twelfth House nobles. Unlike most of Senneth's other relations, no matter how near or distant, Evelyn had not been shocked and repulsed at the news that Senneth was a mystic who could make fire do her bidding. She had offered Senneth a home and unshakable affection, but Senneth had not taken advantage of either one very often during the seventeen years since she had been banished from her father's house. Too much contact with magic strained even the strongest bonds, Senneth believed. She tried never to stay too long in any one place, never to call too often on the reserves of friendship.

"I'm feeling a little bruised and a lot hungry," Senneth said. "Is there food? I'm afraid I won't be able to concentrate on conversation until there is."

"Yes, yes, fresh bread in the kitchen, and the cook will make whatever you like for breakfast," Evelyn said. She led Senneth through narrow back hallways to the small, cheerful kitchen, and they sat without ceremony at a little table pressed against a wall.

The cook beamed at Senneth as she brought over a plate mounded with eggs, potatoes, and some kind of fried meat.

The cook was a sloppy middle-aged woman, beefy enough to slaughter livestock, but she had her own kind of magic when it came to food. "Lady Evelyn warned me we'd need to feed you the minute you came downstairs," she said. "Just call out if you want more."

"Let me finish this first," Senneth said, digging in.

Evelyn poured herself a cup of tea and let Senneth take the edge off of her hunger before speaking again. "You'll be happy to know all three of the cottages are nothing more than cinder and ashes this morning," she said. "Cinder and ashes covered with snow. There wasn't even enough heat left in the coals to melt the flakes."

"I told you the fire was completely out before I walked away," Senneth said.

"Yes, but I didn't really believe you," Evelyn replied. "I mean, how is that possible? They were absolute infernos! Those fires should have taken hours to die down. But you wave your hands at them and suddenly every spark is gone? Two of the boys stood watch all night, just to make sure nothing else caught fire."

Senneth cut another slice of bread and buttered it lavishly. "Well, I'm sorry anyone had to lose a night's sleep because you don't trust magic," she said cheerfully. "But I knew the flames were cold."

"I didn't realize how draining it would be for you, or I might never have asked for your help."

Senneth shook her head. "It shouldn't have been so difficult. Normally, I can set and contain three fires like that with practically no effort. An hour's work or less." She took a huge bite of the bread. *So* good. She spent so much time traveling that, nine days out of ten, she was eating dried rations or stale leftovers while crouched around a solitary campfire. A meal straight out of the oven was the height of luxury.

"Then why was yesterday so hard?"

"The rain," Senneth said. "Everything was so wet. The wood, the walls, the roof thatching. It was difficult to make anything ignite, and once something *did* catch fire, I had to force it to keep burning. That took a lot more energy than I expected."

Evelyn stirred more sugar into her tea and gave Senneth a

shrewd look. "How often does playing with fire leave you so incapacitated?" she wanted to know. "That's a powerful price to pay."

Senneth shrugged. "It's a powerful gift. Maybe if it came easily, I wouldn't value it so much." Although, considering how much she had given up for magic, she supposed nothing about it would qualify as *easy*.

"I don't think that quite answered my question."

"Actually, it's rare," Senneth said. "Mostly I don't get a headache unless I've called up fire while I'm in a rage."

Evelyn looked a little unnerved. "I'm not sure I like the idea of an angry mystic wreaking destruction on the world."

Senneth laughed. "Well, there aren't many who can call up as much power as I can. I've seen plenty of fire mystics who could light a candle with a touch or keep a kitchen fire burning all day without fuel, but I'm not sure any of them could have kept those cottages burning yesterday. And only some of them can put *out* a fire at will, like I can."

Evelyn leaned back in her chair, looking a little quizzical. "Don't take this the wrong way," she said. "But I'm not surprised some people are afraid of mystics."

Senneth nodded. "I don't wonder at it at all."

The untidy cook came back bearing another platter of toast. "Would you like some peach jam?" she offered. "I made it last summer."

"I would love it," Senneth said, and the cook hurried off to rummage through the pantry. "She seems to like me," Senneth remarked. "Apparently *your* servants have enlightened views about mystics."

"She wanted to see those houses burned," Evelyn said. "Her grandmother died in one of them, trying to nurse a young woman through the fever. She's one of the villagers who begged me to pull the cottages down."

It had been simple luck that brought Senneth to this part of Kianlever when there was a hard chore that could be made simpler by her particular brand of magic. Evelyn's modest property was just a half mile from a struggling village that was a good long detour off the major east-west road. An infectious fever had recently passed through the neighborhood, leaving eight dead and three small houses polluted with the detritus of death. The general consensus was that the fever still lingered inside the cottages and no one wanted to risk contagion by volunteering to pull the structures down. But they stood so close to neighboring houses that setting them on fire—the preferred solution—was likely to result in the whole town going up in flames.

Senneth had ridden up two days ago like an answer to a prayer.

She had not been entirely surprised. In her experience, anytime a mystic happened to be in the vicinity, there would develop a need for the very kind of magic that mystic possessed.

Of course, sometimes there would develop a vicious hatred for that kind of magic, too. Senneth had started to hear more and more stories about mystics stoned to death or burned to death or flung into deep water and drowned. She knew she should be afraid. She knew she should operate with more care when she *did* call on her magic. But instead, every time she heard one of those tales, she felt her eternally high internal temperature begin to rise as her anger started to build.

She would like to see someone try to burn *her* at the stake. She would like to have someone bind *her* hands and fling her into a lake. She would cause that lake to boil and evaporate; she would set that whole benighted town on fire.

And then, no doubt, she would suffer the headache of the damned.

The cook returned with a jar of a rich-looking jam, and Senneth complimented her extravagantly on each individual component of the meal. "I wish you would come travel with me and make splendid dishes every night that we camp out," she said.

"I'm not the traveling sort," the cook said. "It would be much better if you stayed here."

She returned to her chores while Senneth polished off yet another piece of bread. All kinds of sorcery used up a mystic's physical strength, but Senneth had to believe she burned through more energy than most other mystics did. She was using her own body as fuel, in a way; she had to replenish or waste away.

Evelyn was looking thoughtful. "Indeed, it *would* be better if you stayed awhile," she said. "You don't have any pressing reason to travel on in a day or so, do you?"

Senneth raised her eyebrows. "Not particularly, no, but I get irritable after I've been in any one place too long."

"Well—how long? A week? A month? I would be so pleased if you would stay a few days. I get the feeling you do not often come to rest."

Senneth grinned. "No mystic does. It's hard for us to sit still."

"But good for you, surely? You could take a little time to—" Evelyn waved a hand to comprehensively indicate Senneth's face and figure. "Clean yourself up a little. Get some new clothes. Perhaps cut your hair."

Senneth automatically put a hand to her head, where her flyaway white-blond hair was still a little gritty from yesterday's ashes. "You cannot possibly turn me into a woman of style," she said. "Don't waste your time trying."

"Do you even *own* a dress?"

"No. Impractical for the kind of travel I do."

"But wouldn't you like to look nice just for a few days?" Evelyn said in a wheedling tone. "I will invite some friends to visit and you will see how enjoyable it is to have urbane and witty conversation."

Senneth burst out laughing. "Evelyn, you're so kind, but I am the worst kind of party guest! I have not sat down at a noblewoman's dinner table for a number of years. I'm strange. I'm antisocial. I have no conversation. Unless you want me to do parlor tricks like setting my tablemates on fire, there is really nothing I can add to any social gathering."

Evelyn smiled. "I think you're missing the point, my dear," she said. "I am not so much trying to show you off as trying to civilize you. I get the feeling that you have not slept on a real bed or eaten off of real dishes in weeks. Months. Years."

"It hasn't been quite that long," Senneth said. "I stop at an inn every now and then. Ariane Rappengrass and Malcolm Danalustrous are always happy to put me up for a few days. And you know I'm in and out of Ghosenhall all the time. The king keeps a room for me whenever I wish it. I have not gone completely feral."

"If you'll pardon me for saying so," Evelyn responded dryly, "it is only a matter of time."

Senneth couldn't decide if she should be irritated or amused, so she shrugged. "I admit I am eccentric," she said. "Hence the reason I make a poor dinner guest."

"I will invite tolerant and genial friends," Evelyn promised. "If only you will agree to stay."

To keep refusing would make her seem wholly ungracious; Senneth saw no choice but to acquiesce. "Very well," she said. "But if it turns out to be the most disastrous social event of your life, you must remember that I warned you."

Three days later, Senneth was wishing she had cared less for Evelyn's feelings and more for her own and had flatly turned down the invitation. It turned out there was a great deal of bustle involved in planning even a small social gathering, and Senneth had been required to participate in most of it. She didn't mind offering her opinion on the menu choices, or even the decorations, but she greatly resented having to deck herself out in an actual gown and matching accessories. Evelyn was completely adamant that Senneth must change out of the men's clothing that she favored—as well as her sturdy boots.

"Since you're a petite childlike thing and I'm practically a giant, I don't know how you think there will be a dress in your closet to fit me," Senneth said when the topic of her wardrobe was brought up on the very day Evelyn proposed the party.

"You're hardly a giant."

"Taller than most men I know."

"I suppose that's why you never married."

Senneth could not smother a crack of laughter. "That and so many other reasons."

"There is a seamstress in the village and her own daughter is quite tall," Evelyn said. "I am certain she will have patterns that will fit you and maybe even a dress or two that could be altered to suit. It would not be exceptionally fine, of course, but *anything* would be better than those trousers."

Senneth was skeptical, but Evelyn was correct. The seamstress herself was big-boned and imposing, a calm, practical woman who seemed quite certain she could produce a suitable dress in the short time available. "Do you have a preference as to color?" the woman asked. She appraised Senneth's fair complexion and gray eyes and added, "Something in lilac or lavender, perhaps?"

"Blue, to show off your Brassenthwaite heritage?" Evelyn suggested.

Her "Brassenthwaite heritage" was one thing Senneth never wanted to show off. She had not been back to that region of the country since her father disowned her. "Something in blue and green," she said. "To celebrate my Kianlever roots."

"I have just the material," the seamstress said.

"Nothing too fancy," Senneth said. "Don't bother with lots of lace and ribbon. And please do not embarrass me with a low-cut neckline."

"Although your figure is very good," the seamstress said. "Not as delicate as the fashion is today, but it's been my impression that men appreciate a more robust girl."

Evelyn was snickering into her palm as Senneth stared at the woman, completely nonplussed. "Well—I don't think I am attempting to attract a man at this event," was all she could think to say. "So no need to show off my charms."

"I will be back with a dress in two days, and we can do a final fitting," the seamstress said.

That was bad enough, but then Evelyn insisted on trying several different styles on Senneth's completely unmanageable hair, calling on the services of her own dresser. "Why do you keep it so *short*?" Evelyn lamented. "It's such an unusual color. You could be so striking."

"It gets in my way if it's any longer," Senneth said.

Evelyn tugged at a particularly ragged lock. "And who cut this for you? Did you do it yourself? It's just a mess."

Senneth grinned. "Hacked it off with a sharp knife. It was hanging in my eyes."

Evelyn released the strands of hair, pulled up a chair, and took Senneth's hands in both of her small ones. She held Senneth's eyes with her own serious gaze. "Senneth," she said. "You cannot keep living this way. Like—like—some kind of animal. Like some kind of madwoman, wandering the landscape, shouting gibberish at the moon. You are—you are losing all the details that make you human. You could slip away from us entirely."

The discreet dresser had busied herself with a jewelry case on the other side of the room, but Senneth was still embarrassed and oddly uncomfortable. Normally she didn't care what people thought of her. So few people *did* think of her, after all.

"I swear to you, Evelyn, it is not as bad as you think," Senneth said. "Just because I cut my hair myself doesn't mean I'm in danger of losing my soul. You don't know many mystics, but I assure you they are all ragged vagabonds. Some of them even worse than me."

"I don't care about any of *them*," Evelyn said. "It is *you* I worry about."

"It's kind of you," Senneth said. "But, Evelyn, I am perfectly happy in my life. I would be sorry to see it change."

Still, in an effort to reassure her hostess, Senneth submitted to the rest of the rehabilitation. The dresser was allowed to give her hair a rather more professional trim and find some narrow ribbons to hold the fine hair from her face. Senneth grudgingly admitted that the style was attractive. She was patient with the seamstress when the woman returned with a flattering green-and-blue-striped dress that still needed to be pinned and tucked against Senneth's body. She allowed her hands and face to be rubbed with scented creams, she tried on dozens of pairs of fashionable shoes, and she agreed to wear a pair of gold earrings that Evelyn found in her own jewelry box, though she refused to take off the simple gold pendant that she always wore. She also declined Evelyn's offer to make up her face.

"Still," Evelyn said, stepping back to survey her, "the transformation is quite impressive. I might almost think you were a Twelfth House serramarra come to give consequence to my little house."

"I certainly hope that is not what your guests are expecting to meet tonight."

"Not at all," Evelyn replied. "I just told them that you were a somewhat distant kinswoman who had been spending an agreeable few days with me."

"Do they know I'm a mystic?"

"Betony does," Evelyn said. "She's my cousin, you know, and we're quite close. She's not afraid of magic, and she can be trusted not to repeat secrets."

Senneth shrugged. "I am what I am," she said, adding, with dark humor, "And if anyone doesn't like it, I'll set them on fire."

"That will not be necessary, I'm sure," Evelyn said. "We will have a very agreeable and civilized visit."

Two

About fifteen minutes into the first luncheon with Evelyn's guests, Senneth was convinced her hostess was right: There would be no need for incendiary theatrics. Evelyn's little group of friends appeared to be very much like Evelyn herself: well-behaved, intelligent, friendly people with just enough breeding to make them gracious but not enough consequence to be insufferable. And despite the fact that it had been at least two years since Senneth had attempted to hold her own in such company, she found that she was having no trouble keeping her place in the conversation. In fact, though she didn't like to admit it, she was almost enjoying herself.

Since this was not a formal meal, Evelyn had made no attempt to keep the numbers even. One set of guests were the Cordwains—Evelyn's cousin Betony, just as small and outgoing as Evelyn; and Betony's husband, Albert, a big man with a ready laugh. Accompanying the Cordwains were their nearest neighbors. Degarde Farthess was a slim, intense, and attractive man about Senneth's own height. His sister Julia, a recent widow, presented an appearance of frailty and confusion barely held in check behind a brave smile. She spent most of the meal trying to get her rambunctious two-year-old daughter, Halie, to sit quietly in her chair, a task that was clearly beyond her. Senneth was a little surprised that anyone would think such a young child would be an asset at a social gathering, but it was clear that everyone in the room was both fond of the little girl and accustomed to her high spirits.

"Do you have children of your own, Senneth?" Julia asked as the first course was being served. Halie was bouncing on Julia's lap, pulling at her mother's hair, and reaching small, stubby fingers out to catch at the servants as they glided by.

"I don't," Senneth said. "I have often thought I would not have the necessary patience to be a good mother."

"It doesn't require patience as much as stamina and iron will," Degarde put in humorously. "You think of children as being small, angelic creatures who will love you with their entire hearts. And instead they are savages intent on nothing but destruction and getting whatever it is they want—and they can *want* with an astounding ferocity."

Julia, sitting across from him, laughed and pulled Halie's curious fingers from her own mouth. Senneth, beside Degarde, turned to him with a smile. "You speak as someone with vast experience," she said. "Do you have children as well?"

"I have not yet had the fortune of taking a bride," he replied. Senneth guessed he was a few years younger than she was—perhaps thirty or thirty-one—certainly an age at which a personable young man with a little property might expect to be married. Perhaps he had suffered a bitter disappointment in love. He went on, "But in addition to Halie, I have three nieces and two nephews among my other brothers and sisters. And all of them, may I say, are just as unruly. It has led me to wonder if I might not be too faint of heart to ever attempt the task of parenting."

"Oh, I found my children a delight at every age!" Evelyn exclaimed. She had two grown sons who were long out of the house. One was a sailor and one was a soldier. "But I admit they were not *easy* children. Particularly at this age."

"Well, nothing worthwhile *is* easy," Albert said. Senneth had the distinct impression he was bored by the turn of the conversation. "Farming—commerce—soldiering—it's all work when you think of it."

Evelyn turned her attention to him. "Indeed, yes, tell us about your recent business ventures!" she said. "Are you still attempting to come to terms with your Lirren traders?"

"*Attempting* is exactly the word for it," Albert said a little ruefully. "We have conversations, they show me the raw gems, I indicate my interest, and yet nothing is ever finalized. I can't determine if they don't trust *me* or if they don't trust anyone from this side of the Lireth Mountains. If the quality of the stones wasn't so fine, and if I didn't already have a buyer in Ghosenhall who's interested, I'd be tempted to wash my hands of the whole idea."

Senneth's attention had been caught by the first mention of the word *Lirren*. The Lirrenfolk were a fierce, close-knit, insular network of families who lived just across the mountain range that marked the boundary of Gillengaria, and Kianlever was comfortably nestled right up against that range. Still, it was rare that the clans crossed the mountains for any reason whatsoever. "How did you manage to scrape an acquaintance with a Lirren man to begin with?" Senneth asked.

Albert offered a booming laugh. "I'd been tracking a wolf that had been hanging around my property, and he lured me up into the mountains, where I got caught by snow."

"I was so worried about him," Betony said.

"I got turned around in the blizzard and went down the wrong slope. Halfway down I came across a campfire and three Lirren men roasting dinner. They were so unfriendly that I figured they'd just as soon kill me as come to my aid, but they let me sit around their fire till the storm passed."

"The Lirrenfolk don't like outsiders," Senneth said.

"Quite obvious!"

"But they are used to offering hospitality to travelers, since that is the only way to cross their land," she added. "There are no inns and cities like we're used to, just these small communities of family homesteads. They can be very generous even to strangers—as long as those strangers aren't from a warring clan."

"How do you know so much about them?" Julia asked.

Oh, this was the first tricky question that could lead to more tricky questions about Senneth's complex and unconventional life. She contemplated a lie, but gave it up as being too difficult to maintain if anyone pressed for more details. "I lived with a Lirren family for a time," she said.

Degarde laid down his fork and stared at her. "*Really,*" he said. "I imagine that is a tale far more fascinating than Albert's account of his blizzard encounter."

"Maybe, but I don't wish to tell it," she said, smiling. "I'd much rather hear how Albert went from unwanted guest at the campfire to potential trading partner."

Good manners prevented anyone from indulging curiosity by asking more pointed questions. "Well, I offered to share my rations, which were accepted, and I laid down my weapons to show that I was peaceful," Albert said. "I happened to be carrying an exceptionally fine dagger, and one of the men at the fire—he looked to be about sixteen—he was quite taken with it. So I said, 'I'd be happy to leave that weapon with you in return for your kindness in sharing the fire with me.' That seemed to please all of them—if you can tell anything by the expressions on their faces—and then we all ate the food. And then we all slept. And the next morning the oldest man said if I wanted to return to this very spot in three weeks' time, he could bring me gems to look over. I formed the opinion," Albert added, "that merely by not trying to kill anyone in the middle of the night, I had displayed some kind of honor or passed some kind of test."

Senneth was laughing. "If you had tried to attack any of them while they were sleeping," she said, "you would most assuredly be dead. They are quite accomplished fighters and always eager to take up weapons. No doubt one of them stayed awake all night, watching to make sure you did not turn violent. Probably the young boy, in fact, who would have happily killed you with your own weapon."

Betony had a hand pressed to her heart. "I'm glad I knew none of this the whole time he was gone!"

"And nothing you say makes me any more confident that I will ever be able to secure their trade," Albert said. "I feel that they are still trying to determine if I am worthy of their business, but I don't know what proof they are looking for. I don't know what they consider important."

"Did you return to that spot in three weeks?" Senneth wanted to know. "Did they have jewels to sell you?"

Albert waved a hand dismissively. "Yes—just a few samples—and I handed them coins and everyone was satisfied, but it was such a meager amount. To really make this worthwhile, we need to trade in quantity. I need ten times the number of stones. But they keep stalling."

"What would you advise him to do?" Degarde asked Senneth. "What would make them trust Albert?"

She thought it over. "What matters to them more than anything is family," she said. "Generations live together in interconnected clan networks, and they can recite for you how everyone is related. While there are a few people who break free of the clans and have respectable positions within their society, for the most part, they distrust anyone who seems solitary or self-reliant." She looked at Albert. "Were you accompanied by anyone when you met with them?"

Albert shook his head. "No, I went alone."

"Then for your next visit, bring along a son or two, perhaps a couple of nephews. A brother, if you have one. None of them need to speak during your negotiations, but they should be very alert and interested in the conversations. And if one or two of them likes to brawl," she added with a laugh, "that is no bad thing. As long as he can handle himself in a fight and acquit himself with skill."

Albert looked bemused. "This is not how business is done among the Twelve Houses. I would never offer violence to a man I was trying to strike a deal with!"

"I'm curious," Degarde said. "You suggested Albert only bring male relatives with him. Are women a liability?"

"Not at all," Senneth said. "You might see a Lirren woman traveling with her brothers and husband and sons—but she would probably be older and married. The Lirrenfolk are very protective of their women. They do not let their girls marry outside the clans. But they greatly value the advice and wisdom of older women."

Albert took Betony's hand in his. "So I should bring my wife along on my next trip."

Betony looked so alarmed by the prospect that Senneth laughed again. "She would be perfectly welcome, but she would not give you as much status in their eyes as a few rough-and-tumble young kinsmen," she said.

"Curtis would be happy to go with you," Betony murmured to her husband. "And Seever! They'd love being told they should pick a fight."

"It seems like odd advice, but I am willing to try it," Albert said. "I am getting nowhere using other methods."

"You should bring Senneth with you next time you negotiate," Julia suggested. She had lowered Halie to the floor and now the little girl was crawling under the table. Senneth saw Degarde hastily scoot his chair back when Halie started prying at the buckles on his boot.

"An excellent idea!" Betony exclaimed.

"Indeed, yes, you could help me translate Lirren notions into rational behavior," Albert said.

Senneth laughed, but then she realized he was serious. "Oh—I'm not sure I would be much of an asset," she demurred.

"Well, you wouldn't be a hindrance," Albert said. "I could hardly do *worse* with the Lirrenfolk than I have done so far."

"Oh, I wish you would!" Degarde said. "Julia and I live a short ride from the Cordwains. We would love to have you among our small circle for a few days."

"What a most excellent idea," Evelyn said, giving Senneth a meaningful look. "How enjoyable for Senneth to spend a week or two among you and your friends. They all live a stone's throw from a most charming town," Evelyn added for Senneth's edification. "You would have a most enjoyable visit."

"Oh, but really—I had no thought of taking such a detour—"

"Are you on a schedule?" Betony asked. "Is someone expecting you? Could you write and ask pardon for a delay?"

This was where the vagabond's life truly failed you, Senneth thought bitterly. It was so empty that it never offered excuses. In fact, she had no deadlines at all—no reason she could not accompany these people back to their little town and live with them *forever*, should the arrangement seem appealing. "Not exactly, but—it is hard to explain," she replied somewhat desperately. "I am so used to my solitude—I do not think I would make much of a guest—"

"We would require nothing of you," Betony said firmly. "You would not even need to join us at the breakfast table if you did not want to."

"Just come with me to bargain with the Lirrenfolk," Albert

said. "You may ignore the rest of us the whole time you're there, and no one will complain."

"Well, I hope you won't ignore *me* completely," Degarde said with a warm smile. "I should like to see you now and then while you are at Albert's."

Is he flirting with me? Senneth thought a split second before the room was rent by the sound of crashing metal and a child's woeful howl. Betony muffled a shriek and Julia jumped up to race across the room. Halie had knocked over a small decorative suit of armor and now stood before the scattered visors and breastplates, sobbing with pitiful abandon. It was clear even before Julia scooped her up that the little girl had suffered nothing worse than shock—which had afflicted the rest of them as well, in varying degrees.

"I think my heart almost jumped out of my chest," Betony said, while Evelyn hurried to Julia to assure the apologetic mother that no harm was done, the suit of armor was more a nuisance than a treasure, and wouldn't Julia and Halie like to come sit down again? The final course was about to be served, and everyone would surely enjoy the fruit cobbler.

Senneth was hopeful that the noisy interruption would have made everyone forget the last few minutes of conversation, but that turned out not to be the case. "So! Senneth! Would you be willing to travel back with us and help me negotiate with the Lirrenfolk?" Albert asked.

"How soon are you expecting to meet with them again?" she said, praying that the lead time would be so long that no one could reasonably expect her to linger.

"Next week!" Albert said cheerfully. "In fact, I told Evelyn we could only stay here two nights because I didn't want to miss my next appointment."

"I think you have no choice," Degarde said. "You *must* come."

The servants entered the room bearing platters of food as the others reseated themselves around the table. Halie squirmed out of her mother's arms the instant Julia took her chair. Senneth was not surprised to see the child duck under the table again.

"I think you should go," Evelyn said.

"I consider it settled, in fact," Albert said.

She could only yield. "Then I will come just long enough to meet your Lirren friends," Senneth said. "I hope I will be able to do you some good."

Betony was tasting the cobbler. "Mmm, Evelyn, this is delicious! How did you get fruit at this time of year?"

Senneth missed the answer because something clutched at her leg through the thin fabric of her skirt. She pushed her chair back and found Halie clinging to her knee.

"Up," the girl said, releasing her grip and holding her arms out. This seemed like the invitation to go to Albert's—impossible to refuse—so Senneth swung the little girl onto her lap, where she balanced precariously.

"Oh—I'm sorry—you can give her back to me," Julia said, half rising from her chair.

"No, I don't mind," Senneth said. Which was only half a lie. The little girl watched her with huge, intent blue eyes and put out a tiny hand to explore Senneth's face. A sticky pat on Senneth's cheek, on her nose, a finger perilously close to gouging out Senneth's eye. Then Halie laid her small palm flat against Senneth's forehead and made a clucking noise.

"Feeber?" she asked.

"What?" Senneth responded.

Julia groaned. "She's asking if you have a fever. I put my hand on her forehead whenever I think she's sick."

"Feeber?" Halie repeated. "Hot?"

Senneth flicked a quick look at Evelyn and glanced away. Senneth's skin was invariably warm to the touch, a consequence of the banked fire always slumbering in her veins. Halie was not so far off. "No fever," Senneth said firmly. "I'm quite healthy."

Julia had gotten to her feet and circled the table to pluck Halie from Senneth's lap. "I keep thinking she'll fall asleep," the young widow said. "Usually by this time of day she's ready for a nap." She set Halie on her feet and said, "Your doll is in the basket in the corner. Why don't you play with her while we finish our meal?"

Halie obediently trundled off, and for a moment they all had leisure to eat and appreciate their cobbler. Talk turned to news about friends and nobles unknown to Senneth, so she was able to drop out of the conversation until Degarde addressed her.

"I hope you will come visit Julia and me while you're staying with Albert," he said.

"Your sister lives with you?"

"Yes—for now, at any rate. Her husband died suddenly a year ago, and Halie, as you can see, is quite a handful. So I moved them into my house, which has been good for both of them, but I think Julia is trying to find a reason to move on." He smiled. "She keeps urging me to look around for a wife, which leads me to think she is looking for a husband. Or else she plans to seize on that excuse if I ever do marry. 'Oh, see, your wife wants me out of the house!' And she'll be gone."

Senneth laughed. "Well, then, you must oblige her!"

He sipped his water. "Prospects have been thin in my neighborhood. Perhaps I need to travel to Kianlever Court and look around."

"Or even Ghosenhall," Senneth said. "Many noble ladies visit the royal city."

He gestured at his clothes with both hands. "I am not so fine a man myself that I require a truly noble wife. Just someone who interests me and has the skills and intelligence to act as a reasonable partner."

Senneth hadn't given much thought to a love match herself, but that description struck her as drearily devoid of passion. It had been clear to her for a long time that she would never marry, but if she *had* been looking for a husband, she would have had wholly different requirements. She would want someone who filled her mind, who shaped her days, someone whose mere presence brought her to life, whose absence felt like death.

She hardly expected to stumble across such a man in her aimless wanderings.

"I would think such a woman would be possible to find," she replied, "*somewhere* among the Twelve Houses."

"So, tell me," he said, "which of the Houses do you call home?"

"Oh, I travel so much that I really have no allegiance to one region," she replied.

He cocked his head to one side, trying to dig beneath the answer. "And no allegiance to the family where you were born, I take it."

She was *not* going to talk about this. "Correct."

He took the rebuff. "Then I hope you have managed to replace parents and siblings with a multitude of friends."

"Indeed, my friends represent quite an astonishing variety! From noblewomen to blacksmiths to Lirren clansmen. I am quite rich in my acquaintances."

"Then I think—" he began.

His words were lost in a sudden hysterical shrieking. Senneth's instant reaction was to leap up and gaze around wildly. She saw all the other guests on their feet and screaming. Evelyn, pointing and fainting. Julia, racing across the room.

Halie, contorted before the fire, her dress blazing around her tiny body, her arms waving in the air, her face a howling mask of terror and pain.

Senneth didn't even think. She flung her hands out and felt the power snap from her body in a great, dark, rolling wave.

Every fire went out. The grate was cold. The candles steamed with smoke. Halie was stunned to silence, her dress falling in charred ribbons from her small frame, her arms still outstretched. Across the width of the room, Senneth could not judge if the girl's skin had been burned, though her face looked untouched.

Julia reached the child a second later, falling to the floor beside her, sobbing and pulling at the incinerated dress. Degarde was moments behind her, followed by Betony and Albert. Evelyn was at the door, issuing orders to the servants. *"Bring us water and salve and dressings!"*

Senneth stood at the table and let her arms fall, feeling the inevitable wash of adrenaline flare up and down her veins, awaiting the next call to action. Halie had started crying again, but it was the hiccupping, nervous kind of weeping that indicated distress rather than pain. Senneth was pretty sure she had doused the flames before they had done any real damage. *But Bright Mother burn me,* she thought savagely. *That child is going to kill herself before she's three years old.*

Senneth estimated she had five minutes before the other guests started asking her questions. She remained standing before the table, waiting.

~

In fact, Degarde broke away only a moment later and crossed the room to Senneth's side. "She is unhurt," he said, his voice threaded with both amazement and relief. "It seems the clothing caught fire but the flames did not have time to reach her skin."

"I didn't even see her approach the fire," Senneth said.

"No. She's very quick. You would not believe the kinds of accidents that occur around her. Well, you have seen two of them today."

"No wonder Julia wanted her brother's assistance to raise the child."

Degarde was watching Senneth very closely. She was a tall woman, but he could look her straight in the eye, and his expression was intent. "You put that fire out," he said. "From across the room. You controlled it."

Senneth would have thought everyone else was still focused on Halie—certainly Julia was—but Betony and Albert and Evelyn caught Degarde's words. Evelyn laid her hand on Albert's arm and pulled him back toward the table.

"What's that? What's he saying?" Albert demanded. The little girl's near disaster had shaken him considerably. His jovial aspect had completely given way to a set look of solemnity.

Degarde gestured toward the fireplace. "Senneth. She waved her hands and the flames went out. *All* the flames in the room. Possibly in the entire house."

"Just this room," Senneth said coolly. She could hear, as if they were melodies being played in different keys, the fires in the kitchen grate and the downstairs parlor and the upstairs bedroom snapping and spitting. She could feel their gradations of heat brush along her skin as if they were breezes wafting in from a long and windy desert. "I can control exactly what my power touches."

"Your power," Albert repeated stupidly. He still had not comprehended what had happened.

Degarde had. "You're a mystic," he said, his voice flat and accusatory.

Senneth nodded. "I am."

Albert actually stepped back at that. "A mystic? A—but that is—you can practice magic? You can cast spells?"

"I can call fire," Senneth said. "And I can put it out. That is all my power encompasses."

That was a lie, actually. A mastery of fire was her ultimate accomplishment, but Senneth had a little skill at some of the other magical talents as well. She could alter her appearance slightly, like a shape-shifter; her hands possessed an ability to heal, if the wound or illness was obvious and simple. It didn't seem necessary to mention these details.

Albert swung his big head to look at Evelyn. "You introduced us to a mystic?" he asked.

Evelyn put her hands on her hips. "Senneth is my kinswoman, and a kinder, braver, more generous person you are unlikely to find!" she said fiercely. "Yes, she's a mystic, but she has been persecuted for no reason! She has just saved that girl's life! If you are so shallow and narrow-minded that you cannot tolerate another human being just because she is different from you, just because you don't understand her, even when she has never done you any harm, and indeed she has done you great good, then—then—"

It was clear that in the heat of her defense, Evelyn had lost the thread of her argument. Senneth patted Evelyn's shoulder. "Peace," she said. "I am not hurt or offended. Do not lose your friendships over me. I'll leave the house. I'm happy to go."

"You will *not* go!" Evelyn said. "*They* will go if they cannot accept you!"

"It is just that no mystic has ever come my way before," Albert said awkwardly. "Everyone says such dreadful things about them—but you are far from dreadful—that is—"

"I have been taught to despise them," Degarde said quietly. "And yet, you are as far from despicable as it is possible to be."

Senneth almost laughed. "Well. I suppose that is a compliment. But I do not want to make you uncomfortable. We can all part now, quite civilly. I will ask no more of you than that you not be so quick to judge the next mystic you meet."

She wanted to step away from the table, out of the room, out of the tense situation, but Degarde deliberately put a hand on her shoulder. "Stay," he said. "You have not given us an opportunity to recover from our shock. You have not given us a chance to express our gratitude. A mystic has saved my niece's life. Therefore, I must feel admiration for all mystics."

Betony and Julia were now crossing the room, Julia holding a sniffling Halie in her arms. The little girl was wrapped in a soft white blanket, since her ruined clothes had been stripped away, but Senneth didn't see any gauze dressings peeking out. Had she truly caught the fire before it had time to scar the child's delicate flesh? That fact alone would sweeten any bitterness this encounter would bring.

"How is she?" Senneth asked.

"Unharmed," Julia said, her voice low and her face haunted. She was staring at Senneth much as Degarde had done previously. "You saved her. Before the flames could touch her."

"I'm a mystic," Senneth said, in case Julia hadn't been paying attention.

"Thank you," Julia whispered. Cradling Halie to her chest with one arm, she threw her other arm around Senneth's neck. The child whimpered faintly between their bodies. "Thank you so much."

Senneth patted her on the back a couple of times and then pulled away. "I'm glad I was able to work so fast. I'm glad she's whole. I hope you are able to keep her out of trouble once you're all back home."

"But you're coming with us when we go," Betony said.

"That no longer seems appropriate," Senneth replied. "A mystic is not so welcome as an ordinary woman."

"She is *twice* as welcome," Degarde said fiercely.

"Yes, yes, please come with us," Julia begged. "I will feel much safer with you nearby. Not that I think Halie will stumble into another fire, but—"

"You will not want to have to explain me to your friends," Senneth said.

Albert seemed to make up his mind. Unlike Betony, who had not been surprised to begin with, and unlike the siblings, who had been converted by gratitude, Albert had seemed to have the hardest time accepting Senneth's change in status. "We will tell them nothing. You are our friend and we have invited you to visit us," he said.

"Excellent. Then that's settled," Betony said, before Senneth could find another reason to protest. "We will be so happy to have you."

"Yes," Degarde said, giving Senneth a meaningful look. "We will be delighted."

~

One good thing about establishing yourself as an eccentric, Senneth thought cynically a couple hours later, was that everyone was willing to allow you some latitude in your behavior. So after the exciting lunch, when Julia and Halie withdrew to recover and the men settled down for a game of cruxanno, Senneth excused herself to check on the project she had considered finished three days ago. With the vague comment that she wanted to examine the destroyed cottages, she paused to resume her ordinary attire and then slipped from the house. She strolled down the main street of the village to find the ruins of the cottages still under a coverlet of snow, though the road itself was cleared, if a bit muddy. She paused a moment beside one of the tumbled structures, imagining that she still could catch a whiff of acrid smoke coiled under the fresh, clean layer of snow.

A few of the villagers who passed made a point of nodding or even coming up to thank her for her service. Senneth was feeling rather pleased with herself when a bent old woman waddled up, leading a shaggy pony.

"So I suppose everyone in town is singing your praises, calling you some kind of savior," the woman spit out, her dark eyes snapping with hostility. "But you're still a mystic! You still offend the Pale Mother! And the goddess will strike you down, never you doubt it."

Senneth usually exited such encounters as promptly as possible, making no attempt to defend herself, but today had been filled with enough emotional reverses to make her a little reckless. Anger seeped past her usually hard-held control. "At least my aim in life is to bring goodness to the world," she replied. "At least I am not screaming invective at complete strangers, or trying to stone them in the street."

The woman's face reddened in fury, and she dug for something buried in a deep pocket. "The goddess wants to cleanse the world of heretics like you!" she cried.

"I am not afraid of the Silver Lady," Senneth said.

Now the woman pulled free a short silver chain hung with a glowing white gem. "But your flesh will still be seared by the touch of the Pale Mother's moonstone!" she cackled and swung the charm so it landed against Senneth's bare arm.

Senneth instinctively snatched her hand away, anticipating the burn, but in fact all she felt was a smooth coolness against her skin. "That's not a moonstone," she said, peering down at the old hag. "That's just a piece of glass. Wait—who are you?" Could it be possible—? *"Kirra?"*

The old woman broke into the most infectious laugh and shook back her thin gray hair. "It's no fun teasing you because you catch on so quickly," she complained. "But I shouldn't have tried the moonstone. I knew it wouldn't work."

Senneth was delighted. There was no antidote to stress more powerful than a visit from Kirra Danalustrous, even when she had shape-shifted into an unrecognizable form. "What are you doing here? Were you looking for me? How did you find me?" She glanced around. "Where's Donnal?"

Kirra lifted a hand to pat the nose of the pony, who shook his head till his harness jingled. "He's right here, of course. Yes, I've been looking for you. I have a message for you from King Baryn. I told him it might be weeks before I could track you down, but then, what luck! I was at Kianlever Court and someone mentioned passing through this tiny little town, where three houses had been burned to the ground with such precision that not a spark misbehaved. So I knew you had to be somewhere in the vicinity."

Senneth grinned. "And having quite an interesting time of it, may I say." She glanced around. "Can we sit and talk for a while? There's a tavern at the crossroads. Would an old woman like you be willing to share some ale with a condemned sinner like me?"

"Go in and get us a table," Kirra said. "We'll join you in five minutes looking more like ourselves."

Senneth had chosen a table in the back of the dark, cluttered tavern and was already pouring ale from a pitcher when Kirra and Donnal strolled in. Kirra was feeling unusually circumspect, apparently, for she was indeed in her natural state— greatly toned down. A serramarra of House Danalustrous,

Kirra had long golden hair and huge blue eyes that turned heads wherever she went, particularly if she was dressed in clothes that played up her charms. But today she wore that marvelous hair tied back from her face and she was dressed in a gray gown so plain it was actually dowdy; the other patrons barely glanced at her. Donnal, as usual, managed to be almost invisible as he followed her. He was slim and short, with dark hair and a dark beard, and a quiet manner that allowed him to deflect almost all attention.

They slipped into the booth across from her and Senneth handed around the rest of the glasses. "So what's the news from Ghosenhall?" she asked.

"Troubled," Kirra said, taking a sip. "Mmmm, this is good. Baryn has heard rumors of unrest among the southern Houses. His spies have reported that Gisseltess and Fortunalt seem to be raising and training troops."

"I was in Rappengrass a few weeks ago," Senneth said. "Everything was orderly as usual around Rappen Manor, but I thought some of the smaller towns and homesteads seemed uneasy. And things were equally tense in Helven. I arrived in one small town shortly after two mystics had been put to death."

"I'm afraid that's a story playing out across the middle and southern regions," Kirra said. "And Baryn is worried. He wants you to investigate the situation for him."

Senneth widened her eyes. "Investigate in what manner? What does he think I can discover?"

"I suppose he thinks you can gain access to sitting rooms and drawing rooms of the nobility," Kirra replied with a grin, "and read for him the mood of the marlords."

"I think it highly unlikely that any marlord would invite me through his doors to discuss his plans for mutiny," Senneth retorted.

Donnal grinned. Kirra bubbled with laughter. "Well, he didn't tell me *exactly* what he wished you to do," she answered. "He merely said he wanted to see you in Ghosenhall as soon as I could find you."

Senneth sighed. "I would love to be able to head for the royal city this very minute, but I have somehow become entangled with Thirteenth House nobles who need me to broker a deal for them with some Lirren traders."

"No! That is too convoluted to even be plausible. Can't you get out of it?"

"Believe me, I tried. And this was *before* they discovered I was a mystic. Now that they've learned the truth, they are even more determined to make me their friend, just to prove to themselves how open-minded they are."

"How did they find out?" Donnal inquired. "Did you set one of them on fire?"

"You know, it's so rare that I actually do that, and yet that's always the first question anyone asks me."

"Because it's so spectacular," Kirra said. "I just love seeing a human being blazed away."

Senneth gave her a warm smile. "I can let you observe the phenomenon from within your own cocoon of flame, if you like."

"She would just change into a bird and dart away," Donnal said. "And so would I," he added when Senneth turned a considering look on him.

"You didn't answer the question," Kirra said. "How'd they find out?"

"Actually, I was *saving* someone from burning. A curious little girl drew too close to the hearth and her dress caught on fire. I was able to put out the flames immediately, of course, but since I was standing across the room at the time—"

"Just as spectacular, but more likely to win you friends," Kirra decided. "But how do the Lirrenfolk fit in the picture?"

"One of the people at the luncheon owns an estate near the mountains and is trying to strike a deal. I offered a little advice and now have been hailed as an expert on Lirren commerce. Apparently we leave tomorrow for a town called Benneld where my new friend has property, and within the week we will meet with his Lirren contacts again."

"Well, wrap up this business as quickly as you can," Kirra advised. "The king is anxious to see you."

"I am not in the mood to linger," Senneth assured her. "Will you be in Ghosenhall when I arrive?"

Kirra looked at Donnal for an answer. Senneth didn't believe they communicated through some kind of wordless speech, but that they knew each other well enough to practically read each others' minds had always been evident. Despite the fact that Kirra was a serramarra and Donnal was a peasant's son, they were inseparable companions. Senneth had met them both more than ten years ago when Kirra's father had hired her to teach his daughter and his daughter's friend the finer points of controlling their own magic.

In no other context did the word *control* fit into Kirra's vocabulary. She was an unchained spirit, even more restless than Senneth, as likely to be roaming the country in the shape of a mountain lion as a woman. Those who loved her were always profoundly grateful to Donnal for loyally following her through whatever hazard or transformation her inclinations took her next.

Kirra turned those blue eyes back to Senneth. "We'll meet you in Ghosenhall," she said. "Who knows? Maybe we'll come with you on this mission for the king."

"That would be fun," Senneth said. "Are you expected back in Danalustrous anytime soon?"

Kirra waved a hand. "Oh, a few weeks won't make any difference to my father."

"And how is your father? And your sister?" Senneth asked. Talk quickly turned to news about family and friends, though Senneth didn't speak to her own family and claimed an odd assortment of friends. Still, it was an exceptionally pleasant way to spend an hour, and Senneth was sorry when the afternoon drew to a close.

"We'll go back to Ghosenhall to tell Baryn we've found you," Kirra said once they were all standing outside the tavern doors. "And if you linger too long in Benneld, we'll come looking for you there. Otherwise, expect to see us in the royal city in about ten days."

Kirra hugged her good-bye. Donnal followed suit, and the two of them set off, heading for the edge of town. Senneth was sure they would scarcely wait till they were out of sight before they changed into shapes more suited for rapid travel. She smothered a sigh of envy and retraced her steps to Evelyn's house.

Three

A day and a half later, a small cavalcade pulled out of Evelyn's drive and headed east at the first crossroads, toward the smoky Lireth Mountains already visible in the distance. Julia and Betony had made it clear Senneth was welcome to share the carriage with them, but Senneth greatly preferred horseback and the open air.

"But it's freezing out here!" Julia exclaimed. Fresh snow had fallen overnight and the temperature had plummeted. Even with their heated bricks and layers of blankets, the women and the little girl in the carriage were quickly going to feel the chill.

"I'm never cold," Senneth said. "In fact, if *you* get too cold, let me know, and I can warm up the air inside the coach."

Julia looked doubtful, but Betony said firmly, "What a most excellent skill to have. I'm sure we will be happy to draw upon it before the journey is half over."

Indeed, even the men, stoic upon their fine horses, were grateful for Senneth's magic when they rested for a few minutes about two hours into their journey. Senneth created a bubble of warm air all around them as they paused on the side of the road. It was so effective that Julia took off her topcoat as she ushered Halie into the bushes to take care of some personal business.

"The longer I am with you, the more I am beginning to appreciate magic," Albert said. "I had no idea mystics could be so useful."

She made him a little bow. "In me you see an ambassador for all things sorcerous," she said. "Just think how other kinds of power could enhance your life."

"I don't believe I know that much about the kinds of magic that exist," Albert said slowly.

"Nor do I," said Degarde, who had drawn close enough to listen. "I didn't even know there *were* different kinds."

So for the next hour of the journey, Senneth described the varieties of magic she had encountered in her travels. "There are plenty of shape-shifters, some with greater ability than others," she said. "I've seen shiftlings who can change so fast they can transmogrify in midair—from a hawk to a butterfly, say. Others take so long to make the metamorphosis that you can actually see them growing feathers on their arms and turning their fingers into claws."

"I might find that a little disconcerting," Degarde admitted. "I apologize for my weakness of spirit."

"It *is* a little disconcerting," Senneth told him. "But I have seen it often enough that I am used to it now. Other mystics can move objects through the air—lift them and throw them. Some can make water do their bidding, cause rivers to slow or underground streams to rise to the surface. I've met one or two who were so sensitive to moods and emotions that they could practically tell what you were thinking—and they could usually tell if you were speaking the truth."

"Another handy skill," Albert said. "Think how valuable such a person would be if you were negotiating with a man you did not trust."

"But consider what a disadvantage you would be at if you were the one with something to conceal!" Degarde exclaimed.

Senneth laughed. "Then I suppose magic would force everyone to be honest," she said.

Degarde gave her a sideways smile. "But aren't there times all of us want to conceal what we are thinking?" he murmured. "Even if we are not precisely interested in lying?"

"Well, take heart," she replied. "I have met very few readers and most of them had only the most rudimentary skills. They might be able to tell in a general way if your bent was for good or ill without being able to pick thoughts out of your head."

"Are there many mystics with magic like yours?" Albert inquired.

I have met no one whose magic was the equal of mine in terms of sheer power, she thought. No need to alarm them with such a boast. "Oh, fire mystics can be found everywhere," she said. "I've often wondered if blacksmiths and cooks—people who work alongside fire every day—might have a little magic in their blood. If that's what draws them to such a profession and makes them particularly good at it."

"How does someone become a mystic?" Albert asked.

She laughed. "One is born that way," she assured him. "It's not a skill you can acquire, like reading, or a disease that you can catch from someone else."

"So babies emerge from the womb breathing fire and splashing water about?" Degarde demanded.

"Some do! Those with particularly strong talents. But some don't display any evidence of magic until they're in their teens."

"And you?" Degarde asked. "When did you know?"

"I can't remember a time I couldn't call fire. It was a gift that came into the world right alongside me, I suppose."

"And your parents? Were they mystics?" Degarde asked.

"No," she said in a tone of such finality that even the curious Degarde realized he had better not pursue the topic.

"This is really quite fascinating," Albert said, and seemed to mean it. "I've never talked with a mystic before."

"You probably have," Senneth said gently. "But many mystics conceal their power, or at least they are careful not to flaunt it. There are too many people in the world who loathe and fear us. It is not safe to show off our gifts."

"Have you ever been persecuted for your ability?" Degarde asked. He was the one who kept asking the most personal questions, Senneth noticed. Albert seemed interested in the general outlines of magic, but Degarde wanted to know how magic had affected Senneth.

"Yes."

Degarde surveyed her. "And yet you seem unharmed. I cannot imagine you were stoned in the streets—and it would seem pointless to try to burn you at the stake—"

"Plenty of things can harm me," she said quietly. "Not the least of them being hatred. I have suffered for my magic more times than I can relate. But it is still the gift I cherish most of all the gifts that have been lavished upon me."

They asked a few more questions, but she was tired of the topic; she managed to turn the conversation to farming and trade, subjects very dear to their hearts. They stopped twice more to take care of personal needs and eat quick meals. There had been some talk of breaking for lunch at a tavern in a small town they passed through, but instead everyone voted to simply pause at the side of the road and bask in Senneth's manufactured summer.

The early dusk of winter was upon them as they came in sight of Benneld. It was a charming town of narrow cobble-stoned roads, well-maintained shop fronts, tidy houses, and an open central square where the residents could gather for important events. Degarde pulled his horse up next to Senneth's to point out the major sights—two taverns, a posting house, and a freighting company in which he owned an interest.

"And if you continue up that road about a mile, you will come to my place," he said, gesturing toward a narrow route that ran north up a wooded incline. "It is a very easy ride. I hope you will make it often while you are staying with Albert and Betony."

"We'll be leaving for the Lireth mountains in a day or so," she replied. *And immediately after that I will be returning to Ghosenhall.* "But I'm sure I will have time to visit you and Julia before I go."

It turned out that the carriage belonged to the Cordwains; Julia and Halie disembarked outside the stables, where their own little gig had been kept during their absence. Everyone parted with fond farewells, and then Senneth, Albert, and Betony turned south on a rutted road and traveled for another fifteen minutes before arriving at the Cordwain house.

It was bigger than Evelyn's and more formal, though still nothing to compare with a Twelfth House mansion. Senneth was shown to a bedroom that was small but filled with light. It was furnished with delicate whitewashed furniture and prominently featured pink accents in the curtains, coverlet, and wallpaper. Her travel-stained trousers and leather vests made a bad match with the frilly decor, she thought, feeling a little oppressed as she hung her clothing in the painted armoire.

She really didn't belong there. Why had she agreed to come?

To do a kind service for a friend of Evelyn's, she reminded herself. *And perhaps to win the hearts of a few people who heretofore looked askance at mystics. It is just a few days out of your life but may have far-reaching consequences for people you do not even know. Do your part with good grace, and then move on.*

～

The two days that needed to pass before Senneth and Albert set out for the mountains promised to be slow and tedious, but in fact turned out to hold more excitement than Senneth could have hoped. The very next morning, Betony took her back to the town proper so they could shop. Since there was a high probability of encountering people who were friends of Betony's, Senneth had donned her green-and-blue-striped dress and tried not to feel resentful.

"I'll have another dress made for you while you and Albert travel, and then you can wear it at the dinner party," Betony said as they stepped into a dressmaker's cozy store.

"What dinner party?" Senneth said.

"The one I shall plan for when you get back. Now, please don't refuse! I look for any excuse to entertain. I won't tell anyone your secret, of course, but I would still like the chance to show you off."

Senneth could only nod dumbly and pretend to show an interest in fabric.

They'd been in the dressmaker's shop about fifteen minutes when a swirl of music and a wave of laughter drew their attention to the window. "Oh, look, a juggler's troupe," Betony exclaimed. All of them, including the dressmaker and her two young assistants, hurried out into the crisp air to watch the performers. They were quite entertaining, tossing balls and clubs and burning torches back and forth with such rapidity that the crowd quickly expanded and often sent up choruses of approval.

There was one juggler Senneth was convinced had mystic blood. He collected toys and dolls from some of the assembled children and flung them in the air, where they hovered so long that it began to look as if they would float above Benneld for the rest of the day. In fact, only when one of the little girls began crying did the juggler let the items fall.

The show continued for about an hour, and then some of the locals invited the performers to one of the taverns for a meal. The crowd began to disperse, but Senneth saw familiar faces in those who were left behind—and they saw her. Degarde waved and carried Halie over to say hello.

"Wasn't that marvelous?" he enthused. "Such coordination! I cannot believe they haven't all been struck on the head or caught their hands on fire trying to grab those burning brands!"

"No doubt they have had such mishaps during their initial practices," Senneth said. "But they certainly presented a fine show this afternoon!"

"We were just passing through town on our way to look for you," Degarde said. "Are you free? Can you come back to the house? I brought Halie with me so Julia could have a couple hours of peace, but I am completely exhausted now and must go home to refresh myself."

"I have more errands to run. But, Senneth, why don't you go with them?" Betony said. "Degarde, you will bring her before dinner?"

"Most certainly I will. I will even get out the gig! We walked down here from the house," he explained to Senneth. "It seemed the easiest way to expend a little of Halie's limitless energy."

"I'm happy to walk," she said, and they set out on the northern road.

The hill turned out to be steeper than it looked, so conversation was a little breathless and Halie refused to make the climb on her own small feet. Degarde swung her up to his shoulder, then held on to her ankles to prevent her from kicking him in the chest. The little girl liked the extra height; she laughed and squealed as she grabbed at tree branches that overhung their pathway. Senneth heard the dry limbs rub and rustle together as Halie caught at them and then let them go.

Degarde's house was picturesquely situated in a slight valley, surrounded by closely planted trees just now denuded by winter. It was built of honey-colored stone so old that some of the edges had darkened with moss or smoke or simple age. But the black roof had the look of something newly installed and the shutters were all painted a matching color, and smoke curling out of half a dozen chimneys gave it an inviting look of warmth. What small portion of the setting was not given over to forest looked to be well-tended lawn, and Senneth spotted at least two gardens as they approached—one surely dedicated to vegetables, but the one in front no doubt riotous with color once the spring flowers bloomed.

"Very pretty," she said.

"It's not fancy, but we find it comfortable," he replied.

"That's a trade I'd make any day," she said.

A servant took charge of Halie once they were through the front door, and Degarde showed Senneth around the main floor. She made suitable comments on the books in the library and the art in the sitting room, but she kept silent about the pieces of decor that really caught her attention. In one window of every room, dangling from ribbons chosen to match the furnishings, hung glowing moonstones as big as walnuts.

Someone in this household was a devotee of the Pale Mother. And the doctrine of that particular goddess held that mystics were abominations.

Senneth felt her skin prickle just from the knowledge that the poisonous gems were so close to her body. She found it difficult to concentrate on Degarde's words as he related which ancestor had added on the north wing of the house, which matriarch had insisted on installing modern ovens.

"My father married late, not having expected to inherit the property," Degarde was saying, "and having made no attempt to ingratiate himself with the local girls! He took a bride from Gisseltess, but my mother was never very happy here. Too cold this far north, she always said. The winter before she died, she spent every spare minute huddled in front of a fire. I sometimes think it was pure frost that stopped her heart."

A Gisseltess girl. No doubt she was the one who had

brought the moonstones here, since the Pale Mother was greatly revered in the southern Houses. It was possible Degarde and Julia didn't even realize what the jewels were—just considered them pretty baubles to hang in the window and remind them of their frail mother, dead too young.

Senneth didn't ask. If he knew, he was being unforgivably insensitive to parade Senneth through his house, inches from anathema. If he didn't, she wasn't about to tell him that the touch of a moonstone could incapacitate a mystic, leave her writhing in excruciating pain. She never handed out weapons carelessly, even to people who seemed benign.

"I myself have never been troubled much by winter," she said, not knowing what else to say.

"Well, no, I suppose you wouldn't be," he said with a laugh. "Since you can scare it off with a wave of your hands."

"Do you spend much time with your Gisseltess relatives?" she asked as artlessly as possible. Not to be too melodramatic about it, she had enemies in Gisseltess. It was not a place she would willingly go.

No, and she avoided Brassenthwaite as well. If she wasn't careful, soon there would be no House in Gillengaria open to her. She shook her head to shake the thought away.

"There are a couple of aunts who used to make their way here every year or so while my mother was alive, but we have not seen much of them lately," Degarde replied. "And there are cousins, I suppose, but I doubt I've spoken to any of them for at least a decade."

That made her warm up to him again, at least a little. "You don't enjoy travel?" she asked.

"Not particularly," he said. "I like to have my own things about me, and sleep in a familiar room, and know what will be on the breakfast table in the morning." He looked a little rueful. "I sound very dull, don't I? I take it you have spent time in every House and acre in the kingdom."

"And time outside of Gillengaria as well," she said. "I have sailed as far as Sovenfeld, though I was not there long enough to say that I really saw the country."

He turned his head to give her a serious, considering appraisal. "You're so exotic," he said at last—and then actually blushed, as if that was a particularly rude thing to say. "I'm sorry. It's just that I have never met anyone like you. You don't fit my notions of—of—ordinary folk. You're not the kind of person I would usually sit down to dinner with. And yet I find you utterly fascinating. I am amazed by how much."

Bright Mother burn me, she thought. *He's not flirting after all—he's convinced himself he's besotted.* She was not good at subterfuge, but she managed to summon an easy smile and a careless answer. "But that is my goal, you see," she said. "To make you realize that mystics are a likable, genial lot—stranger than you're used to, but quite appealing in their way."

He didn't laugh, as she'd hoped. His voice was still quite serious as he replied, "I am far from certain I would feel that way about any mystic but you."

She was grateful beyond measure when Julia took that very moment to step into the room. "Halie was right—you are here!" she said, seeming very pleased to see Senneth again. "Is Degarde showing you the house? I wish you could be here in the spring. The whole place is a little gloomy at this time of year, but once the front gardens bloom it is a completely different story."

"Maybe Senneth will come back and visit us then," Degarde said.

Senneth greatly doubted it. "I am not sure yet what my schedule will be," she said. "I know I am expected in Ghosenhall soon, and after that, who knows?"

"Well, consider yourself invited," Julia said. "Anytime you happen to be near."

They continued the tour of the house, Senneth silently noting the moonstones in the kitchen, in the library, in the playroom upstairs. After they paused to partake of tea and cakes, Degarde reluctantly ordered the gig out and drove her back down the hill, through the town, and along the southern road to the Cordwain house.

"And you leave for the Lirrens tomorrow? How long will the trip take you?" he asked.

"At least three days," she said.

"I hope you will make time for me when you return," he said. "We will certainly have Albert and Betony over to dinner one night, but you and I might go out riding some morning. I promise not to bring Halie!"

"Again, I'm not sure of my schedule," she said. "Betony is already talking of a dinner party, and I must be honest with you. I am not used to so many events all piled together! Talk of so many occasions makes me want to hide in the bedroom or escape out the back hall." She was smiling as she said it, but she meant every word. She had half a mind not to return to Benneld once the conference with the Lirrenfolk was over. She could cut through the southern edge of Kianlever when she crossed the mountains and get to Ghosenhall sooner.

In fact, if she hadn't been commanded to present herself in Ghosenhall, she could stay in the Lirrens for a few weeks. No one would invite her to dinners and dances in that isolated and unwelcoming land. She could be assured of her solitude there.

But she could hardly refuse Baryn's summons. It was not just that she admired him as king and liege, though she did; she appreciated him as a friend, one who had supported her when her own family had cast her out. If he needed her, she would go to him. She would do any chore he asked.

"Don't hide from us, not just yet," Degarde said. "Give us a few more chances to prove that our society can be quite enjoyable."

"I'm sure it can be," she said. They had pulled to a stop in front of the Cordwain house and Senneth paused before jumping down from the gig. "You must understand," she said gently, "mystics are not quite tame. Your first impulse was correct. We are not the sort of folk you would invite to the dinner table—or expect to see there more than a few days running. We can be quite as likable as ordinary men and women! But we are still different."

"I know," he said simply. "I think that is why you interest me so much."

Hopeless. She mustered one last smile, then gathered up her skirts and hopped down before he could think to secure the horses and offer to assist her.

"In three days!" he called, as she waved from the front door. "I will expect to see you then!"

Four

Darkness still blackened the windows the next morning when Senneth was wakened by a furious racket at the front door. She was on her feet with a dagger in her hand before she had even registered what the commotion was about. Loud voices, raised and urgent, and the clattering sounds of footsteps gathering from all corners of the house. She heard someone utter the word *fire*.

She had pulled on a shirt and trousers and plunged out her bedroom door when Betony came running up the stairs. "Senneth—thank goodness you're awake!" Betony cried.

"What's the trouble?"

"The whole hillside north of town is in flames! And the fire is heading straight for Degarde's house—"

Most small towns could form a water brigade from the nearest well or river to put out a blaze that threatened the houses, but a wildfire sweeping through the landscape would only be stopped when it ran out of fuel or encountered a rainstorm.

"Can someone saddle my horse? I have to get closer before I can control it."

"Yes, yes, Albert has already instructed the groom to bring it around."

Degarde was among the small group of men milling about at the bottom of the stairs, and he was the first one to spot Senneth. "Thank you," he exclaimed, catching her hands as she took three steps at once to land in the foyer. "I have exposed your secret, but I didn't know what else to do."

He was streaked with sweat and grime; he must have dashed through the fire itself to reach her. "It doesn't matter, but we have no time to waste," she said, pulling free and running for the door. The groom was just now leading up her raw-boned gelding; she threw herself into the saddle and kicked it forward, trusting it to find its footing in the dark. Dawn was still at least an hour away. There would be precious little illumination to light their way until they arrived at the scene of the fire, when there would be too much.

Degarde was instantly beside her on a horse of his own. "How did the fire start?" Senneth called to him.

"I don't know! Perhaps some of the town boys were hunting yesterday and someone was careless with a campfire. And someone told me there was lightning while we were at Evelyn's house, though it never brought any rain. A small fire could have been smoldering all this time and just now blazed up."

"How big is it?"

"I couldn't see a way around it as I was coming down the hill," he answered. "It stretched too far in each direction."

She nodded and urged the horse to run faster, though they had to slow down as they crossed through town. Anxious villagers had gathered in the cold streets, shawls and cloaks thrown over their nightshirts, all of them staring with dread and fascination at the leaping red wall of devastation slowly climbing its way up the hill.

Even before they were close enough to feel the flames, Senneth could sense her temperature rising. It was as if she was a tightly wrapped bundle of kindling just waiting for a spark. The power began building in her veins; her hands were so hot that she stripped off her gloves and was almost surprised that her fingertips were not steaming in the chilly air.

They were close enough now to make the horses nervous, so Senneth jumped off the gelding and tossed his reins to Degarde. "Hold him," she said. "Stay back."

"What are you doing?" he cried after her, but she paid no attention. She just gathered all her strength and ran uphill as fast as she could, into the heart of the fire.

Every sense was assaulted with heat, scent, sound, vertigo. The air was too hot to breathe. Senneth felt her throat crisp as she tried to inhale, and her uncovered skin felt as if it would melt to the bone. She was surrounded by leaping, chaotic sheets of fire, scarlet and gold and edged with black. Impossible to tell which direction she faced, impossible to determine where the line of fire ended, or if it ran on to engulf the entire country. Around her, trees crashed to the ground, squealing as their highest limbs splintered apart and groaning as their massive trunks were clawed in two. Primitive and triumphant, the blaze roared out an incomprehensible language of jubilant rage.

Senneth raised her hands and spread her fingers wide and gathered all that heat and fury and power inside her.

She felt the fire twist and snap at her like a rabid cur. Calmer than stone, she held her place, bent her fingers back a little to widen the reach of her palms. Inexorably, she drew the fire closer and closer to her. She opened her hollow bones, she emptied her veins, to allow the flames to rush unchecked through her body. Her fever spiked even higher—surely her skin must be glowing. She flung her head back, her blond hair no paler than the yellowest crown of flame, and soaked up the conflagration like so much spilled wine absorbed into a heavy cloth. Around her, the fire stuttered and grew docile. The high, ragged curtains of flame descended, huddled low, collapsed upon themselves in great smoking strips of char and cinder.

Behind her, she heard a growing mutter of wonder and confusion—just as wordless, at least for the moment, as the fire's expression of glory and wrath. Her own orientation was suddenly peculiar; she dropped her hands and straightened her back and felt a little wobbly on her feet. Was she facing uphill or down? Was she sitting or standing? She shifted her weight and looked around her at the blackened and unfamiliar landscape and tried to focus her mind.

Running footsteps behind her made her whirl around and fling out a hand, still red with heat. "Don't touch me!" she warned. "You'll scald yourself."

It was Degarde, of course, who had presumably given the horses over to someone else's charge, but right behind him were about a dozen villagers. Everyone was staring, but some of them looked amazed and some looked horrified. Senneth noticed several of the older residents clutching moonstones in their fists.

"Senneth—are you—do you need—why can't I touch you?" Degarde panted, coming so close he could have swept her into an embrace.

"I am hot with magic," she said, glancing over his shoulder as she spoke to see if any of the townspeople flinched at the words. There were one or two that she noticed, and probably a few she didn't. "It will take some time to dissipate."

"Thank you for saving my house," he said. "For putting out the fire. I still can't—I watched you do it, and I still don't—it seems impossible anyone could have such a gift—"

"Mystic!" someone called out from the gathering crowd. Senneth couldn't tell who spoke, but she saw a few others nodding their heads.

Degarde spun around. "Mystic indeed," he said angrily. "But one who has risked herself to save all of *you* from burning in your beds. You should be grateful! You should thank her! Not call her names."

The muttering mostly subsided, but Senneth saw a few people in the crowd exchange troubled glances. "Never mind," she said in a low voice to Degarde. "I'll be on my way in an hour or so. They can talk about me all they want then."

He looked astonished. "You're still planning to leave for the Lirrens? *Now?*"

"Don't worry. The fire is well and truly out. You and some of the local men might start clearing away debris, but trust me when I say there are no sparks lingering in the wood, waiting to reignite."

He came a step closer, half lifting his hand. It was clear he really wanted to disobey the injunction against touching her. "You misunderstand," he said. "My concern is for *you*. I don't know what toll magic takes on a mystic, but surely such a display must drain you of all strength. Shouldn't you wait a day or two before setting out again?"

Senneth couldn't help laughing. If anything, she felt energized by the encounter with the wildfire; she felt as if she had ingested its elemental exuberance through her pores. "I am not so easily overset," she replied. "In fact, I am more restless than ever and eager to get on the road. I am glad," she added, "that I was here to beat the fire down. I'm not sure how easily you and the people of Benneld would have contained it on your own."

He glanced over his shoulder at the townspeople, most of whom had started to disperse, and then fell in step with Senneth as she began making her way down the hill. "Yes, but there was a cost," he said. "Now you have been identified as a mystic, and there are those who will hate you for that reason alone, no matter how much good you do for them."

She shrugged. "That is the true cost of magic," she said. "And one of the reasons no mystic stays for long in any one place. The welcome tends to disappear very quickly."

"It shouldn't," Degarde said.

They had reached the horses by now, both sets of reins being held by a thin boy who eyed Senneth with frank appraisal. She approached her big gelding with caution, afraid her elevated temperature might cause him to sidle away, but he merely stamped his feet and then turned his head to nose her for a treat.

"Thank you for holding him," she said to the boy as she swung into the saddle.

"I never watched over a mystic's horse before," he said.

"I hope it was not too onerous," she replied pleasantly. She tossed him a coin, since money sometimes helped people forget what they didn't like about someone else, and he gave her a brilliant smile.

"Never been touched by a mystic, either," he said hopefully. She gave him a closer inspection. He looked like he might be ten years old, the curious type who found adventure or trouble wherever he went.

"Eric," Degarde said in a disapproving voice, but Senneth laughed. Her body was still burning up, but she thought she was cool enough now that she wouldn't leave a permanent mark if she touched the boy. So she leaned from the saddle and pressed her hand against his smooth cheek. He gasped but held perfectly still, his face a study in delight, fear, and wonder. When she pulled back, the red imprint of her palm was clearly visible on his skin.

"Now you have," she said. "May you remember the experience a long time." And she kicked the horse forward and picked her way down the hill, back to the Cordwain house.

❧

Two hours later, a party of six set out on the winding eastern road that would take them over the Lireth Mountains. At first, conversation was wholly about the fire and Senneth's miraculous ability to control it, but since she contributed nothing but a smile to that particular topic, eventually her fellow travelers turned their attention to other subjects. Senneth still didn't talk much, but spent the first few hours of the journey forming her opinions of the men Albert had recruited to accompany him on his visit to the Lirrens.

On the whole, she liked them, and she was impressed at how quickly Albert had been able to round up suitable male relatives to enhance his stature with the Lirren traders. One was an uncle, a gaunt, severe man with a watchful face and a quiet way of speaking; Senneth thought he was just the sort who would impress the Lirrenfolk. One was a brother who appeared as genial as Albert, if not quite as prosperous.

Two were nephews born to Albert's sisters. Seever and Curtis were both in their early twenties, friendly, boisterous, and energetic. They reminded Senneth of half-grown puppies whose feet were still a little too big for their bodies. Still, they could both fight, which she learned over lunch when she invited them to engage in battle against her.

"You can call up fire from your fingertips *and* you can wield a sword?" Curtis demanded. "How many skills can one woman have?"

"Apparently, as many as she likes," Senneth replied with a grin. "So, yes, I can wield a sword. Now I want to know if you can."

He looked at Albert, who merely nodded. Albert hadn't seen her fence, of course, but clearly he had come to the conclusion that she could do almost anything. "Very well," Curtis said. "But I don't want to hurt you."

It was obvious pretty quickly that he wouldn't be able to, even though he rapidly abandoned the notion that he had to hold his strength in check. They struck and parried for a good ten minutes before Senneth signaled the fight over.

"Not bad," she said. "You've obviously practiced."

"So have you!" he exclaimed. "Where did a woman learn to fight like that?"

She laughed. "Everywhere I had to." She motioned at Seever. "Let's see what you can do."

Seever wasn't as strong as Curtis, but he was faster and a little more disciplined. She was quite pleased with both of them when she called a halt to the exercise. "I think the Lirrenfolk will like you," she said.

"Will they really want to fight with us?" Curtis asked.

"Most Lirren fighters are fairly skilled," she said. "There's a lot more day-to-day violence than you're likely to see here in Gillengaria, so they have to know how to handle themselves. But fighting is also a sport with them, and they're proud of their abilities. They'll give you a real challenge—so do your best. They'll respect you for your effort, even if you don't beat them."

They were halfway up the mountains by nightfall and made a sketchy camp. "Don't bother with a fire," Senneth said, and used magic to keep them all warm through the night. They were up with the dawn and soon picking their way across the peak. By midday they were halfway down the mountain and within hailing distance of a small party climbing up to meet them.

The two groups came to a halt on a sort of natural terrace, rocky and littered with snow, but relatively level and wide enough to hold them all. There were eight in the Lirren party, including one woman, and Senneth could see on all their faces approval of Albert's entourage.

She hung back to let the men discuss business. She would mediate if anyone wanted her opinion, but she had already given Albert all the advice she could think of, and she didn't have any skills particularly helpful at a negotiating table. So she watched the older men of both groups hunker down to parlay, while the three Lirren boys and Albert's nephews began circling each other and commenting on weaponry. Soon enough, she knew, a friendly scuffle would ensue. At least she hoped it would be friendly.

She approached the Lirren woman, who had picked a spot to begin laying out pans and utensils. She might have been brought along for her sound business insights and good judgment of people, but she was obviously planning to contribute to the success of the expedition by cooking the meals as well.

"I'll help, if you like," Senneth offered. "I know a little about Lirren spices."

The woman looked up from where she was kneeling on the hard ground. Like most Lirrenfolk, she had fine features and a closed, composed expression. These were not people moved to easy smiling. Her hair was a well-brushed brown, just now pulled back in a neat braid. Through the woven plaits, Senneth could make out occasional streaks of lighter blond, dyed into the hair in the pattern of this woman's clan.

"Indeed, I have seen you at gatherings before this," the woman replied.

That sharpened Senneth's interest. She seated herself across from the woman and studied her face more closely. Yes—a little familiar—Senneth might have met her once at a wedding or feast day. "I have kin among the clans, but I don't believe you are among them," Senneth said. "I was adopted into the Persal family."

"I am Derling," the woman replied.

Senneth had to think a moment, but she was pretty sure the Derlings claimed only friendship with the Persals, not blood ties. "A good family," she said. "My name is Senneth."

"Mine is Rinnae."

"Did we meet during the time I lived on this side of the mountains?"

"There was a feast in my sister's homestead that you attended with the Persal family," Rinnae replied. "You helped in the kitchen. There had been rain for days, and yet you made the wet wood burn so that we could bake salt bread and broil the meat."

"I remember that feast," Senneth said. The kitchen had been crowded and cheerful, the older women working tirelessly, the younger ones gathered in the corners to whisper about boys and complain about their mothers. "Even with my help, the wood didn't want to burn! I remember the room being very smoky."

"And yet the meal was delicious," Rinnae said.

Senneth nodded. "As are all meals prepared by loving hands."

Rinnae handed Senneth a small knife and bag of root vegetables. "You might peel and chop those," she said.

It looked like Rinnae planned to simmer a big pot of soup over a small fire, not a meal that was quick to make. Apparently, she expected the negotiations to go on for some time. Senneth pulled out the first lumpy tuber and began methodically to pare it. "I hope everyone in your family is well," she said.

It was a traditional invitation to conversation, and Rinnae obliged, detailing her daughter's upcoming wedding and the antics of her young grandson. "And your family?" she asked in return.

"The last time I heard from Ammet, the Persals were thriving," Senneth said. "I would be happy to hear it if you have any current news."

Rinnae gave her a sharp look from dark eyes. "Do you not have family in Gillengaria?" she asked. "Are all of *them* well?"

The question caught Senneth off guard. It was rare that the Lirrenfolk acknowledged that anyone outside of the clans even existed. "I have not been blessed in my blood family, as you have been," she returned lightly.

Rinnae glanced expressively at Albert and his relatives, now squatting on the ground around some crudely drawn map and arguing in a friendly way with Rinnae's menfolk. "Did no one on the other side of the mountains adopt you as the Persals did? Are you not kin with the men you accompanied here today?"

"They are friends," Senneth said. And not even close friends, by any sort of reckoning. If Rinnae realized that Senneth had known them barely a week, she would be astonished at how much effort Senneth had put into their well-being.

Even without that piece of knowledge, it was clear that Rinnae disapproved. "Do you have no one, then, that you would call on as kin, whether born to you or bound to you by ties of deep affection?"

"I am *bahta lo*," Senneth said. It was a Lirren phrase meaning "above the clans" and usually applied to a handful of restless, solitary women who declared themselves free of family interference. They generally passed their lives as itinerant healers or peacemakers.

"Even a woman who is *bahta lo* occasionally finds a hearth where she can rest," Rinnae said. "Even a woman who is *bahta lo* sometimes needs the arms of the clan about her."

It made Senneth feel peculiar to receive such an admonition from a Lirren matron—a stranger, yes, but part of a tradition that Senneth had learned to respect deeply. She felt chastised, vaguely depressed, clearly in the wrong. So she might have reacted if King Baryn himself chided her for misconduct. "I can claim a few souls who love me," she protested. "I am not entirely friendless."

"It is not right for anyone to be alone," Rinnae said sternly.

"I like it," Senneth said.

Rinnae gave her one long, close inspection before she said, "No. You do not."

There didn't seem to be any answer to that, so Senneth didn't attempt to make one. She and Rinnae worked in near-silence for the next hour, stirring the soup and mixing a loaf of bread. Oddly enough, despite the previous conversation, the silence was companionable, and Senneth felt a sense of deep satisfaction once the meal was ready to serve.

Everyone ate heartily, and, following the lead of the Lirren men, who praised the cooks lavishly, Albert and his relatives thanked Rinnae and Senneth profusely for their efforts. After the meal, the young men engaged in a series of wrestling matches and impromptu duels. Seever and Curtis managed to win about one out of every four contests, which seemed to please everyone, and in between bouts they paused to argue about technique. The older men seemed to ignore the younger ones, but Senneth saw that the Lirren elders always registered when their boys were victorious, and Albert wore a small smile whenever Curtis and Seever triumphed.

It was near dusk, and the wistful colors of a winter sunset were threading their way through the mountains, when Senneth heard the Lirren leader pronounce, "We are agreed, then."

"We are agreed," Albert replied.

"We will return here in ten days," the Lirren man said.

"We will be waiting."

Almost faster than seemed possible, the Lirrenfolk packed up and broke camp. Rinnae gave Senneth a meaningful look as she nodded farewell, but there were no spoken good-byes as the Lirrenfolk mounted their horses and began weaving their way down the mountain. The Gillengaria men stared after them, a little bemused, as the others disappeared into the deepening dark.

"I wouldn't want to travel at night through this terrain," Albert's brother observed.

"There are some Lirrenfolk who can actually see in the dark," Senneth said. "They worship the goddess of night and they feel her protection most keenly once the sun has gone down. Don't be concerned about them."

"Well, *we'll* camp here tonight," Albert said briskly, already turning back toward the fire.

Senneth waved a casual hand at the drooping flames, to revive them against the gathering chill. "I take it you got the deal you wanted?"

Albert laughed. "I suppose no one gets the deal he wants from a Lirren man, but we made an arrangement we both liked," he said. "I must commend you on all your advice. It was clear he was pleased to see my family around me."

"He liked seeing his sons beat us in combat," Curtis said a little despondently.

Albert laughed again. "Maybe, but he didn't finalize the deal until *you* won that last bout. I think he was looking for proof that we are not weak men."

"Strange, isn't it?" Albert's uncle said meditatively. "What *we* wanted from *them* was proof of the quality of their merchandise. Maybe they have the right of it. Learn the character of your potential partner, and that will tell you all you need to know about the goods he trades in."

They busied themselves preparing the camp for what was promising to be a frigid night, though Senneth's presence obviously made that fact a very minor concern. She didn't feel compelled to cook any more meals for the traveling party, so she fenced with Curtis while Albert and his brother put together cold rations. They all talked for a couple of hours before seeking their beds.

Not until she was rolled up in her sleeping blanket, drowsily watching the razor-edged stars, did it occur to Senneth that she was happier tonight than she had been in the past two weeks. She didn't think it was just the fact that she was on the eastern side of the Lireth Mountains, just barely over the border into the Lirrenlands. It was because she was outdoors, on the move, cut loose from formalized social obligations. It was because she knew she would be traveling again tomorrow, and on her way again as soon as she could politely leave Benneld behind.

Rinnae was wrong. Senneth didn't need family. She scarcely needed friends. She needed only motion, and the occasional kiss of magic, and she was content.

Five

They were back in Benneld a day and a half later, having struggled through a snowfall on the western slopes of the mountains. Albert's relatives continued on, waving good-bye and calling out promises, but Senneth and Albert went directly to the Cordwain house.

"Don't you look bedraggled," Betony greeted them at the door. "I'll order hot baths at once for both of you! Was your trip successful?"

"Very," Albert said. "I hope Senneth comes back to advise me the next time I try to negotiate with a Lirren clan."

She shook her head. "I think I've already given you all the guidance I can."

Betony turned to her with a smile. "Senneth, your new dress is ready! Come try it on. I have planned a dinner for the day after tomorrow, so if it doesn't quite fit, there will be plenty of time to alter it."

The day after tomorrow, Senneth thought. *That means the day after that I can leave.*

The new dress was a deep green Senneth liked a great deal, though it was a little too frilly for her taste, with ribbons and lace accentuating the collar and the waist. She had insisted that the neckline be much higher than Betony wanted, with the result that it covered up even the simple gold necklace that she always wore.

"Very elegant," Betony said. "If a little prudish."

Senneth laughed. "But then, I am the demure and retiring type."

Betony inspected her for a moment. "For some reason, I don't believe that," she said. "I have the feeling you could cause no end of turmoil and chaos if you wanted to. You could bring the entire village down with one sweep of your hand."

It was odd to have someone look at her and say such a thing. "I could, I suppose," Senneth said. "But I have never been moved to practice destruction."

"I wonder what it would take to push you to it," Betony said.

Senneth laughed uncomfortably. "Let us hope neither of us ever finds out!"

Dinner was quiet and bedtime was early. Senneth was restless from the minute she got out of bed the next morning. Restless enough that she was even happy to see Degarde when he came calling before the sun had risen very high.

"We saw your group return yesterday afternoon," he told her. "Are you refreshed enough to go riding this morning? I'll understand if you're not."

"I find it much more tiring to sit around doing nothing," she assured him. "Let me just call for my horse."

A few minutes later they were following a rather overgrown trail that led in a southwesterly direction away from the Cordwain house. It was wide enough to ride side by side, though barely, and they had to keep the horses to a walk to avoid any hazards that might be covered by fallen leaves and lingering snow.

"How was your visit with the Lirrenfolk?" he asked.

"Successful, Albert tells me. I didn't participate in the negotiations. Did anything exciting occur in town while we were gone?"

"No, nothing. Even Halie failed to provide excitement, because she was sick in bed the whole time. So she couldn't knock things over or try to put clothing on the dogs or disappear from the estate so completely that every soul on the property had to search for her for hours, terrified of finding her dead in the forest."

"That *was* a stroke of luck," Senneth said. "Though I suppose you and Julia will come down with the ailment next, and no one will be well enough to contain her."

"Thank you for that thought," he said. "It makes me look forward to the rest of the week."

Senneth enjoyed that part of the conversation, but soon enough he was asking her searching questions that she didn't feel like answering. What part of the country had she grown up in? Had she any family at all? What were her plans once she left Benneld? Couldn't she stay just a little longer—another week, perhaps? Would she be traveling back toward Kianlever anytime in the near future?

"If I wanted to get in touch with you sometime," he finished, "how would I do it?"

She smiled, but she felt uncomfortable. Why would Degarde want to get in touch with her? More to the point, why would she want to hear from him? "I am usually back in Ghosenhall at least a couple of times a year," she said. "People who want to reach me can leave a message at the palace."

"I should feel awe that I am speaking to someone who is on such terms of intimacy with the king," he said in his intense way. "And yet, all I can think is, 'Of course Baryn values Senneth! She is so amazing that he would be a fool *not* to appreciate her talents.'"

"It is I who feel gratitude that he allows me to serve him," she said quietly. "He is an excellent king and a good man. It is a privilege to be among those he trusts."

They rode for about an hour, the exercise restoring Senneth to her good mood—which was helped along immeasurably by the appearance of an energetic sun that chased away much of the chill. "Let's go on into town and get something to eat," Degarde suggested just as they came within view of the Cordwain house, and Senneth was feeling cheerful enough, and hungry enough, to agree.

Practically everyone who lived within a five-mile radius of Benneld must have had the same thought, for the streets were crowded with carts, horses, pedestrians, and vendors. They left their own horses at the overflowing stables and promenaded down the main road like everyone else. Degarde introduced Senneth to a handful of people, some of whom she recognized as witnesses to the hillside fire a few days ago. None of them seemed delighted to see her again, though they were civil enough. Eric, the boy who had held their horses, waved at her when she passed, then leaned over to whisper something to a friend. Senneth spotted Julia and Halie inside the dressmaker's shop, Halie with her little face pressed against the window. Even Betony had come to town to pick up supplies, and she laughed as she came across Senneth and Degarde sauntering by.

"If I'd known you were coming here, I'd have asked you to run some errands for me," Betony said.

"I'd be happy to carry home flour and cheese and anything else you might need," Senneth replied.

"No, I think the kitchen is stocked, but I wanted new linens for the table and—Oh, Senneth, your dress won't be ready till tomorrow! I had hoped to bring that back home this morning."

"I can come fetch it tomorrow," Senneth said. "It's not like it's a taxing ride into town."

"Yes, but no matter how careful you are, it is sure to get wrinkled, and it will take some time to iron it out—and I do hope the alterations are perfect, for, you know—"

Before Betony could specify any other problems, she was silenced by a piercing cry from down the street, followed quickly by a low rumble of shouts and questions. Senneth spun around to find the uproar occurring before the confectioner's shop, where a short potted tree was topped with a merry halo of fire. Townspeople had quickly mobilized to put it out, and two boys were already running up with buckets of water sloshing in their hands.

"Bright Mother brand me," Senneth muttered. Next to her, Betony exclaimed, "*Another* fire? Why is everything burning?"

Degarde was hovering at Senneth's elbow. "Can you put it out from here? Shall we get closer?"

"They seem to have it well in hand," Senneth said, not stirring a step. Indeed, the first bucket of water seemed to have doused the flames completely, but two more were tossed on for good measure. Even from the distance of a hundred feet, she could see the townspeople gesture excitedly; one or two of them started scanning the crowd as if looking for someone.

Looking for her. Looking for the mystic.

The woman who set things on fire.

"I think we'd better go home," Senneth said quietly.

But before she could move, there was another shriek, another spurt of flame. This one poked through the bare branches of a decorative shrub planted in front of one of the taverns, which was right next door to the bakery. The fourth bucket was hastily emptied onto the new eruption, and someone had the presence of mind to send more boys off to draw more water.

Which was fortunate, because another shrub caught fire, and then another one, and a stack of boxes outside the dressmaker's shop was suddenly wreathed in flame. The cries of fear became louder; women grabbed their bundles and their children and began fleeing toward the edges of town.

A wagon wheel on a stationary cart was suddenly rimmed with fire.

A bird's nest in a high gutter went up in a swift colorful burst.

A crumpled jacket on the street. Another potted plant. A flag flying outside a storefront. One after the other, brilliant with flame.

"Senneth," Betony said urgently. "Can't you *do* something?"

Degarde was regarding her with something like horror. "Senneth," he said. "You aren't—this isn't your work, is it?"

"Not mine," she said shortly, furious but unsurprised that he even asked, "but it is almost certainly enchanted fire."

Others had come to the same conclusion. More and more townspeople had searched the crowds, trying to locate Senneth, and someone cried out, "There she is!" In the way of mobs, there was a convulsive general movement in her direction and a low, angry muttering that was growing louder by the minute.

"Senneth," Betony said, "we had better get you home."

But Degarde's hand was suddenly around her left wrist. On his face was a curious expression of fear, uncertainty, and uneasy determination. "Perhaps she should wait and answer the questions of our friends."

"Degarde!" Betony said sharply. "How could you for one moment entertain the idea—"

"I don't *think* she has done anything—but I don't know. How can either of us be sure?" he said. "We scarcely know her. I think it is fair that we ask her some questions and listen to her answers."

Senneth couldn't decide which was funnier—the notion that, two hours ago, Degarde was displaying all the symptoms of a smitten suitor, or the fact that he actually thought he could restrain her by merely holding on to her arm. It didn't seem to occur to him that a woman who commanded fire could turn him into a walking inferno.

"Release me," she said to him in a quiet voice. The other townspeople were only a couple of yards away; there wasn't much time. "I will not run, but I can at least put out the fires that are raging now."

He kept his hold. "Even if they are not your own?" he said.

She was too annoyed to answer. Without bothering to argue, she lifted her right hand and made one comprehensive pivot, so that Degarde's arm ended up wrapped around her waist. She felt power flow from her fingertips with a cool and weighted presence. It was as if she covered the entire town with a heavy blanket that suffocated all the existing fires and laid a compound over the rest of the ready fuel that would make it refuse to burn.

"That should hold for a few hours at least," she said to Betony, twisting back around so that she could disentangle from Degarde as much as possible.

The crowd was upon them now, maybe twenty or thirty people, mostly men, all of them shouting. Senneth had to fight down the urge to push them back with a sudden pulse of heat.

"What have you done, mystic?" the nearest one shouted. He was tall and heavy-boned, and his face was red with rage. Senneth remembered that Degarde had introduced him as Baxter. "Are you trying to burn down our town?"

"I'll get Albert!" Betony called, picking up her skirts and racing away.

"I have done nothing," Senneth replied coolly, but her words were lost in the growing rumble.

"Mystic!" dozens of voices cried.

"Burn her!"

"Stone her!"

"Kill her!"

"I have done nothing to any of you!" Senneth shouted, trying to pitch her voice above the angry roar. "This is not my magic!"

"Mystic!" the crowd answered back. "Stone her!"

She saw a few shapes bend and straighten, as if several men had picked up rocks from the street. Something hit her on the right shoulder, and she whipped her head around to see if she could spot who had thrown the missile.

Unexpectedly, Degarde jerked her closer to him and put his free arm around her shoulder. "Let her speak!" he shouted to the crowd, trying to protect her with his own body when more rocks came flying in. "Let her answer! Do not condemn her without a hearing!"

Baxter grabbed a fold of Senneth's shirt and growled, "Speak, then!" into her face.

"This is not my magic," she said again, her voice loud and calm. "But you're right—you are dealing with sorcerous flames. Someone in this town is a mystic and playing with fire."

"You're the only mystic who's come through Benneld!" cried a voice from the back of the mob.

"I'm the only one you know of," she called back. "But there is someone among you who is trying out his power."

Now the muttering changed in tone, and for a moment, neighbors looked at each other with suspicion. Then the big man shoved his red face toward Senneth again.

"Liar," he snarled. "Just like a mystic, trying to start trouble, trying to turn friends against each other."

"Run her out of town!" someone yelled, but other voices called for more extreme measures. "Stone her! Kill her! Kill the mystic!"

Degarde held her even more tightly. "No!" he cried. "You will not harm her! Not without proof!"

"She's a mystic—what more proof do you need?" a woman shrilled out, but a few other voices were raised in favor of a more temperate approach.

Baxter now thrust his face at Degarde. "What kind of proof? We've already seen what she can do with fire."

"We will hold her a few days," Degarde said. His voice was steady, but Senneth, her back pressed against his chest, could feel the heavy pounding of his heart. "We will see if magical fire breaks out when she is not near enough to ignite it."

"I thought a mystic could fling fire from some distance away!" someone called out.

"Yes—I believe so—but we will make sure she doesn't have a chance," Degarde said. Senneth had the sense he was improvising frantically. "We will—we will bind her with moonstones. We will rely on the Pale Mother to mute her power."

"Where will you get the moonstones?" Baxter demanded.

"I've got some!" a woman offered, and half a dozen other voices seconded her.

"My house is protected by moonstones in every window," Degarde said. "And my mother left behind many pieces of moonstone jewelry. I'll slip a moonstone bracelet on her wrist. She will be safe at my house—and *we* will be safe from her."

Senneth jerked her head around to stare at him over her shoulder. "And who do you think would be stupid enough to start fires while I am in your custody?" she said scornfully. "Anyone who is operating under cover of my magic will stay in the shadows until I am free again."

Degarde stared back at her, his face a tortured mask of conflicting emotions. Fear—worry—shame—a lingering obsession—and a willingness to despise her, if she should turn out to be the villainess his neighbors believed. "It is the best I can do," he said. "I do not want them to kill you out of hand."

She was tempted, so tempted, to shoot back a mocking reply: *You have so little idea what I am capable of! I could scorch you and every soul in this town before you have time to gather your pitiful handful of rocks. You are not what holds me here for even another minute.*

"I am content to wait a day, or perhaps two," she said. "Perhaps by then they will be calm enough to realize I am no threat. But I do not think this other mystic will come forward, and I believe your entire town will still be in danger."

"*You're* the danger!" the big man shouted out. "Off she goes, then! To Degarde's house! Who will split the watches with me while the witch is under guard?"

~

It was a loud, angry, awkward procession from the town, up through the singed forest, all the way to Degarde's house. Julia and Halie had arrived ahead of them, though Julia had clearly lingered in the town square long enough to hear the verdict, for she opened the door immediately to Senneth and her captors.

"Mother's old room," she said in a constricted voice, not looking at Senneth. "I think it's best. It's small enough, and there is only the one window."

Baxter pushed past Julia into the house. "Take me there," he commanded. "I will look it over."

The rest of them crowded into the parlor while Baxter explored the house. Someone, Senneth noted, had managed to pause in town long enough to acquire a rope, and he kept coiling and uncoiling the loops in an excited, nervous fashion. They were going to do this up right then. They were really going to keep her prisoner, bound in place and subject to an inimical magic.

If she did not want to risk losing her freedom, perhaps her life, this was her last chance to scatter them all with fire and dash for the door.

She waited patiently, meekly, in Degarde's hold.

Soon enough, Baxter was back, satisfied. "The room will do," he said, "but I myself will see her safely settled."

Degarde, Baxter, and three other men escorted her up the stairs to a small room with worn, faded furnishings and a slightly musty smell. The bedchamber of Degarde's devout Gisseltess mother, Senneth supposed, still looking more or less as she had left it when she died. Yes—a single large moonstone hung in the window and a collection of smaller gems glowed balefully on an oak dressing table.

Baxter immediately started pawing through a jewelry chest and came away with delicate filigree necklaces hung with moonstone charms. He wrapped one of these around one end of the rope, then secured the rope to the foot of the four-poster bed. Senneth watched with interest. Clearly he believed that she would be unable to untie any knots decorated with moonstones. He repeated the process with the other end, and then grabbed her roughly to circle the rope around her waist. Through the fabric of her trousers she could feel the skittering heat of the small gems flickering against her skin.

Baxter turned to Degarde. "You said you had a bracelet?"

Degarde had finally released Senneth when Baxter tied the rope around her middle, and he stood there now looking wretched and unsure. "Yes, but—perhaps we don't need anything more than the moonstones on the rope."

"*Perhaps,*" Baxter said. "And what if you're wrong? She will burn the house down around your head, with all your family inside it."

"The jewels will sear her skin," Degarde said.

"That is nothing compared to what she would do to you," Baxter sneered.

Julia was already at the dresser, going through a small drawer. *She* didn't seem willing to take chances. "Here," she said, turning toward Baxter. Something dangled from her fingertips, icy cool gems of muted white fire linked by coils of silver. Baxter grabbed it with a chortle and stomped over to Senneth.

"Hold out your hand," he demanded.

"I don't think—" Degarde began, but Senneth merely extended her left arm.

When Baxter fastened the bracelet around her wrist, for a moment she thought she would scream. She felt each gem branded against her skin, a separate, specific torture; from wrist bone to elbow, her flesh flushed with an external flame. It was such a strange sensation. She was used to heat, she was accustomed to fevers raging through her blood, but this was altogether different. More like a raw scrape from a rough surface. More like ice so cold it felt like fire.

"That'll keep her from doing any mischief," Baxter said in a satisfied voice.

"How long do you intend to keep her here?" Degarde asked.

"How long will it take to convince you she is the one who has set all these fires?" Baxter retorted.

Julia spoke from the doorway. "There were no fires while she was in the Lirrens with Albert."

"Three days," Degarde said. "If three days pass and nothing else burns—"

"Then what?" Senneth demanded. She was standing very straight by the foot of the bed, her arm still extended to keep the bracelet away from her body. If she breathed quite carefully, she could almost ignore the ongoing pain. At any rate, after the first sweep of agony, the intensity had abated. It was tolerable now, if she held her arm motionless. "What do you plan to do to me?"

Baxter came close enough to leer into her face. His breath smelled of onions. She was tempted to kick him in the groin, just to prove that she didn't need magic to do some damage, but on the whole she thought she was better served by pretending to be submissive. "What usually happens to mystics who have offered harm to innocent people?"

"I think you will not find it quite so easy to kill me," she replied coolly.

"No one is going to kill you," Degarde spoke up swiftly.

Baxter kept his face inches from hers; his smile was evil. "I think a mystic dies as easy as anybody else."

She stared back at him fearlessly. He was only a couple of inches taller than she was—heavier, of course—but she was pretty sure she could beat him in a fair fight, using only swords and no magic. "I am expected in Ghosenhall within the week," she said. "Are *you* going to explain to King Baryn what has become of me?"

Baxter didn't even flinch. "Either you're lying," he said, "or the king doesn't know how dangerous you are. If we kill you, we serve the king and protect the realm."

"We're not going to *kill* her," Degarde said.

Baxter had had enough conversation. "Everyone out," he said, sweeping his long arms before him as if to herd the others into the hall. "Degarde, find something to feed us all while we decide who will stand watch."

Degarde gave Senneth one quick, desperate look. "But—"

Julia put her hand on her brother's arm. "Come downstairs now," she said quietly. "Let us all discuss what we're going to do."

A moment later, everyone had shuffled out the door, and Senneth heard the lock noisily fall in place.

She was alone in a warded room, bound by moonstones, and on sufferance for her life.

Perhaps Rinnae had been right. Perhaps she really did need friends.

She backed slowly toward the bed and, when she felt the frame against her knees, slowly seated herself on the mattress. Just as slowly, she brought her left arm around, holding it at eye height so she could examine the moonstone bracelet. She could still feel each individual gem, both the ones that lay against her skin and the ones that dangled just below her wrist because the bracelet was not particularly snug. But oddly, the jewels were beginning to cool a little—they were still hot to the touch, but not unbearably so—and the smaller gems set in the rope around her waist did not trouble her at all.

This was odd. This was interesting. She had never attempted to keep a moonstone in contact with her skin long enough to learn if its touch would become endurable. She had never heard of any other mystic being able to tolerate the gems— indeed, she had seen mystics with scar tissue from where a moonstone had been pressed too long against their flesh.

She inspected her wrist. Reddened, yes, as if she had carelessly poured hot water over the skin. But even that was beginning to fade.

She narrowed her eyes. "I wonder . . ." Holding out her right hand, palm up, she willed fire to flush from her veins. She had to concentrate harder than usual, and she felt the muscles of her belly tighten with effort, but flame began to build up in her hand. Red and yellow tongues of fire licked between her fingers and snapped upward as if hoping to migrate to the ceiling, or maybe travel as far as the faded drapes. For a moment, as the flames grew brighter, the moonstones on her wrist and around her waist flared with their own contained heat; but then they quieted down again.

"So the Pale Mother's talisman has no real power over me," Senneth said aloud, though very softly, in case one of the guards had been posted at the door. "This whole exercise might have been worth the trouble just to find that out."

That still didn't make her current situation any less precarious. She drew her feet up to the bed and sat there cross-legged a moment, thinking hard.

There was clearly another fire mystic operating in Benneld. Despite the very real possibility for tragedy that had been posed by the blaze in the forest, Senneth had the impression that whoever this other mystic was, he or she was not truly malicious. Today's demonstration of leaping fire had been playful rather than destructive.

"A child, maybe?" she mused. "Just learning what he's capable of? And not entirely understanding how great his power is and how devastating it can be?" She thought for a moment. "And how very much people will hate him once they discover what he can do?"

She had allowed them to take her prisoner—Degarde and Baxter and all the other angry townspeople. She could have escaped them at any point up until the moment they bound her with the moonstone-encrusted rope, could have turned every single body into a living torch. She could have brought the whole town down on them, if she had wanted to teach them not to mishandle a mystic—and if she'd wanted to confirm their worst fears. Hell, she would scarcely have had to do any harm at all if she had just wanted to get free. She could just have ringed them with an enchanted fire that would burn out within an hour, while she grabbed a convenient horse and cantered away.

But she had chosen to stay. She was intrigued by the mystery—and she felt a sense of obligation. To Albert and Betony, perhaps even to intense, bewildered Degarde. She had been welcomed here and treated warmly. She could not allow her new friends to be destroyed by magic that no one else would have a chance of containing once Senneth had left town.

She was not sure how she would uncover the truth. And she was pretty sure she had only three days to find out.

Six

The afternoon passed slowly. Since Senneth had discovered she could still call fire, she didn't even have fear to keep her occupied, and so she was heartily bored. The rope wasn't long enough to allow her full use of the room, but she could make it to a few choice spots, including the chamber pot, the window, and the old woman's dresser.

The chamber pot, of course, was welcome. The window showed very little of interest—a brown patch of worked ground that was probably a garden in the kinder months, a stretch of lawn, and then the edge of the forest that sloped down the hill toward town.

The dresser contained no reading material, which was what Senneth had been hoping for, but a number of small, loose moonstones lay scattered across the top. Senneth picked one up and cupped it in her right hand. At first it brightened with a malevolent white glow, burning like a live coal against her skin. And then its fever subsided to a sullen, sluggish heat.

"It is like it possesses some kind of magic that comes to life when I touch it with *my* magic," Senneth murmured. "That's why it burns my skin. But my power is stronger than the power in the jewel. Or the fire in my blood is hotter." She didn't know. She didn't really care. But she was fiercely glad to learn that she never again had to fear the touch of a moonstone.

The rest of the dresser—the small boxes on its lace-covered top, the six drawers that Senneth opened one by one—yielded nothing of interest. A few baubles, some underclothes, sachet bags so old that no hint of scent remained. Senneth sighed and retreated to the bed again to sit and wait until something might happen.

She had been Degarde's prisoner for perhaps three hours when there was a substantial commotion belowstairs. She jumped up and drew as close to the door as her rope would allow, trying to identify speakers. That one might be Betony— that one most certainly was Albert—and that was probably Baxter, shouting at the top of his lungs. A number of other voices rose and fell. Senneth had the impression two factions had formed in Benneld, one of them strongly opposed to condemning a mystic to death.

That would have been good news if she really had been worried about her safety.

Footsteps pounded up the stairs, so she quickly retreated to the foot of the bed again and took up a demure pose. The lock was thrown, and five people pushed through the door in rapid succession. Senneth barely had time to identify them— Betony, Albert, Baxter, Degarde, and one of the townsmen who had been in favor of stoning—before Betony flew across the room to embrace her.

"Senneth, Senneth, I am so sorry—I am horrified—Evelyn will never, never forgive me if something happens to you—"

"I don't expect anything to happen," Senneth said, patting Betony on the back. It was a little ironic, she thought, that the prisoner would be the one to reassure the visitor.

"It certainly won't," Albert said grimly. "I've already sent Seever with a message to the king. I imagine his majesty will have plenty to say about how badly you've been treated."

There was no chance that Seever could get to the royal city and back in under six days, so there was no hope of rescue from that quarter; but it might give these vigilantes pause to think that a murder would be quickly avenged by the king himself.

"I am not afraid," Senneth said quietly. "Not for myself. I worry for Benneld itself. I believe there is a mystic operating here, who might not know his own power, and who offers far more of a threat than I do."

Betony flung herself away from Senneth to confront Degarde. "And you have tied her up like some kind of common criminal!" she cried. "Have you *fed* her? Have you provided her water and the barest necessities? Shame on you for allowing such a thing to happen! And for treating her so badly!"

Degarde looked even more unhappy. "My sister is bringing her food even now," he said stiffly. "I do not—we have not treated her badly—but she is—there is no way to be sure—I believe there is some possibility that she is the one who has put us all at risk."

"Enough whining and bickering!" Baxter exclaimed. "She is in a safe place, with a fine bed, and no one plans to starve her. But you must see that she is a danger to everyone in this town. She must be restrained until we discover the truth."

Albert gave Senneth a serious look. "I've sent for Curtis and my brother," he said. "The three of us will share the watches here. They will not dare to do anything to you as long as one of us is on the premises."

"I appreciate that," she said. "But Baxter is right, you know. You don't know me very well. You do not truly have a reason to trust me."

Now his expression was set. "I trust you," he said with finality.

"And I swear to you that your faith is not misplaced," she replied.

Betony brushed by the men still gathered at the door. "I'm going to fetch you some food," she said.

"You're not staying here in the room with her!" Baxter shouted after her. "I'm not going to risk having you cut her bonds and set her free!"

If Betony bothered to answer that, Senneth couldn't catch the words.

It was another hour before Senneth was left alone again. She devoured the meal that Betony brought up—she had missed lunch, she realized, and it was now nearly dinnertime—and took no part in the ongoing arguments between Albert and the irate townsmen. Eventually, Baxter insisted they all leave the room to carry on the argument downstairs. Senneth's guess was that she made him uncomfortable, with her unflinching gaze and the somewhat mocking expression she allowed her face to show.

"I'll be back in the morning," Betony promised, clinging to Senneth's hands.

"Perhaps you could bring me something to read," Senneth said. "Or a project to work on. Something to distract me."

"Do you like to sew?" Betony asked, then took in a quick, dismayed sip of air. Senneth could easily follow her line of thinking: *I'll bring Senneth her dress to finish. The dress she was to wear to the dinner tomorrow night! There will be no dinner! What a terrible day!*

"It's all right," Senneth said gently, disengaging her hands. "I told you I wasn't very good at dinner parties."

Truth to tell, except for the boredom, she was just as glad when they all finally cleared the room. It was too exhausting to feel such strong dislike for Baxter, such pity for Betony and Albert—and a growing disdain for Degarde. He could not seem to settle on a conviction, whether for her or against her, and she actually thought the uncertainty was making his situation even worse than her own. Whenever he was in the room, he stared at her hopelessly, joining almost no conversation, but if she turned her sharp gaze his way, he instantly looked away.

Not man enough to defend her, not fanatic enough to condemn her. She wished she was out of his house and never had to see him again.

Night ambled out of the mountains and settled around the house like a well-fed cat. Senneth moved to the window again just for the exercise of crossing the room. Faint rectangular patches of light outlined the foundation of the house, thrown from the bottom-story windows. Occasionally shadows crossed the squares of light—servants, Senneth supposed, or any of the dozen or so townspeople who appeared to be sleeping there for the night. Now and then she could catch snatches of conversation, mostly from male speakers, and she knew there must be a sizable contingent still on hand to make sure she didn't cause any trouble in the night.

It was almost enough to make her want to try a little mischief.

But this was not the time, or the situation, to give in to childish impulses.

She had been gazing out the window for perhaps a half hour when a flicker of movement caught her attention. An undulation of yellow, as if a bright scarf had been left on the grass and just now had been caught up by a random breeze. It disappeared almost immediately. Senneth narrowed her eyes and studied the terrain more closely.

There. At the edge of the dead garden. Another saffron wave, instantly vanishing. And there. A brilliant orange snake coiled through the grass and then burrowed beneath the soil. A red flower bloomed a handspan from the house, then wilted into darkness.

Small fires. Flaring to life, then puffing out. No objects, no piles of rubble or handy little shrubs were actually being set on fire this time. No, the mystic was simply calling flames out of nothing for the joy of seeing the air itself burn.

Whoever this hidden mystic was, he was among the people guarding Senneth at the house.

During the next ten minutes, more bursts of fire flared up and died down, each one a little bigger than the last, lingering a little longer. Senneth stood immobile at the window, torn by indecision. Should she call for Degarde or Baxter and gesture toward the yard? *You see? Fire leaps up even when I am wrapped in moonstones. I am not the cause of your misfortunes.* Should she say nothing, and let the flames grow stronger, until they caught on some highly flammable fuel and turned into a true conflagration? It went against her nature to allow this house to burn merely out of spite, but should she allow the situation to grow dire enough that her jailors were forced to turn to her for aid?

No—it just felt wrong—besides, she wasn't sure they would believe she was innocent even so. They might conclude that fires set in such proximity to her prison cell must have been set by Senneth herself. They would be wrong in fact, but right in theory, since she was fairly sure she *could* have set such fires if she'd wanted to.

Could she put them out, even operating under the handicap of her moonstone accoutrements?

She flattened her fingers against the cool glass of the window and pressed her face so close to the pane that it slowly fogged over. She imagined her hands growing enormous, monstrous, calloused with ice, and then she imagined herself laying each broad palm over a half acre of the land below. She could almost feel the stiff blades of dead grass tickling against her skin, the lumps of dirt, the occasional pebble in the soil. Fire suffocated beneath her touch, and tendrils of smoke trickled between her closed fingers.

She shut her eyes and called up a memory of the whole perimeter of Degarde's house. She pictured herself lumbering slowly around it, a giantess bent half over so that she could touch each separate square foot of lawn with her immense fingers, squelching any remaining flames. Her imaginary hands were cool and damp, even as the palms she rested against the glass grew hot with absorbed energy. She leaned her forehead against the window and envisioned the entire small valley where Degarde's house was nestled, the scattered gardens and the short expanse of lawn that gave way so quickly to forest. She imagined herself, the giant-woman, dropping to her knees and then settling her whole body on the ground, wrapping herself protectively around the honey-white house. Where she lay, pressed against the soil, no flame could ignite. While she guarded this place, no calamitous fire could have its way.

❧

The morning brought Betony, carrying food she had made for Senneth in her own kitchens, as well as a stack of novels and a sewing basket. "There's a pillowcase in there, and thread, if you wanted to embroider," Betony said. "I'm embarrassed to even offer you such a pastime! But sometimes sewing keeps my mind off of troubles—just to have my hands occupied—"

"I appreciate it greatly. I appreciate even more the kindness behind the thought," Senneth said.

"I brought my own projects," Betony said defiantly. "And I am going to stay here all day and keep you company, no matter what Baxter says."

Even though they didn't talk much during that long, dull day, Senneth found Betony's presence a comfort—not least because it kept Degarde from coming to the room every half hour, showing his anxious face. Baxter wasn't much deterred, though. He arrived around noon, planted his feet squarely in the middle of the room, and sneered at Senneth where she sat on the bed, dutifully setting stitches into the fabric.

"So," he said. "We haven't had a single fire since you have been locked in this room, bound with moonstones."

"Not even a candle or a cookfire?" she asked in mild amazement. "How inconvenient for the entire town!"

He jutted his face forward. "I mean, a wayward fire, set to cause destruction."

"Then you've been most fortunate."

"We've been smart," he said. "We've locked up the mystic."

"Well, you've locked up *one* of them," Senneth said. "Not the one who means you harm."

He stamped away, still muttering. Watching him go, Betony said, "He seems calmer than yesterday, don't you think? And Albert says the whole mood of the town is softening. No one is talking about stoning you anymore. They just want you gone, and no more trouble."

"Happy to leave," Senneth said. "But I promise you, there *will* be more trouble once I'm gone."

"I suppose you can't tell who the other mystic is?" Betony asked.

"Mystics look just like anybody else, unless you catch them actively doing magic," Senneth drawled. "That's what makes them so frightening. How can you ever know if your friend is a mystic? Or your neighbor? Or your son? How can you know that *you* won't suddenly develop magic, and turn into the very thing you have always despised?"

Betony showed a little fear at that thought, though Senneth gave her credit for trying to cover it up. "How *do* you know?"

"Most mystics discover their power pretty early—certainly before they're twelve or fourteen," Senneth said. "I'm guessing someone in Benneld has just figured out what he can do and still doesn't understand it. If we knew who he was, and I could talk to him, I think I could help him control his power— at least enough to make sure he doesn't burn down every house for five miles."

"That would be kind," Betony said, "considering the way the townspeople have treated you."

Senneth gave her a warm smile. "Considering the way some of the townspeople have treated me," she said, "it is the least I can do."

A servant brought in an early dinner, since Julia had not bothered to show her face in Senneth's room again. The girl was followed by an elegant yellow tabby with thick winter fur, a disdainful expression, and an attitude of owning the world.

As she set her tray down on a small table, the servant girl said to the cat, "Shoo! Get out!" The tabby ignored her and daintily circled the room, pausing to sniff at Senneth's boots.

"I take it this creature belongs in the barn or kitchen, catching mice," Senneth said with a friendly grin.

"Not even! I don't know where it came from, but it's been hanging around since this morning. Cook wants it gone, because it keeps stealing meat from the platters."

It was clear Betony was not partial to cats. "Well, Senneth has suffered enough indignities in this house," she said coldly. "She should not have to endure *animals* crawling through her room."

But Senneth's eyes were on the golden cat, which had dropped to its haunches and curled its full tail around its front legs. The color of its eyes was a startling blue and the tilt of its head was almost aristocratic. It was staring at Senneth with unblinking intensity.

"I like cats," Senneth said. "Let it stay."

"Well, if you want it to, I guess," the girl said doubtfully.

"They make me sneeze," Betony said apologetically, instantly proving the truth of her words.

"You go on home," Senneth said. "You've been here all day. Come back tomorrow if you like. I can't tell you how much I appreciate what you've done for me."

Betony sneezed again, got to her feet, and hugged Senneth good-bye. "I can't tell you how dreadful I feel about what has happened to you," she said.

"Don't worry," Senneth said. "Everything will be all right."

Betony left with the servant girl. Senneth waited until the lock fell back in place and the sound of the women's footsteps had faded down the hall. The whole time she kept her eyes on the cat, which stared inscrutably back at her.

When she finally judged it safe, Senneth said, "Where's Donnal?"

If an animal could laugh, this one did. It came to its feet, stretched out its lithe body, and kept stretching. Its spine extended; its golden fur turned to golden curls; its sharp, pointed face broadened and refined and turned into a woman's. Within a minute, Kirra stood there, dressed for travel and insouciant as ever.

"He's in the kitchen, nosing around for scraps," Kirra said. She threw herself across the room as if to take Senneth in an embrace, but Senneth flung up her right hand.

"They've bound me with moonstones—you'll burn yourself," she warned.

"What's *happened*?" Kirra demanded, coming to a halt and hovering restlessly next to the bed. "I came to Benneld yesterday to try and track you down, and I found you accused of crimes and put under guard! And wrapped with moonstones? How *dare* they? And how can you stand it? I would be whimpering on the floor by now."

Senneth held up her left hand and inspected the moonstone bracelet, glowing with its usual pale phosphorescence. "I don't know how I can stand it," she said. "They burn, but—not in a way that bothers me. I have to say it pleases me—in a sort of dark, self-satisfied way—to learn that moonstones have no power over me. It was something I didn't know before."

"Well, that certainly makes arrest and imprisonment completely worthwhile!" Kirra exclaimed. "How are we going to get you out of here? There must be something in the room that I can turn into a knife so you can cut the rope."

"I believe the house is full of guards," Senneth said. "Tricky to slip past them."

"I only saw three," Kirra replied. "If we wait till dark, I can take care of one, and I'm sure Donnal can account for two. Unless—I can't tell—does the man of the house side with you or with your enemies? There might be a fourth one to disarm."

"Degarde is not sure how he feels about me," Senneth said with a touch of humor. "Before I was accused of witchcraft, he liked me very well indeed, and even was making some vaguely romantic overtures."

Kirra was instantly diverted. "Oh, *that* must have made you uncomfortable! Was he picturing you presiding over this little house, bearing him sweet babies and settling into a blissful domesticity? The very life you would despise above any other."

Senneth couldn't help grinning. "I will settle into such a life if *you* will."

"Exactly! So did you spurn his advances? Is that why he turned on you and named you a witch?"

Senneth shook her head. "He knew I was mystic and didn't seem to hold it against me—until inexplicable fires kept breaking out whenever I was nearby. Even so, he was more reluctant than some of his fellows to blame *me* for the flames."

Kirra arched her delicate brows. "Another mystic in town, operating in secret?"

"The fires have certainly been magical," Senneth said. "But I don't know who's setting them."

"And I don't care!" Kirra replied. "We need to get you away from here before the entire town turns on you in violence."

"That was the original plan, but Betony tells me that, after thinking it over a day, they are not so eager to kill me."

"Senneth!"

"They won't kill me," she said quietly. "They can't do it." She held up her left hand, the one decorated with the moonstone bracelet, and let fire dance from her fingertips while she talked. "I still have all my power. I could burn the rope off my body, I could set the whole house ablaze and stroll out of here through a corridor of fire, and none of them would be able to stop me. I am bound because I let them take me, and I am here because I have chosen to stay."

"Then you're mad, and I should find a way to get you out of here against your will."

Senneth smiled tightly. "I want to solve the mystery. I want to discover who the mystic is. Or once I'm gone, those who live here will discover it in the most drastic fashion possible."

Kirra had coiled up on the bed beside Senneth, catlike even in human form, but now she jumped up and began pacing. "I am not so convinced you can free yourself, despite what you say," she said. "There is a contingent of King's Riders passing through Kianlever, a half day from here. Donnal and I passed them on the road. Shall I go fetch them?"

Senneth was amused. King's Riders were an elite group of soldiers with an unshakable devotion to the king and very little interest in any other human being. "I hardly think you would convince them to come riding to the rescue of a mystic," she said.

"I could, if I told them Baryn had commissioned you to perform a service for him. Which has the advantage of being the truth!"

"Kirra. I'm not afraid. I'm very glad to see you, and I appreciate your offer of help, but I can handle this by myself. They want to wait one more day and see if any sorcerous flames appear when I am not near enough to call them up. After that, I believe they will release me. I would like to stay till then, just in case the rogue mystic acts again—just in case there is something I can do. But if that deadline passes and there are no more fires, I promise you, I will go directly to Ghosenhall."

Kirra appeared to not even be listening. "I'll go to the Riders—I'm sure they'll listen to me," she said, as if speaking to herself. "But I don't like to leave you here alone." She nodded decisively. "Donnal will stay. He can help defend you if anyone offers you harm."

"Kirra—"

Kirra turned back toward the bed, a smile on her lovely face. "You can't stop me, so don't even try," she said. "Is there anything you need before I leave?"

"No, I'm fine."

"I'll tell Donnal the plan," Kirra said. "He'll come up and spend the night in your room."

Senneth didn't bother asking how Donnal would get in. Both of the shiftlings could transform themselves into any living shape. He might waddle under the door as a beetle or fly in as some kind of insect. "Well, if he takes dog form to sleep on the foot of my bed, it might be hard to explain him in the morning."

Kirra gave her that dazzling smile. "All the stray animals of the estate are drawn to your presence," she said. "How could it be otherwise? I'll return tomorrow one way or the other—with or without Riders at my back."

Senneth stood up to say farewell, carefully wrapping her

right arm around Kirra's shoulders and making sure none of the moonstones touched her. "I appreciate the effort," she said, "but you don't have to worry about me."

"Somebody should worry about you," Kirra informed her as she pulled back. "It may as well be me."

A few moments later, Kirra had transformed herself into a tiny mouse and scrabbled under the door into the hallway. Senneth tried to imagine her route down the stairs and into the kitchen. It was not very late—scarcely full dark—and plenty of people were still roaming the house. A mouse had better be extremely careful if it didn't want to fall afoul of a wide variety of hazards.

Senneth didn't have much time to fret about Kirra. About a half hour later, the same servant returned to collect the dinner tray. The instant she opened the door, a small black sparrow swooped in behind her and fluttered around the room before settling on the curtain rod.

"That bird!" the girl exclaimed. "Got into the kitchen this morning, and the cook chased it with a broom, but it just kept flying around where no one could reach it. I'll call the footmen to come get it out of your room."

"Don't bother," Senneth said. "It'll keep me company."

The girl glanced around. "Where did that cat go?"

"Under the bed," Senneth said without hesitation.

"Maybe the cat'll eat the bird," the girl said. "That would be nice."

"I'll let you know if it happens," Senneth replied.

The door had barely locked behind the servant girl when Donnal drifted to the floor and whirled into the form of a man. Unlike Kirra, he could change shapes so quickly Senneth's eyes couldn't follow the transformation.

"I brought a deck of cards," he said by way of greeting. "Want to play a couple of hands?"

❧

Donnal was always the easiest company imaginable—quiet, good-humored, and undemanding, with a relaxed way of talking that was soothing to a troubled soul. At the same time, his animal instincts kept him extremely alert, and he was never caught off guard by someone barging into the room unexpectedly. Twice he looked up and, without a word, transmogrified himself into something small and unnoticeable before Senneth even heard a footfall in the hallway.

Once the visitor was Baxter, coming to taunt her before retiring for the day. Once it was Degarde, shamefaced and nervous.

"I just wanted you to know—if there are no more unexplained fires tomorrow—the townspeople have agreed to release you the morning of the following day," he said. "There will be no harm to your person. But you will be escorted some distance away and asked never to return to this place."

"Do you imagine I *would* have any incentive to return?" Senneth said dryly.

"I wished—I had thought—I had hoped you and I could be friends," he said miserably.

She tried not to laugh. "There was never any likelihood of that."

"I know that I—I have offended you by displaying my doubt—by not believing in you wholeheartedly—but I considered and reconsidered, and I am sure—that is, I believe—"

She decided to take pity on him. "Degarde. This is why it is very difficult for ordinary men to befriend mystics. Because you are *not* quite sure. Because you will never be quite sure. And even if you were able to thoroughly, completely, absolutely convince yourself that there is no malice in me, despite my ferocious power, everyone around you would always wonder. You would constantly be forced to defend me. It would wear you out, you know. You are much better off not trying to be my friend."

He stared at her hopelessly. "But I wanted to be."

She reached her hand out and let him take it. "At least we will not be enemies," she said. "I hold none of this against you, if that is any comfort to you."

"Some," he said in a low voice. "But very little."

She pulled her hand away. "One way or another," she said, "I will be gone soon. Try not to brood too much about how sadly everything went awry."

"They won't hurt you," he burst out. "I won't let them. They will banish you from Benneld, but no one will raise a hand to strike you or—or worse."

"I am not afraid," she said. "No one in this town has the power to destroy me."

It was perhaps too confident a thing to say. Doubt flickered in his eyes, and then he turned away. "You will be held here one more day," he said, his voice muffled. "And then you will be sent on your way."

Degarde had not been through the door more than five seconds before Donnal was standing before Senneth again. "Rather a pathetic excuse for a man," he commented.

Senneth laughed. "I am trying not to despise him, but in truth he is something of a lost soul."

"But will they really set you free the day after tomorrow? What if no mysterious fires sweep through the streets? They will say it is only because the mystic is locked up."

"I know."

"Maybe I should collect some rags and kindling," Donnal suggested. "I could get quite a convincing blaze going without much trouble, and you would be nowhere near it."

"Tempting," she said. "But unnecessary. Just stay to keep me company—or to take a message to Kirra if something dire befalls me."

"If something dire befalls you," Donnal said, "Kirra will expect me to remain beside you to help you fend it off."

Senneth laughed. "Very well," she said. "Then deal the cards."

Seven

The following day was windy and cold, though the skies were breathtakingly bright. "It feels like the sun is mocking us," Senneth remarked to Donnal a little before noon. "It *looks* very warm out there, but the window is cold as ice beneath my hand, and it rattles in the casement like it's about to come loose and shatter on the floor."

"Maybe the weather will be better tomorrow once we're on our way to Ghosenhall," he said.

"I don't mind cold," Senneth said. "But I do hate to travel against a wind. Or in the rain."

"I don't like wet weather, either," he said. "One time Kirra and I were in Coravann when a storm came through—" He paused and cocked his head to listen. "Someone's coming—no, a lot of someones," he said. "And they're agitated."

Senneth turned to face the door squarely. "Can you tell what's wrong?"

Donnal didn't answer. He was already back in bird shape and circling the room at the level of the crown moulding.

The door was flung open and people poured in, all of them yelling. At first it was hard to distinguish any words except *fire* and *market* and *main street*. Senneth flung up her hands.

"One of you! Tell me what's happened!" she commanded.

Degarde, holding a knife in his hands, pushed himself to the head of the delegation.

"Fire!" he panted, running over to start sawing through her bonds. He didn't make headway very quickly. "The tavern is burning—and the dress shop—and two of the houses."

"And it's spreading!" someone shouted from the door. Other voices joined in.

"We can't keep up—not enough buckets—too many fires—"

"Come quickly! Please, you must help us."

Degarde looked up at her, his hand clenching on the rope. "Please," he whispered. "Even if you hate us all. You must save us."

With an exclamation of annoyance, she twitched the rope out of his hand and set it to burning at a point very close to her body. Degarde jumped back and everyone crowded at the door gasped in surprise and dismay. As soon as the rope had charred through, Senneth doused the fire. The loop wrapped with the moonstone necklace was still knotted around her waist. "Let me pass," she said, striding for the door, and everyone scattered before her.

Baxter was just outside the front door, holding a horse. Senneth jerked the reins from him and threw herself into the saddle. It was a tricky business racing downhill on a track half-mud and half-ice, but the horse obeyed her urgent commands until they drew close enough to town for him to see the flames and smell the smoke. Then he began to slow and pull sideways, resisting her exhortations. She didn't waste time— she just swung out of the stirrups and hit the ground at a dead run. She could already feel the heat beginning to pool in her hands.

The instant she was close enough, Senneth lifted her arms and began to try to reel in the flames. Still pounding forward, she made a winding motion with her hands, as if rolling loose twine into a ball. Some of the flames bent her way; some of the smaller blazes blew themselves out.

In a few moments she was in the market square and fire cavorted all around her, rebellious and beautiful. Senneth spread her arms as wide as they would go, and then slowly, slowly, fell into a crouch. Resisting every inch of the way, the fire sank along with her. It dropped to the height of a man's head—to a woman's hips—to a child's ankles. Senneth fell to her knees and flattened her palms against the dirt.

Every single fire abruptly died.

She stayed where she was, arms splayed beside her, head bent, listening, waiting. All around her she could hear the excited buzz of conversation—astonishment, anger, accusation, bewilderment. *What happened? Who did that? Is that the mystic?* Someone was weeping uncontrollably. Someone else was offering loud prayers to the moon goddess.

Still touching her fingertips to the ground, Senneth lifted her head and gazed around her. Townspeople were clustered in ragged groups near the smoking ruins of half a dozen buildings. Some were gazing at their lost property, some were crying in each other's arms, some were staring at her. She spotted Albert, Betony, Baxter, the boy Eric, and other somewhat familiar faces.

Her attention returned to Eric. A few days ago, he had been enthralled by her display of power; he had wanted to feel the touch of a mystic's hand upon his skin. Now he was gazing around in fascination, his narrow face intent. As if remembering what each building had looked like before it had burned down, as if admiring the efficient handiwork of the flames, as if wondering what else might catch fire . . .

As Senneth watched him, he reached up to feel the charred edges of the dressmaker's front wall. She saw him pinch the blackened wood to dust between his fingertips and almost smile.

Behind her, a woman's voice rose in a desperate scream.

Senneth leapt to her feet and whipped around to see a small tumbling shape turn into a fireball and somersault into the bakery. Instantly the wood of the doorway began to smolder; the lace curtains at the windows were suddenly webs of flickering red and yellow.

"Halie!" a woman shrieked and raced in after the small child.

The whole building was suddenly engulfed in flame.

"No!" Senneth shouted. She couldn't have said which of them she addressed—the mother running after her child, the townspeople who surged forward to rescue both of them, or the fire itself, roaring into sudden, ravenous life. *"No!"*

She flung her hands out again—she sucked in a great gulp of cold winter air. She gathered all the flames to her in one roiling, untidy mass. Her body spasmed with a sudden access of heat; her skin crackled as if her very blood ran with fire. For a moment it seemed as if she herself was an inferno, a swirling storm of primitive destruction. Then she wrapped her arms tightly around her body, smothered the mad flames against her skin, and felt the temperature around her drop by twenty degrees.

Julia staggered out of the shop, her face streaked with soot, clutching a squirming Halie in her arms. Julia was sobbing, kissing Halie's cinder-swept hair, crying, "My baby, my baby . . ."

"Put her down!" Senneth called, starting in their direction. "Julia! Set her down! She is not safe to touch!"

Julia didn't seem to hear. She knelt in the middle of the street, frantically patting Halie's face and hands and clothing, looking for the burn, the mark, the scar. "Halie, my baby, are you all right, are you all right—"

Halie reached out a small, pudgy hand and set her mother's shirt alight.

Julia screamed and fell backward, slapping at her shoulder. Free again, Halie chortled and took off at a run toward the stables.

Senneth caught her in five strides and scooped her up. Instantly, Halie began to wail, and she beat at Senneth with her small fists. Her hands were encased in fire; wisps of flame licked around her face, mingling with her hair.

"Down!" the little girl cried. "Want down!"

Julia had struggled to her feet and was limping up to Senneth as fast as she could. *"What are you doing to my baby?"* she shrieked. *"You're setting her on fire!"*

Senneth squeezed Halie tight enough to hold her motionless and tamp down her unruly magic. "No," Senneth said, her tone as compassionate as she could make it. "Halie is setting herself on fire. Halie has practically burned down the entire town. She's a mystic, Julia, and she has just discovered her power."

❦

The next twenty minutes were a chaotic jostle of loud voices, angry words, shoving bodies, and ongoing excitement, all made more urgent and more exhausting by the acrid overlay of smoke and heat.

Senneth continued to hold Halie in her arms, despite the little girl's determination to wriggle free, despite Julia's fierce clasp on her arm, Julia's continuing insistence that her child was *not* a mystic, there had been some kind of misunderstanding. But a number of townspeople had seen Halie set one fire or another, and dozens had seen her burst into flames and run inside the bakery, to emerge unscathed a few minutes later.

"It's your little girl. It's your Halie," Baxter said heavily. "She's the mystic. She set the whole town on fire."

By this time, Donnal and Degarde and the rest of Senneth's erstwhile guards had clambered down the hill and joined the people milling in the center of the ruined town. Donnal hung back from the rest, but Senneth saw him scanning the crowd, staying alert in case there was any trouble. Degarde pushed his way through the mob and took Julia in a comforting embrace. She turned and wept against his shoulder.

"My baby, my baby," she cried.

Degarde gazed at Senneth over his sister's shoulder. "How did this happen?" he demanded. "How did Halie become a mystic?"

"The way any of us do," Senneth said. "She was born magic."

"She never showed a sign of it until we met *you*."

Senneth nodded, not allowing his hostility to anger her. This revelation had shaken his world; who knew if he would ever recover? Julia looked unlikely to accept the truth anytime soon, although until she did, there would be no way to start Halie's education. "She touched me while we were all dining at Evelyn's," Senneth said. "I'm guessing that the fire in my blood woke the fire in hers."

"You poisoned her—you turned her," he said flatly. "You made her this way."

Senneth shook her head. "If my touch was capable of turning random individuals into mystics, you and your sister and Albert and Betony and the whole of the Lirrenlands would be rife with fire mystics. Halie has always had this ability lurking in her veins."

"But until we met you—" he began again. Senneth interrupted him.

"Your house is shrouded in moonstones. No doubt they kept her power mostly in check. You notice that none of these fiery episodes occurred within your walls—not yet, anyway. Now that she has discovered what she is capable of, she will continue to experiment. She will soon learn how far from the influence of a moonstone she must stand in order to summon fire."

Her words made Julia sob even harder. Degarde spent a moment trying to calm her, whispering in her ear. Then he gave Senneth a long, somber look. Finally he asked, "What do you advise us to do? Neither of us knows how to deal with a mystic child."

"You must find someone who can help her control her power. There are mystics in Ghosenhall who can teach your sister how to raise a child with magic in her blood."

Degarde swallowed. "Can you stay? Can you help us?"

Senneth hesitated. "I am needed in Ghosenhall and I must be on my way today. You can travel with me, if you like."

He looked helpless. "Today? But I can't—there is so much to do to prepare for such a trip—"

"Tomorrow, then," Senneth said. "But I cannot stay any longer than that."

Julia gulped and pulled herself shakily from Degarde's embrace. When she turned to look at Senneth, her face was so red and swollen that she was almost unrecognizable. "I will take her to my mother-in-law's," she said, with a forlorn attempt at dignity. "I believe she is a woman with some magic of her own."

Degarde looked astonished, but Senneth nodded. "No doubt. Magic tends to follow bloodlines, and if no one in your family is mystic, then it is a trait brought to your daughter through the marriage bed."

"My mother-in-law lives only a day's ride away," Julia said. "Much closer than Ghosenhall."

"But how will we get Halie there without setting the entire countryside on fire?" Degarde asked.

"Bind her with moonstones," Senneth said. "They will check her power."

He stared at her, his eyes going first to the bracelet on her left wrist, then the frayed noose of rope hanging from her waist. "They did not check yours."

She smiled. "I'm different," she said. "In fact—" She balanced Halie on her left hip and started a slow, careful fire through the loop of rope still knotted around her body. She said, "You can use these moonstones to dampen Halie's power while you return to the house. Otherwise, I imagine the forest will catch fire again before you even make it home."

Halie stretched her arms out to Julia. "Mama! Mama!"

Julia reached for her, but Senneth pulled away. "I cannot release her until she is bound," she said quietly. "Trust me, Julia, now that she has learned what she is capable of, you can never leave her unguarded."

The severed rope fell to the ground at Senneth's feet. Degarde retrieved it and slipped off the jeweled chain. "Wrap it in cloth before you give it to her," Senneth directed. "Or it will burn her skin."

This condition met, Senneth finally felt safe handing Halie back to her family. The little girl laughed and chattered in her mother's arms. Julia pressed her lips against Halie's smooth cheek and turned away from Senneth without speaking.

Degarde remained at Senneth's side, his face a study in wretchedness. "What a terrible day," he said. "What a terrible week."

"I am sorry for you," Senneth said. "It is no easy thing to learn that someone you love has been touched by magic. Make no mistake, Halie's life will be difficult. There are people who will despise her without even knowing her—people who would destroy her because they fear what she is. I hope *you* are not among those who hate her. I hope *you* will help her learn that magic can be a blessing and a gift."

"She is my niece," he said. "I love her. I will defend her with my life."

Senneth put her hand out to touch him on the shoulder. "Then Halie is luckier than I was," she said. "And I am proud to call you my friend."

Before Degarde could answer, Donnal stepped up behind

him. "Senneth," he said. "There's a group of men on horse-back coming up the road. Strangers."

Senneth dropped her arm. "I suppose the smoke and flames were visible for miles," she said. "Maybe travelers have come to investigate."

"I must go to Julia," Degarde said. He offered Senneth a deep bow, paused to give her one last look of regret, and pushed through the clusters of townspeople to follow his sister.

Senneth turned her attention to the steady clopping sound of hoofbeats coming from the east, but the haze from the burned buildings was still thick enough that it was a moment before she could make out any travelers coming up the road.

Then one man materialized through the curling gray smoke, appearing like a shadow that took solid shape and substance as she watched. He was a big man on a big horse, and he carried a naked sword in his right hand. Except for the pride of golden lions embroidered across his sash, he was dressed all in black. His eyes and his hair were almost as dark as his jacket; there was nothing resembling softness or humor on his severe face. While he rode, he cast a quick, comprehensive look around the smoldering town, seeming, with a single glance, to read the entire story that had played out on the streets.

"I understand that there is a mystic in this town who is being held against her will," he said.

Behind him, three more horsemen trotted through the smoke. They were similarly attired and similarly armed for action, swords in their hands and resolve on their faces. Senneth recognized both their distinctive livery and their air of confidence. Kirra had fetched the King's Riders, after all.

"I am the mystic. My name is Senneth," she said, stepping forward and addressing the large man in the lead. "But I am no longer being held prisoner."

He glanced down at her and his gaze was coolly assessing. She had the oddest sense that she could tell exactly what was going through his mind. *She does not look like a physical threat, and yet she is a mystic. Perhaps she is the one who set this place on fire. That makes her dangerous. Therefore, I must be on my guard.* "I am Tayse," he introduced himself. "My companions and I are King's Riders."

Before she could answer, Kirra swooped in, a bright yellow songbird who transformed herself swiftly into a woman. Senneth could hear the uneasy murmurs from the nearby townspeople—*More magic! More unnatural behavior!*—but the expression on Tayse's face never changed.

"Senneth, these are the Riders I told you about," Kirra exclaimed, coming close enough to put her hand on Senneth's arm. "They have come to help you."

"I appreciate that. But as you see, I am no longer in need of any aid," Senneth replied.

Kirra was looking around at the charred and tumbled buildings. "What a mess it is here! I take it you were not the one who started these fires."

Senneth shook her head. "A small child, just now learning what she can do."

Kirra gave her a shrewd look. "Some poor mother has just had her heart broken, I suppose."

"Exactly so."

Tayse shifted in his saddle, sheathing his sword and bringing his horse around so he could look straight down at Senneth. "I understand the king has sent for you and wants you in Ghosenhall with all speed."

"Yes, that's what I understand as well," she said.

"If you are ready to leave, you can ride with us," he said. "We will protect you for the rest of your journey."

She almost laughed. "Thank you, but I don't need protection."

Donnal came a few steps closer. "But there's no reason to stay," he said softly. "And I imagine these folk would be happy enough to see you gone."

Senneth sighed. "You're right. All I need to do is gather my belongings and find my horse, and then I can go."

"We'll wait until you're ready," Tayse said.

Senneth cast him one short, exasperated look. "I told you, I don't need your protection."

Kirra, all golden hair and big blue eyes, was smiling up at the Riders. "Speaking for myself, I will feel so much safer if we have soldiers around us on the journey," she cooed. It was sheer flirtation; even less than Senneth did Kirra need someone to defend her on the road.

The big man shrugged, supremely indifferent to either

Kirra's wiles or Senneth's protests. Senneth had the sense that once he had made up his mind, it was very difficult to dissuade him. He would not argue; he would not fume. He would merely do as he intended, and anyone nearby would fall in line. She could tell already she was fated to have his escort for the rest of her trip.

"You may as well ride with us to Ghosenhall," Tayse said. "We're going straight home."

M474T0310